NOTHING
TO
LOSE

STEVEN SUTTIE

I'd like to thank my loyal readers for buying this, the seventh DCI Miller story. I really appreciate your support and your positive reviews on Amazon, as well as your endless likes and shares on social media. It really means a great deal.

I hope you enjoy the latest Miller adventure. And please, if you do like it, bob off to Amazon and bung a review on if you can. If you don't like it, I promise to try harder next time!

If your name appears at some point in the following pages, or it has done in any of the previous Miller stories; that's my small way of saying thank you for your support.

Cheers
Steve

Prologue

Will Clarke was 24 years old when he took his own life, by driving his little Ford Fiesta off the edge of a cliff.

At first, it looked like a tragic accident. But in the months that followed, a very different picture began emerging.

Widely acknowledged as "the life and soul of the party," Will was the last person that his family and friends would expect to commit suicide. He had always been such good fun, he was happy-go-lucky and very kind-hearted.

In the weeks and months following the "accident" a completely different and unrecognisable version of Will Clarke's life began to emerge. A version that nobody close to him could comprehend.

The coroner's report into his death was initially dismissed by his parents. Joe and Margaret Clarke, already trying to cope with the devastating grief of losing a child, were now being presented with a file at the inquest and the details within it made them believe that there had been a monumental mix-up.

The file in question was essentially a list of debts, bank transactions and most surprisingly of all, a police charge sheet in relation to the theft of a watch from a friend's house. Will owed more than £60,000 to pay-day loan companies, credit card providers and banks. In a further troubling twist, it transpired that Will had taken over £1,000 from the butcher's shop he worked at on the day that he died.

Every penny of the money that he owed had been spent on gambling.

The Coroner had concluded that these factors, coupled with the details of a very dark Facebook message to his former girlfriend, as well as the forensic examinations of the crash scene, was strong enough evidence to determine that Will's death was no accident.

Although there was no suicide note, the Coroner was satisfied that the crash was deliberate and that Will Clarke had intentionally killed himself. It concluded that his gambling problem was "most likely the reason."

Until the inquest into their son's death, Joe and Margaret Clarke had no idea that Will had any problems at all, which made these shocking revelations even harder to accept.

Chapter One

"Emergency Service. Which service do you require?"

"Fire brigade, shit, quick..." the young man on the phone sounded shocked, scared and out-of-breath.

"Putting you through now."

"Greater Manchester Fire and Rescue Service." Said a different voice on the line.

"Yeah, there's a fire, it's proper bad, a shop on Windmill Lane, Denton." His voice was unclear, it sounded as though he was struggling to catch his breath.

"Do you have a postcode for that location please?"

"No, no, it's... top end of Windmill Lane, motorway end, it's called Bet-a-days bookies. Denton end, you need to hurry up. Seriously, it's bad. People are trapped upstairs. They're screaming."

"Okay, I'm organising a response now, I just need..."

The caller was making a strange noise and it took a few seconds for the emergency call handler to realise that he was retching. He gasped, before speaking again.

"You'll need an ambulance, you'll need a few ambulances... aw fucking hell, this is so bad..."

"Are you at the location now, Sir?"

"No, no... I've, I'm not..."

The call ended. The call handler tried to reconnect with the public phone-box, but it rang out. Whoever had made the call had gone. The fire service operator logged the call time and saved the audio file. Just as the recording was being locked in the system, several other calls began coming in, reporting the same fire and all of the callers were in a distressed state, making the conversation extremely difficult. The people inside the burning building could be heard down the line, screaming for help.

It was becoming clear to the staff in the control room that this one was a very nasty shout.

Chapter Two

DCI Andrew Miller was fast asleep, snoring loudly as his phone began vibrating on the bedside table. His wife, Clare shoved his shoulder.

"Eh? What's…" He quickly realised that his phone was ringing, the glow from the screen was lighting up the bedroom ceiling.

"Time is it?" he asked.

"Shut up Andy and answer your phone."

Miller answered the call. His eyes began focusing a little better and he noted the time. 3.14 a.m. The call was coming in from his deputy, DI Keith Saunders.

"What's up?" he asked into the phone, as quietly as he could.

"Hi Sir. Got a horrible job on, arson, young family. The mum's managed to get out with the daughter but neither of them are in a good way. The dad and his little lad are dead, fire brigade found them cuddled up in the bottom of the lad's wardrobe. It sounds very grim this one, boss."

"Where?"

"Denton. Windmill Lane."

"When?"

"It was reported a couple of hours since."

"Why have we got it?" asked Miller as he pulled himself up on the bed, making a loud groaning noise as he did so.

"Andy!" said Clare. The tone that the DCI's wife used conveyed so much more. By simply saying 'Andy,' she had also managed to say "get up and get out of here right now, you annoying bastard!"

Miller understood his wife's message loud and clear, and scrambled out of the bed. "Soz, just a sec," he whispered into the phone which he started using as a torch as he found his clothes and some underwear, before heading out of the bedroom. He closed the door quietly behind himself.

"Sorry, where were we?"

"I was just…"

"Oh aye. Why has it been handed to us?" asked Miller,

still whispering.

"Tameside CID have escalated it, as soon as they arrived. The entire building's been destroyed apparently."

Miller's team, the SCIU were responsible for investigating the most serious crimes in the Greater Manchester area. It was extremely unusual to have a case handed up to them right from the very start. The vast majority of cases that they dealt with had been thoroughly investigated and exhausted by the city's local CID teams before being handed up to the SCIU. It was usually during this "dying" stage in an investigation that the SCIU were mobilised and asked to scrutinise the case and look for additional information with fresh eyes and their "neutral" standpoint.

"Jesus. Are you there now?"

"No, I'm on my way there, about ten minutes away."

"Right, well, I'll just have a quick piss and I'll be on my way. Cheers."

Chapter Three

"Good morning, Happy Monday, everybody," said DS Jo Rudovsky as the rest of the Serious Crimes Investigation Unit officers took their seats before her.

"I want to appeal against your decision that it's Monday already!" said DC Peter Kenyon.

"Morning!" DC Helen Grant was the only cheerful voice.

"Ma'am!" said DC Bill Chapman, aware how much the name Ma'am grated on the young DS.

"Now, I've been asked to take this morning's team brief as our superiors, DI Saunders and DCI Miller have been called out on an urgent job."

"What's the job?" asked DC Mike Worthington.

"That fatal fire last night in Denton. It was arson. They've been at the scene since half-three this morning."

"What, are we taking that on as well?" asked Kenyon. He didn't seem pleased at the prospect.

"I'm not sure yet Pete, it'll all become clearer later. But in the meantime, we're not making great progress with the Graham Hartley case, so let's crack on with that eh, and see what Miller and Saunders say when they get back?"

Each member of team nodded and the newly promoted DS was pleased to see that there was a collective sense of positive energy amongst the DCs. The case that Rudovsky was talking about had been an intense investigation involving every member of the small, tight-knit team of detectives who investigate Manchester's most serious and problematic cases.

And the murder of Graham Hartley had indeed proved to be a problematic investigation. Graham had been beaten to death three weeks earlier, whilst jogging in countryside between Swinton and Eccles. The area, known locally as Eccles Field, stretches out over a two-mile area in between the two major towns within the City of Salford. Eccles Field is extremely popular with dog walkers, a fact made clear by the amount of dog turds which decorated each side of the tarmac pathway which runs the entire length of the area.

Graham had been discovered lying in a pool of blood

soon after the attack. The dog walker who had contacted the emergency services had been talked through CPR by the call handler and was still working on Graham when the police arrived, followed several minutes later by an ambulance crew. The paramedics worked relentlessly for half an hour on trying to save the 40-year-old's life. But sadly, it was to no avail and they pronounced him dead at the scene, after finally accepting that his injuries were not consistent with life.

The crime scene was a complete disaster, from a forensics point of view. The dog walker who had discovered Graham had been shouting so loudly that he had managed to raise the alarm on the nearby housing estate where he lived, which backed onto the field. Alerted by the commotion, dozens of local people had come out with torches to see what was happening, several of them dropping to their knees to assist with the resuscitation efforts.

Whilst this was an excellent example of a community coming together to help somebody in need, it had completely devastated the crime scene in terms of cross-contamination of any evidence which may have been left at the site.

Graham Hartley had been attacked with a golf club. The initial blow had been to the back of his skull and had shattered his cranium. There followed a sustained and savage attack in which thirty-eight devastating blows from the golf club had shattered bones in almost every part of Graham Hartley's body. The attack was so brutal, several police officers in attendance had been seen to vomit near the crime scene.

This horrific attack had taken place shortly after 7pm on a cold November evening, close to the village of Monton which sits around halfway between Swinton in the north, and Eccles to its south. There were street lights all along the path way, they'd been erected to prevent anti-social behaviour close to the houses, but the light that they gave off had not been sufficient enough to alert Graham Hartley of the danger that he had been jogging towards. This appalling crime had left the local community in a state of panic and terror since it had happened.

It was so serious that it had topped the list of the most serious crimes in Greater Manchester, and as such, it was handed over very quickly to the SCIU department, mainly because DCI Andrew Miller, who runs the unit, is widely-regarded as Manchester's top detective and therefore, the safest pair-of-hands to take control of an investigation of this nature.

"We've been making slow progress, as you all know," said Rudovsky to the team. Her DCs, Helen Grant, Bill Chapman, Mike Worthington and Peter Kenyon all had their own aspects of the investigation to work on and were helping to make several question marks disappear with each passing day. But they weren't getting any closer to the killer, or a motive.

"So, let's recap. We know that the attacker is a male, stocky build, escaped in a northerly direction, heading away from the area towards Swinton. We know that a bike was used, as several witnesses at various points along the path saw him riding towards them in the moments following the attack. We have also established that there is no operational CCTV at any point along that path, or at any of the pathway's junctions into Swinton. However, we do have the CCTV footage of a cyclist riding across the East Lancs Road not long after the attack was phoned in. Those images have been circulated to the press, but as we all know, the images were recorded in the dark and don't really tell us very much at all. But just to keep it all fresh in our minds, he is of a stocky build, quite a big lad, it's hard to put a height on him but we're thinking six foot. He was wearing a dark coloured hoody and the bike turns out to be a very common model, a Carrera, a mass-market bike manufactured by Halfords."

Rudovsky was standing by the investigation wall, which was filled with photographs, maps and important details and calculations. She was pointing at the picture on the wall, it was a grainy, almost black and white image which didn't offer very much information about the cyclist other than what Rudovsky had mentioned.

"He just looks like any other scrote on a bike. But as we all know, he isn't, he is a very evil man. To commit a crime of such sickening violence, and then ride off calmly, letting on to passers-by as he rode past, tells us that he is a very dangerous individual. So, let me throw it out to you guys. What do we know about the victim, Graham Hartley?"

Rudovsky stepped across towards the window and grabbed a hold of the giant A1 notepad stand, before shuffling back into the centre of the room with it. The height of the A-Frame really exaggerated how short Rudovsky stood at 5 feet 5. She folded the last page over the top of the stand and started a fresh sheet, writing HARTLEY at the top. When she turned around to face the detectives, she was glad to see that they all had a hand raised in the air.

"Go on Helen, ladies first." Rudovsky pointed at DC Helen Grant, the partner of DI Keith Saunders, both professionally and domestically.

"Positive discrimination!" shouted Kenyon with a wide smile on his face.

"Shut up Pete. Go on, Helen."

"Lots of interesting intelligence is coming to light on Hartley, boss. The most common theme that is consistently coming back from his family and friends is that he was a very insular person, kept himself to himself. He was financially secure, owned his own property and drove a tidy car, but there seems to be a glaring lack of a significant other. He's never had a long-term relationship, no kids or anything. He was seen as a keen ladies man, but he never seemed keen to settle."

Rudovsky was making notes on the board as Grant continued.

"Professionally, he was described as very popular. He worked in retail management, so that in itself is quite rare." The comment received a laugh from everybody. Behind the humour lay a pretty universal truth, most managers are disliked – rarely are they described as very popular.

Once the laughter had subsided, Grant continued. "As you know, we've seized his PC, his phone and his work i-pad. There's nothing on any of them which arouses any suspicion, like threatening texts or e-mails, or iffy websites he's been looking at. Nobody we've spoken to can explain what's gone on or offer any kind of plausible theory for what happened. We've found no criminal links in his past, no domestic problems in his present, his post-mortem showed no signs of drug or alcohol abuse. I hate to say it boss, but it looks like a worse-case scenario. The facts that we have are pointing towards a motiveless, random attack."

Grant was right. This was the worst-case scenario. The idea of a random attacker carrying out such an horrific attack on a perfect stranger was unthinkable.

Rudovsky nodded, she knew that the facts pointed towards the conclusion that Grant had just suggested. But she wasn't happy to accept that just yet. "We need to keep going, keep digging, turn Graham's private-life upside down. I'm just not prepared to accept that this was a totally random act, the level of violence just isn't consistent with that. The severity of the injuries tells us that this was an attack powered by raw hatred and passion. We don't stop looking into this man's life-story until we know for certain that Graham Hartley should receive a post-humous award for being the nicest bloke ever. Okay?"

"Sarge!"

"No problem, boss."

"Ma'am!" said Chapman, trying as always to piss his new superior off.

"Imagine how much physical effort would go into battering another person to death with a golf bat. We all know how exhausting it is to do shadow boxing for 60 seconds from our PT examinations. Imagine what went into swinging that bat. 38 separate swings of it, using every ounce of strength you could muster. In fact, I want to prove a point on this."

Rudovsky walked across to the corner of the incident room, where all of the team's tactical equipment was kept. She began throwing police-issue batons to each of her officers, which they caught, whilst looking at her with quizzical expressions. With the last one thrown in DC Grant's direction, she instructed her officers to spread out and start attacking the seat of their chairs, with as much power as they could muster, thirty-eight times.

"Come on, I want you to hold the baton in two hands and whack your chair as hard as you can. Imagine it's David

Cameron's head."

After a few dubious looks, they finally got started after following DC Kenyon's lead. Each member in the SCIU department, Rudovsky included, went about hitting their chairs as hard as they could. They were all keeping individual count as each powerful whack from the batons rebounded loudly against the soft foam inside the upholstery. If anybody walked in here now, they'd be excused for thinking that the SCIU detectives had lost the plot.

But it was a good exercise to carry out, that much was clear from the exhausted, out-of-breath and sweat soaked detectives as they finished battering their chairs thirty-eight times. They were all knackered, including Rudovsky and Grant who were widely acknowledged as the fittest members of the team.

"So... you get my point!" Rudovsky was breathless and pouring with sweat. "Thirty-eight heavy whacks takes a lot of effort and energy. But the person kept going and kept going, presumably until he had nothing left. This adds weight to my theory that this attack was not random, the hatred and anger required to carry out such a physically exhausting attack was being fuelled by something and we cannot solve this mystery until we know exactly what that is. So, off you pop and find out!"

"Are you going to order us up some new chairs?" asked Kenyon, breathlessly.

investigators. Amongst those police officers are two of the best-known detectives in the city, DCI Andrew Miller and DI Keith Saunders from the Serious Crimes unit, we've seen them walking around the area all morning. So, the fact that the two most senior members of that department are here tells us a lot, I think."

"Yes, it sounds like it Nick. This will of course be the fifth incident within the region, involving a betting shop. Over the past fortnight, we've seen four other bookmaker premises being completely trashed. This would appear to be connected, from what we are hearing?"

"Very possibly and I'm sure that will be the thought running through the minds of the police officers here this morning. But as you know Alan, we are only news reporters and can only really provide official information, so myself and many other colleagues who are here, reporting for various other news agencies are eagerly waiting to hear the official news. However, what I would say is that if this tragic incident does prove to be connected to the previous attacks against betting shops, then it would mean that things have suddenly become much more serious."

"To recap those other incidents, starting a fortnight ago, on November the fourth, the Welcome Bet shop on Bury Old Road, near Heaton Park was targeted by vandals. The entire shop was trashed, the betting machines and television screens were smashed up, the electrics were ripped out and the people responsible had left the taps running throughout the night so the entire shop was flooded by the time that the staff arrived in the morning. Three days later, on the seventh of November, the Mintbet premises on Liverpool Road in Eccles were also trashed in very similar circumstances. Four days after that, another bookies was targeted, the FreeBets shop in Romiley, once again, the store was completely smashed up by the intruders, and the shop will require a complete re-fit before it will be able to trade again. And that attack was followed up just a few nights ago, on November the fifteenth at GoWin betting shop on Bolton Road in Farnworth, once again, smashed up and left needing some major building work. Now, with last night's shocking and tragic incident, things are becoming extremely concerning."

"That's right Alan, and I'm sure as the day goes on, we will learn a lot more about these incidents, and what exactly the police are planning to do to catch the people responsible. If they are involved in the incident before me, then the criminal charges have just moved up considerably from vandalism and burglary, to arson and from what I can gather, murder."

"Okay Nick Forbes-Warren, I'm sure we'll speak to you again soon. In other news now, and the Conservative MP Nigel Evans has created a storm by publicly complaining about the lack of police in his Ribble Valley constituency, despite consistently voting for the police service cuts himself…"

Chapter Five

Miller and Saunders looked quite preoccupied as they entered the SCIU department, heading straight into the DCI's office without so much as a hello or a smile for their colleagues. Saunders closed the door behind his boss and took a seat across the desk as Miller sat down. The rest of the SCIU officers were looking through the glass walls, trying to lip-read the conversation.

"If we could all stop gawping at the boss and carry on with our own tasks, that will be great!" said Rudovsky, to nobody in particular.

"Just trying to work out if we're going to be switching cases, Ma'am," said Chapman.

"Yes, Bill, I know what you're doing. But what you are supposed to be doing is finding the killer of Graham Hartley. I'd prefer it if we got that case sewn up before we start looking for another one."

Chapman looked down at his desk and as he did so, a frosty atmosphere suddenly enveloped the office. He had always had a very turbulent relationship with Rudovsky and it was no secret that he didn't like her much. Nobody really knew why, as Rudovsky was a good detective and she was a popular member of the team with everybody else. Some of the staff put the hostility down to Rudovsky's success at such a young age. Bill Chapman had twenty years more experience than Rudovsky and hadn't managed to get past the DC rank. Other staff thought that Chapman might have issues with Rudovsky's sexuality, being an out-and-proud, flag-waving member of the gay community. Rudovsky herself put it down to bitterness on Chapman's part, because she was funnier, more popular and she didn't have a beer belly the size of a Space-Hopper.

Rudovsky wasn't keen on the bad vibes that were hanging ominously in the air. She walked across to Chapman's desk. "Bill, got a minute please, mate?" she asked quietly, before turning and heading towards the conference room on the opposite side of the office floor. Chapman huffed quietly and got to his feet, walking slowly behind his newly promoted DS.

Once inside the conference room, with the door firmly shut behind both detectives, Rudovsky wasted no time in coming to the point.

"Bill, I know it's a bit of a pisser for you that I've gone from your daily sparring partner to your gaffer…."

"No, it's… that's not…"

"Let me speak please, Bill. Now I think we need a day out together, just me and you. What are you into? Walking, cycling, fishing, playing golf?"

Chapman looked down at his feet, his bulbous face was visibly heating up. "No, I'm… we don't need to go for a day out…" He looked a little sheepish, not sure how to react to such a bizarre suggestion.

"What about a few pints and a game of darts then. Or pool, you beat me last time we played." Rudovsky was smiling, and Chapman broke a smile too.

"Honestly Jo, we don't need a game of pool."

"I think we do Bill. I really think that if we spent a bit of time together outside work, away from the others, we might start to get along a bit better. We need to find a way of getting along."

"We get along fine."

"Bill, listen, I just made a very reasonable comment in there, about concentrating on our current case. If Miller had said it, there wouldn't be an issue. Same goes for if Saunders had said it. But because I said it, there's suddenly a load of hostile friction and animosity in the room. If we are going to work together, we need to keep it positive and constructive. Now, I know I'm guilty of giving you a bit of shit here and there over the years, we've both been as bad as each other. But I can't behave like that in this job, as you know, I'd be guilty of workplace bullying or some bullshit if I said the kind of things that I used to say."

"What, like when you said that you're jealous of people who don't know me?"

"Yes, yes, that kind of thing…"

"Or when you said that I'm so fat I should go to the beach and sell shade?"

Rudovsky looked down at her feet. It was true, she had been quite brutal towards Chapman in the past.

"Yes, I admit, I've used you for practising my best put-down lines. But don't forget that you said that I'm the reason the gene pool needs a life-guard."

The two SCIU officers smiled at one another. They had been quite equally matched in the insults department.

"But those days are over now Bill, okay?"

Chapman nodded.

"So, like one of the Four-Tops, I'm reaching out to you, saying we need to bury the hatchet, and not in each-others heads."

"Jo, seriously, it's fine. There's no hatchet to bury." Chapman wasn't making eye contact, he seemed sincere and it looked as though he was a little embarrassed by this conversation.

"Listen Bill. The day I got this job, I said I don't want anybody calling me Ma'am, because I'm not the fucking queen. Do you remember?"

Chapman nodded, with a smirk.

"And every day since, you've called me Ma'am. Now it might be a bit of banter, but it's shit banter."

"I'll stop saying it, I'm only pulling your leg."

"And what about if I give you an instruction? Do you promise to stop having a hissy-fit?"

Chapman looked up at Rudovsky and nodded.

"Alright, let's shake on it. I'm not saying that you can't take the piss out of me Bill, you know I'm not. But please stop trying to undermine me in this new role. The job's hard enough as it is without somebody chucking obstacles in front of me."

"Okay. Sorry Jo, it wasn't intentional."

"Thanks. I know that you are a brilliant detective, and I'd rather we were focusing on you showing me and the rest of the team that, instead of using all your energies in trying to piss me off."

The comment about being a great detective seemed to have hit home. Chapman looked as though he had tears forming in his eyes as he looked down at the floor. He looked as though he'd needed that vindication.

"Well I'm glad we've had this chat. Let's start again, starting now, okay?"

"Absolutely, you've got my full support."

"Cool. Because if I haven't, you're coming raft building with me on a team-building weekend. I'll pay!"

"It won't come to that. Believe me!" Chapman smiled widely, and Rudovsky touched his shoulder gently.

"Thanks Bill. I know you and I have been at war in the past. But the best days lie ahead."

"Sounds like you've been at a positive thinking book?"

"Yeah, I have as it goes. How about this one 'if you want the light to come into your life, stand in the sunshine and welcome it."

"Doesn't really work for Manchester, does it?"

"Nah. It's a pretty shit one that, to be fair."

"Right, well, let me prove I'm not a total bum. Okay?"

"Deal. Thanks Bill."

"Ma'am... ah, shit, sorry... Sarge!"

Chapter Six

Despite reprimanding her team for gawping into the office, Rudovsky was guilty of the same crime. She'd glanced across several times to try and figure out what Miller and Saunders were planning. As things stood, there was absolutely no way that the department could handle another case, not whilst there was the very real threat of a mad-man killer on the streets, supposedly attacking at random.

But she couldn't make out what her senior officers were discussing. Rudovsky realised that she'd just have to wait and see. She glanced back at her paperwork and sensed a presence hovering by her desk. It was DC Bill Chapman, just twenty minutes after their clear-the-air chat in the conference room.

"Sarge, do we know if Hartley jogged along that route regularly?"

Rudovsky was impressed. Chapman had managed to call her Sarge, without her ever suggesting it. He sounded genuine and respectful. Best of all, the rest of the team had all heard him. That was an excellent start to this new working relationship pact.

"Oh, do you know what, I don't know." Rudovsky looked across to DC Peter Kenyon.

"Pete, do we know if Graham was a regular jogger?"

"Er... just a sec," Kenyon started looking through his file. A few seconds of silence passed before he nodded at his paperwork and looked back in the direction of Rudovsky and Chapman.

"It says here, witness statement from his sister... says he tries to do an hour of jogging every night. Erm, says he was training for a marathon."

"Anything about keeping to a specific route?" asked Chapman, still standing by the DS's desk. Kenyon continued to scan over the report. A few more seconds passed before he replied.

"Nah, doesn't say anything about that..."

"What are you thinking Bill?" asked Rudovsky.

"Well, I don't jog much myself these days…" The comment received a big laugh from Chapman's colleagues as he patted his enormous stomach. "But I imagine that somebody who does it regularly is likely to stick to the same route. It'd make it easier for keeping track of your speed and progress and that."

"You sure you don't jog Bill?" asked DC Mike Worthington, Chapman's regular partner in investigations.

"No, don't be a dick, look at me, I'd look pretty stupid in a running vest! I look like a giant egg." Chapman's self-deprecating gag received another good laugh from his colleagues. He waited for the laughter to subside before continuing. "I'm just thinking, we're all worried that this is a random attack. But if Graham Hartley was in the habit of going on a specific route, at a similar time, it wouldn't be too hard to keep tabs on him for a few days, learn his routine and then wait in the bushes along the route."

Rudovsky clapped her hands together. "Spot on! Nice one Bill, I think you're on to something here. Have a ring around his family, his colleagues, see what his routine was around the running. Brilliant suggestion Bill, well done."

"Yeah, nice one Bill," said Kenyon.

Chapman headed back to his desk and picked the phone up from its cradle, looking pleased with himself. Rudovsky looked on, feeling glad that her little pep-talk had seemed to have worked like a charm in adjusting Chapman's attitude towards her, and it would appear, to his work too.

*****

Inside Miller's office, there wasn't a lot of talking going on. Both of the SCIU's senior detectives were reading through the case-notes from each of the betting shop attacks which had taken place over the past few weeks.

Until today, each attack had been the responsibility of the local CID teams in their corresponding divisions. Bolton, Salford, Middleton and Stockport detectives had been dealing with each incident. Although "dealing with it" was a bit

killer."

"And we'll know that it wasn't a random attack, too."

"Brilliant. This is the breakthrough we needed. We've already got the locations of every available CCTV camera around the crime scene. I think we need to get a hold of it all for the past few weeks, build up a picture of the whole route and see what other cameras he comes into view of. We know he's well covered for the East Lancs Road, might be a big gap along the canal though…" Rudovsky was making notes as she spoke.

"There are a few pubs along there, plus a few apartment blocks coming into Monton. There's the Co-Op store at Worsley Road as well." DC Helen Grant was familiar with the area.

"Okay, I'm going to see the gaffer, see what he suggests is the best method of capturing this CCTV and reviewing it. Back in five minutes."

Rudovsky headed across to Miller's office and knocked lightly. Miller looked up from the report he was reading and waved her in. The mood was flat, and the atmosphere was heavy.

"Everything alright?" she asked.

"No, not really Jo. We've been to a horrific job this morning. Young dad and his seven-year-old son were killed in an arson attack in the early hours."

"Aw fuck…"

"And we've just learnt that the little girl rescued by fire officers has passed away in the last half an hour. The mum doesn't know yet that her family are all gone." Miller looked as though he was tearing up. Rudovsky looked down at the carpet tiles. She couldn't think of anything to say. What could she possibly say to that?

Saunders sensed that his colleague was speechless at that devastating announcement and decided to fill the dark silence. "So, these daft attacks against betting shops have now become a triple murder enquiry. And we've been given the case."

It was clear to Miller and Saunders that Rudovsky's first thought was "how the hell are we going to manage that?"

Miller decided to get straight to the point. "Keith and I are currently working out a strategy on how to deal with the logistics of this enquiry Jo. I want you and the team to get this Graham Hartley case boxed off, so please continue with that. I'm going to put forward a proposal to pool resources with the divisional CID departments from each crime scene and spread the workload evenly between each division. That will leave you and the team free to pursue the killer of Graham Hartley. Okay?"

"Yeah, sure, that's... well, that's what I wanted to hear to be honest. Are you two okay though?" Rudovsky could see that both of her senior officers were upset.

"Yes, we'll be alright," said Saunders. "Thanks for asking like."

"Yeah, thanks Jo. We'd been pretty confident the little girl was going to make it, so at least her mum would have had that..."

"Fuck. Oh fucking hell boss, that's just awful. Any idea what this is all about?"

"Well... there's a couple of theories we need to look into, but for now Jo, I don't want to distract you from your case."

"Oh, yeah, sure. I can't help myself can I?" Rudovsky smiled, attempting to lighten the mood. But it didn't work.

"So, did you want me for anything?"

"Yes, God, I almost forgot. Chapman's come up with an interesting line of inquiry."

"Go on."

"He's discovered that Graham Hartley ran most nights of the week, setting off at a similar time, seven pm. He stuck to the exact same route. I'm just thinking that we could pull in all the CCTV from the past few weeks and check the footage and see if we can identify anybody who might have been sussing out Graham's routine."

Suddenly, Miller seemed to come alive. "That's brilliant. Even if it doesn't present anything, that outcome will support the theory of it being a random attack, so we can't lose. It's perfect. Pull in the CCTV feeds from the street view cameras, local businesses and any domestic systems along the route.

Work backwards from the day before Hartley was attacked."

"It's going to be a big task, Sir."

"I know. But you've got Bill, Pete, Mike and Helen. That's five of you… if you dedicate your day to this task alone you'll make some progress. Tell them to log car registrations of any vehicles that seem to be loitering, screenshot all individuals riding bikes and everybody walking in the direction of Eccles Field in the thirty minutes leading up to Graham's run."

"Sir."

"And all people leaving Eccles Field in the fifteen minute period after he'd entered, each day. This could be the case closed Jo."

"Great, okay. No point asking for additional support staff? Even if it's just to retrieve the CCTV footage."

"I can ask Dixon if he can pull a few levers… give me ten minutes."

"Cheers Sir."

Chapter Seven

"This is Sky News at lunch-time and our top story this hour. A father and his two children have been killed in an arson attack in Denton, Greater Manchester. As our footage shows, this was a devastating fire which has completely gutted the building where it took hold in the early hours of this morning. The names of the victims have not yet been released, but the police and the fire service are treating this incident as an arson attack which means that a triple-murder enquiry has been launched by Manchester City Police."

The footage on the Sky News screen was a very bleak and upsetting view of the burnt-out building, accompanied by the vibrating sound of the fire engines which were still in attendance. A crowd of shocked and distressed members of the public stood by the cordon line tape. Black soot covered the surviving wall at the end of the row of shops. The betting shop and the flat were unrecognisable now, there was nothing but a pile of burnt-out rubble in a heap with several fire officers still scrambling through the debris looking for evidence.

"This scene of utter devastation and tragedy in Manchester is very hard to recognise as an end-terrace shop and living premises. But as you can see from the Google Street View on your screens now, until the early hours of this morning, this property was a very normal looking building which consisted of the Betadays bookmakers shop on the ground floor, with a neat and tidy looking flat above it."

The Street View picture really brought home the level of destruction, it looked as though a bomb had gone off at this address.

"Our reporter Catherine Palmer is at the scene of this tragic incident. Catherine."

"Yes, I'm joined by Greater Manchester's Chief Fire Officer, Nina Thompson. What can you tell us about the cause of this devastating fire?"

The screen changed from the reporter to a shot of the very distressed looking fire chief.

"Well, I've been a fire officer in Greater Manchester for

almost thirty years and I can honestly say that this is one of the worst incidents that I have attended, and many of my officers are currently struggling to deal with the horrendous scenes which greeted them here in the early hours. As you can see behind me, there is nothing left of this property. Our investigations into the cause of this tragedy are ongoing, but I can confirm that this was a fire which had been started deliberately. Our initial examinations have revealed that a flammable substance which we believe to be petrol, was poured into the property through the shop's letterbox and then ignited. From the way that the fire has spread throughout the lower floor instantaneously, we believe that a large amount of this substance was poured into the property, we're thinking that something in the region of twenty litres was used, and then the vapours were allowed to build up for several minutes before the source of ignition was dropped through the letterbox. The sheer power and the resulting blast of the fire would have been similar to an explosion. This resulting explosion has quickly burnt through the suspended ceiling in the shop area and through the wooden floorboards into the flat above."

"And there was a family sleeping up there when this fire was started?"

"Yes, that's…" the Fire Chief's voice faltered as she began to speak. The raw emotion was impossible to miss. "That's very sadly the case, and as you are aware, lives were lost here this morning."

"What can you tell us about those people who were in the flat?"

"Well, as you are probably aware, we can't reveal too much information about that yet, as family and friends will obviously need to be informed. But there will be a press statement released with those details in due course."

"What role does the fire service now have at this scene, I see that several fire appliances are still here and dozens of officers are still working hard behind me in the rubble?"

"Our priority here now is to check for any other people who may have been in the flat. This is a painstaking operation which involves moving the debris away from the scene in a very careful and meticulous way, whilst at the same time ensuring that structural integrity of the remaining sections of the building are not compromised. Once that section of the operation has been completed, our next task will be to organise the demolition of the gable end wall, so the road closures in place will continue for the foreseeable future until the scene of this tragic incident has been made safe."

"So, you anticipate that you will be here for a while yet?"

"Yes, we'll certainly be here for a couple of days at least."

"Chief Fire Officer Nina Thompson, thank you."

*****

"Jo, have you got five minutes, please?" Miller was standing in his office doorway, summoning his DS over.

Rudovsky stood and walked across the large office floor space and followed her boss in, closing the door behind herself.

"Hi Jo," said Saunders, without looking up from the file he was reading.

"Sir."

"Right, Jo. I've had a chat with Frosty." That was the forbidden nickname for DCS Dixon, in reference to his massive white eyebrows which made him look like he'd just been playing Santa at the local infant school and had forgotten to take them off.

"Good news?"

"Yes. I'm surprised to say. I think he realises that we're over-stretched with having the two most serious cases in the region to manage with a skeleton crew. He's instructed Salford's duty Inspector to organise retrieving the CCTV data from all the addresses you want. So, I need you to come up with a list of all the cameras you want the footage from pretty sharpish."

"Already got it Sir. I can e-mail it across to you right away."

"Brilliant. Well, better still, send it straight to Dixon. How many addresses are we talking about?"

"Over twenty in Monton, about seven in Swinton, four or five in Worsley."

"Okay. It's a lot of footage to go through, though..."

"It is, but you know that it only takes one decent lead and it's not such a needle-in-a-haystack once you find summat and have a specific time-frame to work around."

"Good. Okay, well, without trying to put you under too much pressure..."

"Oh, just a second... I don't fucking like the sound of this!"

Saunders laughed at Rudovsky's tone.

"...we really need a lead on the Hartley case. If you get something that looks tasty, I can flick it over to CID at Salford to do the donkey-work."

"What, hand them all my glory?" Rudovsky looked a little disappointed.

"Well, not that so much, it will just clear our desks so that I can incorporate all of the team into this." Miller pointed down at the files on his desk, a photograph of the burnt out, collapsed building was sitting on the top.

"What's the plan, with this I mean?" Rudovsky nodded at the macabre photograph.

"Keith and I are meeting with senior CID officers from each division that has had an incident involving a bookies. At this stage, temporarily I hope, we are going to be managing each CID department. This will be good for getting all the leg-work done, but I want to sack them off and use my own guys for stage two. So, now more than ever, I need something to materialise in the Hartley case. I'm relying on you Jo, all of my faith is being entrusted in you and your amazing detective skills. Me and Keith were just saying, only you can save us."

"Oh wind it in Sir! Or I'll arrest you for gross insincerity!"

All three of the unit's senior officers laughed at Rudovsky's plain-talking response to Miller's over-the-top brown-nosing.

"Right, go and do that e-mail for Dixon. Me and Keith are heading back to the crime scene to meet the other CID officers, not sure when we'll be back."

"Why are you meeting them at the scene of the fire?"

"The mobile incident room is there, plus a load of TV and press reporters are still on the scene so Dixon said it will show how involved we are while we stall the preliminary press conference."

"Okay, well, good luck with it. I'll go and e-mail Frosty."

Chapter Eight

The CID staff from the police stations affected by the betting shop attacks were waiting to meet Miller and Saunders at the agreed location, a few streets away from the scene of the previous night's tragedy.

Following some brief introductions, Miller led Bolton, Salford, Tameside, Stockport and Middleton division's most senior detectives around the red-bricked terraced streets which led out to the cordoned-off road.

Several fire appliances were still on site, as were numerous police vans and cars. A number of PCSO officers were explaining the road diversions to frustrated drivers who were making it very clear that they could do without all this hassle. Apart from the emergency services personnel and the odd spectator by the cordon tape, the only other people around this eerie, solemn place were the members of the press who, understandably, were trying to get more information about this devastating fire. The return of Miller and Saunders to the scene, joined by five other familiar looking DCI's and DI's was a major development as far as the assembled media were concerned and a very welcome sight.

Miller was talking as he walked with his entourage, explaining the facts as they were understood, starting at the front of the collapsed building, where the betting shop's door had been situated, and where the petrol had been poured through the letterbox.

The scene which lay before the detectives was impossible to make sense of, so Miller was explaining the situation using a Google Street View picture, which showed how the building had looked up until the fire. Miller was waving his arm around, explaining the geography of the site, pointing out reference points from the photograph and these gestures were providing interesting footage for the photographers and cameramen.

Miller was showing his colleagues the photos and pointing at the only surviving wall, the gable end. He was trying hard to explain how the building had been set out and describing the way that the staircase to the flat had run parallel to the seat of the fire, and how the fire had subsequently engulfed the stairs, which had been the only escape route that the family had access to. He also explained that as this was a traditional, Victorian-era built shop parade, the height of the first-floor flat had prevented the occupants to jump to safety. By modern building standards, he explained, the height of that window would almost be the equivalent height to that of a standard house's roof.

Miller appeared oblivious to the press attention as he talked to his new team leaders.

"Right, so, in terms of forensic evidence, this place is an absolute write-off. The only piece of decent evidence we have is a CCTV camera on the back of the Hat Factory which shows four people walking away from this area shortly after the fire started, a couple of minutes before the first emergency call came in. We've also got a potential lead with the person who made the initial emergency 999 call, although that person has yet to be traced. I'll show you some stills from the CCTV and play you the call once we get in the truck."

Miller was referring to the Force's mobile incident room, which was parked close to the scene of the fire. The huge white truck housed all of the communications tools required to co-ordinate a major incident response, as well as containing a private conference room at the back. DCS Dixon had been keen to see Miller and the others using this facility, right under the media's noses, to reassure the public that the city's leading detectives were on scene and were busy trying to track down the individuals responsible for such an unthinkably evil crime.

As things presently stood, it was too early to present a press conference because the information was still being patched together and a full, rational explanation of the incident was not yet possible.

Understandably, there was a huge desire to hear the police's response, particularly from members of the local community. But, the media staff understood that the information would only be released the moment the police were happy to do so, and not a second earlier.

"The entire building has been condemned by structural engineers," said Miller, pointing to the blackened, soot covered remainder of the terrace which had consisted of three houses and another shop at the far end. "So, we've got an absolute nightmare of a case here, two kids dead, as well as their dad, a mum with no family or home to go to if she survives. Then we've got the incidental victims of all this. Four families have been made homeless, the other shop and its owner have lost their livelihood. And all for what? A cowardly attack on a bookies shop!" Miller couldn't hide his contempt for the perpetrators.

The other detectives stayed silent as Miller explained the extent of the damage. He'd spent a good ten minutes, walking all the way around the terraced building with his new team, commenting on various aspects of the SOCO investigations, and talking them through the plans that the fire service had for compiling their own reports and publishing their findings.

Once the site recce had been completed, the TV camera crews continued filming as Miller showed the detectives up the steps and into the mobile incident room. This was where the real work was to begin.

"Okay, well, I think we should take this opportunity to introduce ourselves properly," said Miller as he sat down at the table at the back of the converted truck. "I'll go first, I'm DCI Andy Miller, head of the Serious Crimes Investigation Unit. I've been put in charge of this investigation by instruction of DCS David Dixon, acting on behalf of the Chief Constable. As you are all fully aware, DCS Dixon has decided that this investigation requires the full support of the city's CID departments where betting shop attacks have occurred in the past few weeks, which hopefully explains why you are all here."

Miller nodded to his number two, DI Saunders, who had taken the seat to Miller's right.

"Hello, I'm DI Keith Saunders, also with the Serious Crimes Unit. As things stand, there are only two officers available to work on this case from our department, that's myself and DCI Miller. The rest of our team are working on the Graham Hartley murder, which I'm sure you'll all be aware of from internal communications as well as the substantial press coverage that the case has attracted."

There were nods all around the table from the five officers. Saunders gestured the person to his right to introduce herself.

"Hi, I'm DCI Katy Green from Tameside CID. I'm here because this incident has taken place within our division, and I'm looking forward to working with you all."

The next detective spoke. "Yes, hello. I'm DI Nadeem Iqbal from Salford CID. Our division had an arson attack against a betting shop on the seventh of November, the Mintbet bookies in Eccles. That incident was obviously much less serious than this one in that nobody was hurt and the incident caused only cosmetic damage inside the shop."

Miller nodded to the next detective.

"Hi, DCI Bob Cryne from Central. Our department investigated the first of these attacks, which was initially put down to bored kids but of course we are now realising that there is potentially something much more sinister going on. The shop was near Heaton Park, it was completely trashed and flooded, that was on the fourth of November, three days before the incident that Nadeem was just talking about in Eccles."

"Hello, DCI Sue Sutherland from Bolton. Our incident took place just a couple of nights ago at the Go-Win betting shop in Farnworth. This was another case of vandalism that has basically put the shop out of business for the foreseeable future. As you'll probably be aware it has attracted quite a lot of media interest as the link began to be made about the fact that these shops were being targeted. Looking around this site today has been shocking and I'm looking forward to doing everything I can on this investigation to help get the bastards responsible for this locked up."

The last of the detectives spoke. "Hello, I'm DI Lee Burrows from Stockport. Our attack was the third incident, on the eleventh of November, at the FreeBets store in Romiley. This was initially treated as vandalism, we had reached the conclusion that it was youths running amok. The store was completely trashed and our witness reports suggested that the whole incident was carried out in under five minutes. There wasn't any flooding at this address, but the FreeBets managers have said that it will take many months before the damage is made good and the shop reopens."

Miller smiled and nodded. "Thanks everybody. I think we can all agree that these crimes weren't previously viewed as the most serious incidents in the city up until last night's. That said, I can sense a shit-storm brewing from the press. I imagine that they'll highlight our lack of progress in arresting the people responsible after the first four attacks, and ultimately use that as a device to blame us for the deaths here last night."

"Standard response," said Saunders under his breath.

"Anyway, I'll deal with the press, so please point any enquiries my way. My priority for today is to discuss our objectives and for us all to leave here with a game-plan. The incidents in your own divisions will need to be looked at again, naturally. I'm confident that by treating the earlier attacks much more seriously, we're bound to get something. Please don't take this as a criticism, I'm acutely aware that your teams will have had much more pressing incidents to investigate than these shops being smashed up. But it goes without saying that we need to push this right to the top of our priority lists now. I want to see thorough, no-stone-unturned investigations, including CCTV searches, door-to-doors, fresh forensic examinations, we really need to throw the kitchen sink at it. Is that understood?"

Miller smiled appreciatively at the faces around the table. They were all nodding enthusiastically. Miller knew exactly how much pressure these people were already under before this had been landed on their laps and was pleased to see a positive response and no moaning.

"Okay, back to the CCTV footage we managed to get from the factory around the corner." Miller pulled out a photograph of four people who were walking away from the fire. Based on the physical profiles of each individual on the image, it looked as though all four were male, but their body-types didn't look particularly young. "It's not that clear on these photos," Miller started handing out the grainy CCTV images which had been filmed in the dead of night. "Based purely on watching the moving footage, which I will e-mail across to you all later, I'm guessing that these four individuals are male and are aged over thirty."

"What makes you say that?" asked DCI Katy Green.

"You'll see for yourself when I send the footage, but they don't walk like young people. Their body shapes don't make them look like youths. One seems to have a bit of a limp. I may be wrong entirely, but I just don't think that these are the body movements of nimble youths. I'm sorry I can't play the footage here, but rest assured you'll all have it on e-mail by the time that you get back to your desks."

The detectives continued to look at the photographs, swapping them around across the table-top.

"The other interesting thing that we have to think about is the nine-nine-nine call. The tech team are doing some tests on the fancy software they have, apparently they can put an approximate age on the voice by measuring the frequency of the hertz range, or some dorky stuff. But the caller needs to be identified as a matter of urgency, he can be heard puking up during the call and he sounded extremely disturbed, so there's a strong possibility that he was involved, then panicked when he realised that there was a family trapped above the burning building. I'll have more information on that later, but I can tell you that it is going to be a major element of the initial press conference."

"When's that happening?" asked DI Nadeem Iqbal.

"Soon. Just waiting for clearance from the press office who are making sure all loved ones and extended family members are aware of the situation. It's proving tricky as the family are from Latvia. So, it's been quite a challenging job to inform the nearest and dearest, I'm told."

The five detectives sensed that Miller was done. Now all they wanted to do was get back to their own police stations, and their own teams and begin co-ordinating their own investigations.

"Any questions?"

All five of the detectives averted their eyes from Miller's. That was a no. They just wanted to get out of here and get cracking on the tasks they had to oversee.

"Okay, well, thank you for being so supportive and understanding. I realise that it's not ideal, but we should have this sorted out within a few days. I'll send you all the e-mail correspondence I've been talking about just as soon as I get back to my office."

And with that, the chairs scraped back and the detectives all stood, before filing out of the major incident room vehicle one-by-one, unbeknown to them, live on the Sky News and BBC News networks.

Chapter Nine

Several reporters had clocked the direction that Miller and his entourage had appeared from an hour earlier, and some of the more enthusiastic ones had investigated further and discovered where he and the divisional officers had parked. It was easy enough, six newish silver Vauxhall Insignia cars, all parked in the same street. It had been a bit of a give-away.

"DCI Miller! What can you tell us about the motive for this tragedy?"

"Any news on the fatalities?"

"What time are you expecting to give a press conference?"

Miller walked calmly towards them, whilst the other CID officers that he'd been meeting with got into their vehicles and headed back to their respective police stations. Saunders got into the SCIU car and started the engine.

"Hi, alright?" said the well-known DCI as he confronted the small group. They all nodded and said hello. "Alright Lee, has your missus had the baby yet?"

"No, still a few weeks to go!" said the Granada Reports crime correspondent, appearing pleased that Miller had taken an interest.

"Yes, I can tell. You look like you've had a good night's sleep. I'll know when the baby's here because you'll have the new dad look of despair! There's no way of hiding it, I've tried myself."

Lee laughed as Miller switched his attention to the rest of the reporters. "Listen everyone, I know we've been pretty quiet today and not fed you much but it'll all become clearer in a bit. I just need you all to be patient for a bit longer."

The press appreciated Miller's no-bullshit response. He was always good with them, and treated them as colleagues rather than nuisances, which was the way most senior police officers treated the press. The respect that Miller showed them was appreciated. They all knew that if he had something to tell them, he'd have let them have it by now. Incidents such as this one were always shrouded in a cloak of secrecy until the formalities had been taken care of.

"It's bad though, isn't it? Horrific crime scene."

There were nods and grunts from the small crowd.

"I hope you're all ready for a busy time of it though, once we've had the go-ahead for the press conference?"

"Any idea when it will be Andy?" asked one.

"Not sure... but it will be today, probably after tea. So, I'll probably see you all later on. Cheers for now guys."

Miller smiled warmly and returned to the last remaining Insignia on the terraced street. Saunders had the engine running and pulled the clutch up as soon as his boss sat in the passenger seat.

"Bless 'em."

"Who? Them?" asked Saunders, looking across at Miller as though his boss had lost his marbles.

"Yeah, must be shit doing that job, waiting around all day for us to tell them what they already know, but can't actually say."

"Well there are worse jobs. I went to college with a lad whose brother had to pull turds and rubber johnnies and dead cats out of drains. All day, every day. His nickname was Michael shit-fingers."

Miller smiled. In the grand scheme of things, that was a much worse job than being a reporter.

"So, what do you reckon?" asked Miller.

"About the fire?"

"Well yes, obviously Keith. I'm not interested in your thoughts on Michael shit-fingers."

"Well, my theory is that the people who did this had no idea that the family were in bed above the shop. I think they will all have woken up to the news and will be going insane now with guilt. Once you've done your press conference, I think they will hand themselves in."

"Really?"

"Yes. How can anybody live with that? They'll want to explain, try and cleanse their conscience, make sure everybody knows that it was a tragic accident, that they're not monsters. That they're just fucking stupid, not evil." Saunders tapped the indicator and pulled onto the motorway slip-road before pressing his foot hard on the accelerator.

"I hope you're right. That will make our jobs a lot easier."

"I've seen it happen before. I just can't imagine anybody being able to justify it in their minds. If it was one person, I'd feel a bit different, but four of them? Four people who all know what they are guilty of, killing two little kids and their dad in the most terrifying of circumstances? There's no way they can try and carry on as normal."

"Is that the way you think I should present the press-conference?"

"It wouldn't do any harm. Play the sympathy card, tell them that you know they never meant it... yeah, definitely. I think we'll have them in custody tonight."

Miller wasn't so sure. He trusted Saunders completely, and valued his opinions, after all, his DI was very rarely wrong. But the idea that the perpetrators were just going to walk into the police station and beg forgiveness was taking it a bit far in Miller's estimations, they were all facing life sentences for last night's activities. Life sentences with the label 'kid-killer.' It wasn't necessarily going to be a softer option to confess and spend the next twenty years being beaten and abused in jail.

"Well I don't personally agree that they'll walk in, but I think I will construct my press conference around that basis, get in touch, cleanse your soul. I might add in a bit of scare-mongering too."

"What like?"

"Well, you know, if you suspect that you know who did this, I am appealing to you to phone the police, under no circumstances must you go round there and take the law into your own hands. That kind of thing."

"Genius. Creating a sense of complete and overpowering mental anguish. Nice touch."

"Any idea what it's all about, Keith?"

"No, not really. I've a couple of theories swimming about in my head but nothing too solid."

"Go on, I'd like to hear them."

"Well, there are still a few anomalies in each version. First, I was thinking that this might be a gang-land issue, a protection racket. Pay us a grand a week or we'll put your shop out of action."

"Could be a strong theory."

"Yes, it ticks a few boxes. The only trouble is, looking at the CCTV footage of the blokes walking away... they're not gangsters, are they? They walk more like geriatrics."

"To be fair Keith, we don't know that's them. They could well be eliminated as soon as the footage is made public."

"Yes, I get that. But I doubt it somehow. Why would four blokes be walking up the middle of the road at one a.m. just after a major fire has been started around the corner?"

"I see what you're saying, but we don't know where they came from, do we? It could be that they'd had a lock-in at the Working Men's Club. That would also explain the laboured walking."

"Doesn't explain the dark clothing and their hoods up."

"No... no, that's a good point."

"So, my theory about gangsters running a protection racket on the bookies still has a few missing links."

"What was your other theory? You said you had a couple."

"Yes, the other idea I had is just as tricky to nail down. I was thinking that there might be a group of disgruntled gamblers who have decided to take their frustrations out on the betting shops where they've lost all their money."

"Wow. I like the sound of that idea."

"Yes, well, it would explain the general view that the four people on the CCTV aren't looking very nimble."

"I like this... this is a good theory mate."

"Yes, but there are a number of flaws with it. Firstly, the geography of the shops that have been targeted. They are so random, they sort of circle the Greater Manchester map. Bolton, Middleton, Denton, Stockport and Tameside. If this was a group of angry gamblers, why would they target bookies in such random places?"

"Don't know."

"Plus, each shop belongs to a different chain."

"Good point, so we can rule out a vendetta against a certain brand of bookmakers."

"Precisely. So as I say, these theories present more questions than answers at the minute."

"Besides, going back to the geography... its not as though there's a shortage of betting shops in the area." Miller took his phone out of his pocket and opened the internet browser. He did a quick search. "Here we go... how many bookies do you think there are in Greater Manchester?"

"Fifty? Sixty?" said Saunders, not sounding very confident.

"Over three hundred!"

"Seriously?"

"That's what it says here..."

"Bloody hell. How many bakers?"

Miller searched again. It only took a few seconds to get the answer. "One hundred and eighty-two."

"Holy macaroni! So there are almost twice as many bookies as bakers?"

"That's what Google reckon."

"Yeah, actually, thinking about it. How many betting shops are there in the average town? Five, six..."

"And only one Greggs!"

"This makes me think that the second theory is even more unlikely. If these attacks are being carried out by bitter gamblers, they wouldn't have to go as far as Bolton to find a bookies to trash, or burn down."

"Well Keith, I still like it. I think you might be on to something there, this could form a significant line of enquiry. We need to look at the locations of the shops that have been targeted and see if we can work out why that particular shop was chosen. Was it because it was remote, isolated, away from prying eyes, handy for an escape, far away from CCTV? I think we should start building a picture up of each location and see if there's a common theme."

"Well, last night's was certainly in a remote location. There are other betting shops in Denton, there are four up at

Crown Point, but there's lots of CCTV and traffic all night running through the town centre." Saunders indicated and pulled the car off the motorway as Miller's phone rang.

"It's Dixon. Hello, Sir."

"Hi Andy, its Dixon."

Miller smiled at the familiar greeting and wondered if his boss knew how stupid he sounded introducing himself like this in the digital age when his name pops up on the phone screen.

"Where are you?"

"Just coming into town, about five minutes away. Why, what's come up?"

"Oh, I've just had clearance from the family liaison officers. It's okay to speak to the press now."

"Oh, that's good news."

"Yes. So, I'll book the media-centre for... shall we say five?"

"Yes, that sounds okay Sir. Thanks."

Miller hung up and let out a heavy sigh. He hated press conferences.

Chapter Ten

DCS Dixon's instruction to the Divisional Inspector at Salford Division had yielded an amazing result. The amount of CCTV footage which was being delivered to the SCIU from Salford's police officers, detectives and PCSO's was incredible considering the request had only been made a few hours earlier.

DS Rudovsky had built up a list of business and domestic addresses around the route of Graham Hartley's regular run and had then sent the list to Dixon. It was almost as though the Salford Inspector had asked all of his available officers to drop everything and grab the footage as a top priority. It certainly demonstrated the power of a senior rank. If Rudovsky had asked for this favour alone, she was confident that it would probably take several weeks to accumulate this much footage, if she ever received any at all.

Rudovsky's desk was cluttered with envelopes and evidence bags which contained USB memory sticks. Each parcel included the dates and times of the CCTV footage downloaded, along with the address of the source. She started sorting the USBs into piles, starting with the addresses closest to Hartley's house on Francis Street in Monton. The next pile of USBs, the biggest pile, was made up of footage from addresses along the main Monton Road, the thoroughfare between Swinton and Eccles which made up the hub of the village.

Monton has witnessed a huge amount of regeneration over the past fifteen to twenty years. In that time it has seen a very ordinary, very northern road of charity shops, takeaways and pubs transform into a popular social hot-spot filled with restaurants, cafes and wine bars with outdoor dining, which stretches all along both sides of the road for half a mile. It's not quite Paris, but Monton has managed to pull-off a remarkable make-over since the turn of the millennium and has become a very trendy place to be seen. The district attracts lots of Premier League footballers, celebrated musicians as well as well-known actors and TV presenters from the nearby Media-City development a mile or so away.

It was thanks to this make-over and modernisation that

the SCIU team now had hundreds of hours of CCTV footage from all along Monton Road to be examined, looking for anybody who might be following or spying on Graham Hartley each night when he set off on his 7pm jog.

The mood was a peculiar mix of excitement and dread. This operation had the potential to confirm that Hartley was attacked completely at random, or to prove Chapman's theory, that the attacker will be seen on CCTV working out his logistics for battering the jogger to death with a golf club in the lonely darkness of an isolated path behind a housing estate.

"Right everybody, look at the state of this," said Rudovsky, pointing at the Monton Road pile of envelopes. "I have never seen so much evidence which has overwhelmed me so much that I am having dark thoughts about throwing myself onto the motorway."

"How have you got all that so quickly?" asked Chapman, looking at his watch. It was almost five, knocking off time.

"I have no idea. Dixon asked the Inspector at Salford to co-ordinate it."

"Jesus. That Inspector must have a point to prove!" said Kenyon, walking across to have a better look at the huge pile on Rudovsky's desk.

"He wants a promotion!" said Chapman.

"So, just a heads up, tomorrow you will need your specs and your Optrex eye-drops as we're all going to be staring our computer screens out all day."

Chapman wandered across to the desk and looked at how Rudovsky had laid the piles out. The first pile, which contained just two envelopes was labelled "Francis Street."

"Sarge, is it okay if I get cracking now?" asked Chapman. Rudovsky's initial thought was that DC Chapman was taking the piss, after all, it was literally minutes before home time. But she quickly realised from his expression that he was being deadly serious.

"Yes, Bill, course. If you want?"

"Thanks. I'll start with Francis Street, if that's okay?"

"Sure. Fill your boots." Rudovsky handed the two

packages across to Chapman and smiled widely.

"So, we're checking for Hartley leaving the house and then creating a log of any people or vehicles that he passes?"

"Yes. And any other activity that might look odd, like people sat in cars or loitering around bus stops. If anybody is waiting at a bus stop when Graham runs past, we might want to speed it up and check that they actually catch the bus when it arrives, that kind of shit."

All of the SCIU officers were familiar with CCTV investigations, so Rudovsky didn't have to lay it on too thick, she knew that they had enough experience to carry out a thorough search through the footage without too much supervision.

"Right, well, I'll make a start. I'll start on Francis Street on the night of the attack and work backwards one day at a time."

"Brilliant. Thanks Bill."

There was a slight sense of mirth in the office. The other detectives, Kenyon, Grant and Worthington glanced at one another, trying not to laugh. This enthusiasm, particularly volunteering for overtime, was most uncharacteristic of Bill Chapman. Rudovsky was clearly impressed by this new attitude.

"Right, well, sorry but I'm going home. I've got to pick the kids up from after-school club." DC Mike Worthington was the first to draw his line in the sand regarding overtime.

"That's fine," said Rudovsky, her eyes fixed on the back of Chapman as he organised his desk ready for a CCTV session.

"But I'll come in early..." added Worthington, keen to show that his commitment to picking the kids up was not a reflection on his enthusiasm for finding out who was responsible for that horrific attack on Hartley.

"No worries Mike. See you in the morning."

"I've got to go as well," said Kenyon.

"That's fine, don't worry about it. I didn't think we'd see all this lot until tomorrow afternoon at the earliest anyway. See you tomorrow Pete."

Kenyon left the office with Worthington. It looked as though they both felt awkward as they abandoned the team.

"I'm alright to stay for a bit..." said DC Helen Grant once

the departing officers were through the door.

"Oh right, nice one Helen."

Rudovsky handed an envelope to Grant. "This is the CCTV footage belonging to the Park Inn." She turned and pointed at the map of Monton village on the wall. "This is the pub on the corner, next to the entrance to the crime scene. The attack happened a good two hundred and fifty yards away from here, along the path. But this is going to contain the last footage of anybody leaving or entering the path through Eccles Field."

"We've already had this, haven't we?"

"Yes, obviously, but only for the night of the attack. We had footage of Hartley jogging that way, and our search of the footage didn't show anybody fitting the attacker's profile, riding a Carrera bike in the hours leading up to the attack. So, we came to the conclusion that the attacker had come from the other side of Eccles Field."

Grant remembered. "Okay, well, I'll start from the previous day, and work backwards, like Bill."

"Excellent. Well, I'll let you make a start and I'll make us all a brew."

Chapter Eleven

It was always obvious when the Manchester police were holding a major press conference. The road outside their huge modern HQ building near Hyde Road was littered with outside-broadcast vehicles, parked illegally on double-yellows, ironically. Half a dozen of the vans with huge satellite dishes on their rooves blocked out sight of the entrance to the building, as the broadcasters tried to get their transmission kit as close to the media-centre complex as possible, to minimise the cable runs to their cameras and sound equipment.

Every major broadcaster was here, vans from ITV News, BBC, Sky, Global, RT and PA gave a visual indication of how just big this news story was. The shocking images of the devastated building in Denton had made up the news headlines all day. Now it was time to hear what the police had to say about it.

"Good afternoon ladies and gents," said Miller as he sat down on the platform before the cameras and sound recorders. It was clear that the usually charismatic DCI was in a sombre mood. The reason soon became very clear, as Miller launched into his press-conference in a shocking manner.

He didn't say anything, he just pressed a button on the laptop on the table-top. Suddenly a photograph of a happy, smiling young family appeared on the huge screen to Miller's right. The parents looked mid-twenties, the beautiful, smiling children looked angelic as they showed their perfectly white baby teeth, their faces were beaming with joy.

Miller let the media personnel look at the photograph. He was in no hurry to start talking. He made a mental note of the "on-air" lights above the Sky and BBC TV cameras. The realisation that this was being broadcast live encouraged him to keep the silence going for a little bit longer and add even more of an impact to what he was about to say.

Eventually he spoke. His voice was cold and emotional. "The photograph that you are looking at there, is a picture of the Ozols family, taken during the family's summer holiday at Pontins in Southport. The dad, Andris, the little lad, Juris, and the little lass, Inga, were murdered in their beds last night."

Miller's voice faltered as he delivered the news. There was a very audible sound of emotion amongst the media personnel, too. The sight of this happy, care-free family smiling at them all was a very powerful image which chilled them all to the core.

"The mum, Marija is currently in a very poorly condition in hospital. We think that she knows that her family have died, but we haven't had the opportunity to speak to her yet as she is very poorly and is presently in a medically induced coma while doctors try to figure out a way to heal her severe burn injuries."

A fresh wave of sadness washed over all of the men and women in the packed media-centre, many of whom were parents themselves.

"It was a deliberate arson attack, which killed three members of this young family. But before we talk about that, I wish to make an appeal to the person, or persons responsible for this tragedy. I am of the opinion that you did not know that there was a young family sleeping in that property when the fire was started. I want to offer you my word that I am quite prepared to keep an open mind that the heart-breaking outcome of this horrendous incident was unintentional. So, if you were there, I want you to get in touch with me. I'll put the number up on the screen in a few minutes, but before I do, I want to tell you all a little bit about this family. They have lived in Denton for three years, they moved here from Latvia. Dad, there, Andris, worked as a butcher at Bretherton's butcher shop at Crown Point. Mum, Marija worked part-time at the Subway store in Denton whilst the two children Juris and Inga were at school, at St Anne's Primary. This family have been described as happy, friendly, hard-working and very good neighbours. Andris' boss at the butchers has said that he has never known a more hard-working and conscientious employee in over thirty years in the trade. Marija's manager at Subway described her as extremely hard-working, friendly and very popular with the store's customers. Juris and Inga's headteacher at St Anne's has today described them as adorable, happy little children who were loved by everybody within the school community."

Miller stopped talking and looked up at the

photograph. It was clear that he was very upset about this tragedy himself, despite his image of being a hardened police detective with years of experience of disturbing crimes.

"I know that you have all been linking last night's arson attack to the other attacks which have been carried out against betting shops in the area over the past fortnight. As most of you have reported today, this fire was started in the Bet-a-Days betting shop. The family lived in the flat above, and all the evidence we have so far suggests that the Ozols family were the innocent victims of a crime which was intended to damage the shop."

Miller pressed a button on his laptop and the screen changed from the family photo, to an image of the four betting shops which had been targeted.

"Now, a major line of enquiry centres around these attacks. It is not our only line of enquiry, I must stress. But it is significant, and we are very hopeful that these four crime scenes will provide some important information about the people who did this."

Miller stopped for a moment to take a sip from his glass of water. Every person in the packed-out media-centre was staring at him, waiting to hear his next sentence, desperate to know what was going on. "I want to make something very clear, if you know of anybody who has been involved with these activities against betting shops, I am appealing directly to you to contact me. I am quite sure that the people behind this will have mentioned it to others in the community. If this is the case, I am urging you, please do not take the law into your own hands. If you know who these people are, or just one of them, please, contact the police and let us deal with this matter. You can also contact Crime-Stoppers where all calls are treated confidentially."

Miller pressed his laptop again, and the phone numbers of the incident room and of Crime-Stoppers appeared on the screen.

"This is obviously a major investigation, and I am working in conjunction with the divisional CID departments all around the city. I can make a promise to everybody here, and most importantly, to Marija Ozols, who is gravely ill in hospital, the young woman who has just lost her whole family, and who has done absolutely nothing wrong. That promise is that I will get to the bottom of this crime, very quickly. If you are one of the individuals responsible for this, my advice to you is to hand yourself in right now, because at this moment in time, we want to help you to come to terms with what you have done."

The DCI took another sip from his glass before looking back at the media staff. "Okay, the fire last night was phoned in at 1.07 am. The caller phoned 999 from a phone box on the corner of Windmill Lane and Hyde Road, which is roughly fifty yards away from the property which was on fire. I'm now going to play you this telephone call, as it is of the utmost importance that we identify the caller and speak with him as a matter of urgency. If you recognise this voice, I need you to contact my team straight away."

Miller pressed another button on his computer and the audio began playing. The DCI sat, looking at every member of the press, watching their expressions carefully as they listened to the shocking audio. The man, possibly a youth, sounded upset, scared and traumatised. The incident which he was reporting had clearly had a very deep effect on him, this detail was made clear as he could be heard retching during the call.

Miller waited until the call ended. The entire thing only lasted twenty-eight seconds. But it felt much longer.

"I need to know who that is. I need to talk to him. I need to understand why he was in the area. I need to know why he ran to a phone box, rather than use his mobile phone. He is quite possibly just an innocent bystander, somebody who did the right thing and alerted the emergency services to the fire. But until I speak to this person, I cannot eliminate him from my enquiries. At least one person watching or listening to this broadcast will know that voice. I need that one person to phone the number up there," Miller pointed at the screen. "And tell me who he is."

There were a few moments of quiet chatter and whispered discussion amongst the media personnel, before Miller opened his mouth again.

"Any questions?"

The respectful mood in the room quickly gave way to a barrage of noise and shouting. It took almost a minute for the rabble to settle down and for a single question to be made out.

"Jill Bennett, Manchester Evening News. DCI Miller, there is growing criticism for the police's rather lackadaisical response to the four previous incidents. A manager from one of the bookmaker shops has claimed that the police have shown no interest in catching the people who wrecked his betting shop. What is your response to this very serious claim? It does imply that if the police had treated the previous incidents a little more seriously, this tragedy might not have happened last night."

That was a good question and had been anticipated by the DCI. Miller had to stall his answer for a few seconds as he thought of the appropriate response. He passed the time taking another sip from his glass.

"That is a very good question, Jill. Thank you. I wasn't involved in the investigations into the previous incidents..."

"Well, with respect - it sounds like nobody was!" Said the reporter, keen to go in for the kill. Her vicious counter attracted a wave of chattering throughout the room.

Miller waited for the fuss to die down and was glad of the opportunity. This rabble bought him extra time to plan his reply. He knew that it was a valid point which was being made. He just didn't need the aggravation of a bollocking from his superiors for answering it wrong.

"Well, as you know Jill, our officers have to prioritise the seriousness of crimes that are reported. Crimes which don't involve injury or worse are not prioritised as highly as, let's say for example a burglary where the home-owner was hurt or threatened. It's not ideal, but let's keep a sense of perspective. I don't think that any of Manchester's police officers could ever have imagined that these incidents would escalate to the horror that I have personally witnessed today, the horror that Marija Ozols is going to have to wake up to."

"DCI Miller! Helen Reeves, Tameside Radio, I accept that police officers have a difficult job to do..."

"Thank you." Said Miller.

"But that said, I have to ask the same question. If resources had been thrown at catching these individuals, last night's tragedy could have been avoided."

Miller looked at the reporter, and he looked sad as he spoke. "I agree. But we deal with thirty-five thousand reported crimes a month in this city. We have to prioritise the seriousness of them, and quite frankly, vandalism against a shop would not normally attract the same level of investigation as a mugging or an armed raid, or a rape or an arson attack. I wish we did have the resources to tackle every single crime with the same amount of investigation, but despite the circumstances that this point is being made around, we have to be realistic."

"But you accept that if these crimes had been investigated as top priority, last night's tragedy might not have happened?" The reporter was pressing Miller. He was getting bored of this, it felt as though this was more about the media people getting their voices on the national news bulletins, than genuine outrage at the police's culpability for the tragedy. Miller decided to call this witch-hunt out for what it was.

"Can I remind you that I'm investigating the deaths of two children and their father? The mother is lay in a hospital bed with nothing to wake up for. I really don't think this is an appropriate time to try and get a sensational headline about policies that have nothing to do with me, or my colleagues. Go and talk to the politicians about these concerns, talk to the Mayor, talk to the Prime Minister. Please don't attempt to use this tragedy as an excuse to attack the people who are working tirelessly to keep this city safe, in spite of the policies which restrict our capacity to thoroughly investigate every crime that comes in."

Miller's strong, to-the-point outburst managed to quieten the hecklers. Another familiar face in the audience held up his hand.

"DCI Miller, Paul Mitchell, Sky News. Sorry to repeat the same theme, but recent figures released by your own police force state that fifty-five per cent of all reported crimes in Greater Manchester are not investigated. What can you tell us about this worrying statistic, a statistic which says that if you are a victim of crime, there is only a forty-five-per cent chance that the police will look into it?"

Miller was beginning to look disappointed by the questions. He knew that every single member of the press knew that these matters had absolutely nothing to do with him. Everybody in the room knew that this was just the media pushing a political point.

"Cheers Paul. You know that question has nothing to do with me, or my department. I'll take a couple more questions, but no more about politics please." The DCI pointed to BBC Northwest Tonight's crime correspondent Ellie Bradshaw, who had her hand in the air.

"Ellie."

"Thank you, DCI Miller. You said earlier that there were a number of lines of enquiry, the previous betting shop attacks being only one of them, plus the phone-call presumably is a second. What can you tell us about the other lines of enquiry?"

"Great question Ellie." Miller was glad to finally have a question about his work rather than police funding or resource management. "As with any investigation of this nature, we have to start with an empty page. Naturally, the other incidents at betting shops will form a significant part of this investigation and we are throwing everything at that. To put that into some sort of context, we have five CID teams working around the clock on this, and we are very confident that lots of information will come in over the next few hours following this broadcast. But, we have to explore every possibility and right near the top of the list is the question of the nationality of the victims. We have seen a ten-fold increase in xenophobic attacks against immigrants in the UK, and it is not beyond the realms of possibility that this may have been a racially motivated attack, and nothing at all to do with betting shops. There's nothing to say that this fire wasn't an insurance job, after all the building was very old and in a poor state of repair. We have a whole range of possibilities to look into and I can assure you all, and the public at home, we will explore every single one of them."

Another hand was up, and Miller pointed at Ian Appleby from Piccadilly Radio.

"Last question please, Ian."

"Thank you, DCI Miller. Regardless of the motive for this attack, there are growing concerns from the community following this appalling crime. What reassurance can you offer the community, in Denton, and across the wider city, that the police are doing everything they can to prevent any further attacks on betting shops?"

"Well, firstly Ian, I hope that everybody in the city, and the wider area realise that this horrific incident last night is being treated with the utmost seriousness by Manchester City Police. One thing is absolutely clear from me, my officers, and the CID teams working across Greater Manchester tonight – we will find the people who did this, and we won't stop until we do."

"Yes, but that doesn't really…"

Miller stood up. He'd had enough for today. "Thanks everybody, I appreciate your support." With that, he stepped down off the raised platform and headed out of the media-centre, leaving every single person under no illusion that the DCI was completely pissed off with their attempts to trivialise the situation, attempting to turn this appalling tragedy into a political football to knock around.

Chapter Twelve

"Nice press conference, Sir!" said Saunders as Miller entered his office.

"Did you think?"

"Yes, very powerful."

"Seriously?" Miller seemed surprised by Saunders' feedback. "I thought it got a bit watered down by all the shite the reporters were asking about political bullshit."

"Well, yeah, to be fair it trailed off a bit with all that, but your bit, the bit that will be cut into all the news reports for the next twenty-four hours was rock-solid. I think we'll see some great reaction from the public after that."

"Reckon?"

"Would I be saying it if I didn't mean it? You know if you do a shit press conference, I just say I haven't seen it." Saunders smiled as Miller laughed loudly.

"Wait a sec... you always say that you missed it..."

"See!"

The two men laughed at the daft banter. It had been a really shitty day in so many ways and it was nice to have a bit of a distraction with some stupid bitching and piss-taking. It always lightened the load. But it didn't take Saunders long to change the topic back to the fire.

"Anyway, Sir, have you got a minute?"

"Yes." Miller grabbed a chair from a nearby desk and wheeled it across to Saunders' desk. "What's occurring?" he asked as he sat.

"Just been Googling the betting shop attacks. I've excluded all news reports from my search preferences to see if anything came back from other sources. Just have a look at this stuff that's come back."

Miller leaned in towards the screen. There were a number of blogs, discussion forums and indie websites listed on the results page. He grabbed the mouse and scrolled to the bottom of the screen. There were at least another ten pages of similar results.

"This one here," Saunders pointed to the screen,

prompting his boss to move the pointer and click the link. "This is a discussion board that originates from a separate website. Have a look at the comments on the screen."

Miller leant in even further and started to read the content. The first comment on the thread, at the top of the screen said, "Three Betting Shops in Manchester Put Out Of Business By Vandals. Thoughts?" The comment had been made by a member of the forum called FrogEyes1981.

"Three shops?" said Miller under his breath.

"Yes, this post was started the day after the third shop was done, the FreeBets in Romiley. The attack happened on the eleventh, this post is dated the twelfth.

"Right... so..."

"Well, the point I'm making is that this didn't really get into the news until the thirteenth, that was when the Manchester Evening News made the link between the three betting shops being targeted. The other local news reporters picked up on it after that, BBC Manchester, Granada Reports, Key 103. When this post was published, it was a day before the media started talking about it."

"So, to be perfectly clear, you're suggesting that Frog Eyes has made the connection before the media?"

"Yes. It doesn't mean that he is the attacker. But it does inspire a few questions. Firstly, how did he make the link before the M.E.N, who presumably noticed it after looking through our duty logs and just happened to clock that three betting shops had been smashed up within a week, before looking into it a bit deeper in the hope of finding a story."

"Yes, I see your point. But where's this going?"

"Look, just read the comments. Shall I do a brew while you're having a look?"

"Yes. Nice one Keith."

As Saunders stood to leave, Miller moved in closer to the screen and began reading. Over a dozen comments had been made underneath the initial one from Frog Eyes.

"Looks like it's started." Said Hotel Whisky 76.

"Hope so!" added another user.

"Trust me. This is it, the fight-back has begun!" added

Hotel Whisky 76.

"I'm not a betting man these days lol. But if I was, I'd say this is going to be the fight-back! About time too."

The thread went on like this, comments from users with completely random names, or "handles" making light of the attacks, and in some cases congratulating the perpetrators. Miller continued reading.

"This is going to be fkn epic!" said a user called BobTheBuilder.

"Hope they keep going!" added another unidentifiable name on the screen.

Saunders arrived back at the desk with two cups and placed them down. "What do you think?"

"Hmmm. Not sure. It's a bit wanky, isn't it?"

"Yes, that's a good word for it. But it seems like these people were expecting something to happen. Look, there." Saunders pointed at the top of the thread, the "looks like it's started" comment.

"Yeah, saw that."

"Well, I'm intrigued. I was going to start searching back through these message boards and see if a discussion has taken place earlier on, at some point before the first attack. What do you think, Sir?"

"What would you be hoping to find?"

"Well, if a few of these stupid names keep popping up, talking about starting some sort of campaign of vandalism against betting shops, it might bear fruit."

Miller looked thoughtful. He definitely understood the point that his DI was making. He just couldn't see how it could trace back. "Okay, let's say you find something... let's say that you find the person who instigated all this. How are you going to find out who they are from all these dickhead names?"

"There's ways. There's always ways, Sir."

"Go on."

"Well, if we adopted the same procedures that they do for child porn investigations, it wouldn't be too hard to find out who is hosting the website, and from there we will find the account holder, and once we have that information, we can seize the server and download the IP addresses of all these random names. It will be a big piece of work, don't get me wrong. But it's achievable."

Saunders was talking about the Internet Provider address which every internet connection uses. It may just look like a series of random numbers to the average person, but to a data communications engineer, IP addresses were traceable from the green BT street cabinets, straight to the router inside the owner's house, or factory, or wherever it was located.

"Frog Eyes might think his stupid name provides him a cloak of anonymity. But he can't hide his IP address, even if he's using a mobile phone to connect with the website."

"Is this on the dark web?" asked Miller, referring to the really murky world of internet browsing, the "hidden" internet which only attracted those who were interested in browsing the dark things, the kind of things that get you locked up, on their internet browsers.

"No, it's not the dark web Sir, it's just plain old Google. But the fact is that these lot are having a good yack about the attacks against betting shops as though it's been on the cards for a while."

Miller's phone vibrated in his pocket. He took it out and saw that he had a text message from an Inspector in the MCP call-centre. 'Got something interesting Sir. Please pop down asap.' Miller looked pleased by the message, but returned his gaze to his DI.

"Okay, tell you what Keith, you crack on, see what you can find in amongst this lot. If you find something, I'll have a word with Lloydy in Child Exploitation, and ask him to have a look. He'll be able to advise on the tech support we're likely to need."

"Great stuff. Thanks boss."

"What is this website, anyway?"

"It's a gambling addict's support group, Sir."

Chapter Thirteen

Miller arrived in the call-centre less than two-minutes after receiving the text message. The huge, bustling room which contained thirty-five officers and civilian call-handlers was situated on the first floor, directly beneath the SCIU offices. The noise and chatter in the place always came as a surprise to Miller, the rest of the Manchester police HQ was a rather calm and composed environment. But there was no calm, nor quiet inside this large, stiflingly-hot room as the thirty-five call-handlers spoke to the constant stream of callers who were dialling in their report of crimes, or to report missing relatives or making bizarre requests for police support regarding a late pizza delivery or missing remote controls. This department also managed the non-urgent calls on the 101 number as well as any "incident room" calls.

The Inspector who had text Miller was waiting by the side of a call-handler's desk. He quickly gave a pair of headphones to the DCI and pressed a playback button on the computer screen. Miller listened to the call which had come in only minutes earlier.

"Hello, Manchester City Police Incident Room."

"Hi, yes, hello. I'm... I wanted to report that I know the voice that was on the news."

"Is your call in relation to the fatal arson attack in Denton last night?"

"Yes, that's right, just heard about it on North West Tonight." The caller was an elderly female with a deep, gravelly voice. She sounded as though she'd had a life-time addiction to cigarettes.

"Okay, well if I can just take some details."

Miller listened as the name and address of the caller were logged down.

"And what did you want to tell us?"

"Well its... I'm not a grass..."

"Okay."

"Just wanted to make that clear?"

"Yes, that's fine..."

"If you're concerned about somebody, you know, about the people they are hanging around, well, that doesn't make you a grass, does it?"

"No, of course not. Quite the opposite in fact."

"I know, that's what I thought. But I'm about a hundred-per-cent certain that the voice on that phone-call is my grandson."

"Really?"

"Yes, plus, he only lives a five-minute walk away from that phone box."

"And you're definitely sure that it's him?"

"Yes. Like I say, I'd bet my life-savings."

"Can you give me his name and address please?"

"Yes. He's called Lewis Braithwaite, he lives at number two hundred and eleven, Egerton Street, Denton."

"And how old is your grandson please?"

"He's nineteen, no, twenty. It was his birthday a few weeks ago. Twenty."

"And have you told Lewis that you are contacting us?"

"No. I don't speak to him. We don't get on."

"Okay, well, thank you for calling. I'll make sure that the investigating officers are aware of this information straight away."

"Good. He's been hanging around in the wrong crowd. He needs to get away from them."

Miller patted the call-handler on the shoulder. "You are a legend young man! Thanks very much."

The young man smiled widely as Miller turned to the Inspector who was running the call-centre. "That's absolutely brilliant that. Thanks for getting it to me so quick. I'll go and fetch this Lewis Braithwaite in right now before his granny tells anyone that she's grassed him up."

*****

Saunders was busy working away in Miller's office, keen to stay away from the rest of his officers. It was inevitable that he'd be badgered constantly about the Hartley case if he was within earshot, and that would dramatically hinder his progress as he kept digging through the threads on the discussion boards. He was frustrated that he couldn't find a single comment which gave any clues. There were lots of vague remarks about "payback" and "vengeance" and "retribution" but no specifics. It was all very ambiguous and nebulous, like the mainstream media's ongoing suggestion that British Labour voters all hate Jewish people.

The web page contained lots of keyboard-warrior style statements, such as "I'm up for this. If I can't have my money back, these cunts aren't having it neither!" That remark by a user called "Atlantean" had received 47 "thumbs up" from other members of the online forum.

After half-an-hour of scrolling through the same, stupid, often childish remarks, Saunders was becoming frustrated.

"Welcome to the world of the brain-deads!" he muttered to himself. He decided that there was nothing but bullshit here, so opted to become proactive. He logged onto Google and searched for a "free e-mail address." Within a second, the screen was filled with links to websites offering new e-mail addresses. Saunders clicked on the first one, "Outlook" and started thinking of a fake name to use. It didn't take him long to come up with John Smith, as he started filling out the boxes on screen. His new name was accepted and the e-mail company offered him various versions of it. Saunders wrote the e-mail address in his pad, and then jotted down the password that he had chosen. Password1.

Within seconds, Saunders was back on the forum page, and was signing up as a new member. He decided to go with John5mith, which was accepted. After a few tick boxes were checked, Saunders was now an active member of the page which hosted such inspired comments as "goes around comes around lmfao karma bitches."

The DI went back to the thread that he had shown to his boss half-an-hour earlier and checked to see if it had any new comments. It hadn't. Nobody had made a single comment today, despite the issue of betting shop attacks being the number one news story in the UK. This detail didn't stack up.

"Well that was a fuck up idea, did they not know there was a family inside. Kids. RIP to the Ozols family is all I can say." Saunders pressed return on the keyboard and sat back in his seat as the comment by "John5mith" appeared on the virtual "wall" of the forum.

*****

The three remaining SCIU detectives in the office, Chapman, Grant and Rudovsky were getting on with their tasks in silence while the clock wound itself on. Time seemed to move very quickly when rewinding, reviewing and logging CCTV clips.

"Bloody hell! Look at the time," said Rudovsky, sounding stunned to see that it was almost eight pm. "Are we going to call it a night soon, or what?"

"Sweet baby Jesus! How did that happen?" Asked Grant.

"I know! I'm going to be getting my ears chewed off from Abbi," said Rudovsky. "Right, well, I'm off," she said as she made some final notes of where she was up to.

"Yes, I'm packing up too," added Grant. "My eyes are starting to get pissed off with me."

"I'm going to stay, if that's okay?" said Chapman, without looking around. Rudovsky and Grant glanced at one another and almost laughed at the bewildered expressions that each was exaggerating for comic effect.

"Are you sure Bill? You'll get square eyes staring at that screen all night."

"Yes, I'm sure. I think I might have something here."

"What about your tea?"

"Oh, I'll ring summat. Don't worry about me. You guys get off and I'll see you in the morning. Hopefully I'll have something for us..."

"Really? What have you got?"

"Well, nowt concrete yet. But I'm working on it." Chapman seemed a bit defensive and Rudovsky read the situation well.

"Okay, well, I hope it follows through Bill. See you in the

morning."

"Night." Said Chapman, without altering his eyes from the flickering black and white CCTV footage of a quiet terraced street. The footage he was examining had been captured by a camera on the corner of an Italian restaurant on Monton Road. The camera's primary objective was surveillance around the side of the property, where the kitchen door offered a vulnerable spot for burglars. But the periphery of the camera's lens also took in the entire length of Francis street and was providing Chapman with some extremely valuable footage of the dead man's street.

Once Chapman's colleagues had left, he walked across to the kitchen area and had a look at the various takeaway delivery menus which were pinned up on the noticeboard. It didn't take him long to decide on a twelve-inch spicy meat-feast pizza and a portion of cheesy chips with a carton of chilli sauce. As soon as he'd phoned it through and made a cup of coffee, he headed back to his PC monitor, determined to come up with something solid for the following morning's team briefing.

*****

Miller was parked outside Lewis Braithwaite's address, waiting for a custody van to join him. He'd phoned Tameside, the nearest police station and asked for a van on the hurry-up as he'd made his way to the address. He'd anticipated that it would be nearby by now, but it wasn't.

The house was a typical post-war Manchester council-house, built from the hardest Accrington NORI bricks, so they could last forever. The property was situated close to the junction with Corporation Street, a main road through Denton and Audenshaw. The lad's granny had been correct, the phone box where Lewis had allegedly made his 999 call was about five minutes away from this house on foot.

All of the lights were on inside, including the upstairs. Miller was pretty sure that he had seen a young bloke in the smaller upstairs window when he'd pulled up, but the silhouette figure hadn't returned while he'd been sitting in his car, waiting for the meat van.

A few tense minutes passed, before Miller finally saw a police van enter Egerton Street at the far end. He flashed his lights numerous times in the oncoming vehicle's direction to alert them to his location, as well as to tell them to kill the blue lights and siren. They got the message and Miller got out of his car as the van parked up.

"Hiya, alright? Just a routine one this." Said Miller to the two police officers as they stepped out of the vehicle and closed the doors. "Person of interest is twenty-year-old Lewis Braithwaite, I think he's in the address. One of you cover the back-door, the other stay with me in case he starts kicking off."

The officers followed Miller through the gap where a garden gate had once stood. The first officer continued around the side of the house as Miller knocked on the front door.

A woman in her forties answered, she was dressed smartly in a Barclays Bank uniform.

"Yes?"

"Hello. I'm DCI Miller from MCP. I need a word with Lewis. Is he in?"

"Yeah, why, what's..."

"Can you get him for me, please?"

"Lewis!" she shouted up the stairs.

"Whaa-aat?" came the moody reply. Lewis sounded like Kevin the teenager from the Harry Enfield sketches.

"Come down here, now. There's a policeman here to talk to you."

Suddenly, there was some noise upstairs, banging and feet moving around quickly. Miller rushed past the mother and ran up the stairs. The police officer stayed at the door.

"What's...what the fuck man?" said Lewis as he saw Miller bounding into the little bedroom towards him.

"What are you doing?" asked Miller, noticing that he was pushing something into a cupboard.

"Nowt. Get off me. I haven't done fuck all!"

Miller looked into the cupboard and pulled out a rucksack. That was the item that Lewis had been trying to conceal. He placed it on the floor by his feet.

"Have you got an evidence bag in the van?" shouted Miller down the stairs.

"This is fucking bollocks man. Persecution and shit!"

"Yes Sir," shouted the policeman downstairs.

"Go and grab it for us, cheers."

"Fucking total bollocks!" said Lewis.

Miller stared at him, doing his scariest, most intimidating glare. He held his finger up to his lip to shush the young lad. It worked. Whatever this Lewis was, he wasn't a fighter, he was a soft-arse. He looked down at the floor.

The police officer came rushing up the stairs.

"Bag that please." Said Miller as he took his cuffs off his belt. "Lewis Braithwaite, I am arresting you on suspicion of murder, you do not…"

"Murder? What the actual fuck?" pleaded Lewis as Miller read him his rights. He looked completely stunned.

"Will be taken down and…"

"Fucking murder? Mum, come and tell this dibble, he says I've murdered someone! Mum!"

Miller fastened the hand-cuffs behind Lewis' back and began walking him onto the landing, towards the top of the stairs.

"What the hell is going on?" asked the lady who had opened the door a couple of minutes earlier. She was trembling as Lewis and Miller walked slowly down the stairs towards her.

"Tell 'em mum! He's arresting me for fucking murder!"

Lewis' mum fell to her knees by the front door, holding her hands to her face.

*****

Fifteen minutes after Saunders had left his comment on the gambling addicts chat-room page, a reply appeared. It was written by one of the earlier correspondents who had last posted on the page several days ago.

"Well it obvs wasn't supposed to kill a family was it you numpty."

Saunders was staring at the comment, trying hard to

think of a response that wouldn't blow his cover. As he was trying to come up with something, another comment appeared.

"Not seen you on here b4 m8. Who r u?" The comment had come from a familiar name on the group, FrogEyes1981.

Saunders began typing. "Hi, I'm just pretty gutted about that fire. It fucks everything up now."

Several minutes passed, though it felt even longer. Finally, Frog Eyes replied. "Doesn't mean its over. But it will probably die down for a few weeks, maybe months BUT ITS NOT OVER!!!"

Saunders smiled. In his heart of hearts, he hadn't thought that he'd actually get anywhere with this. But Frog Eyes' comment was invaluable in suggesting that people knew what this was all about. And if they knew that, they probably had a good idea of who was behind it, too.

The DI was getting ready for going home, but decided to roll this dice one last time. He shook his fingers above his keyboard for a few seconds before starting to type, "Its over. Total fucking failure."

As soon as it appeared on the screen, he shut the PC down and knocked Miller's office light off. It was twenty past nine and Saunders was starting to feel tired for the first time today, despite his day beginning at 2am after just a couple of hours sleep. As he stepped out of Miller's office, he was shocked to see DC Bill Chapman still at his desk on the opposite side of the office-floor.

"Bill?"

Chapman span around on his chair.

"What are you doing here?"

"Oh, alright. Just doing a bit of CCTV work on the Hartley case."

"Fucking hell!"

"What?"

"Oh nowt. I thought you'd died or summat, still sat in here after five o'clock!"

"Very good!" said Chapman, turning back towards his PC screen. Saunders walked across to him.

"So, what have you got?"

"Oh, I'm just trawling through the footage on Hartley's street. I think I might be on to something actually."

"Well, listen, don't let me start distracting you. I need my bed."

"Night Sir."

"Yeah night Bill."

Saunders walked out of the SCIU offices and onto the stairs. "Never thought I'd leave the office before Chapman!" He said to himself as he descended.

Chapter Fourteen

Tuesday. 9am.

"Okay guys, I think we need a team briefing to catch up with everything that's happened over the past twenty-four hours." DS Jo Rudovsky looked excited as she spoke to her team, gesturing them enthusiastically to join her by the incident room wall, which contained much of the story so far in the search for Graham Hartley's killer.

The SCIU detectives stayed seated and pushed their chairs along the floor using their feet as they formed a semi-circle around their DS.

"Right... things are moving at an excellent pace, and things are really starting to fall into place."

"If you could make your next sentence rhyme, that would be fucking ace!" Kenyon grinned widely as his colleagues laughed at his wise-crack.

"Very good Pete! One-nil to you. Right, on a serious note, Bill has unlocked a treasure trove of leads with his suggestion about the jogging route. We're now looking at the potential for an arrest in the next couple of hours so I think that it is vital that we all have a good understanding of what's come to light."

Rudovsky stepped across to a black and white photograph on the wall. It was a CCTV still of a car pulling into Francis Street, the road that Hartley had lived on, in the centre of Monton village.

"Okay. This car, a dark grey Vauxhall Vectra has been coming and going during the week prior to the attack, roughly around the time that Graham Hartley arrived home from work. It has stayed in the street until Hartley set off jogging and has subsequently left shortly afterwards, following the direction that Hartley was jogging. The vehicle is not registered to an address in the Monton area, and our CCTV footage confirms that the driver does not leave the vehicle at any time, on any of the visits. The vehicle enters the street, turns around at the bottom, then parks and waits."

"That's a bit weird." Said DC Helen Grant.

"It gets weirder, believe me. This vehicle parked in or around Francis Street on three occasions in the week leading up to the attack on Graham Hartley. So, as we had almost a month of CCTV footage from the security cameras on the Italian restaurant at the top of Francis Street, we decided to do a scroll through each day, looking for this vehicle."

"Sounds like a ball-acher, that!" said Chapman, the DC who had stayed until the early hours working on this brain-numbing task.

"It was worth it though Bill, as you well know!"

"True."

"What Bill discovered was that this car initially started appearing in the street soon after another vehicle had." Rudovsky pointed to another black and white camera shot, this time of a smaller car.

"This vehicle, bizarrely, was registered to the same address as the suspect vehicle. Anybody want to guess the rest?"

DC Grant put her arm up first.

"Go on Helen."

"Well, my first instinct is that the smaller car, what is it, a Corsa?"

"Yes."

"Well I'd guess that the Corsa driver is up to something they shouldn't be, and the Vectra driver is doing a bit of amateur detective work."

"Ten out of ten Helen. Spot on. The Corsa driver is being driven by the wife of the Vectra driver. We have the names of both from DVLA records. The Corsa driver recently changed addresses. So, what we are actually witnessing here is a marriage break-down, where the newly estranged wife has been embarking on a new relationship with this man." Rudovsky patted the photograph of Graham Hartley as her team made comments and noises which conveyed their surprise, as well as their excitement that this case looked close to being cracked.

"Nice one Bill!" said Kenyon.

"Yes. Good shout Pete. This is all down to Bill's

suggestion in the first place," said Worthington. "I think we should make a big point of that." Chapman's regular partner was keen to remind the team that this was Chapman's finest hour in recent times.

"Okay, well let's not start wanking each other off just yet." Said Chapman, typically deflecting the well-deserved praise.

"To cut a long story short," said Rudovsky, regaining some authority, "the Corsa driver is this person." She pulled out a photograph of a fair-haired lady. "Thirty-two-year-old Lindsey Nolan." Rudovsky pinned the photo up on the wall and wrote the lady's name beneath. "She recently split from this man." Another photograph was held up. "Thirty-seven-year-old Billy Nolan. His address is number eleven, Worsley Road, Swinton. Can anybody tell me how this address is significant?"

Once again Grant held her hand aloft.

"Go on Helen."

"That CCTV photo of the attacker..."

"This one?" asked Rudovsky, touching the grainy image which showed the attacker heading up the East Lancs Road on his bicycle in the minutes following the attack.

"Yes, that image was captured close to the junction for Worsley Road."

"Once again, top marks Helen. Now I'm sure we can all agree that as things currently stand, this man is our prime suspect."

The chattering started again, along with encouraging and positive noises from the detectives.

"We now need to plan our arrest. Obviously, we're going to need extra operational support, and we're going to need Miller and Saunders on this as well."

"Where are they, anyway?" asked Kenyon.

"Tameside, working on the arson job. They're interviewing a person of interest. But I've asked for an urgent meeting and one of them will be coming back shortly. The biggest question mark which remains is regarding this person." Rudovsky patted the photograph of Lindsey Nolan. "I want to know why she hasn't made contact with the police, bearing in mind that the biggest news story in this area has been the brutal murder of her new boyfriend."

It was a good question, and all of the detectives agreed that it was extremely odd.

"What's her new address?" asked Chapman.

"She moved into a rented flat in Boothstown a couple of months ago, a couple of miles away from her former home in Swinton, and an equal distance from Hartley's address in Monton. I don't want us going round there until we've got Billy Nolan locked up in police custody, just in case we give the game away too early and it all starts going tits up."

"Makes sense," said Kenyon, nodding.

"Any ideas on how we want to proceed with the interview with Billy Nolan?" Rudovsky was standing by her giant notepad on the A Frame, a fresh sheet of A1 paper was waiting for some ink.

"Well, if I was doing the..." Chapman had been the first to speak but Rudovsky cut him off.

"You *are* doing it, Bill."

"Oh. Right. Nice one." Chapman was wearing a very rare smile.

"Go on," said Rudovsky, pleased to see that Chapman was one-hundred per-cent engaged in his work. It had been a long time in coming.

"Well, I think I'd present a half-story interview. I'd act stupid, asking him about his wife's car and his car, try and torture him emotionally, asking things like 'why do you think your wife was visiting Francis Street, does she have any family or friends there, what was her reason for going there so often.' I think that will make his fuse blow."

"Yeah, that's incredibly cruel Bill. I like it."

"Then, I'd try and make it out as though his wife is the prime-suspect, try and gauge his reaction to that. I think it would be best to encourage him to think that we haven't got a fucking clue what we are doing, then give him a bit of thinking time in his cell to reflect on the clues we have slipped him. Then, a few hours later, present an alternative version of events and watch his little world cave in."

"Excellent, Bill. Anybody else?"

DC Peter Kenyon waved his hand before speaking. "Well I think we should really concentrate our efforts on finding some evidence that places him at the crime scene. That would be the ace card. What have we got along those lines?"

Chapman replied. "That's proving to be a problem in all honesty. There's nothing forensic at all. There's a CCTV camera on the side of The Park Inn pub in Monton, which is next door to the entrance to Eccles Field. I've been back through it for the date of the murder. We've got hundreds of people coming and going, dog-walkers, cyclists, kids, mums with prams. We've got every face, but nobody fitting the attacker's physical profile and nobody with that bike." Chapman pointed up to the black and white photo on the wall.

"What about at the other end?" It was DC Helen Grant who raised the question.

Chapman and Rudovsky both looked a little stumped, but Grant continued.

"We know that his address is in Swinton, and that he went back that way on his bike. It stands to reason that he will have passed the same CCTV cameras in Swinton on his way to the crime scene."

"He didn't go that way, the whole day was checked on the East Lancs camera that he appeared on. Which was done when we found the images of him coming back." Chapman looked a bit irritated by the suggestion that he'd been looking at the wrong camera. He was more irritated that Grant was right. It was stupid to check the camera next to the entrance of the field when it was already established that Graham Hartley's attacker was from the opposite side of the field.

"Should we check that again?" asked Rudovsky. "I don't think it can do any harm, Bill."

A sudden frostiness filled the air. Rudovsky sensed it quicker than anybody else and went for damage-limitation. The last thing she needed was to piss on Chapman's chips when he'd come up trumps.

"Who checked that CCTV on the East Lancs in the first place?" She asked the question, fully aware that it had been DC

Worthington.

"Me, Sarge."

"Well, sorry Mike, but can I ask Bill to give it the once over?"

"What.. you..."

"Just in case, mate. We all know how easy it is to miss something when we're staring at CCTV footage all day."

Worthington looked a bit put-out by the suggestion that he'd screwed up. But Rudovsky wasn't too fussed about that, her overriding priority was to try and keep Chapman on side.

"Come on Mike, we're on the verge of nailing this. Nobody is going to take the piss out of you for missing a lone cyclist, before we even knew we were looking for one! Suck it up, butter-cup. Bill, can you give that another pair of eyes please?"

"Yes, no problem Sarge."

"Brilliant. Okay, finally, back to the Park Inn at Monton. I'll bet any money that Nolan has gone that way on foot at some point, after parking his car up nearby. We need to go through the Park Inn footage for each day that Nolan's car was seen in the area. I'll bet you all a sloppy Guiseppe that he walks past there. If we have his face, plus the CCTV on the East Lancs before and after... well, we've got the evil fucker bang to rights. Agreed?"

The DCs all nodded and looked enthused by the simple tasks they had to carry out. The conclusion to this grizzly case suddenly felt very close.

Chapter Fifteen

Miller and Saunders were at Tameside police station, preparing to question Lewis Braithwaite, the 20-year-old who had been identified by his grandmother, who'd contacted the police after hearing his voice on the regional news.

Lewis had spent the night in the cells in Ashton. It had been a long and very scary night for the young man, his first experience of police custody. The noise in the cell-wing had scared him half to death, the shouting, the aggression, the kicking and punching of doors, accompanied by the constant comings-and-goings of custody officers clanging open the steel hatches and the slamming of the solid doors had left him in a constant state of panic and anxiety. And that was before he could even consider the gravity of being arrested on suspicion of murder.

When Miller arrived on the detention wing to collect the young man from his cell, he saw a very frightened and vulnerable kid, a far-cry from the angry, cocky young adult who had been trying to give him lip in his mother's house some twelve or so hours earlier. This morning, Lewis Braithwaite looked like he was about to cry.

"Morning Lewis." Said Miller, in a warm and friendly manner. "How was your stay?"

Lewis looked broken.

"God, it wasn't that bad was it? Mind you, I've seen some of the Trip Advisor reviews for this place. Apparently the breakfast leaves a lot to be desired!"

"Good one." Said Lewis, looking down at his bare feet on the cold mezzanine floor.

"Right, anyway, it's interview time. Follow me please." Miller set off walking and sensed that his prisoner was following behind. "I've been looking at your police records, Lewis."

"I've not got any!" Said Lewis, in a voice which was severely lacking in confidence.

"I know! That was a big surprise to me. Usually, people have a bit of a journey through the police computer before they arrive at the destination you have. Normally starts out with anti-social behaviour, then affray, then drunken-disorderly or drug possession, intent to supply. That sort of thing." Miller was talking very casually, an old trick of trying to affect his prisoner's state of mind before they reach the interview room.

"Seriously, how can I prove I'm not involved with a murder? This is absolutely fucking insane."

Miller stopped and turned around to face Lewis. The youngster stopped walking and looked pleadingly into the face of the detective. "Well if that's what you want, I'm here to make it happen. You go in that interview room, and you answer all my questions. If you are not involved, you'll be out of here in a couple of hours."

Lewis nodded. He understood.

"Come on, nearly there. Where are your socks?" asked Miller as he held open a door onto the corridor.

"I don't wear them."

"Why not?"

"It's not cool."

"Well, I'm no fashion victim mate, but I can assure you that wearing a fresh pair of socks every morning will help stop your feet stinking of parmesan cheese."

"My feet don't smell..."

"They do. Just saying. I'm going to ask the Sergeant for a pair of socks before we go in that interview room. Otherwise, I'll be confessing to murder, just to get away from you!"

Lewis looked down at his feet. He couldn't smell anything.

Miller held open the interview room door. Saunders was sitting inside, looking at his phone. "Detective Inspector, just watch him a minute, I'm going to find a pair of socks." Miller turned back to Lewis. "Stay here a sec. Have you got a girlfriend?"

Lewis looked confused by the question. "No, I... I used...we split up."

"How long were you going out?"

"About six months."

"What's her name?"

"What... Chardonnay Shufflebottom. Why?"

"Nowt. Have you not had a girlfriend since?"

"Nah." Lewis looked to the floor again.

"Since you stopped wearing socks?" Miller was smiling but Lewis' eyes were still fixed on his pale size nines. "You'll never get a lass when you've got smelly feet. They're not into all that. Wait here, I'll go and fetch you some socks."

"Get him a bottle of Dettol as well, Sir." Shouted Saunders as Miller walked along the corridor. The DCI laughed loudly.

The lad's feet didn't even smell. Not noticeably, anyway. This was all a load of bollocks to figure out the suspect's attitude, his body language, his voice patterns when he was talking about real-life issues. It would prove useful later, to judge when he was being genuine, and when he wasn't.

"Fucking Norah! They are worse than a dead body's!" Saunders swept his hand in front of his nose as he appeared in the doorway and stood next to the suspect.

Lewis was feeling embarrassed and a little confused. He was supposed to be here for murdering someone, and the police were just banging on about how bad his feet smelled. It seemed weird.

"Don't worry. He'll find you some socks. I bet he'll come back with two gas masks as well!" Saunders laughed to himself. "So, where are you from, Denton?"

"Yeah."

"Whereabouts."

"Near Egerton Park. Do you know it?"

"Yes, I know Denton. You had those two kids who threatened to blow up the school there didn't you?"

"Oh, fucking hell yeah, I remember that. It was Audenshaw High School, and they were going to blow up the shopping precinct as well. I was only a kid then."

"Yes, it will be about ten years ago. I worked on the case."

"Really? No way."

"It's stunning around there though, isn't it? Beautiful place."

"Where. Denton?"

"Oh, no. I'm getting mixed up with the Cotswolds. Sorry."

Miller came bounding along the corridor clutching a fresh pair of socks.

"Where did you get them from, Sir?" asked Saunders as Miller handed the socks to Lewis.

"In the spare sock cupboard, where do you think? Right, let's get cracking."

Miller talked for a few minutes about the legal stuff while Lewis Braithwaite put the socks on, unaware that they'd just come from the DCI's car boot. Miller always had an overnight bag packed away in the boot ready for the unexpected all-nighters.

"Okay, so, Lewis, do you know why you're here?"

Lewis looked straight at Miller and his eyes were filling up. He looked extremely scared and immature.

"You said suspicion of murder. But that's all I know…"

"You seemed quite shocked by that, when I came round your house last night."

"Yeah, well, obviously. Because I've not fucking killed anyone."

"Lewis, to be clear, this is relating to the deaths of three people. It's triple-murder that we're talking about. What do you know about it?"

Lewis' eyes were streaming with tears and his nose was snotting. He wiped it all away with the back of his sleeve.

"Is it to do with that fire the other night?" He was trembling.

"Yes Lewis. Two little kids and their dad were killed in that fire."

The youth put his arms on the table-top and buried his head into them. He was sobbing heavily, the sound was genuine and his shoulders were heaving. He was obviously very upset and both Miller and Saunders offered him some encouraging words. After a minute, Lewis took the tissues that Saunders was holding out and cleaned his face up.

"In your own time, mate," said Miller softly.

"What?"

"What can you tell us about the fire?"

"Just a sec, right, why am I being arrested for it? It was fuck all to do with me!" The tears were coming back, and it didn't look like they were tears of self-pity. Lewis was genuinely upset about the fire. A haunted, jaded look had aged him dramatically. His eyes looked hollow and his sadness was unmistakable.

"You're here because of the phone call you made. We've had five calls identifying you as the person making the telephone call to the fire service."

"Yeah, it was me. I'm not denying it. But I didn't do anything. I just saw the fire, ran over..." He broke down again. "...I wanted to help. But I couldn't get near the place, windows were blowing out. I could..." He hunched over the table-top again. "I could hear them screaming, begging me to help them."

Once again, Miller and Saunders had to sit and wait. This lad had been through a major ordeal. They just needed to know what he was doing in this remote part of Denton at one o'clock in the morning. They waited until Lewis had composed himself.

"Remember what I said Lewis, tell me the truth and you'll be out of here in no time."

"I am."

"Okay, well, I appreciate that. And I can see that you're struggling with what you saw. Now let me make it a bit easier for you, okay?"

"How?"

"Well, in the time you've been here, our detectives have managed to track your movements on the CCTV cameras around the M60 and M67 motorway junction. They capture you walking up towards Denton from the direction of Sainsburys. Then, you were captured on a town-centre camera situated on the junction of Seymour Street and Hyde Road. These images show you walking in the direction of your home, before suddenly turning and sprinting in the opposite direction towards the fire. One minute later, we see you running back and going into the phone box outside the church."

"So that proves I didn't do it."

"Correct. But it doesn't prove anything else. We can eliminate you as a suspect in relation to starting the fire..."

"Yeah?" Lewis' eyes were now showing some signs of hope.

"But for all we know, you were just a look-out for the person who did start it." Miller looked on sympathetically as Lewis began to cry once again.

"I fuckin... I swear down. I wasn't a..."

"What were you doing there at that time Lewis?" Saunders had asked the question, and his tone had become a little harsher.

"I was just... I was coming home. I'd been out."

"Where had you been?"

"Just mooching about."

Miller looked disappointed in Lewis' rather vague explanation of what he'd been doing in the area at the time an arsonist had killed three people and severely injured a fourth. He took a photograph out of the file on the table-top.

"Is this your bag, Lewis?"

Lewis nodded, before looking down at his lap.

"For the tape, I am showing Lewis a photograph of a Berghaus ruck-sack, and he is nodding to confirm that the bag belongs to him."

"Can you tell us what is inside that bag please?" It was Saunders asking again, his tone still quite stern.

"Look, right, all I've done was phone a fire engine. Now you're going on about what I was..."

"I am showing Lewis a photograph of the bag, along with its contents. What can you tell us about these items?"

The suspect looked at the photograph which Miller was holding up.

"They are cans of spray paint."

"That's right. For the benefit of the tape, the photograph shows seven aerosol cans, all of which are cans of car paint in various colours. Gold, silver, blue, black."

"What can you tell us about these cans of paint Lewis?"

The young man shrugged and started making a circular motion on the table-top with his fingertip.

Miller decided it was time to wrap this up. This poor bastard had been through enough.

"Listen Lewis. If you have a bit of a job on the side at night, that's not a matter the police would be interested in. But we do need to eliminate you from the enquiry. So, if you can tell us what you were doing, walking through Denton in the dead of night with a ruck-sack full of spray-paint, we'll be able to let you go."

Lewis continued doodling with his fingertip. Saunders and Miller looked at one another, they exchanged a glance which confirmed that they were both thinking the same thing. The lad was a bit dim.

"So," said Saunders, in a bid to help Lewis out of his hole. "Is it correct what DCI Miller has suggested, that you have been moonlighting in a garage, painting cars to earn a bit of extra money?"

Suddenly, the penny dropped. Lewis looked up at the two detectives who were smiling at him.

He started nodding enthusiastically.

"For the tape, Lewis is nodding."

"Okay, well, I think that answers all of our questions for today DI Saunders. Are you happy to conclude the interview?"

Saunders looked at his boss. "Yes, I don't have any further questions, Sir."

"Okay. Interview terminated at zero nine thirty hours. Lewis, you are free to go." Miller switched the tape recorder off.

"Spray painting cars! Whatever! Come on Lewis, lets go and get your smelly trainers and book you out. DI Saunders will drive you home."

"Right. Nice one. Can I have my paint back as well?"

Miller and Saunders looked at each other and laughed loudly. Lewis looked on, he appeared slightly confused.

"Don't take the fucking piss, mate."

Chapter Sixteen

Saunders dropped the young lad off at his home in Denton, before heading back to HQ to keep his promise of meeting with DS Rudovsky regarding the Hartley case. He felt quite wretched as she had asked for a chat first thing, but he'd been stuck in the interview with Lewis. He decided to give her a quick call to let her know that he was on his way.

"Jo, hiya mate, sorry. Been stuck in an interview. We found out that he had nowt to do with the fire about half an hour before we went in. Just needed to be double-sure. I'm on my way over to you now."

"Oh, right. Good news. We're looking good on this, might have it boxed off today."

"Really? Bloody hell. That's a turn-up."

Rudovsky walked across the office floor, closer to her officers. She wanted a certain detective to hear what she was saying to her superior officer.

"Yes, well, it's all down to Bill. He's stayed here all night and he's turned up some magic."

"No way! I was taking the piss out of him last night. When I saw he was still at his desk, I asked him if he'd died."

Rudovsky forced herself not to laugh. That wouldn't sound good after she'd just been praising Chapman. She quickly thought of something to say. "Absolutely, I'll pass that on. So how long will you be?"

"Oh, is he there? Soz. Right, I'll be about fifteen minutes."

"Cool. Can we talk in the gaffer's office?"

"Yes, just go in and wait for me. I'm looking forward to hearing about the developments."

*****

Miller was heading into the CID department at Ashton nick. The Tameside detectives had been working non-stop on the investigation into the fatal fire. DCI Katy Green was heading the investigation into the case and was reporting directly to

Miller, who was overseeing all five of the investigations into the betting shop attacks.

Katy was a young, but very ambitious woman. She was viewing this chance to work with Miller and the SCIU team as a very positive opportunity. This pleased Miller greatly as it often went the other way and divisional bosses could be quite hostile and negative when having to report to a different department. Katy was quite small, with a very slight build. She was waiting for Miller when he arrived back from custody.

"Hello Sir."

"Hi."

"How did it go?"

"Yes, as I expected really. He's got no connection whatsoever to the fire."

"So, his reluctance to stay around at the phone box was down to the spray-paint in his back-pack?"

"Yes. But I decided not to pursue that. It's just paperwork and time. I managed to get him to confess to painting a car at his mate's garage."

Katy didn't look as though she approved. Miller noted the expression. It told him that DCI Katy Green was a stickler, who liked to do things by the book. But there was no time for that kind of bullshit as far as Miller was concerned, not on this case anyway.

"So...." Said Miller, keen to move things on.

"Yes, we've had a major break-through."

"Right?" Miller looked delighted to hear this news.

"I think you'll like this."

DCI Katy Green took Miller through to her office and invited him to sit down before explaining the break-through that her officers had managed to come up with overnight, and during the time that Miller had been down in the interview room.

Over the next ten minutes, Miller learnt that Katy Green ran a very efficient and productive team. They had managed to come up with the first set of clues as to who was responsible for the tragic arson attack which had shocked the nation. It was an extremely good response in such a short period of time and Miller was visibly impressed.

"Bit of a geography lesson to start with, I'm afraid." DCI Green handed Miller a map which she had printed off. "This is the scene of the fire, at the junction of Windmill Lane and Seymour Street." She pointed at the location on the map. "This road, Windmill Lane starts off as a built-up urban area at the Denton end, lots of terraced streets left over from the days of the mills. But as you can see, the terraces give way and the road soon turns into the main thoroughfare of a large industrial estate."

Miller was studying the map as DCI Green continued. "Windmill Lane is a very lonely place at night, just empty factories and industrial units surrounded by spiked metal railings. As a consequence, the area does attract a fair amount of burglars who are keen to try and take advantage of how secluded the area is at night. This criminal activity has seen a major investment in CCTV systems, security patrols and all night security guards in the area."

"Okay..." Miller wasn't sure where this was heading, but he was familiar with Manchester's industrial estates after dark. This one in Denton wasn't particularly special.

"Sorry, okay, so the reason I'm making this point is to highlight the fact that we believe this betting shop was targeted specifically for its location. In essence, it appears that it was chosen primarily due to the ease of getting away from the crime scene relatively quickly.

Good, thought Miller. This is going somewhere, finally.

"My team have checked the factory's CCTV cameras all along Windmill Lane and we have discovered that four people, believed to be male, headed up this road, past all these factories and got into a vehicle, here." DCI Green had been tracing her finger along the map to illustrate the route that the four people had taken.

Miller was a little confused by the place where DCI Green's finger stopped, the bridge above the M60 motorway.

"So... why did they park so far away from the betting shop, that's got to be, what half a mile?"

"Close, its just over. But the car was actually parked on the M60."

Miller looked closer at the map.

"They've jumped the fence, run down the embankment and got into their car, which had been abandoned on the hard-shoulder."

"What?" Miller looked and sounded stunned.

"Here's a photo we've taken from CCTV on the motorway. The car was parked in that spot with hazards on for almost twenty-five minutes. It would appear that they've faked a breakdown."

"That's totally ludicrous!" Miller was confused by the utter stupidity.

"Well, that was my first thought too, Sir."

"But?" Miller looked interested to hear what DCI Katy Green's second thought had been.

"Well, it was actually genius. Had these individuals been stopped by police patrols, there's literally no better alibi for walking around the streets of Denton in the dead of night, carrying petrol cans. Is there?"

*****

"Hi Jo. So, what's been happening?" Saunders was asking questions before he'd even closed Miller's office door. This sudden burst of enthusiasm was much appreciated by the DS. She'd been feeling a little abandoned on this case and in turn, had started to feel frustrated that the case was pretty much cracked, but none of her senior officers were involved, or were even taking an interest.

"Well, before I say anything, I just need to get summat off my chest."

"Go on." Saunders looked concerned as he sat down next to the DS, he knew from the tone of her voice that she was being serious.

"This has all come about because I had a bit of a heart-to-heart with Bill. We've buried the hatchet..."

"Shut up!" Saunders was smiling. Rudovsky and Chapman had been sworn enemies since day one. They just didn't work well together, like Liam and Noel Gallagher.

"Seriously. We've started again, with a clean slate and he's been absolutely amazing. He's single-handedly cracked this one."

Saunders had a weird look on his face. This was a very unlikely scenario. "Okay, well, hats off to Bill. Better late than never!"

"To be fair, he's never been the same since Karen..." Rudovsky was talking about her former boss, DI Karen Ellis who had been shot dead in front of Chapman's eyes. The comment reminded Saunders of a very dark time in his life, and Rudovsky instantly regretted bringing it up. An awkward moment passed slowly before Saunders composed himself and tried to move the conversation on, despite that rather insensitive reference to the worst day of his entire life.

"Sorry, Sir."

"It's alright. I'd not thought about that for at least a day. Go on, what's the point that you were leading up to?"

"Right. Well," Rudovsky took a deep breath. "I've been instructed that once we have a potential lead on this case, I've got to hand it over to divisional CID to clear it all up."

"That's right. So that the whole team can jump on this triple-murder arson case."

"I know. I get that, totally..."

"But..."

"Well, if we do that, just at the point that Bill's turned over a new leaf, it's just going to piss him off and we'll be back at square one with him."

Saunders looked as though he was starting to see the point.

"It's Dixon who's..."

"I know. I'm just saying, you've got half of Manchester's CID departments working on the arson job. Can we please just have another twenty-four hours to shut this down? Just so Bill can make the arrest and claim the glory. It's really important."

"Okay, fucking hell! I submit!"

"So, we can?"

"I didn't say that. But I'll ask the question."

"When?"

"As soon as you've told me what Bill's managed to uncover."

Jo looked across at her boss and folded her arms across her chest.

"What?" Saunders looked puzzled and slightly bemused by Rudovsky's weird body language.

"Come on Sir. Go and ask Dixon now. I'll come with you. I can't tell you the problems this is going to cause if Bill's case is handed over to division for them to get the victory parade. Don't forget this was the biggest case in the city until the fire."

Saunders thought about what his colleague was saying. He could see that it was an awkward position for her to be in. "And you are refusing to tell me what the developments are?"

"That's for me to know and for you to find out."

"Are you blackmailing me Detective Sergeant?"

Rudovsky grinned sarcastically. "Maybe. A little."

"Right. Fuck's sake." Saunders took his phone out of his pocket and looked for Dixon's number. He pressed the call icon and took a deep breath as it connected.

"Hello Keith. Everything okay?" Dixon sounded like his usual, grumpy self.

"Ah, yes, hello Sir. Just wondered if Jo Rudovsky and I could pop up and see you for five minutes?"

There was a long pause. It was Dixon's typical boundary-setting exercise, designed to remind whoever he was long-pausing, that he was a really big deal. That was his intention anyway. In reality, people just thought he was a bit of a knob.

Eventually, just as Saunders was about to curl his toes, Dixon replied. "Yes, yes, I suppose that will be okay. Where is Andy?"

"He's in Ashton, Sir. I should be with him, but Jo needed to update me and sound me out about her case. With DCI Miller otherwise engaged, I thought it might be best to contact you directly."

Another stupidly long pause passed by. "Okay, well, if you can come now, I'll see you. Otherwise it will have to wait until three o-clock."

"We'll be two-minutes. Thank you, Sir."

Chapter Seventeen

Saunders and Rudovsky were walking up the stairs to the top floor of the MCP head-quarters. They both felt quite on-edge and nervous, it was always a bit tense going in to see Dixon. He always ensured that a visit to him felt like a visit to see a V.I.P.

"Right, Jo, listen, I'll do the introduction into what's been happening with Bill. Then you jump in and talk about how he's the greatest copper working today. And then we'll ambush Dixon with your demands. Okay?"

Rudovsky laughed nervously and nodded.

Saunders opened the door to the top-floor using his fob. Only he and Miller had the correct security clearance to get up here, the floor which housed the most powerful people in the MCP force, including the Chief Constable and his Deputies.

DCS Dixon was responsible for all of the city's CID departments. He'd started out as a detective himself and had worked his way up through the ranks over a thirty-odd year career. Nowadays, he was a glorified, over-paid administrator who rarely got involved in any of the cases that his officers were working on.

The two SCIU senior officers paused outside his door and waited for the signal to enter. It was a hard job not to laugh when Dixon repeated the same ritual every time. He'd look up through the glass door, see who was waiting outside his door, before glancing back down at his desk, waiting a few seconds before saying "come."

Saunders and Rudovsky walked into the musty smelling office which was filled with ancient books on police procedure and law stuff. The shelves stacked with hundreds of obsolete volumes was the source of the weird smell, which reminded most visitors of a school headmaster's office.

"Okay, thank you Keith and Jo for coming along at such short notice." This was another of Dixon's stupid boundary setting exercises, making sure that the two people before him knew that he was the main man.

"Thank you, Sir."

"Take a seat and tell me how I can help."

Saunders started. "Well, as you know Sir, DCI Miller and myself are overseeing the divisional..."

"Yes, Keith, I'm quite aware of our operations."

"Of course. Well, the thing is, we've left Jo in charge and she's been working tirelessly on the Hartley case."

"Very good." Dixon stared at Rudovsky and nodded approvingly.

"Well, one major challenge that Jo has had since her promotion has been trying to manage a difficult working relationship with DC Bill Chapman."

"Yes, well, I think we have all had an issue with Bill over the past couple of years. Andy talks to me regularly about the personality complexities within your department."

"Really Sir?" asked Rudovsky, trying to sound more interested than she was. She just wanted to get this conversation to the point.

"Oh yes. I've been quite shocked by the deterioration in Bill Chapman's attitude and work ethic. You do both realise that it was I who put him in the department when we started it up?"

Rudovsky and Saunders nodded. They knew that Chapman hadn't been Miller's choice of team member.

"Yes, well, I have to say, I thought that he'd have made DS by now, at least. But something has happened to that man. I'm aware of his divorce, that hit him hard. Plus, he's piled the pounds on over the past decade. I'm very sad to see that he's become something of a slave to the liquor as well. It's a real shame."

The two visitors nodded sympathetically.

"I've had him up here once or twice, you know, to discuss things."

"Well, the thing is, Sir. Bill and I have always clashed, it's just been one of those things. But over the past few days, I've seen a real change in him. He's positive, conscientious, he appears to be trying hard to be a team-player. He stayed ridiculously late last night, working on the Hartley case."

Dixon grinned. Even the man who had put his faith in Chapman all those years ago was shocked by the over-time detail. "How late?" he asked, his exaggerated expression of surprise made his visitors laugh politely.

"Well, he hasn't said what time exactly, but he'd sent me several e-mails over the course of the evening, the last one was just after one in the morning."

Dixon smiled widely. "Well, I can only congratulate you on your excellent people-management skills Jo. I know you can manipulate your suspects in interviews like a genius. I'm not surprised that you can transfer the same skills to your new role in man management." Dixon meant the compliment, but it sounded a little insincere and a bit too much like a forced conclusion to the discussion regarding Chapman. Instead of accepting the praise and the intended closure, the DS felt that she had no option but to press further.

"Well, you see Sir, I have tried really hard with Bill, and I've also taken responsibility for my own conduct with regards to how difficult our relationship has been. But I made a deal with him, that we'd have no more bad vibes. And I'm absolutely blown away by how positively he has taken my offer of an olive branch."

"Yes, yes, as I say, this is very welcome news, and I congratulate you whole-heartedly." Dixon looked as though he was becoming a little tired of this conversation.

"I think the point that Jo is trying to make," said Saunders, aware that Rudovsky was tying herself up in knots, "we feel that we need to reward Bill's hard-work on this case. Show him that his positive contribution is being acknowledged."

Dixon leant forward and rested his chin on his hands. "I'm sorry, Keith, I'm not quite…"

"No, no, sorry Sir, what I'm trying to say is that Bill Chapman has cracked the case. His determination to show Jo that he wants to commit to this new working relationship has resulted in him single-handedly solving the mystery surrounding Graham Hartley's murder.

"Ah, I see. Well, that is significantly good news!" It was clear from Dixon's face that he was suddenly interested.

"But if we are to follow your orders and hand our file over to Salford CID to make the arrests and bring the charges, well Jo and I are both concerned that this will have an extremely negative effect on Bill's attitude going forward."

"Yes, yes, I can see that. How confident are you in the work that Bill's done with this?" Dixon was staring directly at Saunders. The DI handled himself well.

"Well, I think Jo is probably the best person to ask about that." Saunders' reply was good and his poker-face was strong. It sounded so much better than the truthful answer, 'I don't know, Sir, she won't tell me!'

Rudovsky spent the next five minutes explaining the facts and circumstances surrounding Hartley, his girlfriend, and her estranged husband.

Dixon was impressed. This case had been a real pain for the police service, which had been bombarded daily by local journalists and news editors, who it seemed were absolutely determined to keep their fear-mongering about a random killer stalking Manchester's streets on their front pages and in the top-of-the-hour news bulletins.

"What I am asking you for, Sir, please, is to allow us to see this through to the end. I want to make it clear right now that I understand the logistical sense of handing this file on to Salford. But I fear that the short-term gains from that approach will be lost on the longer-term aims that I have for nurturing and developing a better work ethic from DC Chapman."

Dixon looked at Rudovsky and nodded. He stayed like that for several seconds, which made the DS uncomfortable, she was seriously starting to doubt her judgement as the silence hung ominously in that musty room.

Finally, Dixon spoke. "Twenty-four-hours you say?"

"Give or take." Rudovsky's typically cheeky reply was met with a raised eye-brow. She decided to keep digging the hole she felt she'd started. "I mean, I'm extremely confident that we can have him banged up this afternoon, interviews done and CPS reports filled out by tomorrow morning, based on what I currently know. But I'm sure you'll appreciate that I can't give you a cast-iron guarantee."

Another cringeworthy silence passed. It was Dixon doing his big-bollocks act. "Okay. Based on the circumstances you've explained, I think the benefits of letting Chapman make this arrest far outweigh the negatives. But I will not extend this any longer than end-of-play tomorrow. I hope you realise that this is a one-off, and that I'm not known for changing my mind. I must say that you are both extremely fortunate that you've caught me in an unusually pleasant mood today."

"Oh, thank you, Sir. I really appreciate your support."

"Thank you. Let me know the plans for the arrest and the tactical requirements you will need within the next half-an-hour."

"Sir."

Chapter Eighteen

DCI Katy Green's revelation about the vehicle on the M60 had come as great news, but Miller had soon learnt that he was in for a disappointment. Ideas of a fast conclusion to this investigation were to be dashed as DCI Green revealed further information.

The vehicle involved, a dark silver Vauxhall Zafira had been found burnt out on wasteland close to the Peak Forest canal in Hyde. The car had been driven using false plates, DVLA checks revealed that the registration plates used on the vehicle which had been parked on the M60 corresponded to an identical vehicle which had been scrapped several months earlier.

Miller scribbled some points down in his note-pad as he listened to the rest of DCI Green's information. He was surprised to learn that the car which had been used, and subsequently burnt out, had been reported stolen one day before the fire, from a business address in Rochdale. The vehicle was owned by an Asian gentleman, and had been an MOT failure. It had been parked up outside the MOT garage for several days, whilst the mechanic tried to get some second-hand parts from eBay in a bid to save the owner some money. He'd arrived at work in the morning and noticed that the Zafira had gone. After ringing the owner to ask if he had taken the car, and learning that the owner had no knowledge of the car's disappearance, it was reported to the police as stolen.

"So, just let me get my head around this. Whoever started that fire had gone to the enormous trouble of nicking a car, then finding some fake-plates for a similar model at a scrap-yard, before burning it out, all within thirty-six hours?"

"That's how it appears."

"I can see how parking it on the motorway, pretending it's broken down is a good cover for walking around with petrol cans…"

"Yes." DCI Green was listening intently.

"But I'm struggling with the rest. Putting fake plates on from a car which has been scrapped is like something off

Britain's dumbest criminals. It's the fastest way to get a traffic cop pulling you over. As soon as a traffic car's ANPR camera saw that registration it would have flashed it up as scrap, and the traffic car would be on its tail and pulling it over faster than you can say Free Deidre Rashid." Miller was tapping his pen against his head as he looked at his notes.

"Yes, I agree that this detail is quite puzzling. I can only assume that the people responsible were unaware that the car had been scrapped."

"Which would rule out the suggestion that they've gone around the scrap yards looking for a similar coloured Zafira?"

"I think so."

"Well let's find out for sure. Find out which scrap-dealer signed the log book when it was scrapped and let's see what they have to say about it."

"My officers are already on that, Sir."

"And?"

"Well, it's one thing on a long list of others." DCI Green looked a little embarrassed as she realised that this should really have been at the top of the priority list.

"Anything else to report at this moment in time?"

"Yes, Sir. I've got my officers looking at the route that the car took after it set off on the motorway, in the moments after the fire started. I've got a strong suspicion that it will have come off the sixty at the next junction, which is Bredbury, and would have made its way to Hyde via Woodley."

"Stockport Road?"

"Precisely, Sir. My officers are currently looking through the CCTV cameras along that stretch. It's a long-shot, but I'm hopeful that we might get a look at the occupants as they made their way to the waste-land where they burnt it out."

"Good call. Presumably, the waste-land has no CCTV anywhere near?"

"No, Sir. Not really. It was the site of an old cotton mill, pulled down after a fire a few years ago. It's in a very remote spot between the canal and the river, and only accessible by the old road to the mill which has become quite overgrown now. It's a cracking little place to burn a car out, we see two, maybe three a month there."

"Okay, well, I doubt we'll be able to get very much from the scene. But good luck with the CCTV, there's every chance you'll find something with that line of enquiry. Go and gee your detectives up with regards to finding the scrap yard. I think I should pay the owner a visit."

"Yes, Sir."

"Do you mind if I stay in here?" Miller was mindful that he was taking over this DCI's office and he wanted to be polite about it. It would do his head in if the shoe was on the other foot.

"Of course not. Make yourself at home, Sir."

DCI Green headed off to talk to her officers as Miller picked up the map of Windmill Lane and the motorway. He thought that there was a lot more to this bizarre idea of the pretend break-down. Either the people involved were total fuck-wits, or they had been duped by a third-party into buying the fake plates. Whichever it was, Miller was pleased that he finally had something that he could look into. His gut feeling was that this group of individuals had gone to a hell of a lot of trouble to cover themselves whilst burning down the betting shop. Too much trouble, if he was being honest. He smelled a rat, but his train of thought was interrupted by his phone ringing. It was Saunders.

"Hi Keith, alright?"

"Yes, all good. Got some excellent news on the Hartley case."

"Oh?"

"Yes, are you sitting down?"

"I am as it happens. Why?"

"Well, it's shocking news. Bill Chapman has cracked it!"

Saunders spent the next five minutes filling Miller in on the developments, and on Dixon's decision to keep the SCIU team on the case for the next twenty-four hours."

"Wow, well, that is a development. How did Jo manage to get Dixon to agree to that?"

"Jo felt, well, we *both* felt it was worth making the case

that Chapman should make the arrest."

"Seems fair enough."

"Yeah, well, she's trying to make amends with him, and everything could back-fire if he had to hand his breakthrough over to another team."

"Yes, no, I totally support the move."

"So, it doesn't cause too much disruption there?"

"No, not at all, this DCI at Tameside is brilliant, she's had some real developments. It's all very positive."

"Right, good news. So, what about me?"

"What about you?"

"Shall I stay and assist Jo with this lot, or come back to Ashton?"

"Oh right!" Miller laughed loudly. "I thought you meant, what about you, as in, I'm replacing you with DCI Green!" He laughed again.

"You can't replace me. You might as well call it a day if you haven't got me on your team, I'm the one who consistently makes you look good and we both know it. You'd be hopeless if you didn't have me! Back in uniform within months!"

"Alright, don't get too giddy Keith. Fucking hell fire."

"So, what am I doing? Coming back or staying put?"

Miller thought for a moment and the line went silent as he did so.

"Well, if it's just making the arrest, you don't need to be there. It will do Jo good to oversee the whole operation."

"Okay..."

"Thing is, I need your brains over here. Got a right head-scratcher on the table here."

"Oh?"

"Yes, so my thoughts are that you come and make me look good and leave Chapman to enjoy his moment. It sounds well deserved."

"Okay, understood, see you in about half an hour."

*****

Miller was looking through his case-notes as he passed

the time waiting for Saunders. He was feeling very positive as he plotted the sites of the previous betting shop attacks, checking the geography of each location with the help of Google maps. He was making reams of notes in his pad as he studied each incident. There was no solid consistency between the sites other than the fact that they were all located in the quieter parts of the town. None of the five shops were in the town centre or anywhere near the main streets and thus, weren't covered by town centre CCTV systems.

The location of each shop did share one similar characteristic in that they were all close to the edge of town and these remote locations offered several options for escape. Miller began plotting the locations on the map software, looking all around each shop for isolated places that a car could be stashed close by, or used as a meeting point should the perpetrators of the attacks find themselves being separated or chased.

Every location, at Eccles, Romiley, Bolton, Middleton and the fatal fire in Denton shared similar characteristics in this regard. But that was all there was. This was where the similarities ended.

Miller popped out of the office and across to DCI Katy Green, asking her to get one of her officers to print off a map of Greater Manchester. A couple of minutes later, Miller had an A3 print of the city. He went back into DCI Green's office and started drawing dots on the map, each dot marked the locations of each shop.

Miller began looking at each location's proximity to major roads, police stations, town centre CCTV systems and also the motorway system. The WelcomeBet shop, near Heaton Park ticked every box, it was close to the main Middleton Road which led traffic from the M60 motorway straight into Manchester city centre. It was also close to Middleton police station, and there were plenty of CCTV cameras along that stretch of road. He made more notes in his pad, a wave of enthusiasm was rushing through him as he realised that he was making some long-awaited progress.

Safe in the knowledge that DI Saunders was on his way back, the adrenaline was starting to pump and Miller allowed himself to imagine that some tangible progress was finally being made after the initial sense of confusion. It had been a frustrating and emotional first 24 hours on this case, but the DCI was starting to believe that there was still plenty of stuff to look at, whilst reminding himself that the people behind these crimes were pretty dim. Dim people were the best kind to investigate in Miller's experience, due to the fact they leave lots of silly clues lying around. Investigating hardened, experienced criminals was a different kettle-of-fish altogether. Time-served cons knew all the tricks of the trade, from covering their tracks at a crime-scene, evading CCTV and other surveillance systems, to knowing exactly how to perform in the police station should they find themselves under arrest.

But these characters, parking up on the motorway half-a-mile away from their crime scene, using fake-plates from a car which had been scrapped, combined with the way that they carried themselves on the CCTV told Miller that he was dealing with complete and utter fuck-wits on this one. They were evil, sadistic people who had committed one of the most appalling crimes imaginable. But they were fuck-witted imbeciles and this realisation brought with it a warm, fuzzy feeling to DCI Miller.

Chapter Nineteen

Rudovsky had sent her arrest plan to DCS Dixon within fifteen minutes of getting the green light to pursue the operation. The plan was a simple one, an undercover officer was going to keep an eye on the address and as soon as the suspect was eye-balled, the address would be ambushed by tactical aid officers, front and back, doors smashed off and the full weight of the law would go in there, pin Billy Nolan down and then take him into custody. There would follow a full search of the address by SOCO, looking for any evidence of Nolan's link to Hartley and if possible, but extremely unlikely, try to discover the murder weapon and the Carrera bicycle at the address.

Dixon approved the request and phoned Salford's Inspector, instructing him to release two tactical aid teams to assist the operation. He then e-mailed Rudovsky to instruct her to proceed.

"Okay guys, squeaky-bum time!" She briefed her team; DC Bill Chapman, DC Peter Kenyon, DC Mike Worthington and DC Helen Grant. She explained that the confrontational work would be carried out by tactical-aid, and that once Nolan was in cuffs, Chapman would go in and make the arrest. The mood in the SCIU was fever-pitch. These types of operations were always good for getting the blood pumping, but without Miller and Saunders here to oversee everything, there was an added sense of jeopardy and excitement.

"Okay, listen, I'm prepared to bet next month's wages that Billy Nolan is the man responsible for the brutal, sickening murder of Graham Hartley. But before we go out there and bring him in, we need to all agree that without Bill's excellent work on this, we would still be sat here scratching our heads. So well done Bill!"

"Yeah, nice one Bill, brilliant job."

"Top man Bill."

Chapman looked slightly embarrassed, but also very pleased. Rudovsky thought that she saw a tear forming in the corner of his eye.

"Come on, let's go and take this sick bastard off the

streets."

*****

Swinton is the civic hub of Salford, where the city council has its offices and where the main police station serving the city of 234,000 people is located.

Worsley Road, at the rear of Swinton town hall, is well known for its traffic jams, as all of the traffic that attempts to leave the busy town ends up stuck here at the junction with the East Lancs road.

Worsley Road is also well known in the area for being the childhood home of Ryan Giggs. Britain's most successful footballer of all time grew up here, not far from the traffic lights that everybody knows so well. He still lived in his childhood home for several years after becoming a first-team Manchester United player at the age of 17. In the early days, fans young and old would tap on the door and ask for Ryan's autograph. Some were stunned to see Paul Ince or Andy Cole answer the door once or twice, who would solemnly announce that Ryan wasn't in, before closing the door in the stunned fan's face. It's rumoured that Bryan Robson and Alex Ferguson once answered the door together, playing the same trick. The United legends would then close the door on the uninvited callers and loud laughter would be heard coming from inside the modest little house where Ryan lived with his mum. It was the stuff of legend around Swinton, a fierce United supporting town well inside the red side of Manchester.

About half a mile up the road from Giggsy's former home, a BT engineer was knocking at the door of number 11. His white "Open-Reach" liveried van was parked just outside the small, terraced property. He had to knock a few times before the door was eventually answered.

"Hiya mate, sorry to trouble you. I'm having a bit of a nightmare with the lines to these houses. Just wondered if you've been having any problems?"

The man at the door looked puzzled. "What, with the phone?"

"Yeah, phone, internet. I can't get my head round it, because some houses are alright and others are reporting faults, but all these houses are fed from the same cabinet so it's not making much sense really. Can't get my head round it."

The man thought about it for a few seconds. He was a well-built man, around six feet tall, with close-cropped ginger hair. "Nah, everything's sweet, in fact, I've just been on the internet then, when you knocked on."

"Alright mate, no worries, thanks a lot, I'll ask them next door. Cheers mate, sorry for disturbing you."

"No problem, pal."

Billy Nolan closed the door on the friendly BT engineer, who turned and started talking quietly into his chest. "Suspect home, positive ID, over to you guys. Stay safe. Over."

Within seconds of the under-cover policeman's alert, a huge, dark blue police van pulled up on the kerb outside the address and six officers jumped out, fully suited up in helmets and riot gear, one of them was carrying a bright red battering ram, known amongst officers as "the enforcer." They began running towards the front door.

Round the back of the address, another team of 6 tactical aid officers were taking their positions in the back-yard, listening to the radio for their next instruction.

"Use the big red key! Go! Go! Go!" came the order from the TA sergeant. As soon as this order was issued, a tactical aid officer swung the huge battering ram and smashed the front door off its hinges.

"POLICE!"

"THIS IS THE POLICE!"

"ARMED POLICE!"

The officers ran into the address. Billy Nolan was standing in the living room with his hands up in the air. The officers were loud and aggressive.

"GET DOWN!"

"GET ON THE FUCKING FLOOR!"

Billy Nolan looked like he was going to shit himself as he got down on his knees, his arms still high in the air. His mouth was wide open, it looked as though he couldn't take in what was happening.

"LIE DOWN! PUT YOUR ARMS BEHIND YOUR BACK."

Within seconds, the suspect was cuffed and was getting a close-up view of his front-room carpet.

"Okay, all secure, nobody else in the property, suspect detained. Over."

The SCIU officers were sitting in their cars a little further down the road, outside Joan's Corner Shop. Rudovsky was in her car, with Chapman in the passenger seat.

"Okay! That was intense! Come on Bill."

Chapman had to do a bit of a jog to keep up with Rudovsky as the SCIU officers reached the front door. Some of the TA officers were standing outside, taking off their helmets.

"Thanks guys, nice one," said the DS as she rushed past. She was shocked to see how pathetic Nolan looked, sobbing into his carpet. This was far from the mental image she had built of the man who had unleashed such sickening and sustained violence against another human being.

"Go on, Bill."

"William David Nolan, I am arresting you on suspicion of murder. You do not have to say anything…"

Chapter Twenty

Miller was pleased to see Saunders arriving back at Tameside CID. DCI Katy Green also looked quite pleased to see him, so Miller decided to mention his colleague's girlfriend at the earliest possible opportunity.

"Ah, nice of you to join us DI Saunders!"

"Hello, alright?"

"This is the trouble with senior officers dating their detective constables! How is Helen, by the way?"

Saunders laughed off his DCI's remark. "I didn't even see her!" he said, reading between the lines. DCI Green looked as though she got the message too, as her cheeks suddenly reddened slightly.

"So, anyway, lots of interesting developments to tell you about Keith. DCI Green here runs an excellent operation, her detectives are on it!"

"Oh, brilliant, that sounds positive." Saunders smiled warmly.

"Where shall we start?" said DCI Green, without reciprocating Saunders' friendly smile.

Fifteen minutes later, DI Saunders had been brought up to speed with the details about the attackers, their car, and the extraordinary lengths they had gone to, which ironically, looked likely to be their downfall. It would be anyway, if Miller had his way.

"So, DI Saunders, I think we should go and visit the scrap yard where these plates appear to have come from. DCI Green, have your officers found the details on that, yet?"

"Yes, Sir." DCI Green handed a piece of paper to Miller. "The scrap yard isn't too far away. Shawcross Street in Oldham. The owner is a 38 year-old Polish man called Piotr Tchorzewski."

"Oh, that's great stuff. Well, we'll head over there and have a chat..."

"I wouldn't advise that, just yet." DCI Green had a serious expression on her face.

"Why not?" Miller looked puzzled.

"There's another side to this Piotr Tchorzewski's

business operation, it appears. He's currently flagging up on the NCA's organised crime database as a person-of-interest."

"Really?" Miller looked gutted.

"Yes, there are no specific details listed, but there is a note on there which instructs any investigating officers to speak to the NCA before engaging with this individual." DCI Green had a serious expression on her face.

"Well, under the circumstances, Katy, I'm going to pretend that I never heard that."

The Tameside DCI was visibly shocked by Miller's reply. "What's... how do you mean?"

"Thing is, the National Crime Agency stick those flags on a lot of people. In my experience, it never ends well. Not for me, anyway."

"I'm sorry, I don't follow." DCI Green folded her arms across her chest and maintained eye-contact with Miller. It was becoming increasingly clear that she preferred to play by the rules.

Saunders picked up on the body-language and came to his superior's rescue, aware that she wouldn't approve of Miller's response, she just wasn't from that school-of-thought. He decided to play the part of the diplomat.

"Well, DCI Green, in our experience, the NCA tend to block any requests that you make to them, keen to protect their own investigations. It always seems like a conflict of interest when a CID department ask to get involved with anything linking back to an NCA inquiry. The very best case scenario, certainly in my experience, is that they'll take at least forty-eight hours to get back to us, and even then it could be just to say that they would prefer us to stand down. Unless of course the information we had was likely to assist their own enquiry."

"Understood. But I am not prepared for me, or any of my officers to have any part in a deliberate attempt to ignore a written directive from the NCA. Absolutely not."

This was an impressive stand to make, and both Saunders and Miller respected DCI Katy Green's assertiveness.

"Under the circumstances," said Miller. "I feel we have come to a bit of a cross-roads here. I'm sure we're all agreed that we want to arrest the people who started that fire, and killed Juris and Inga, and their dad, Andris?"

Both Saunders and Green nodded. Miller noted that DCI Green's arms were still folded firmly across her chest, he interpreted that this unconscious stance implied that she was feeling very defensive judging by her body-language.

"But the thing is, the NCA won't give a Tinker's cuss about any of that. It's perfectly natural, I suppose. Their default position is to try and protect whatever it is they are investigating. All we want to know is, who bought those registration plates? It's not going to affect the NCA in any way, shape or form. Is it?"

DCI Green still looked unhappy with the suggestion.

"Listen, boss. I'm with DCI Green on this. We could end up getting into some serious paperwork, or even worse if we ignore the flag." Saunders looked hard at Miller, almost staring him out. "And let's face it, when did a scrap-yard owner ever give any useful information away? I've never known it to happen." Saunders relaxed the steely-stare. Miller had understood what it meant, and he was confident that DCI Green hadn't even noticed it.

"Ah, you're right. I'm just so keen to arrest these bastards, I'm getting way ahead of myself." Miller looked frustrated.

"Well, I'm glad you've started to see some sense. I don't like to get into treacherous waters, it never sits well with me." The Tameside DCI relaxed her arms and rested them by her sides. "Okay, well, I'll go and speak to my team, see what's developing out there, I'll leave you to work on a plan B." DCI Green turned and left the two SCIU officers in her office. The paperwork with Piotr Tchorzewski's details was still on her desk. Saunders took his phone out of his pocket and clicked the camera icon, before taking a photo of the document.

"I thought you were starting with me, then." Said Miller with a smile.

"Nah, just wanted you to back off. You weren't going to get anywhere with her. She's a goody-two-shoes."

"So, what's the plan?" asked Miller.

"There's a way we can do this without the NCA being approached."

"Go on." Miller loved it when Saunders was taking charge.

"We send somebody unconnected with the enquiry down to this scrap-yard, looking for a gear-knob for an X-Type Jaguar."

"Why?"

"Because my dad needs one, the numbers have all rubbed off on his."

"And what are they going to be looking for?"

"The Vauxhall Zafira with no number-plates. If we know that much, we'll have a stronger case to take to the NCA and we can insist on an immediate arrest warrant for Piotr Tchorzewski."

"Who's going to do it?"

"What about that PC you ring up for favours from time to time?"

"Nah. Could drop him in the shit. It'd be a bit dirty that. We need somebody who isn't involved with the police in any capacity." Miller looked as though he was deep in thought.

"What about a grass?"

"Like who?" Miller suddenly looked interested.

"Well, I don't know. What about Big Fat Kev?"

Miller smiled. He loved the nickname that Saunders had given Kevin Howarth, a small-time wheeler-dealer who bought and sold dubious goods. He had become an excellent informant after his lock-up had been raided and an impressive amount of stolen goods were discovered. His excuse was that he just rented the space out, providing a storage facility for some very unsavoury characters who had items which were far too hot to move. To save his own bacon, he had "sung like a canary" and supplied the police with a great deal of information. The excellent intelligence that Big Fat Kev had provided regarding a number of Manchester's scummiest villains had resulted in him facing no charges, but had in turn left him extremely vulnerable to any police officers who needed a favour by way of black-mail.

"That's a very good shout Keith. Big Fat Kev won't look

out of place wandering around a scrap yard, will he? Tell you what, go down to your car and phone him, it'd be a shame for DCI Green to overhear you."

"Sir." Saunders smiled and stepped past Miller, and out of the office.

Chapter Twenty-One

"Good afternoon, this is BBC Radio Manchester, and some breaking news which is just reaching us from Manchester City Police." The presenter sounded quite excited about this, but it was hard to tell if it was because of the content she was about to deliver, or if it was because this was a brilliant opportunity to get rid of 91-year-old Wilma from Gorton, who was on the line describing all the cats she'd ever had during her life. It was suicide inducing radio, and this breaking story was the perfect excuse to terminate Wilma's sweet, but painful call.

"It relates to the major police investigation into the horrific murder of Graham Hartley in Monton, a story that we have been covering extensively here on BBC Radio Manchester for the past three weeks. Our crime reporter Kelvin MacDonald joins us from the crime-desk, Kelvin, please update us."

"Yes, thank you. This is a major development this hour, and one which will no doubt bring a huge sense of relief to many people in the Greater Manchester area. In the last half-an-hour, police have detained a man in relation to the extremely brutal attack against Graham Hartley, the 40-year-old man who was beaten to death as he went jogging near his home on the first of November. It would appear from the language used in this press-release, that the detectives involved in this arrest are extremely confident that they have detained the man responsible for this crime."

"It is quite unusual for the police to reveal information like this, before any charges have been brought, Kelvin."

"Yes, that's absolutely right. And I think that detail alone demonstrates that the police are keen to quash these rumours about a random attacker on the streets. That theory is backed up by one line in the press release, which states, "our investigation into this horrific attack has identified several links between the attacker and the victim which gives us enormous confidence that this was not a random attack. We hope that this news will be of reassurance to the general public of the city and that they will regain the confidence to go about their daily business without the sense of fear which has been hanging over the city all month."

*****

With Billy Nolan booked into police custody at Swinton police station and the SOCO team currently carrying out a deep search of Nolan's home, the SCIU team had another task to fulfil. They needed to question Lindsey Nolan, the estranged wife of Billy. As things stood, she was currently facing a charge of assisting an offender as an accessory after the fact. This was because she had failed to report her relationship with the murder victim. In plain English, her failure to inform the police of her relationship with the dead man had effectively concealed the crime that her estranged husband was suspected to have carried out. This is a serious crime in normal circumstances. But in these circumstances, where the murder had made national news, and had been the number one news story in the local area for several weeks – there was literally no defence for her decision to stay silent.

As soon as Billy's cell door was slammed shut, Rudovsky instructed Chapman and Worthington to start working on their interview plan. She then went back to her car with Kenyon and Grant and the three headed to Lindsey's new address, four miles away in Boothstown.

Fifteen minutes later, the unmarked police car parked up outside the flat, which was situated above the Spar shop in the neat little village between Worsley and Astley, a bonny little place best known for its canal marina at the start of the Bridgewater canal. This unique waterway looks like tomato soup, famed for its bright orange appearance which is due to particles of iron ore which are found deep in the coal mines all around the area and which the Bridgewater canal was built to serve.

"Okay, listen up. As we discussed, we'll be playing the soft-touch, showing lots of sympathy as we talk to Lindsey, nice and gentle, telling her about Billy's arrest and asking her if she knows about a violent side to him. Most importantly, as far as she's to know, we don't have any clue about her connection with Graham Hartley. I think this is the best way to start proceedings, see what kind of a hole she starts digging for herself. Understood?"

"Sarge!"

"Crystal clear boss."

"Okay, let's get this ticked off the to-do list. We'll let her say stuff that will be hard to reverse out of later and then charge her for accessory and perverting the course of justice."

The DS got out of her vehicle, followed by her detectives and the three of them headed around the back of the convenience store. There they found the door to the flat. Rudovsky knocked loudly, but there was no response. The place was silent. The DS looked at her watch, it was almost half-past five.

"She might not be back from work yet." Said Rudovsky, annoyed by this halt in proceedings. "Pete, do us a favour, go in the shop and ask them if they know what time she normally gets home from work."

"No worries." Kenyon walked back around to the front of the property.

"Her car's there." Said DC Grant, pointing at the Vauxhall Corsa which they'd seen several times on Chapman's CCTV stills.

"Yeah, I noticed that." She hadn't.

Rudovsky knocked again, louder this time. Nothing.

"She's not in."

"Unless she's heard about it already?"

DC Kenyon came back. "They don't know her, said she keeps herself to herself. But the woman behind the counter said that her car hasn't moved for ages and it's taking up two spaces. She said she'd put a polite note through her door asking her if she wouldn't mind trying to park a bit more sociably!"

Rudovsky smiled. "That's not polite, that's passive-aggressive!"

"Yeah, that's what I thought." Said Kenyon, laughing at the same joke.

DC Grant wasn't joining in with the conversation. She had a serious look on her face as she walked over to the letterbox and looked inside. There was a pile of mail on the doormat. Suddenly, she pulled her head back as a toxic smell pinched her nostrils.

"Fuck!" she said as she recoiled from the door.

"What?" asked Rudovsky.

"She is in there. But judging by the smell, she's not alive."

Rudovsky stepped across to the letterbox and lifted it, she crouched down to take a sniff and pulled her head away quickly.

"Shit!" Rudovsky retched. It was a completely involuntary reaction to the odour which had hit her nostrils, so strongly that it stung.

"Is it bad?" asked Kenyon, stepping over towards the door.

Grant nodded, grateful that she had not taken as much of a deep inhalation as her DS had.

Rudovsky was taking deep breaths and trying to calm her smell senses down. Eventually she spoke, her eyes still watery from the retching. "Yeah. It's about as bad as it gets Pete. It's the raw sewage and boiled egg smell of several weeks of decomposition."

"It's a good reason to explain why Lindsey hasn't been in touch about her relationship with Hartley," said Grant.

Rudovsky took her phone out of her pocket and dialled DCS Dixon.

"Come on, come on," she said as the phone rang and rang.

"Who you phoning?" asked Kenyon.

"Dixon."

Kenyon raised an eyebrow before nodding as he remembered that Miller and Saunders were on another job. "He'll have gone home now. He only works Dolly Parton hours."

"Fuck's sake!" Rudovsky hesitated, wondering if she should phone Miller, or Saunders, or either. She didn't want to make it look like she couldn't cope or make decisions. Her finger was hovering above Miller's number.

"What you thinking about, Jo?" asked Kenyon, who had been Rudovsky's regular partner for the past six years, before she'd got her promotion.

Rudovsky looked at him. "I'm just thinking... Miller and Saunders are up to their necks in it with that arson job. I'm just not sure I should disturb them."

"Well it's your call. But it's a major development, it's not like you're bothering them because you can't find the stapler."

"I agree with Pete, Sarge." Said Grant. "They're not going to mind you phoning about this, and after all, you tried Dixon first."

Rudovsky nodded. "Yeah, you're right. I'll ring Saunders. Come on, let's get in the car in case we're overheard." The three SCIU detectives walked back around to the front of the building and sat in Rudovsky's car as her call connected.

"Sir, hi, yes, sorry to bother you... I know you're busy. I tried Dixon first but he's gone home. There's been a development."

"What's up, Jo? Are you okay? You sound proper stressed out."

"Yeah, well I am actually. We're at Lindsey Nolan's house. She's not been seen for a few weeks and there's a very unpleasant smell coming from her flat."

"Shit."

"Smells worse than that."

"Right. Miller's in with the DCI from Tameside at the minute. I think you should... what's the address again?"

"Boothstown."

"That falls under Salford, doesn't it?"

"Yes. It's slap-bang on the border with Wigan division but I'm pretty sure it's within Salford's division."

"Okay, tell you what to do, ring Salford's Inspector and explain the situation. It's going to have to be investigated by them, Dixon wants this all tidied up by tomorrow. And that's not going to happen now."

"What, not necessarily, Sir."

"What do you mean, Jo?"

"Well, it looks pretty obvious what's happened here, doesn't it?"

"Do you think?"

"Yes, totally. He's killed her lover, then he's come round here to tell her all about it, then killed her. That's my theory, and I'm one-hundred-per-cent on it. And I've not stepped foot inside and seen the murder scene yet."

"It's plausible. But the SOCO investigations at the property are going to take a good bit of time up. There's no way you'll be in a position to charge Nolan tomorrow, which was your original plan. This development changes everything."

"Well, I'm snookered then aren't I?"

"It looks that way Jo. But anyway, stay there, phone Salford and explain your suspicions and get the Inspector to log the job as a potential murder scene and then they'll automatically have the ownership of the job, that will cover your arse. There's nothing to stop you hanging around and seeing what you can find out."

"We're still going to be taken off it."

"Not necessarily. As soon as Miller comes back I'll update him and get him to give you a call."

"Right, cheers. How's yours going, anyway?"

"Yes, looking quite positive on this one, got a tasty lead so, looking good."

"Right. Okay, cheers Sir, speak later."

Rudovsky ended the call and looked through her phone contacts, selecting DTY INSP SLFRD. The call connected a couple of seconds later and Rudovsky explained the situation.

"Okay, that's on a priority one, we won't need a warrant to force entry due to your suspicions that a serious incident has taken place. I'll await further information from my officers and proceed from that point."

"Thanks, but I can assure you, you might as well ring the pathologist as well."

"Thank you DS Rudovsky, I take on board your comments. I suspect my officers will be with you presently."

Rudovsky hung up and looked at her colleagues. "Shit. This suddenly got a lot darker, didn't it?"

Kenyon and Grant nodded and a heavy silence suddenly descended on the car. The mood was low, this conclusion had never been considered by any of them, the plan had been to try and frighten Lindsey with the threat of criminal charges and then bargain with her to become the star witness in her ex-husband's murder trial.

But judging by the unmistakable smell of human decomposition which was wafting from the young woman's letterbox, that idea was finished. It was depressing for all three of the detectives to consider how much they had misjudged Lindsey's motives and in turn, how they had automatically assumed her guilt, when all the while she had been a victim of this psychotic bastard herself.

Chapter Twenty-Two

Kevin Howarth parked his car at the end of the road, making sure to lock it. This was a dodgy-looking area, the actual road itself didn't even exist, it was just a long, dusty, pot-hole ridden dirt-path covered in old rags, rubbish and oil-spills. It was as though the authorities had forgotten this place existed. This neglected old road was the polar-opposite of Britain's Best Kept Village and could easily be a strong contender for Britain's Shittiest Shit-Hole.

Both sides of the dirt-track road had huge scrap-yards running along as far as the eye could see, hidden by collapsing concrete panel walls which were daubed in graffiti and topped with barbed wire. Shitty old bangers littered both sides of the road, waiting to be taken inside one of the yards and stacked on top of all the other battered old motors.

Big Fat Kev had decided he was going to visit all of the scrap-yards, rather than heading straight into the one that DI Saunders had phoned him about. He knew how these little places worked, he was well aware that all the scrap yard owners talked to one other so Kev had reached the conclusion that he'd appear a bit more genuine if he started looking around all of them. He wrote a list of bits that he was looking for, just in case he was asked. His list included an X-Type gear knob, which DI Saunders had requested.

As he entered the first scrap yard, he was approached immediately by a rough-looking, filthy mechanic in his early 30's.

"Alright mate, what are you after?" He asked, holding a massive spanner by his side.

"Oh a few bits mate. Got any MG ZR's in?"

"Yeah, there's one on the second row, a red one, about half-way down. Go and have a look. Don't start climbing on anything though, you fat fucker!" A wave of loud laughter came from the small office behind where the mechanic stood. Kev smiled, mostly out of embarrassment and headed off in the direction he'd been pointed.

He pretended to look at the cars and spent a minute or two looking at the ZR, looking for a part that it definitely didn't have, to avoid any aggro on the way out. He felt nervous as he walked back towards the office, his nervousness manifested itself into a little trip as he neared the office. There was more laughter from inside. Kev hated these kinds of places, the rules of normal civilisation didn't exist down these dodgy back-streets, a fact made clear by the staff smoking indoors, sitting beneath porno-mag pages which had been pinned up on the walls inside the little office. He was glad to be out of there as he stepped out onto the third-world road and headed on towards the next scrap-yard.

He wasn't challenged at this one, he just walked straight in and started looking around the cars. He was working out that he only had another one of these to look around before he arrived at the one that DI Saunders had asked him to have a look around. All this for fifty quid, he thought as he finished his charade of walking around the piles of knackered old cars in the second scrap yard. He managed to leave without anybody quizzing him, which he was pleased about.

The third scrap yard felt a bit more hostile as he approached. There was a group of four young lads wearing mechanics overalls, all standing by the gates.

"What you after mate?"

"What you looking for?"

The young lads looked as though they were desperate for something to do, so Kev decided to recall the most obscure vehicle he'd thought of on the way here, just to avoid stepping another foot in the yard.

"Alright, I'm after a two-litre diesel engine for a Sherpa minibus, 1988 model."

The young lads laughed loudly.

"Nah mate, no minibuses here. You'll be lucky getting anything from the last century in here mate!" said the most sensible looking one.

"Alright lads, well, thanks anyway."

"You'd be better off looking on eBay mate." Said another lad. They looked quite intimidating, but they were alright really, Kev had been pleased to discover.

"Yes, I have, nowt doing. Someone said there was one

in one of these yards. You don't know which one, do you?"

"Nah mate, nothing that old down here."

"Alright, well thanks anyway."

As Kev walked slowly away from the young lads, he realised that he was now finally arriving at the yard that Saunders wanted him to look at. He felt his nerves kick in as he reminded himself of the vehicle that he needed to find. There was extra money, Saunders had said, if he managed to get a photo of the Zafira, and the VIN number from the windscreen. But he'd been warned to be very discreet about it and make sure that nobody from the scrap-yard was aware of what he was doing. "Don't take any risks!" Had been Saunders advice.

Kev walked into the yard, it was identical to the others, a thick, oily residue covered the mud-tracks of the ground. Inside the compound, the cars were stacked four or five high, models of every colour with their wheels, doors, bonnets and windscreens missing. Kev had hoped to get straight in, as he had at the second scrap-yard. As he side-stepped the office and approached the first row of cars, he began to relax a little. He began walking around, conscious of some loud talking in the portacabin office just behind him. He heard the phone ring, it was wired up to a Tannoy system and he felt a huge sense of relief when he heard it ring off, and a voice in the office started talking on the phone. The accent sounded Russian, or Eastern European. Kev felt the pressure mounting and decided to just walk around the yard, find this Zafira, if it was here, and then get the fuck away from this horrible, scary, shit-hole of a place.

On the third row of cars, Kev found what he was looking for. It was a dark silver Zafira, all the doors were off, but it was still easy to see that it was the car that DI Saunders was interested in. Kev continued walking around, looking to see if there were any other Zafiras in, and also to see if he was being followed by any of the staff. There wasn't any other Zafiras, and he wasn't being followed, he had the place to himself. He decided to head back to the third row, grab a photo of the car that he'd been sent here to locate, and then get as far away as he could from here. Kev took his phone out of his pocket, activated the camera and pointed it in the direction of a completely different car, ensuring that the Zafira was in the corner of the shot, but not so that it was obvious if anybody saw him and asked to see the photo. Kev's paranoia was overwhelming him and his hands were shaking slightly as he held his phone up, trying to be as discreet as possible. He took two quick photos, switched off the camera and put it back into his pocket, before heading back towards the gates.

"What you looking for?" asked a big bald guy, standing by the office door. Kev felt his adrenaline kick in.

"Oh, nowt."

"Well what ya doing then?" The man looked like a body-builder and he had an intimidating stare. He didn't seem like a particularly pleasant character.

"Oh, er, well I'm after a gear-knob for a Jag. X type." Kev felt that his voice had sounded nervous.

"No, not here. Go to eBay to buy."

"Yes, I'll try on there. Thanks."

The big man just turned and stepped back into the office and said something in a foreign language to somebody else. Kev didn't understand the language, but he knew instinctively that it was the foreign equivalent of "stupid fat fuck." Kev began walking, trying hard not to make it look as though he was in a hurry. But he *was* in a hurry. He just wanted to get away from here as quickly as possible, then get these photos sent over to DI Saunders and hopefully, he wouldn't hear anything else from the dibble for another six months, at least.

*****

Saunders was busy working on his laptop in DCI Katy Green's office when he heard his phone ping in his pocket.

"Okay, here we go," said Saunders to Miller as he opened up the text message from Big Fat Kev.

"Has he got anything?"

"Yeah, wait a sec. Two photos, the Zafira is still there, and look, so are the pissing number-plates." Saunders passed his phone across to Miller, the look of frustration was unmistakable.

"What the hell?"

"That is definitely the right number-plate, isn't it?" asked Saunders, his voice giving away the sinking feeling that he was experiencing.

"Let me check." Miller grabbed his file off the desk and leafed through the pages until he found the intelligence file that DCI Green's team had built up with information concerning the car on the M60 motorway at the time of the fire. He found the photograph of the vehicle, taken from CCTV stills on the motorway. "Here we go, the reg was ML09 AHW."

"Bingo. There you go, the registration plates are still on the scrap car in the scrap yard. They didn't take the plates off the real car, because they are clearly still attached. This lead has just come to a dead-end." Saunders looked gutted. Miller, on the other hand looked confused. Neither spoke for several minutes as they thought about the next line of enquiry.

"Thing is though…"

Saunders looked across at his boss. He was encouraged that Miller wasn't finished with this.

"What?"

"Well, the fact that this car, used for such an horrific crime, was parked on the motorway with fake plates on has never made sense to me. I didn't think that whoever was responsible would be stupid enough to take some plates off a similar looking vehicle that's been scrapped. That detail has never added up."

"I agree. Go on."

"So, we need to know how they found a similar vehicle's registration plates and managed to get some plates cloned within 24 hours of the Zafira being stolen. The Zafira in the scrap yard was logged down as scrapped on the DVLA computer in August. That's three months its been off the road. How did the arsonists find the registration plate for a similar looking vehicle, which they obviously assumed was still on the road?" Miller was staring hard at the file on his lap. Saunders was listening intently, trying to think of possibilities.

"Speak to the owner of the stolen Zafira. Ask him a few questions about the car, where it used to be parked, what it was used for, did anybody else drive it, who knew where it had been parked when it was stolen, all that kind of stuff. I strongly suspect that there's a connection there somewhere. There's more to this Keith, I can feel it."

"I feel the same. Something's just not right."

"I'm not letting it go just yet, there are too many questions and not enough answers."

It went quiet again as the two detectives thought about this strange situation. Saunders disrupted the silence.

"I've just had a thought."

"What?"

"Well, we know that the stolen Zafira had the fake plates on it when it was parked on the motorway?"

"Yes, and that they were still on when the car went through Woodley, Katy's officers have found a clip on the traffic monitoring cameras."

"And just after this, it was burnt out, not far away."

"Yes. I know."

"But do we know if the plates were still present on the vehicle when it was burnt out?"

"No, I don't know. There's not usually much left of a car after it's been burnt-out though, other than the metal carcass, is there?"

"I disagree. Thinking back to my time on the beat in Salford, we were called out to burnt-out cars every day. Joy-riders would rally the tits off them all night and then torch them when they'd run out of fuel in order to destroy any evidence of them touching it."

"Yeah. So?"

"Well nine times out of ten, the number plates survived, that's how we identified the vehicles and reported the outcome to the owner. So, I'm just thinking that there is a strong possibility that these plates might have survived the fire and if they did, there might be some evidence to be gathered. Any idea if the plates are still on it?"

Miller looked again at DCI Green's file. There was no mention of any number plates in relation to the burnt-out car, and annoyingly, there were no photographs of the vehicle in its current state, either. "Nope, nothing here about that."

"Right, well, I think I'll go down and have a look for myself. I take it the car is still there?"

"Yes, as far as I know. I can't see why anybody would have taken it away, it was burnt out on a patch of wasteland apparently."

"Do us a favour, get me the details of the location. I've a got funny feeling about this."

Fifteen minutes later, Saunders was on the edge of Tameside, close to where the borough borders with Stockport. It took him a few attempts to locate the route through to the waste-land. Bushes and weeds had grown all around this location which was once the entrance to a grand old Victorian cotton mill. Today, it just looked like another part of the city that had been completely forgotten about.

Saunders eventually sussed out the way to get his car through the undergrowth, building in confidence the further along the track that he drove. He could see the tracks that the stolen car had made, where it had crushed the undergrowth. Eventually, he reached the clearing, which he assumed had once been an out-building belonging to the mill. It was a flat, concrete square with three burnt-out cars marking the spot. The few remaining sections of wall were covered in graffiti, some of it very good and some of it less so. The ground was covered with hundreds of empty beer cans and cider bottles, they were scattered everywhere. It looked to Saunders as though this was a prime spot for kids to come and hang out and get pissed, as well as an ideal location for local toe-rags to burn cars out without risk of being challenged.

He parked his shiny new CID car up. The only light was coming from the loading bay floodlights on a factory on the opposite side of the canal. Saunders left his car headlights on, putting the full beam on to better illuminate the area he wanted to inspect. He got out of the car, walking straight over to the soot blackened Zafira. As he walked, he could see that the top-half of the car had practically burnt away, the heat from the blaze had completely gutted the interior and all that remained was a burnt out, stinking shell. As he got a little closer, he saw that the external damage was not as bad, particularly around the bottom third of the car. It was still possible to see the original paint colour all around the sills and around the wheel arches. This was definitely the same colour and model as the dark silver car which had been abandoned on the M60 for twenty-five minutes, with its hazard lights flashing.

Saunders crouched down at the rear of the vehicle, he was glad to see that the back bumper was still attached. It was black with soot, but it hadn't melted and remained attached solidly to the car. There was no number plate. He took his phone out of his pocket and started to take some photographs of the flat space on the bumper where the registration plate was supposed to be. He looked on the floor, getting down on his hands and knees, and switched on the torch function to assist him with his task of looking for the screws. He couldn't see any. He got to his feet and walked around to the front of the fire-damaged vehicle. Once again, the front bumper was relatively intact, but there was no sign of the number-plate. Saunders took some more photos and checked on the ground amongst the broken glass and debris beneath his feet but he couldn't find any screws. One thing was for sure though. Both the front and rear number plates had been taken off this vehicle before it had been set alight. And that detail didn't make any sense at all.

Chapter Twenty-Three

Outside the Spar convenience store in Boothstown, the alarming police presence was sudden and intense. Several police cars and vans all arrived within seconds of each other, their blue lights and sirens lighting up the neighbourhood. The sudden burst of loud and visual activity had the curtains and blinds twitching at almost every window.

The police officers were all assembling around the rear of the Spar, awaiting further instruction. The only job that any of them had been given so far was to cordon off the area and prevent any members of the public from gaining access to the rear of the building. From the side wall of the Spar store, a POLICE LINE DO NOT CROSS tape had closed the side-street which was used as the shop's unofficial car-park. Officers were receiving lots of "aw for fucks sakes" and "you've got to be fucking jokings" from drivers who were appalled by the news that they had to park fifteen metres away from their usual spot.

One or two members of the community had wandered across to try and get hold of the gossip, but the police officers were cautious to reveal the true reason for their sudden and unmistakable presence in this normally quiet area. So, they tried fobbing the nosey neighbours off.

"What's going on, officer?" asked one anxious looking woman as she approached the cordon line.

"We have received intelligence that there is going to be a half-price sale on the donuts in this store. We are not letting anybody past until we have bought them all."

"Are you taking the piss?"

"No madam. This has come from a very reliable source."

Finally, some ten minutes after the first patrol cars had arrived, the incident commander pulled up, a duty which had fallen to the Inspector that Rudovsky had spoken with on the phone.

Rudovsky was at the back of the shop, standing near to the door.

"Hello, I'm Inspector Johnson. Are you the DS that I

spoke with?"

"Yes Sir, DS Jo Rudovsky, SCIU."

"Okay." The Inspector stepped past Rudovsky and crouched down by the letter-box. He seemed to take a few seconds before he lifted it and had a sniff. He closed it very quickly, within a second of the toxic scent hitting his senses.

"Mother fucker!" He said, standing up straight. His eyes were watering. "Yes, I think that's definitely a fatality."

Rudovsky nodded sombrely.

"I think you can leave this with us Detective Sergeant. There's nothing you can do now."

"Well, sorry Sir, I was just hopeful to get a look at the scene. We're about to interview the suspect we believe to be responsible for what's happened here. I was hoping to find something..."

"Is this connected with the guy we brought in today, from Swinton?" asked the Inspector. He knew all about it, he'd managed the Tactical Aid support.

"Yes Sir, Billy Nolan. The lady who lives here is his ex."

"I see. Okay, well, I'm not prepared to let anybody in there just now apart from my Pathologist and my Forensics officers. You may as well go back and get on with your interview regardless. The details of our findings from this location will be sent to DCI Miller later on."

"But, Sir..."

"I'm sorry DS Rudovsky. That's my final decision. Stand down."

"Sir." Rudovsky nodded and walked away calmly, but she was fuming. It wasn't as if she particularly wanted to go into that flat, and see, and smell the horrors which lay within. But it would have been useful for when she was sitting down with Billy Nolan.

"Fucks sake!" said Rudovsky as she got into her car. Kenyon and Grant were waiting inside, out of the cold.

"What's up?"

"The Inspector has just fired me off. Told me to fucking stand down!"

"Stand down? God I've not heard that for yonks! What

a dick." Kenyon sounded pissed off on Rudovsky's behalf.

"Right, anyway, fuck him. We'll just have to do the interview about Graham Hartley. There's plenty to talk about anyway. We'll have to talk to him about Lindsey tomorrow." Rudovsky pushed her key into the ignition and started the engine, putting the fan on full blast to de-steam the windows.

"Who's doing that?"

"What?"

"The interview with Nolan."

"Well, it's Bill's arrest. So, I was going to go in with him."

Kenyon didn't say anything and Grant remained silent on the back-seat.

"Why? Do you want to do it?" asked Rudovsky after several seconds.

"Well, normally, it'd be me and you, wouldn't it? The dream team! The deadly duo! The..."

"Get on with it Pete, fucks sake."

"Well, we know how to play off each other, where to set the traps and that."

"Yes, I know that Peter. But it's Bill's job this. He's worked really hard for it. I can't take him off it now. It wouldn't be right."

"I know. I'm telling you to stand down! I'll go in with Bill, try and find out what this Billy Nolan character is all about, get him used to me and Chapman, and then you can go in and pull him apart tomorrow."

Rudovsky smiled. "Now that is a very great idea! I like that. Absolute magic!" She started wiping at the windscreen with her sleeve, in a bid to speed up the de-steaming process. "They've got video-monitoring at Swinton nick, haven't they?"

"Think so. They'll have at least one interview room with video-link. Why?"

"I think I'll spectate the first interview. Don't tell Bill I'm watching though, you know how nervous he gets about stuff like that."

"What, technology?" asked Grant.

"Yes. Well, he's from the generation before ours isn't

he?" Said Kenyon.

"Hey, credit where its due please. We wouldn't be sat here now, with Lindsey Nolan's rotting flesh still raw in our nostrils if it wasn't for his very capable use of technology. Give him a break, eh?" Rudovsky put the car in gear, eased the clutch up slightly and the three detectives were soon on the move, away from this major crime scene and headed for Swinton police station.

"Never thought I'd see the day though." Kenyon didn't want to let it lie.

"What?" asked Rudovsky, annoyed by a patch of steam that wasn't budging.

"You sticking up for Bill. I'm not saying it's a bad thing, just seems weird."

"Well, I'm a big girl now Pete. DS in the best CID department in the city. I've had to accept my own failings with regards to my relationship with Bill. We've put our past differences aside, and it's working out well. Like I say, he's nailed this case, so as I always say, there's nothing positive about being negative."

"Jo! When have you ever said that?" Kenyon was laughing at Rudovsky's blatant bullshit.

"I say it all the time, thank you very much!" The DS had a sly smirk on her face, it was illuminated by the oncoming headlights.

"Bollocks! Helen, back me up here. Have you ever heard Jo say that phrase before?" Kenyon was straining round to see the DC who was sat on the back seat.

"Never!" said Grant, with an unmistakable smile in her voice.

"I say it all the time!"

"You lie! Gonna start calling you Roxanne Pallett."

"Right, anyway, enough of your jibber-jabber Pete. I need a bit of quiet time, need to think about stuff."

"How do we know if that's even true?"

"Shut up now, or you're walking back."

*****

Rudovsky was sitting in an adjacent room to interview room 5 at Swinton police station. This room had four video monitors on a desk, along with a small bank of controls which she could use to alter the volume and zoom in on Billy Nolan's face during the interview.

Chapman and Kenyon were sitting in the interview room, waiting for the prisoner to be brought down from his cell. Chapman seemed nervous. He'd worked bloody hard to get this result, and he was terrified of screwing anything up now, at this critical stage. Kenyon sensed the tension and decided to try and lighten the mood, just for his own sake. He knew that Rudovsky was listening in to everything that was being said from her vantage point next door.

"Tell you what, Bill, what I noticed today when I was with Jo."

"What's that?" asked Chapman, without looking up from his interview plan.

"Her arse is getting fat! Sweet baby Jesus! I thought I was walking behind Jabba the Hut! I think somebody should have a chat with her. She's been at the sausage rolls from Greggs again I think. By the fucking tray load!" Kenyon looked up at the camera and smirked.

"Haven't noticed, Pete."

"God, have you not? She's going to have to get a sign fitted on her back soon. Wide load."

"I bet you wouldn't say that to her face," said Chapman nonchalantly, he was more interested in checking over his paperwork than listening to Kenyon's random waffle.

"Nah. Probably not. I'll leave that job for you."

"Pete, shut the fuck up please mate. I've read the same line three times here."

"Sorry."

Rudovsky was holding a V sign up at the video monitor, but stopped when she heard a knock at the interview room door through the sound system. The door opened and Billy Nolan was led into the interview, dressed in a grey police-issue jogging suit.

Suddenly, Rudovsky stiffened up and grabbed her pen,

ready to observe and take notes.

"I'll be just outside." Said the custody officer who had brought Nolan from his cell.

"No solicitor?" asked Chapman of the officer, who shook his head. That was good news.

"Okay, thank you officer." Said Kenyon.

Nolan sat down on the seat facing Chapman and Kenyon. He was a big lad and he had an attitude about him. He looked like the kind of bloke who could handle himself, and he displayed the confidence to back it up.

"So, William..."

"Call me Billy."

"Is that your preferred name?"

"Yeah."

"Okay, well, lets just get the formalities out of the way, using your birth name, and then we'll call you Billy. Alright?" Chapman appeared confident, which pleased Rudovsky in the room next door.

After a few minutes of legal talk about Billy's rights and the procedure of the interview, Kenyon started the tape recorder and all three people waited for the long beep sound to finish.

"Okay, the time is nineteen-forty-eight, present in the interview room is William David Nolan of 11 Worsley Road, Swinton in the city of Salford, DC Peter Kenyon and DC Bill Chapman. William Nolan has declined the offer of legal representation. Is that right William?"

"Yeah, but like I say, I'm called Billy."

"Okay Billy. Well, I'd like to start by asking you where you were between six pm and eight pm on Wednesday the first of November?"

Nolan didn't look remotely phased by the question. "What year?"

"This year, Billy. Three weeks ago."

Nolan shrugged. "No idea mate."

"Well, just to remind you, it was the night that there was a very vicious murder, not far from your home, on Eccles Field. Do you remember that?"

"No idea mate. There's always summat happening round here."

"This murder has been front page news ever since, its been covered on TV and radio news."

"Yeah, well, I might have heard summat about it."

"Do you know anything about the man who was attacked?"

"Nah. Why would I?"

"Well, we have information that suggests that he was a friend of your wife's."

"Like I say mate, I don't know anything about him."

"Did your wife say anything about him? Perhaps he was a colleague from work?"

"Don't know. She lives her life, I live mine."

"But, well, I'm just thinking, it must have come up in conversation, that her friend had been murdered."

"Nah, she's not said anything to me about it."

"Does she have a lot of male friends?"

Nolan was leaning back on his chair as though he didn't have a care in the world. His body language was relaxed and he looked more like a bored employee in a health and safety meeting.

"Not sure what you're getting at mate. If you are asking me if Lindsey was a little slag who puts it about with any bloke she meets, then yeah. She's been Rogered more times than your police radio probably has."

There was a silence. Both Kenyon and Chapman had picked up on the comment about Lindsey, used in the past tense. Nolan had said that she *was* a little slag. Not is. That was a big moment, and Rudovsky had picked up on it from the next room, too.

"You said that Lindsey *was* a little slag. Can you tell us what you meant by that comment?"

Nolan's relaxed body-language didn't alter as he answered. "Well, I think you know what I meant. She likes to put herself about, you know."

"You said she was a slag. Does this mean that she's not a slag now?"

"Listen mate, don't try and get clever. You know what I meant. You know exactly what she's like."

"Do you think that Lindsey was having a sexual relationship with the man that was murdered on the first of November?"

"Well how would I know?"

"You're separated, aren't you?"

"Yes."

"Did this relationship commence after your marriage had ended, or during?"

The idea behind these questions was to try and stress Billy Nolan out and make him volatile. But it wasn't working. He appeared to be completely relaxed.

"No idea mate. I don't even know if she knew this fucking Graham bloke. It's you that said it."

Another silence hung heavily in the air. Nobody had mentioned Graham Hartley's name. Nobody until Billy Nolan just had. Rudovsky had instructed Kenyon and Chapman to keep Hartley's name out of it, as though he was just an unidentified body. That decision had just paid a big dividend, Billy Nolan had named a man who'd been murdered, in an incident that he had previously stated that he knew nothing about. That was two fuck ups in two minutes, and Chapman was feeling extremely pleased with how things were going.

"Going back to the evening of the first of November. Can you tell us what you were doing that night?"

Billy Nolan didn't move an inch as he replied, "no idea mate."

"Are you a football fan Billy?"

"Yeah. But what's that..."

"What team?"

"Well I live in Salford, don't I? So you should know..."

"So, you're a red?"

"That's right. Glory Glory Man United!" Nolan raised two arms in the air, his fists were clenched and he was wearing a huge smile.

"November the first was the night that United played against Paris St Germain in the Champions League."

"Oh right, yeah, I remember what I was doing now. Watching the match. One nil to the reds, Jesse Lingard scored off a volley in the second-half. Fucking brilliant goal as well."

"Where did you watch the match?"

"At home."

"By yourself?"

"Yeah, why?"

"Because we need to eliminate you from our murder inquiry. And if you had just said that you were watching the game at Old Trafford, or in the pub, or with somebody else, we'd be letting you go out the door in five minutes."

"Nah, I always watch footy on my own. Can't stand listening to other people's opinions and their annoying fucking commentaries. I always watch footy on my own."

"But I'm guessing that you can see why it's a problem for us?"

"Nah, not really."

"Well, you're saying that you were alone, with no witnesses."

"Yeah."

"At the same time that somebody was beating your wife's friend to death on Eccles Field."

Suddenly, Billy Nolan sat up and leaned forward. His relaxed, care-free bearing had become much more serious, in the blink of an eye.

"Let me get this straight, yeah? Because I was watching football on my own, that makes me a suspect in this murder bullshit?"

Chapman wasn't phased by Nolan's sudden aggression, and kept strong, confident eye-contact with Nolan.

"Well, that's not exactly the situation. But we have a reason to believe that you have a motive for this attack. The link between the victim and your wife…"

"Ex."

"Okay, your ex-wife. So, we've got a problem here Billy. We need some proof that you were watching the match."

"Tell you what yeah, I've heard what you've said, I've played along with your little game. And now I've found out that all you've got to link me to this crime is because of Lindsey. Good luck in court. Now are you charging me or what? I need to go home and fix my fucking front door after your lot have fucked it all up."

Kenyon had been silent throughout the interview. He'd spent the time watching and listening, assessing Billy Nolan. His assessment was done and he felt that it was now time to get involved.

"Thing is though Billy, cards on the table, you know we can't charge you with anything based on what we've told you."

"I know yeah, exactly!" Billy Nolan clapped his hands together and laughed. "I like you! You're alright by me." Nolan flicked his eyes across to Chapman. "You should listen to this one, knows his stuff!"

Chapman locked stares with Nolan. He knew what this bastard was all about, and he wasn't losing a staring contest against him. Kenyon was looking through the paperwork file on the desk. After several seconds he pulled out a photograph and held it to his chest.

"Have you ever heard the phrase 'over-confidence sinks the ship?'"

"Nope."

"You've seen Titanic though, haven't you?"

"Obviously."

"Well, the guy who was driving that boat got a bit too over-confident didn't he? Smashed it into an iceberg and sank it."

"I fell asleep after the bit where Kate Winslet flashed her titties. What are you saying all this shit for anyway? Trying to sound cool or summat?"

"Nah, I'm just saying that you remind me of the Titanic."

"Nice one. Can I go now?"

Kenyon placed the photograph down in front of Nolan. "Do you recognise this car?"

"Looks familiar. I've seen one like that outside my house a few times."

"It's your car Billy. It's registered to you, it's insured in your name. The tax is paid by direct-debit every month from your current account."

"Ah! That will be why it looks so familiar then! Can I go now?"

"Can you explain what's happening in these photographs?" Kenyon started placing the CCTV photographs down on the table in front of Nolan. He placed four different photographs down, with the date and time stamps visible in each corner.

"What you are looking at here is your Iceberg Billy."

Billy Nolan wasn't listening to Kenyon. He was staring down at the black and white photographs of his car in Graham Hartley's street, just yards from the dead man's front door.

"Tell you what DC Chapman. I'm starving. Shall we call it a day? Leave Billy to think up a plausible explanation for this evidence of him stalking the address of his wife's lover on four separate dates in the weeks leading up to Graham Hartley's brutal murder?"

"Yes. That sounds like a good idea DC Kenyon. Could you hear my belly rumbling?"

Billy Nolan was staring down at the photographs, paying particular attention to one especially. The one where Billy's face was clearly visible through the driver-side window. Kenyon started picking the photographs up off the desk and stacked them neatly before placing them back in his file.

"Interview terminated at twenty-ten hours." Chapman pressed stop on the recorder and waited for the familiar ear-piercing screech of the machine alerting the officers that it had stopped recording.

"Right Billy, I think its past your bed-time mate." Kenyon stood and knocked on the door. As he did so, Billy Nolan leapt out of his chair and punched the detective solidly in the face, knocking him off his feet with a punch that landed with a sickening crack. Kenyon crashed in a heap in the corner of the room as the custody officer entered the interview room.

Bill Chapman jumped off his seat and grabbed Billy Nolan, wrapping his arms around Nolan's chest, trapping his arms by his sides. The custody officer pressed the panic alarm strip on the wall and within seconds the heavy sound of foot-steps on the corridor confirmed that the panic alarm was in good working order. Nolan was struggling with Chapman, repeatedly flinging his head back in an attempt to head-butt the DC, and kicking his feet backwards, trying to injure Chapman. But the DC wouldn't let go from his solid body-grip, despite Nolan's attempts to break free.

The first of the police officers burst in through the door, followed by five other officers. They very quickly subdued Billy Nolan and had him pinned to the floor, face-down within a few seconds of entering. Nolan was shouting and struggling, but he didn't have the strength to wriggle away from the police officers who were kneeling on his legs, his back and upper torso. He was quickly cuffed, and his legs were strapped, before being lifted-up by the shoulders and carried out of the interview room and back into his cell.

Chapman knelt down to see if Kenyon was okay. The DC was knocked out, and Chapman attempted to wake him up as Rudovsky ran into the room.

"What the fuck?" said Rudovsky as she dropped to her knees and assisted Chapman in trying to rouse Kenyon.

"Come on Pete, wake up mate." She said as she patted his face.

"He needs an ambulance," said Chapman, checking Kenyon's pulse.

"CAN SOMEONE PHONE FOR AN AMBULANCE?" Shouted Rudovsky into the corridor.

Chapter Twenty-Four

The ambulance had arrived pretty quickly, just seven minutes after the custody sergeant had phoned. Kenyon was awake by the time the paramedics entered the interview room. He was sitting on a chair, looking dazed, confused and a little embarrassed.

"You alright mate?" asked the first paramedic as he approached the sorry-looking detective.

"Yeah, I'll be alright in a minute. Never been knocked-out before."

"Your jaw is looking pretty swollen there, can you say ahhh?"

"Ahhh!"

"Open your mouth wider please and say it again."

Kenyon did as instructed. The paramedic started feeling the detective's face, then began shining a torch into his eyes, giving him instructions of where to look.

"Okay, I think you'll live, but you'll have to come in for a check-up."

"Aww for fuck's sake..."

"Shut up Pete, you're going." Said Rudovsky. "It's procedure anyway, if you don't go you'll be on a disciplinary."

"It's gonna be six hours, it's gonna be about two in the morning when I get out." Kenyon seemed more annoyed about this than he was about the punch in the face.

"I'll come with you. We can pass the time with me showing you how to fight, you big pussy."

Kenyon stood, groaning in pain as he realised that he'd hurt his leg as well as he'd crashed into the wall. "Come on then, the sooner we get there, the sooner I'll get out." He started walking out of the interview room, and onto the corridor. Chapman and Rudovsky followed behind the paramedics.

"Well, that was a dramatic climax to the interview." Said the DS.

"You can say that again." Chapman looked as though he was still in shock.

"You did brilliantly there Bill. If you hadn't gripped him,

God knows what could have happened. I bet he would have jumped on Pete's head."

"I know. He's a strong bastard though, I'll give him that."

"Well he wasn't strong enough to get away from you, so well done."

"Cheers Sarge."

"You did a great job of the interview as well."

"Yes, he's a bit of a thick bastard this Billy Nolan, isn't he?"

"I loved where he named the victim of an attack he didn't know anything about!"

"Ha ha, I know. Shit for Brains. Right, well, I'm going to get off home now, I'm knackered. Have fun at A and E with Pete, and I'll brush up on my notes for tomorrow's interview. I might wear a boxing helmet though!"

"Oh, on that Bill. Just to warn you, we might not get the chance to interview Nolan again."

"What..."

"Well, Salford division have taken over the investigation surrounding Lindsey Nolan. And Miller's desperate for us to ditch this case now you've cracked it. He wants us to leave Salford to do the tidying up."

Chapman looked a bit disappointed. Rudovsky knew that look, and she was expecting him to start kicking off about it.

"Fair dos. At least we managed to bang him up. Might as well leave Salford to do the donkey-work now." Chapman smiled, aware that Rudovsky hadn't quite anticipated that response.

"Nice one Bill."

"I'm quite eager to get on with this betting shop one anyway, it looks pretty interesting."

"Right Bill, now I know you're just taking the piss!" Rudovsky toy-punched Chapman in the arm and they both laughed.

"Anyway, I'd better follow this ambulance. See you tomorrow."

"Night."

Hope Hospital Accident and Emergency was rammed. The big TV screen in the corner said that the estimated waiting time was 4 hours and forty-five minutes. The department was filled with people, some crying in pain, some laughing at jokes, others looking thoroughly miserable and pissed off.

Kenyon looked the most pissed off. Rudovsky tried to keep his spirits up, but it was a big task.

"I didn't see that punch coming Jo. First I knew of it was when Chapman threw that cup of water in my face."

"Yeah, it was a cowardly punch that, he waited until you were at the side of him so you wouldn't see it. He's a fucking horrible bloke, real nasty piece of work."

"He's alright once you get to know him."

Rudovsky laughed loudly at Kenyon's gag, which made him laugh too.

"Aargh, don't make me laugh. It kills."

"Serves you right this, anyway." Rudovsky suddenly had a serious expression.

"What?"

"You getting twatted, it's karma for saying to Bill Chapman that I had a fat arse. Wide-load, you cheeky bastard!"

Kenyon laughed again and reached his hand up to his jaw as the pain seared through his face once again.

"Soz. Right, I won't make you laugh again. Wait here, I'm gonna go and see if we can hurry them up a bit."

Rudovsky stood and walked around the back of the checking-in desk and followed the corridor around to where all the cubicles were. Every single one had its curtains drawn, with unpleasant sounds of crying, moaning or vomiting coming from each cubicle. Eventually, Rudovsky found the area where all the nurses, doctors and auxiliary staff worked from. She stood and patiently waited to be spoken to. All of the staff were busy discussing cases, or checking medical notes. Finally, a nurse looked up at Rudovsky.

"Can I help?"

"Hiya, yes, I hope so. I'm detective sergeant Rudovsky.

One of my officers has been brought in, he's been attacked, he was knocked unconscious. He's okay, the paramedic didn't think it was anything too serious, just a swollen jaw. Thing is, its procedure that he has to be checked over. I was just wondering if we might be able to jump up the queue?" Rudovsky knew that what she was asking was very cheeky and pulled an embarrassed face as she finished talking, which made the nurse smile.

"Well, we're currently dealing with some urgent-care jobs, we've got a teenager with serious burns, a suicidal young mum, a man with two broken legs and an elderly patient who is receiving end of life care. We've also got a serious RTA coming in in about five minutes, so with the best will in the world, all our staff are extremely busy and they are not going to be able to drop what they are doing to check a swollen jaw. I wish we could help, but it's not likely to be any time soon. Sorry."

"Fair enough. Sorry to be a dick."

"No, no, it's fine. I know you have to follow procedure and come in, even when you don't think it is necessary. We would normally boost you up the list, but it's just not going to happen tonight."

"Alright, I'll go and tell him."

As Rudovsky arrived back in the crowded waiting room, she was surprised to see Miller and Saunders sitting on either side of Kenyon.

"Oh, alright. The cavalry has arrived!" Rudovsky was smiling but Miller and Saunders seemed concerned about their DC.

"Hello Jo. Just been finding out what happened from Pete." Said Miller.

"Yes, I've just been to see if we can get him seen a bit quicker but it's not happening, they've got a lot on."

"I've told yous, I'm fine. I just want to go home and have a beer."

"Hey you'll be getting about five grand compo for this Pete, so cheer up!" Saunders was smiling.

"Yes, that's true," said Miller. "You'll be able to buy some decent clothes!"

Kenyon laughed, then grimaced as the pain shot

through his skull. His hand flew up to his face again.

"Looks pretty bad that," said Saunders. "It's swollen pretty bad. They'll probably want to x-ray it."

"The paramedic had a feel, he doesn't think it's out serious. I'm just here to tick the boxes."

"Fair dos. Well, don't worry, you won't have to meet with Billy Nolan again, we're officially off the case now." Miller looked slightly anxious as he broke the news.

"Oh?" said Rudovsky. It was quite obvious that she had been expecting the announcement.

"Yep. Out of my hands I'm afraid. Salford are taking full ownership. It *was* Lindsey in the flat, she'd been battered to death. Nolan's absolutely fucked, he made no attempt to clear up after himself, the whole scene has his forensic signature all over it so I guess he realised he was fucked and took it all out on Pete."

"Gutted." Said Rudovsky, looking down at the waiting-room floor.

"What, about Lindsey? Or being taken off the case?"

"Both."

"I know, I knew you'd be annoyed, but at least Chapman made his arrest. Any success in court will have Chapman's evidence all over it, so he'll have to give evidence and will be credited with his arrest. So, its marginally better than we'd anticipated earlier on."

"True."

"Besides, we are getting somewhere with the betting shop case, so it'll be great to have the full team on the investigation from tomorrow morning."

Lee Riley's Story - Part One

Lee Riley was staring out of his living room window, out across the stunning, rolling landscape of the Calder Valley. It was this view which had first attracted him to this house. He wasn't fussed about the retro salmon coloured bathroom which would need ripping out and replacing. He wasn't particularly phased by the creaks of the floorboards or the squeaky doors or any of the various other jobs that had helped to make this property the cheapest on offer in Hebden Bridge. The work which needed doing to the place hadn't bothered him in the slightest, he was a builder by trade and a bit of hard work never worried him. It was this sensational view that he was most interested in and he had put in an offer as soon as he'd seen the offering from this front window.

It was an old terraced house, at the end of a row of twelve other identical homes, built from huge blocks of York stone a good 150 years earlier. These houses had been built during the industrial revolution and still stood solid today, albeit with certain issues such as damp and mould, creaks and groans and the occasional slate sliding off the roof and smashing into a hundred pieces on the pavement below. But the view, from Lee's end-terrace was mesmerising. Everything was there, the woods, the windy moors at the top with the scattered farm-houses dotted along the country-roads, beneath them stood church steeples, old mill chimneys and streets and streets of similar looking houses to his. From this window, Lee Riley could see almost every part of Hebden Bridge, the schools, the town centre, the pubs and shops. Whichever way he looked, the beautiful view was framed by stunning countryside and the long, meandering Calder Valley which carved a gigantic V shape through the area. It looked as though it went on forever.

Lee was Hebden Bridge born and raised. The little market-town in West Yorkshire sits around halfway between Halifax and Todmorden. These were good, strong Yorkshire towns which had made their fortunes around the time Lee's house had been built. The industrial revolution had seen the fortunes of hundreds of northern towns change beyond all recognition within a generation, when the production of cotton yarn was simplified following the invention of the Spinning Jenny. The new factories and mills sprung up everywhere, replacing the only other jobs that had existed around these parts, which had largely been agriculture based.

Tiny little villages suddenly became booming towns with new houses, factories, mills and of course, canals and railways, which were built to connect theses new towns with the ports, as global demand for the north's cotton produce soared. All along the Calder Valley, and across the north of England, the population boomed ten-fold within a decade as people travelled from every corner of the UK to find work in these new industrial towns which were being powered by their endless supplies of coal.

The cotton industry has all but died in Britain now, as has the coal-mining which fuelled it. The last half of the previous century saw almost all of the mills in Hebden Bridge and those in the surrounding towns and cities in Lancashire and Yorkshire close down one by one, as the industry slowly admitted defeat as other parts of the world "cottoned" onto what the industrial north had mastered for almost two centuries. With the introduction of electricity at the flick-of-a-switch, cotton-yarn production no longer relied on the north's coal-fields and the mills were replicated in warmer, drier countries all across the globe, in sunnier locations which were much more suitable for the job. The U.S, India and China now dominate the industry, collectively exporting many millions of tons of cotton products every year.

Most of the former mill towns in the UK have declined, their populations have plummeted and their strong community values have fallen by the way-side as mass unemployment and depression took a firm hold in neighbouring communities such as Burnley, Blackburn and Accrington on the Lancashire side of the Pennines, and Halifax, Sowerby Bridge and Bradford on the Yorkshire side.

But Hebden Bridge is widely acknowledged as the

exception to the rule that former mill towns have become deprived. The town is well known and respected as a very special and extremely unique place. It has continued to be a bustling, busy little town, refusing to die and become what so many of its neighbours have, which is commonly termed as a "shit-hole."

Hebden is quite the opposite, thanks in part to the former hippies who were attracted to the area by the rock-bottom house prices when the mills began to close down in the 1970's. The hippies, it's said, brought with them a very bohemian attitude which explains the relaxed pace-of-life in this picturesque little market-town. That bohemian attitude is now getting into its third generation and has produced an extremely laid-back, peaceful and tolerant community. It was the chilled-out influence of the hippies, so local legend suggests, which in turn influenced the way-of-life which has become the town's main selling point, attracting huge visitors numbers to sample this relaxed and cheerful place which sits in between some of Great Britain's most depressed and declining places. Hebden Bridge is like a gold tooth in a mouth full of decay and infection.

The place is filled with actors, writers, artists, poets and all manner of creative people. It's also known as the "Lesbian capital of Britain" thanks to its well-populated and thriving gay community, which is testament to the tolerant and progressive attitude of the people in this part of the world.

Unique, independent shops selling exclusive products have made Hebden Bridge a town well worth visiting on day trips. In amongst the usual bakeries, charity shops and butchers that every northern town has, Hebden is crammed full with interesting and quirky shops selling everything from antiques, afghan rugs and locally produced artworks to arts and craft shops, along with vintage clothes shops and vegan stores. The locals are fondly regarded for their happy nature and strong community spirit. Many towns could learn a great deal from this random little place on the road between Yorkshire and Lancashire, but they would have to accept that it takes about fifty years for the hippies to turn a dying, former mill-town into such a prosperous, harmonious and peaceful community.

Lee Riley never experienced the area's industrial heyday, it was all over and done with before he was born. At 28 years old, all he really knew about it was that when he was a lad, there were dozens of derelict old mills that he and his friends could play in. It was fantastic, especially on rainy days, of which there were many in this part of the world. The old mills would be full of kids, running around and chasing one another up and down the stairs. They would build dens out of all the old items that had been abandoned, each den containing at least one chair from the old canteen and a handful of ripped-out pages from a dodgy porno mag. Occasionally, another gang would come along and smash the dens up, and in turn, Lee's gang would go along and smash up their rivals dens, in their mill, at their end of town. It was certainly a lot of fun growing up in an area that was in the process of adapting to enormous social and economic change.

Lee, and all of his friends left school and found other industries to work in. The mills and the mines which had kept his father's generation in work were all gone now, and young people learnt to work in the service industries, building, plumbing, sales and retail. Lee became a builder, starting out as an apprentice and slowly but surely learning his trade. Now, at the age of 28, he had his own van and tools and had built up a strong reputation as a reliable and conscientious contractor. As a result, Lee always had work on and was making a very good living.

But today, Lee was staring out of his window, out across the view that he loved so much. Today, the scenery was out of focus, it was just a huge merge of greens, browns and greys. He looked as though he had tears in his eyes as his girlfriend Olivia opened the front door.

"Hiya love, alright?"

"Oh hiya. What are you doing home so early?" asked Lee, surprised to see her home at half-past two. He didn't seem his usual, chirpy self.

"Oh, it's dead at work, no more appointments booked for this afternoon so I decided to close early, can't be arsed sitting there waiting to see if I get a walk-in."

"Oh right."

"What's up with you anyway, misery guts? Why are you home early?"

"Oh, it's… Why are you calling me a misery guts anyway?" Lee smiled widely, but it didn't really affect the low mood he was giving off.

"I've just been watching you as I walked up the hill. You look like you've lost a tenner and found a dog-shit!"

Lee smiled again, but it looked fake. "Nah, just, there's nowt wrong with me mate! I'm just thinking about this job I'm on at the minute."

"Why are you home early anyway? It's not like you."

"Oh, I'm going back in a minute. Just came home for a chill for five. Right, well, I'd better get off then, get back to it."

"Well… we could… you know…" Olivia had a cheeky look in her eye as she made her flirtatious suggestion.

Lee laughed. "Ha ha, no, nice idea, but I need to get on. See you in a bit Liv."

"What seriously? You're knocking me back? You'd rather build a wall than…"

"Ha ha, don't be like that. I'll see you later." Lee walked over to the door and tried to kiss his girlfriend of four years, but she pulled away, faking offence at her partner's rebuttal.

"See you later then. Love you."

"Love you too. The band."

Lee went out of the house, and down the steep stone steps to the cobbled street and jumped into his van, tears were streaming down his face. His hand was trembling as he put the key in the ignition and started the engine. The van pulled away and drove down the street. He kept driving, down into town and kept going. He drove his van up the hill out of Hebden Bridge, up Peckett Well and onto the tops of the moors which led over to Keighley.

Olivia was confused by Lee's strange behaviour. It wasn't like him to be home during the day. And it certainly wasn't like him to refuse a spontaneous offer of hanky panky. He'd been acting a bit weird for a few weeks now, but today's odd behaviour had really got to her. She decided to call Lee's sister and share her concerns.

"Hiya Joanna."

"Hi Liv, how are you love?"

"I'm alright, I'm just... well the thing is, I'm a bit worried about Lee. He's acting weird." Joanna could tell from her sister-in-law's voice that she was genuinely concerned.

"Why, what's been going on?"

"I don't know. But summat's up. He was fine this morning, his usual annoying self. But I've just got home from work and he was here, just staring out of the window like a zombie. He didn't even notice me walking up the street, I was waving at him and everything."

"Did you ask him what was up?"

"Yeah, course. But he just denied it, said he was fine. He just went back to work, and I was sure he had tears in his eyes when he got in his van."

"Are you sure? That's not like our Lee."

"I know. I just thought I'd ring you and see if you knew what was up with him. I know how close you are."

"Yeah, yeah, I know, we are. But he's not spoken to me about anything. Honestly. What do you think is up with him?"

"I don't know. Haven't got a clue. I've started worrying though, you know, thinking it's me..."

"What's you?"

"Well, that he's getting sick of me or summat."

"Don't be so bloody daft!" Joanna laughed loudly down the phone. "Lee adores you Liv. You know that! He's madly in love with you, all his mates take the piss out of him, saying he's punching above his weight having such a gorgeous bird!"

They both laughed, but Liv still sounded stressed and Joanna picked up on it.

"Tell you what, I'll give him a ring. If something's bothering him, he'll tell me. That's what big sisters are for. Right?"

"Well, don't make it out as though I've been gossiping. But yeah, if you wouldn't mind. I'm feeling a bit weird about it."

"No problem. Enough said. I'll ring him now, and I'll ring you back after I've had a chat with him. It's mum's birthday in a few weeks so I'll use that as an excuse for ringing him. I'll phone you back in a bit Liv, try not to worry love. Okay?"

"Aw thanks Joanna. Cheers."

Joanna hung up and stared at the phone for a moment. That had been a very strange conversation. Her brother was a fun-loving, happy-go-lucky type of guy, he never dwelled on stuff. His generic response to any problem was "it'll be right." After speaking to Olivia, she was now feeling extremely confused by the call, and her first thought was that maybe Olivia had done something which had upset her brother. After all, she is a stunning young woman with no shortage of male admirers. What if that call had been to try and find out if Lee knew something that she didn't want him to know? Joanna's mind was suddenly whirring as she looked up Lee's number in her phone and pressed the call icon.

It rang about ten times before it went to answer phone. "Hello, you've reached me, Lee, of Lee Riley Construction. I'm either driving or grafting. Leave a message and I'll call you back as soon as I can."

Joanna didn't leave a message. She rang again. She knew that her brother always had his phone in his pocket so he'd feel the vibrations soon enough. But it went to answer machine again. She dialled again and after the fourth ring, he answered.

"Lee? Hiya love, you alright?"

"Yeah, course I am, why what's up?" His voice sounded flat, and sad.

"Are you sure you're okay? Where are you?"

"I'm alright Joanna. I'm fine."

He didn't sound fine and Joanna's intuition was always spot on. She trusted her gut.

"Where are you?"

"What, I'm... I'm just out for a drive."

"Where are you?" Her voice sounded stricter this time.

"I'm just on the tops, getting a bit of fresh air."

"Where?"

"At the bus terminus. Why, what's all the fuss?"

"Stay there. I need a word." With that, Joanna hung up,

grabbed her car keys off the kitchen work-top and scribbled a note on the pad by the kettle. "Had to nip out, make a butty and do your jobs. Back soon. Mum xxx."

Joanna got in her car and headed through town, cursing the slow drivers who were dilly-dallying looking for parking spaces. As she got through the tiny town centre, and onto Keighley Road, she put her foot down as her car speeded up the hill, which stood high above the town.

Five minutes later, she arrived at the bus terminus, a huge piece of tarmac where the buses turned around and headed back down into town. Lee's van was there and he was sitting in the driver's seat. He looked pale.

"Right mate, what the fuck is going on?" asked Joanna as she stepped up into the van and sat in the passenger seat.

"What, seriously, what the…"

"Something's up. I could tell by your voice…"

"There's nowt wrong!"

"So, you're just sitting here, chilling out?"

"Yes, that's all."

"But you blanked my calls?"

"I didn't hear…"

"Lee, you're starting to freak me out. What in God's name is going on?"

Lee opened his mouth, he'd been about to protest that all was well, but he thought better of it. He knew that Joanna wouldn't stop asking until he told her. A harsh silence filled the cab of the van. Joanna wanted to prompt him to speak but she knew it would be better to wait.

Eventually, he spoke and his voice broke with emotion.

"I've… I'm in trouble. A lot of trouble."

This was a strange thing to hear Lee say. He wasn't the kind of bloke who got into trouble. Never had been.

"Go on."

"Aw, it's… God, I can't even say it." Lee started to cry, something that she hadn't seen him do since he was a little lad.

Joanna was starting to panic. This whole scenario was unbelievable. She wanted to know what he'd done, what he'd got mixed up in. But at the same time, she was scared. She wasn't that sure that she wanted to know. It was obviously bad, and she was genuinely fearful of what Lee was going to say.

"Come on Lee. There's nothing we can't sort. Come on, tell me what's gone on." She reached over and touched his hand. The touch of his big sister's hand, along with her reassuring words broke him down completely and he began sobbing. He was in a state, tears and snot were streaming down his face as he said "oh God," over and over again.

Joanna reached into her hand-bag and found a packet of tissues and handed several to her baby brother.

"Come on mate, clean all that snot off your face."

Lee laughed humourlessly as he took the tissues, he felt embarrassed that he was making such a spectacle. Joanna stared out of the windscreen whilst Lee got himself together. She was focusing on the grass in the field opposite as the wind bashed it all around. Her hands were shaking, as her mind raced with different thoughts and scenarios that her brother could have got caught up in. Her first thought was that he was having an affair, but she couldn't give that idea too much credibility. She knew in her heart that he would never do anything that would hurt Liv. Her second thought was that he might have got mixed up with the wrong crowd. There were a few dickheads knocking about Hebden Bridge, dickheads that Lee knew from school. It was no secret that they were involved in drugs and violence with other dickheads in Halifax and Sowerby Bridge, just up the road. But again, that didn't seem right. Lee was too clever to fall in with that lot.

Joanna handed another tissue to Lee. "Come on, get that big booger off the end of your nose!"

Finally, Lee had calmed down.

"A problem shared is a problem halved" said Joanna, but that dread of what Lee was going to say was still there.

Lee took a deep breath. It was a massive breath and it stressed Joanna out even further, her adrenaline was bursting through her veins. He raised his hands and gripped the steering wheel.

"Basically... I've... God, I can't even say it."

"Come on Lee, I'm shitting myself here. Please, just tell

me what's gone on."

He moved his hands up to his face and held them there for a minute. Joanna returned her attention to the grass which was lying flat one way as the wind drove across it, then trying to stand up straight again before another blast of air flattened it all down again. A cyclist raced past, pedalling as fast as he could down the hill, curling himself into a ball to increase his speed.

"Right, fucking hell I just need to say it. I've lost all my money. All my savings, all my credit cards, all my advances for materials. I'm broke. Totally broke. I'm finished Joanna."

This announcement was met with a slight sense of relief by Joanna. This was bad, sure, but nothing like as bad as she had imagined.

"What... how..."

"Gambling."

"Gam..."

"I know. I know, it's fucking stupid, I don't need anyone to point it out. Now I've blown five grand that I had for materials for a farm-house extension." Lee's voice had got colder and he too was staring out at the grass across the road.

"Five grand?"

"Yes. Every penny. Trying to win back what I lost. Now I'm absolutely fucked. I'll have to close the business. I'll have to tell the lady whose money it is that I've gone bankrupt and her money is gone."

The sheer magnitude of Lee's confession took a while to take on board. A heavy silence filled the air before Joanna spoke, softly.

"How long has this been going on for?" asked Joanna, mindful not to say anything stupid like "are you a fucking moron?"

Lee laughed at the question. "That's the best part. Three weeks."

"Three weeks?"

"Yes. I've lost about fifteen grand altogether, in three weeks."

"Fucking hell Lee!"

"I went down the bank at dinner to try and get a loan,

but I need Liv to sign for it because she's on the mortgage."

"And what did you want the loan for?"

"For these materials. The woman I'm working for gave it me in good faith, to buy the stuff I need for her extension. I can't believe I've blown the lot. Lost it. Every penny." Lee lifted his hand to his face and took a huge intake of breath before exhaling loudly.

Joanna was about to speak but Lee kept going. "It started when Gaz, one of the lads I was working with asked to pop in the bookies one dinner-time. We were only going to the chippy, but he said come and have a go on the machine. He put three quid in and won a hundred quid."

"Did he?"

"Yes, so I had a go, put a fiver in and won. Not as much as him, it was about thirty quid or summat. But I loved it, it was proper exciting and we had a good laugh about it. Gaz said he always wins, best he'd got was a grand for a two quid bet. Anyway, we went round to the chippy, got our lunch and went back to the site. I was thinking about it all afternoon, it proper gave me a buzz."

"I bet it did! But they bookies always win in the end. Everyone knows that Lee."

"Well, I'm finding that out now. I went back that night, after work. Put the thirty quid that I won back in, came close to winning five hundred quid a couple of times. But anyway, I just thought, right, I've lost my winnings, time to go home. But the buzz I got, honestly, I can't tell you what it felt like. I felt alive, this daft little ball was bouncing around on the computer screen, and the roulette thing was slowing down and the screen was flashing with all the amounts I'd win if it stayed in that slot. It would say five hundred, then one hundred, then twenty-five, then a grand. It was proper exciting. I put another twenty quid in, I couldn't resist it."

"Aw Lee, that's how they suck you in, mate!"

"Yes, but I won a hundred quid!"

Joanna could tell that Lee's mood was lightening, he was getting stimulated, just by recalling the event.

"I went home with my hundred quid, absolutely

buzzing. It wasn't the money, it's not like a hundred quid was a life changing amount, it was just the thrill of the game. I decided on the way home I was going to get a shower and take Liv out for a meal. I was planning it all, a surprise at The Olive Branch, you know the little Turkish place in town."

"Yeah…"

"Anyway. When I got in, Liv was out, she'd left a note saying she was round at Lucy's next door and my tea was in the microwave. I got out of my shitty work stuff and showered and had my tea, still buzzing about the casino game. Honestly, it's… I can't describe it. It's… you feel alive!"

Joanna was concerned that Lee was talking affectionately about this game, when he should be furious with it, and himself. She remained silent, encouraging him to carry on with his story.

"Next thing I knew, I'd downloaded the app on my phone and put my card details in. I lost a few times, but I worked out that I was still a tenner up, I'd lost the thirty quid, then twenty quid, but the hundred gave me a profit of forty-five, so I just thought, fuck it."

"Lee!"

"I won a grand!"

"Bloody hell!"

"I know. The buzz was even better then, God, I swear down I've never known a better feeling than that moment in my whole life. It sort of spins around for ages at the end and the ball moves from one slot to another, and then, right at the end, it landed in the grand slot. It was amazing."

"So, what happened then? Did you carry on? Or stop?"

"Stopped. I was chuffed to bits! I withdrew the grand from my online wallet and put it in my account. It was when I took Liv down to London for our romantic weekend."

"Oh, right! I thought it was weird that you did that out of the blue!"

"I know! Had the best weekend ever, posh food in the Shard, no expense spared! Still spent an extra seven hundred quid down there like, but it was a brilliant weekend."

"So, something good came from it?" Joanna was trying

to stay positive but all the while she was trying to work out her brother's mind-set. He was clearly in bits about the problems he now faced. But his voice was filled with enthusiasm for the game which had got him into all this trouble. It was a worrying contradiction.

"Yeah, something definitely good came out of it. And also, I was a bit worried about how quickly I'd got the bug, so I thought, it's been a laugh, but I need to stop it, quit while I'm in front."

"And presumably you didn't?"

"Yeah, I did Joanna. Honest to God, swear down. I deleted the app off my phone, and next time Gaz asked me to go down the bookies, I just said no, just told him what I wanted from the chippy. I wanted to go with him, like I say, it gave me a really strange buzz! But I said no I'm not doing it again, after I'd won the grand, and he stopped asking me after that. But about a week after, I started getting these e-mails from the bookies. I was just sat at home watching telly with Liv and I heard my phone go. I had a look and it was an e-mail from Spin Win. It had the graphic of the roulette wheel, and it was flashing saying 'free £50 bet."

"You're joking?"

"No. I got dead excited again, could feel my heart-beat racing. But I just thought it was stupid so I deleted the e-mail and forgot about it."

"Good for you Lee. No, that's really good."

"A couple of days later, same thing happened, it was about eight o'clock at night. Liv was at her mate's house and I was watching some shit on telly. This e-mail was offering a free credit of a hundred quid. To get it, all I had to do was reinstall the app and upload my card details."

"And you did?"

"No. Swear on my life. I thought, it's a con this, why would they give me a hundred quid, but they need my bank details? I deleted it, but that excitement was there again, I was thinking about it for ages afterwards." Lee started tapping his hand against the steering wheel. "Couple of days later, same e-mail pops up, offering me three hundred quid credit!"

"And did you delete it?"

"No." Lee's face suddenly dropped again. "That's when everything started to go tits up. I took the three hundred quid credit and started playing, and I won a couple of fifty quids. I was so close to a grand a few times, and I was proper excited again, I mean, proper excited. It wasn't even my money I was playing with, so I wasn't arsed if I won or lost really. Anyway, I came close to big money a few times, almost got ten grand, but it popped out at the last second and fell in the twenty-five quid slot. I was absolutely gutted!"

"Lee, mate, this is how they get you!"

"I know, fuck me Joanna, I definitely know. Within an hour of taking the free credits, I'd spent a hundred quid of my own money."

"Oh shit."

"Anyway, that hundred quid turned into two hundred. I didn't even think about it. It was the game, that was all I was thinking of, the game, and how much I was going to win. I ended up spending another hundred quid, so they had their three hundred quid back. I never thought about it at the time, but the next day when I was at work, I was proper fuming about it. Seriously pissed off with myself. I couldn't get it out of my head, that I'd blown three ton on a fucking computer game!"

Joanna rested her hand on Lee's arm. She thought he was a complete prick for doing this, but she could understand how he'd fallen into the trap.

"All day long I was just thinking, I need to finish work, get home, win that three hundred back before Liv finds out, then delete the app, block the e-mail address, and learn a good lesson from it all. So, I started off with twenty quid, won back fifty. I thought I'd spin that fifty, try and get it to five hundred. Didn't happen. Lost it all, the twenty, then the fifty. So like a dick, I put another twenty on. Then another. I finished up losing another hundred and forty quid." A coldness had returned to Lee's voice. "So, I was four-hundred and forty quid down now. I had nothing left in my current account. And here's where I fucked up. Instead of just accepting my loss, and putting it all behind me, I transferred two hundred quid out of my savings, and put that on."

Tears were forming in Joanna's eyes, as she listened to her brother's depressing story. She really felt for him, and to a certain extent, she understood how he had got himself into this mess. He had been played by the betting company, and he'd fallen for it, hook, line and sinker.

"You put two hundred on? In one go?"

"Yeah. I was sure I was due a win, I'd never gone this long without one, so I thought if I put the two-ton on, the least I'd take back was a grand. And then I'd be done."

"But you didn't?"

"No, it bounced out of the twenty-five grand slot and into zero at the last second." Lee did a fake, humourless laugh and started tapping the steering wheel again. "Next morning, I was getting ready for work and I was feeling really pissed off with myself. I kicked off at Liv for no reason, just because I was in a mood. She looked dead upset, but I just stormed out. I couldn't believe I'd now lost six hundred and forty quid. I was so gutted, it was all I could think about. I'm at work, snapping at the other lads, just being a total dick all day. I just wanted my money back now. I wasn't interested in the buzz of the game, I was past that stage now. I just wanted the money back. So, guess what I did?"

Joanna nodded slowly as she looked at the side of Lee's face. "I think I can guess, mate."

"You can't. You can't guess this. I took five hundred out of my savings, transferred it into my online wallet. I won! Five grand!"

"Aw for fuck's sake Lee!" Joanna sensed what was coming, and she was dreading hearing it.

"I was buzzing. Really, really buzzing. These pricks had tried to have me over, and I'd had the last laugh, I'd absolutely skanked them! That's what I was thinking. I transferred four grand back into my bank, and left a grand in my wallet. I had a good feeling now, I was up, well up on what I'd lost. I felt like I'd beaten them. So that grand I had left in my wallet, I put it on! Almost won fifty grand! The buzz was mad, oh God, I'm telling you now Joanna, you've never felt anything like it! It was like a million orgasms at once!"

"Lee!"

"I know, sorry. But it's impossible to describe. Anyway, I transferred the four-grand back. Don't ask me why, because I swear to God, I do not know the answer. I've played it over in my head a hundred times. Why didn't I just leave one grand in the bank, and transfer the three? I know, I've been over it and over it. But anyway, for reasons that I can't understand, I played with the four grand, one bet, convinced I'd be getting a hundred grand back. And it landed on zero." Lee's voice had been getting excited again, as he described the big money stakes. But as his story reached its conclusion, the tempo of his voice had slowed dramatically.

Joanna didn't know what to say. A very heavy silence filled the gap which had been plugged by Lee's sorry tale. The only sound between them was the wind blowing against the side of Lee's van, high up on the moors.

Chapter Twenty-Five

"It's ten past seven, you're listening to Talk Radio UK, I'm Alex Cooling and our hot topic of discussion is the news this morning that a group calling itself "Odds on Revenge" has claimed responsibility for the spate of attacks on betting shops in the north west of England. The announcement came during the night through a series of Tweets sent to Manchester City Police, and the group's primary message was the announcement that they were not responsible for the fire-bomb attack in Denton two nights ago, which left two children and their father dead, and has left their mother in a critical condition in hospital. We are still waiting to hear the reaction to these Tweets from the police. Our crime correspondent, Becky Willis has this report."

"At twenty-five minutes past two this morning, a new Twitter account was set up, with the name Odds on Revenge. Just three minutes later, the account began sending a series of six tweets to the Manchester City Police Twitter account, the first one of which read, 'Dear MCP, we are very shocked, angry and saddened by the tragic fire in Denton. This cowardly and evil act against an innocent family is unforgivable.' Two minutes later, a second Tweet was sent, which read, 'We are a peaceful group of many hundreds, protesting against the unscrupulous, depraved and totally irresponsible activities of the gambling companies who are making billions of pounds each year through the shameless exploitation of their customers.' A third Tweet was sent two minutes later, at two-thirty-two. It read, 'We are a nation-wide group who have come together to highlight the malevolent activities of gambling companies, and to force a change in government legislation around gambling.' All of these tweets appear to have been written prior to their publication, as the gap between each one ranged between one and three minutes. The fourth Tweet was sent at two-thirty-two am. 'We are keen to admit our activities with the first four betting shop attacks, where we deliberately caused damage to those shops in order to disrupt their business. We plan many more similar attacks.' The fifth tweet was sent three minutes later, and it stated, 'We are quite prepared to accept the punishments for our actions if and when we are caught by the authorities. However, we will not accept responsibility for the tragic incident in Denton. This was awful crime was in no way connected with us, or our campaign.' The final tweet was sent one minute later and it stated, 'we are confident that investigators will find that our attacks and the attack in Denton were carried out by different people. It had nothing to do with us. RIP to the Ozols. We hope you catch the bastards responsible.'

"Well, that was quite an announcement, Becky!"

"That's right Alex. The individuals responsible for this extraordinary communication with the police are taking a huge risk in publishing these Tweets, and looking through the social media pages this morning, I am seeing that the public appear quite split on whether the group Odds on Revenge are making a genuine announcement about the attack in Denton, or, as some are commenting on Twitter this morning, this is nothing more than a stunt to divert the investigating officers attention away. It's certainly an interesting development in this troubling story."

"No news as yet from Manchester City Police?"

"Well, not really. Their press office have released a statement saying that they are looking into this matter and that a more detailed response will follow in due course."

"This is a very unique situation though, Becky, the fact that people like ourselves are discussing these Tweets, possibly before the investigating officers have even arrived at work!"

"That's right Alex, but there is a lot of hope that the publication of these Tweets will help the police to find the people who are behind this group. It is certainly a very unorthodox situation, where criminals are communicating directly with the police on a social media platform."

"Interesting. We do however know that social media companies such as Twitter and Facebook don't exactly have a good track record in helping the police."

"Yes, that's a very good point Alex. Even the Government have failed to convince social media companies to assist the authorities in criminal investigations. There is a possibility that the people behind the Odds on Revenge account have realised that this loop-hole exists, and that they could, perhaps, remain anonymous behind the Twitter account name. One thing that we do know is that it is extremely simple to sign up for a Twitter account, all you would need is an e-mail address and you can literally write whatever you like, to whomever you like, within a matter of minutes. One thing which has been a surprise this morning is that the account remains active and has not been deleted. It has already attracted over ten thousand followers, and the six tweets have been shared over twenty thousand times."

"You mean that you'd have expected the account to have been deleted?"

"Absolutely. The longer that it remains live, the greater the chance of the police locating the information they need to find the people responsible. If this group have delivered the message they wanted, then there is no logical reason to have left this account live."

"Unless of course, they want to tell us something else?"

"Well, that's a very strong possibility. The public of Great Britain are just waking up to this news, so I'm sure that if there is going to be another Tweet from this group, it will be coming very soon, and then the account will be deactivated."

"Very interesting developments in this story this morning Becky, thank you."

*****

"This is Sunrise on Sky News and following on from the story we've been bringing you about the Odds on Revenge group, which has admitted responsibility for four out of the five bookmakers shop attacks in Manchester, I'm joined by Rhian McFarlain, our Consumer Affairs correspondent. Good morning Rhian."

"Good Morning Sophie."

"Tell me, Rhian, have we ever heard of this group before?"

"Well, short answer. No. The first that anybody appears to have heard of Odds on Revenge was in the middle of the night, when they sent those six Tweets to Manchester Police."

"Quite. And they seem quite sure about what they are about, don't they? In their Tweets, they talk about campaigning against the book-makers, and the government. Fill us in on what you think these statements refer to please, Rhian."

"Sure, well, there's not a massive amount of information within those six short messages. But one thing that we can gather is that this is a group who have decided to try and disrupt the activities of British bookmakers, by smashing up four of their shops."

"And they are of course denying any involvement in the fifth attack, which killed three people and has seriously injured a fourth?"

"Yes, well that's what these Tweets are predominantly about. This group are admitting that they did smash those four shops up and make a less than subtle hint that they intend to smash up others, too. But it is very clear that they want the police, and I'd assume the public too, to understand that they are not responsible for the attack in Denton, which as you say had very tragic consequences."

"There could be some truth in that statement, bearing in mind the stark differences between the fire-bombing in Denton, and the four other attacks which were far-less serious in nature. Indeed, we were criticising the police only days ago, for their apparent lack of interest in investigating these four shop attacks. It does appear to stack up, what this group are saying, doesn't it?"

"Well, yes, I'd say that it does have some credibility on the face of it. However, it is also a very strange coincidence, and I'm sure I'm not alone in making that connection."

"That's a good point and it will be interesting to hear what the police have to say as the day goes on. But Rhian, please tell us what you think this group, the Odds on Revenge group have against these bookmakers shops."

"That's a very good question. Over the last few years, we have seen an increased criticism of betting shops and gambling outlets for what many describe as their irresponsible behaviour. Indeed, this criticism comes at a time when gambling has never made so much money, last year sixteen billion pounds was spent in the UK on gambling."

"Sixteen billion?"

"Yes, it's quite a figure. In fact, it is exactly the same amount of money which was spent in shops and supermarkets on alcohol over the same period."

"Good heavens! Is that correct?"

"Yes, it's absolutely correct. Gambling has become a very popular pass-time in Great Britain, and, well the fact that its income is now competing with alcohol sales tells you quite how popular it has become."

"I find this an extraordinary figure. Sixteen billion pounds. Surely there has been some mistake, Rhian?"

"Well, I can see why you would say that, but there is no mistake. Alcohol has for many years been the most popular consumer product in Britain, outselling its closest rivals of shelf foods and chilled and fresh foods. What this means is that spending on gambling is now greater than what we spend on our most popular items in the supermarket."

"This is quite an eye-watering amount of money we are talking about. And presumably, those kinds of figures are resulting in good returns to the tax man?"

"Absolutely, gambling companies contributed four billion pounds to the Treasury last year, that's enough money to build something like six hundred new schools, or around sixty-five thousand council houses. So, to be clear, these are very significant sums that the gambling companies are contributing to the British economy. Looking at the economic benefits of this gambling trend in the UK, there is further good news beyond just the tax revenues. These gambling sector companies provide over one hundred and six thousand jobs, which as you will realise, adds another significant revenue of around two billion pounds which feeds into the economy annually."

"One of the Tweets that was sent through the night suggested that the group calling themselves Odds on Revenge are protesting to the government's legislation on gambling. What do you think they mean by that?"

"Ultimately, based on the nature of the attacks that

they are claiming responsibility for, which involved destroying the gambling machines and causing as much damage to the premises as possible, I would make the assumption that this group are making a protest against the huge profits that these companies are making at the expense of their customers."

"But what does that really mean? For instance, Tesco make huge profits from their customers, but nobody seems to want to trash their shops and disrupt them."

"Yes, well the nature of gambling is very different from buying groceries. In the past ten years, since the gambling laws were dumbed down in this country, there has been a significant rise in something that professionals refer to as 'problem-gambling.' These professionals argue that too many people are gambling because of addiction, rather than fancying a quick flutter on the horses. There have been a number of studies into the rise of problem gambling and there is absolutely no doubt that it is a very serious issue and that it is the reason we see the public health warnings all over gambling adverts, most notably of which is that memorable phrase, 'when the fun stops, stop."

"And is this a major issue?"

"Oh, undoubtedly, the rise in gambling addiction has become an enormous problem over the past decade, and it is estimated to cost around two billion pounds to the economy each year. There are a number of charities which have been set up to tackle the issue, and these charities suggest that there are as many as half a million people suffering from this acute addiction in Britain today, which leading professionals say is no different to any other kind of addiction, and takes very similar treatment to that of an alcoholic or a crack addict to break the habit. So yes, it's a very serious issue, albeit a relatively new and emerging problem in this country."

"Well, very interesting and informative as always Rhian, thank you. We'll be following this story throughout the day here on Sky News, but to other news now and police in the West Midlands are appealing for help..."

Chapter Twenty-Six

DCI Miller looked quite calm and collected as he entered the MCP media centre and sat down on the raised stage area, beneath the gigantic Manchester City Police emblem. Many of the media representatives were intrigued by his bearing, he usually looked stressed and a little anxious before the press briefings. But today he looked remarkably relaxed.

"Good morning, thanks for coming along so early. I hope you've all taken advantage of the free coffee?"

There was a few minutes of idle chat between the press people and Miller, who was saying hello to the familiar faces before him. Once everybody had settled down and a natural silence fell, Miller began his press conference.

"I've got a couple of cases to discuss with you all this morning. The first case is the Graham Hartley murder enquiry, which as you are all aware, has been at the top of my department's agenda for the past three weeks. We are all extremely relieved to be able to announce this morning that we have made an arrest, and that the suspect remains in police custody. This arrest was made thanks to the excellent work of one of my detectives, DC Bill Chapman who has done some absolutely sterling work in gathering evidence against the individual who is currently in custody. So I'm sure you will all agree that this is excellent news, and I can almost guarantee you that you will have more information regarding charges within the next twenty-four to forty-eight hours."

The media were indeed delighted to hear this news. Graham Hartley's murder had been the only story in town for the three weeks leading up to the fatal fire in Denton.

"As this case has now pretty much been concluded, my team have been relieved of our duties on this case, so any enquiries regarding the Graham Hartley murder investigation should now be forwarded onto Salford CID, who I'm sure will be making their own announcements at some point today." Miller took a sip of water and waited for the journalist's whisperings and mutterings amongst themselves to die down.

"My team will now be concentrating one-hundred-per-cent on the betting shop attacks. Now, I'm aware of the activities on Twitter through the night, and naturally, we will be looking into these Tweets as a matter of urgency. But one thing that I think is absolutely crucial to tell you, is that my own investigations into these attacks have already suggested that the first four instances of vandalism at the betting shops, are unconnected to the fifth incident, which as we all know had a very tragic outcome."

This was a hell of an announcement, and the sudden noise from the press highlighted what a major statement it was. Miller allowed the press a few more seconds of whispers before he continued.

"What we appear to have here is a very unique coincidence, in that the Ozols family lived above a betting shop. Had the shop beneath their flat been any other, then perhaps the link would never have been made. But I can confirm that there are no similarities between the four betting shop attacks, and the arson attack in Denton two nights ago. I'd like to show you this video footage, taken from cameras on the M60 motorway, around half a mile away from the Ozol's flat." Miller pressed a key on his laptop and started playing some grainy CCTV footage on the huge screen to his right.

"Keep your eyes on this car which appears to be slowing down on the hard-shoulder of the motorway. The car is a dark silver or metallic grey Vauxhall Zafira, the registration plate is locally registered in Manchester, MT15 FPG. Now, as you can see, the car pulls up, the driver puts the vehicles hazard lights on, and four people get out of the vehicle. Now keep watching, the four people go to the back of the car and open the hatchback door. Then it closes, and we can see the individuals climb over the barrier and walk up the embankment, up towards Windmill Lane. As you can see, they are all carrying petrol cans, that's what they were taking out of the back of the car."

Miller waited again, as the press staff discussed this extraordinary footage amongst themselves.

"I'll forward the tape on twenty-five minutes. And as you can see, the four people return to the car, still carrying their petrol cans. They get in the vehicle, and the car pulls off." Miller closed the video and started another one playing.

"Eleven minutes later, here comes the same vehicle, driving up Stockport Road between Woodley and Hyde. The vehicle was found burnt out at the former Jubilee Mill site on the outskirts of Hyde."

Miller presented the photos that Saunders had taken.

"Now, as stated - we are quite convinced that this incident has no connection to any of the four betting shop vandalism attacks in Eccles, Romiley, Farnworth and Middleton. Whilst we are still looking for the individuals responsible for putting those four shops out of business and we are very keen to see them punished for their actions, I must stress that the over-riding priority for my team is to apprehend the four individuals in the Vauxhall Zafira, and I am appealing to you all to help us to publicise this footage and help us in our appeal for information. We want to know who these four people are, as they are all wanted for the murders of Andris, Juris, and Inga Ozols. Any questions?"

Suddenly, the noise was deafening as every journalist, reporter and news presenter shouted out their questions. Miller took a sip of water from his glass as he waited for the familiar barrage to die down. He never understood why they all did this, it just slowed things down.

Finally, things quietened down and Miller pointed to Henry Talbot from BBC Radio Manchester.

"Thank you DCI Miller. Have you any clues at all about the identities of the four people?"

"No Henry, at this stage, we do not, but that is likely to change over the coming hours. I'm hopeful that your listeners, and the tv viewers and newspaper readers will all share these images all over their social media networks in Greater Manchester. I'm quite convinced that somebody out there will know who these four individuals are from the mannerism of their walk and the way that they stand. It's a real shame that we don't have any better footage at this stage, the camera which took these images is almost a quarter of a mile away from the car, so we are extremely lucky to have the images at all. But unfortunately, there is no way of making out their faces."

"DCI Miller, Isi Mahmood, Manchester Evening News. As the car was burnt out not too far away from Denton, are you of the opinion that the arsonists are local to the area?"

"Yes, good question Isi. I'm quite sure that they are local. The car was stolen the previous night from an address in Rochdale. So we think that these people are certainly from the Greater Manchester area."

"Helen Jones, Piccadilly Radio. DCI Miller, I understand the reasons why you are treating the attack in Denton separately from the other betting shop attacks. However, I'm a little confused about whether you are still looking for the betting shop attackers?"

"Hi Helen. Yes, of course we are looking for those individuals as well, and I am being supported by all of the CID teams in all of the four divisions where these attacks occurred. But, let's be brutally honest, my number one goal is to arrest those four men on the motorway. These are very dangerous and ruthless individuals and the sooner we get them locked away, the better for everybody in the city, especially Marija Ozols, who is still in a medically induced coma in hospital as staff try to heal her horrendous burns."

"DCI Miller! Kenny Bates, Granada Reports. Is there no other CCTV footage available, other than what you have shown here this morning? Naturally, we will be featuring this as our top story, but I have to say that the images we've seen are not very helpful."

"Yes, I totally understand your issue there Kenny, but I'm afraid that is all we have for public use at the moment. There is some footage that we have from a business premises close to the scene of this fire which is not being released at present, as the footage does contain some details which will make up a significant part of the evidence in the court case and we wouldn't want this footage to become public until that time. But that said, we have got all of our teams scrutinising many hundreds of hours of CCTV and we are hopeful that we'll have something else soon. But for now, this footage has told us a lot, and we are extremely grateful to have it. Okay, thanks everybody, busy day ahead, but I'll keep you all up to speed as our investigations continue."

Chapter Twenty-Seven

The local news teams in the north-west were having a busy day. Just an hour after Miller's press conference, most of the reporters had travelled over to Salford police station, waiting to hear from the divisional inspector who had scheduled a short news briefing outside the station's doors.

The briefing expanded on the news that Miller had revealed earlier, regarding the murder of Graham Hartley. But, there was more, as the inspector explained that the suspect, Billy Nolan had been charged with murder for the attack on the first of November, but then he revealed the shocking news that Nolan had also murdered his estranged wife, and had left her body to rot in her flat, most probably around the same time he had battered Graham Hartley to death with a golf club.

Lindsey Nolan was a very popular and well-known young woman in the Swinton area, and the news of her murder hit the local community extremely hard. Within minutes of the announcement of her death, a whole new story began emerging on Facebook, as Lindsey's best friend, Michelle Christian wrote a status update which was to go viral.

"OMFG so sad I can't even describe. Just heard the news that my best friend in the world has been murdered. Lindsey has been my BFF since Grosvenor primary school and I've been trying to find out where she is for weeks. I've phoned the police loads of times but they wouldn't do anything. Said I need to get next of kin to ring, but I told them she's only got me. Can't believe this, it's not sunk in. RIP my angel Lindsey, my heart is shattered."

By lunch-time, Michelle's status update had been shared over 15,000 times, as Facebook users shared their disgust at this poor young woman's heart-break, whilst voicing major criticism at the police for ignoring her pleas for help. Whichever way this devastating story was going to be dressed up by the police powers-that-be, it wasn't looking good.

The local and national news gatherers were suddenly facing an explosion of news stories, and it was hard to decide which one of them should take the number one spot. It was excellent news that the man who had instilled a sense of terror over the city for the past month was safely behind bars, and in normal circumstances, that story would be the number one. But the news about Lindsey Nolan, and her friend's Facebook status confused everything. Most frustratingly for DCI Miller and his team, his story, regarding the four people on the motorway had slipped right down the pile and was hardly getting a look-in.

Quite unexpectedly, Manchester City Police were now finding themselves at the heart of a major scandal, not dissimilar to the criticism they had been receiving for not investigating the betting shop attacks earlier in the week. But this one was so shocking, and the thought that this poor woman had lay dead in her flat for so long, whilst her best friend had tried her level best to alert the police, well, it was a PR disaster and it didn't look as though it was going to go away any time soon.

Miller was watching Sky News' reaction to Michelle Christian's Facebook status. He was shocked himself, this was completely unforgivable. He stepped out of his office and called his team over.

"Everyone, stop what you're doing. Over here please." Miller had a very strange look on his face, it was as though he was shocked, annoyed and bemused at the same time. The DCI rarely encouraged any drama, so this sudden request was met with alarm.

"What's up?"

"What's going on?"

Miller waved them all through into his office.

"Watch this. I think we might be getting a new Chief Constable soon."

Miller's team watched the news report in silence. Not one of them could believe what they were hearing. They just stood and listened as the Sky News reporters launched a full-on assault against the Manchester City Police. They had managed to organise a phone interview with Michelle Christian, and it was heart-breaking to listen to as she broke-down all the way through it. The most resounding message that came through the interview was the news that she had phoned the police three times, and three times they had fobbed her off and refused to make a missing person's report. This was bad enough, but the story got even darker as Michelle explained that she had warned the police that Lindsey's ex-husband was violent and wasn't happy about her moving out of the marital home.

Not only was this a deeply upsetting story in itself, hearing the raw heart-ache and grief in Michelle's voice, it was also a major scandal, one which was attracting an overwhelming reaction from the public. The report made extremely depressing viewing for every member of Miller's team. As the news segment ended, Miller summed it up.

"We all just need to be glad we've been taken off the case. I don't think I could handle the backlash that this is going to get."

Rudovsky nodded, realising that although she'd been gutted that her team had been taken off the enquiry, she knew that this had been a near-miss.

"How many people are going to get sacked for this?" asked Chapman.

"Don't know. But I suggest we keep our heads down because this is going to go nuclear. This is going to have the Prime Minister involved, I'm telling you now."

"What do you mean by keep our heads down?" asked Saunders.

"Well, we've been the public face of this inquiry since it started. We've been taken off it just a few hours before it's turned into a major scandal, so we are bound to be approached for comments by the press. We say nothing. Understood?"

Miller's team all nodded sombrely.

"They'll try their usual tactics to engage one of us in conversation. We are not to say anything at all about the Hartley case from now on. It might be tricky, because we're still going to be in the public-eye while we're running the bookies investigations. So I need you all to stay sharp, and no comment any questions regarding this shit-storm." Miller pointed angrily at the Sky News feed on his PC monitor. "Okay, as you were. Cheers."

*****

"What the hell is going on in this country?" Read the headline from the Daily Mirror's website. This was not a sub-editor's choice of headline, but a quote from the leader of the Government's opposition party. In a long and damning TV interview, the politician slammed the state of the nation's most vital services, specifically the police, in a long and often bitter response to this appalling news coming out of Manchester.

"It is an incredible thought, that a poor young woman has been murdered, and her best friend has tried to get the police to investigate her disappearance, and this lady's requests for help have been ignored by the very people who are employed to be there for us. I have been a politician for a long time, over forty-years, but I have never known of such a scandal as the one which we are currently hearing about today. I find it inconceivable that this once great country, the very country which invented the world's very first police force in 1829, can today find itself so under-funded, under-manned and over-stretched, that it cannot satisfy a most-basic task of police work, that a missing person's report has been denied on the basis of a technicality. What the hell is going on in this country? We've got record levels of crime and disorder, we have murders on the streets of our cities every day, we have youths running amok, knowing that there are no police officers to challenge them. No matter which political party you support, we should all be angry, furious with the way things are going in this country, a time when our Chief Constables are campaigning for a ban on fireworks because whole communities are being terrorised by a small handful of yobs. We should be incensed that we have opened the door to disorder and criminality in order to save money. We have lost over twenty-five thousand police officers at a time where our population is growing faster than at any time before, our communities are becoming more and more fragmented and divided. This matter has to be addressed right now, and I am calling for a root and branch inquiry into the death of Lindsey Nolan, and the role of the Manchester City Police in the handling of her friend's missing person's report. I call on every person watching this, or reading this, to tell the government that enough is enough. I'd like to send my deepest condolences to the friends and family of this poor young woman."

*****

The news was everywhere, assisted by the photographs of the beautiful, promising young woman who'd lay dead in her flat for three weeks. This was a tragedy which pulled at the heart-strings of the nation. Sky News was the network with the most hours of live broadcast to fill each day. As a result, they were in the habit of adopting a particular story for maximum discussion. This news had all of the hallmarks for a Sky News Special Report.

It was a very tricky job to do, discussing a murder case before a trial, and as such, the broadcaster could say very little about the alleged killer, Billy Nolan, until after the trial had ended, which may be anything between three months and a year away. It was helpful, from that point of view, that Sky had another element of this tragic case to focus on.

The full glare of the national broadcaster was now on the activities of the police and they had dozens of journalists looking at all of the nation's 47 police forces, looking for any other stories where the basic level of policing had been refused. The story regarding police negligence had already been a topic for discussion earlier in the week, when it had been revealed that fifty-five per cent of all reported crimes in Greater Manchester are not investigated.

This latest announcement was destined to reignite the debate into the police service cuts which were having a devastating affect on the service. As a publicly funded organisation, paid for by the people who relied on it, there was not much sympathy when the service was being exposed as a failure.

There had been a similarly shocking and disturbing incident in Scotland a few years earlier, when a young couple had lay undiscovered in a car-wreck for three days. Lamara Bell, 25, and John Yuill, 28, both died following the accident on the

M9 motorway near Stirling, despite the incident being reported to Police Scotland at the time. Lamara was still alive when the car was eventually found in a wooded area by the side of the motorway, after the couple had been reported missing. It was an incident which brought with it huge sadness and shock, as well as anger at the failings of the police in investigating the reports of an accident. Had they done that, it is believed that Lamara, the young mother of two, could have survived.

This news coming out of Manchester had shocking echoes of that case, and the news reports into the Stirling tragedy were being replayed as commentators made their comparisons. Politicians from all sides of the House of Commons were condemning the failure of the police to investigate the disappearance of Lindsey Nolan and this story was becoming far bigger than Michelle Christian had ever anticipated, a fact made clear by the broadcast vans and camera crews who had set up their base outside her small, terraced home in Swinton.

Miller switched off his Sky News feed in his office, feeling a range of emotions. He was shocked and embarrassed that the police force he had always felt a great pride in, appeared to be guilty of such an inexcusable failure of duty. He also felt deeply sad for Michelle, whose heart was publicly breaking. And he felt selfish because he was gutted that all of this was clouding the information that he had released to the press that morning. The information that he had released just hours earlier was now off the collective news agenda, and in Miller's experience, it was unlikely to rise to the top again. He'd learnt a long time ago that you don't get to do a press conference twice. News is only news once. Miller decided that he should go home, on time for a change. He switched off his computer and packed his briefcase, feeling as though the day had been wasted.

He switched off his office lights and said goodbye to his team who were all working away at their desks. It wasn't great leadership, but he was only human. Miller wanted to get away from here, switch off for a few hours and spend some time with his family.

Unbeknown to DCI Andy Miller, the matter of attacks

against betting shops would soon be thrust back into the news, in spectacular fashion.

Chapter Twenty-Eight

Miller arrived home ridiculously early. It wasn't even five yet.

"Daddy!" shouted the twins as they came running towards him as he entered the front door of his neat little semi-detached house in Worsley, about four miles west of Manchester city centre. He'd beaten the rush-hour gridlock and he felt victorious.

"Hello my small friends!" said Miller, falling to his knees and embracing his five year olds in a huge hug.

"Andy! What on earth are you doing home at a reasonable time?" asked his wife, Clare as she walked into the hall, her glowing smile was the first thing Miller saw as he looked up in her direction.

"I came here to see if anybody wants to go to Crocodile Pete's!"

"Yes!"

"Yes please daddy!"

"I'd prefer Nando's!" said Clare, half joking, half serious.

"Well... let's vote. Everybody who wants to go to Crocodile Pete's, put your..."

The twins already had their hands in the air. So did Miller.

"Sorry mum, it's three votes to one! We're going to Crocodile Pete's!"

"Yay!"

*****

DI Saunders was at home, sitting on the settee with his girlfriend, DC Helen Grant. Helen was becoming increasingly annoyed at Keith's constant messing with his phone.

"Are we watching this, or not?"

"Yes. I'm listening to it and looking up now and again."

"That's not watching it!"

"Don't be passive-aggressive." Said the off-duty detective inspector with a smirk, without looking up from his screen.

"What? How was that passive-aggressive?"

"You are trying to force me to put my phone down and stare at the TV, by using subtle hints that you are unhappy with me looking at my phone. You are compromising my safe space, you psycho."

Helen threw a cushion at Keith's face.

"Now that was just plain aggressive!" he said, smiling.

"Are we watching it, or can I put something I want to watch on?"

"Just give me a sec. I've got something here. Might be a lead."

"You're always working Keith. Do you never just switch off?"

"No."

"I know, stupid question. What's the lead, anyway?"

Keith Saunders looked up for the first time and made eye-contact with Helen. "The other night, I joined this web forum. It was all about the gambling companies, and all these dickheads were on there going on about how the bookies were going to get their comeuppance someday. It was a load of shit really. But I joined up and made a comment about the fire, saying that the people who'd done it were sick bastards."

Helen paused the TV. "Right?"

"Yes, well, I didn't think very much more about it. Anyway, I've just had a reply from one of them."

"Let's have a look."

He handed the phone over to Helen and pointed at the part of the screen where his comment was.

"John Big Bad?"

"Yes."

"Great name!"

"Just read it, you turnip."

Helen read her partner's comment before reading the reply out loud. "So, this is from Gomch81. It says 'Everyone knows that fire was nothing to do with the fight back. The boss has put out a twitter message anyway, so the police are now aware as well. I take it you've not registered???"

Helen glanced at Keith, she had a puzzled look on her face. "What's that supposed to mean?"

"I've got absolutely no idea. But I'm trying to think of a decent response and you keep trying to make me watch The Apprentice."

"What are you going to put?"

"I'm thinking along the lines of... something like 'if it's proved that the fire has nothing to do with us, then I probably will.' Something like that. What do you reckon?"

Helen liked it and nodded enthusiastically. "What's the worst that can happen? They ignore you?"

"Yes. Well, no actually. The worst that could happen is they realise I'm an undercover detective snooping around and I get booted off the web-page. If that happens, I'll be snookered."

"Bollocks love. If you get booted off the site, you can just sign up again. But choose a better bloody name next time, John Big Bad!"

Within five minutes of sending his reply, Keith's phone pinged with a new notification, forcing Helen to roll her eyes and press pause on the TV remote again.

"Aw don't be like that. Gomch 81 has sent me a response. Here we go. It says 'don't be a fool. Why would anyone start a fire? How many other fires have been started? Don't believe everything you read in the press. We need all the help we can get so join in rather than make snide comments. You can sign up here." Beneath the message was a long website link. Saunders clicked it and his phone screen quickly loaded with a new website. It was very basic, there were no fancy graphics or pictures. The website was called "Just Justice." It looked more like a word-processing document than a website.

Beneath the page's title was a short paragraph. It read;

"Welcome. You didn't arrive here by accident. You cannot find this website through conventional search engines. We have hidden this page from all of the search engines. The very fact that you are here means that you are interested in signing up to our newsletter, which will give you access to your local justice network. Please sign up by submitting your e-mail address in the box below. Do not share this link with anybody else unless you know that they feel the same way that we do."

"What the hell is this?" asked Keith. Helen was leaning against his shoulder, reading the same paragraph, thinking exactly the same thing.

"That has got to be the vaguest message I've ever read!" said Helen.

"It's assuming that the person who is reading it already has a bit of an idea what its all about. I think Gomch 81 might have just fucked everything up for his mates!"

"Bless him!" said Helen, realising that this could be of major significance to the enquiry.

Keith leapt off the settee and stepped across the living room, grabbing his work bag. He crouched down and took out his jotter pad, flicking through the pages.

"What are you doing now?" asked Helen, half collapsed on the sofa where Keith had just been sitting. He was supposed to laugh at her awkward position, but his attention was elsewhere.

"Keith?" she tried again, lying at a funny angle on her side.

"I'm just trying to find the e-mail address I set up to join this forum. Oh, it's alright, here it is." He stood up and walked back across to the sofa, finally noticing the uncomfortable position that Helen had landed in after he'd jumped up. He sat back down, trapping her twisted torso behind his back.

"Get off me you saggy gonad!" pleaded Helen. Keith began typing the e-mail address into the page as Helen struggled out of her awkward position. A few silent moments passed before Keith spoke, with a real enthusiasm in his voice.

"Right! Sorted."

"What now?" asked Helen, seeing that Keith had submitted the e-mail address and pressed the "register" button.

"Now, we watch The Apprentice." Keith switched his phone off and threw it onto the settee opposite.

"Correct answer!"

The couple sat and watched as the candidates on the TV show argued and bickered amongst themselves about who should be sacked from the show. Keith was fidgeting, biting his nails and shaking his leg. Helen knew the signs, she could see that the DI was thinking about the case and wasn't watching TV at all.

"Right, well, I'm going to go to bed."

"Why? It's not even ten o'clock?" asked Keith, appearing surprised by Helen's sudden announcement.

"Well, it's obvious that you want to get on with your work, and I can't stand any of the contestants on here this year. So I'm just going to go to bed and try to stop myself from breathing."

Keith laughed loudly. "Bloody hell! That's a bit melodramatic!"

"Well, I guess this is goodbye." Said Helen as she stood up and grabbed her glass of water off the coffee table. "Just so you know, I want Dancing Queen and I'm in the Mood for Dancing on as the main songs at my funeral."

"Why?"

"So that whenever any of my friends or relatives are at a do in the future, those songs will come on and their night will be ruined with sad thoughts about my passing."

Keith laughed again. Helen bent down and kissed his forehead. "Goodbye. Forever."

"Oh, don't be so depressing. Night H. Love you."

As soon as Helen left the room, Keith leapt up off the sofa, and grabbed his phone off the other, switching it back on as he walked through to the kitchen to make a brew. He was pleased that he was getting this opportunity to do a bit more work. It was just like the old days, when he was miserable and lonely and wished that he had a girlfriend to share his life with, cuddle up on the sofa and watch a bit of telly with.

Lee Riley's Story - Part Two

Joanna had listened quietly to her little brother's problems for the past hour. The wind was getting worse up on the top of Keighley Moor, and the van had begun shaking from side to side.

Joanna was the person who everybody went to in a crisis. She was strong, dependable and the kind of person who could fix problems, finding practical solutions, no matter how big the mess. It was really saddening for her, listening to all of Lee's troubles and it hurt a little that he hadn't come to her for help. She'd had to go to him and practically forced him to come clean about the problem. She understood, she totally got it that this was a pretty embarrassing position to find yourself in. But it still bothered her that he hadn't come to her. She felt confident that things wouldn't have got this out-of-hand if he had of.

Lee was crying again, and Joanna felt that everything that needed to be said, had now been said. She felt it was time to start the job of fixing this problem, time to make it go away.

"Well, love. I think we need to stop sulking about it now. It's horrible, what's happened, no mistake about it. But I think you've learnt a very harsh lesson. Haven't you love?"

Joanna put her hand of Lee's and left it there. He nodded.

So, come on, push your tits out, stick your shoulders back, big smiles. We need to put it behind us, look to the future."

Lee smiled. It was reassuring to hear Joanna talking like this, instead of calling him a fucking dick. In his heart, he knew that Joanna would always be supportive, she was good like that. But he wouldn't have blamed her if she had called him a fucking dick.

"This woman's five grand. Is this all that it boils down to in the end?"

"Well, yes. I guess. I just don't know how I can tell her."

"So if we had the five grand, everything would be okay?"

"Yes. Well, I mean, eventually, yes. But I'd need to tell Liv, so she can sign for the loan."

"I get that Lee. But if you tell Liv, you'll have to tell her about your savings as well. She might not be too understanding about that."

"I know. This is what's going through my head. It's like a pneumatic drill in my brain. I can't switch it off." Lee started crying again.

"Right, listen, stop crying now mate. If you cry again, I'm going to video it on my phone and I'll post it on the Hebden Gossip Facebook, with a comment saying this is what Lee Riley looks like when he's lost an arm-wrestle with his sister."

Lee smiled again and wiped his face with his hands.

"I might be able to get the money."

Lee turned his head and stared at his big sister. "What?"

"Might. Not definitely, but I might be able to. If I can't get the full amount, it'll be pretty close. So you can get the materials you need and carry on as if nothing happened. Our little secret."

"Jo, you can't…"

"Shut up. You can pay me back in bits, when you can afford it. But it stays between me and you, nobody else. Right?"

"Jo…"

"Shut up Lee. This is the only way. But if Tony finds out, I'll be getting a divorce, so I need you to keep it zipped. You'll be over this in a few months, and we'll be joking about this by your birthday. Right?"

Lee nodded, but he looked tearful. Joanna was the kindest person he'd ever known and he knew that he was extremely fortunate to have her as a sister. She'd never had money to splash about, so her talking about lending him five grand was not only a shock, but also a reminder of how amazingly generous she could be when somebody needed her help.

"Right, I need to get home. The kids will have all the bloody lights on. Give us a cuddle." Joanna leaned over and held her brother tightly. "It stays between us, yeah. Nobody else needs to know."

"Thank you."

"It's alright. Now get your arse back home and tell Liv that you're sorry you've been a knob but it's because you've felt a lump in your balls and you've been worrying about it."

"Eh?"

"It'll explain your mood swings, and also, she'll have a right good feel of your balls as well. Win win."

Lee laughed loudly. It was the first time he had laughed properly since Joanna had arrived, and it made her feel good. She got out of the cab and closed the door before getting into her own car and starting the engine. She blew Lee a kiss before driving off, heading back down the hill towards the town below.

*****

"What's for tea, mum?" asked Ellie as Joanna closed the front door.

"Oh, hello! What a wonderful greeting!" said Joanna as she took off her coat and hung it on the bannister post at the bottom of the stairs.

"Hi mum!" shouted her eldest, Ben, from upstairs. "What's for tea?"

"First of all! It's not tea, it's dinner. Tea is a drink!" shouted Joanna up the stairs, trying once again to encourage her family to adopt the posh name for tea into this household, aware that it was a losing battle.

"Second of all, have you done your jobs?"

"Ellie said she was doing them!"

"No I did not!" Shrieked Ellie up the stairs.

"She did mum! She said she wanted to help out more and begged me not to do any jobs."

"That is a total lie! Liar!" Ellie ran up the stairs loudly and a huge row started. Joanna couldn't really hear the details as she went through to the kitchen and started running the hot tap, muttering "teenagers" under her breath. She filled the sink with hot water and washing up liquid, before going back to the foot of the stairs.

"Right! Ben! Ellie! Down here now and do these pots before I put you both in a children's home."

Joanna went through to the dining room and opened the drawer in the Welsh dresser which held all the family business documents. The drawer was filled with letters, bank statements and pay-slips. She pulled out her savings book for the Post Office. It showed a balance of £828.

"Shit." She said under her breath, she'd been sure that there was more in there than that. Next, she pulled out her ISA folder and checked the balance. The last statement was from a few months ago, but it said that the account had £2,487 in. She did a quick sum and realised that she had about £3,200 altogether. Joanna grabbed her phone out of her bag and logged into the online banking app. She'd been paid a few days ago, so most of her wages would still be in. Her balance was £1,400.

"Fucks sake!" she said under her breath, as she realised that she didn't have enough money. The bills were still to go out anyway. Joanna cleared the paperwork away and pushed it back into the drawer. Even if she gave every penny to Lee, he would still be about £400 short of the money he needed.

"The Whisky bottle!" said Joanna, excitedly, as she remembered the savings bottle which her and her husband put their spare coins into. She opened the dresser door and saw that the huge whisky bottle was about two-thirds of the way full. They only put "decent" coins in these days, the pounds and fifties and twenties. She thought about how much might be there, it had been about £200 last time they'd emptied it, but that was with all the shit coins, the 1ps, 2ps and 5ps as well. Joanna began to feel quietly confident that she might just have enough.

"What are you doing, mum?" asked Ellie in the doorway.

"I'm just checking something. Have you done the pots?"

"Ben's washing, I'm drying."

"Right, well, off you pop."

"Where's dad?"

"He's working late. He'll be back about seven. Now go and do your jobs young lady!"

Joanna started emptying the huge bottle, it had taken all of her strength to hoist it up onto the table top. The noise from all the coins bashing against the inside of the heavy bottle, and landing on the table top brought Ben and Ellie through from the kitchen.

"What are you doing, mum?" asked Ben.

"I'm just sorting this out."

"What's for tea? I'm starving!"

"Have you done the pots?"

"I'm doing them now."

"Well clearly, you're not! You're in the wrong part of the house for a starter!"

"Just waiting for the contact time."

"Contact time?" Joanna laughed loudly.

"Yeah, we learnt about it in home economics. When you're washing up, you have to leave the pots for five minutes contact time with the water. Hygiene!"

"Right, well, that's a new one on me Ben."

"What are you doing with all that money? Is this to thank me for washing up?"

"No. I'm just having a sort out. If you go away and leave me alone, I might give you some for the chippy though."

Ben disappeared back into the kitchen as Joanna began making piles of coins, stacking up the twenty pence coins into £5 piles, stacking up the one pound coins into stacks of tens. After about twenty minutes, she could see that there was well over two hundred pounds piled up on the dining table. She felt pleased, knowing that there was still about half of the bottle to be counted.

She grabbed a stack of the £1 coins and handed five to Ben and five to Ellie. "Right, thanks for doing your jobs. Go and get yourselves a chippy tea, Dad's not home until about half seven."

"Chippy dinner, don't you mean?" said Ben as he took the coins. "Thanks mum."

"Yeah, thanks mum!" said Ellie as she took her cash.

Joanna went back into the dining room and sat down, determined to count the coins and have them all bagged up and stashed away before Tony got home.

*****

The following day, Joanna banked £312.70 from the whisky bottle. The huge bag of coins which she had taken into the Natwest was attracting tuts and sighs from the customers queuing behind her. But she didn't care, it was hardly her fault that there was only one person serving, she thought, as the tuts and huffs got louder behind her. It took almost twenty-minutes to bank all the cash, each bag having to be weighed separately by the bank clerk, who looked just as pissed off about the whole thing as the people in the ever-lengthening queue.

Joanna's next job, now that she'd got rid of the heavy bag, was to go into the Post Office and withdraw her savings. Once that job had been done, Joanna headed round to the Pawn shop, having a careful look around before stepping inside, she didn't want anybody gossiping in this closely-knitted community.

"Good morning, madam," said a seedy old bloke behind the counter.

"Hi, I, er, hope you can help. I need to borrow a hundred pounds. Only for a couple of weeks."

"I'm sure we can help you with that. What were you planning to leave with us?" The old guy spoke like a robot, it was apparent that he'd had this conversation a million times before, just by the insincere delivery of his patter.

Joanna's eyes were filling with tears as she wriggled at her wedding ring, trying to pull it off her finger, her mind was whizzing as she tried to pull it off. She couldn't remember the last time she'd taken it off. After an embarrassing few silent seconds, she finally presented her wedding ring to the pawnbroker. He held it up to the light and smiled.

"Yes, I think we can arrange a hundred pounds for this. But it will cost you one hundred and thirty to buy back."

"Yes, yes, that's fine," said Joanna, her voice breaking with emotion. She'd not considered that this transaction would stir up so much emotion within her.

"There's a few forms I'll need you to fill in, shouldn't take long." Said the man. Joanna didn't like him much. She filled out the forms and showed her ID, that heavy sense of emotion was still hanging over her, and she had no idea where it had come from. She knew it was a bit iffy, pawning her wedding ring. But it was for a good cause, it was to help her brother who was in need. Her gentle internal argument made her feel a little better about things as the pawnbroker handed her the cash.

Finally, she went back to the bank and paid in the funds from her Post Office account, and the Pawn shop. She then instructed the bank-clerk to transfer all of her available funds to Lee's account, handing the clerk her brother's account and sort-code details. She felt good, knowing that her efforts would get Lee out of the trouble he'd found himself in. She just hoped that Tony wouldn't find out before Lee paid it all back.

As she got back in her car, she took her phone out of her handbag and wrote a text to Lee. "Five grand just been transferred into your bank our kid. Your problems are over. Love you xxx." As soon as she'd sent the text, she deleted it. It would cause World War Three if Tony ever got to hear about this. It wasn't as though Tony didn't like Lee. Far from it, he thought the world of his brother-in-law. But lending money wasn't Tony's thing, and it certainly wouldn't go down well that Joanna was lending money to a man who had three decent holidays a year, when they struggled to pay for one. It would just be better all round if Tony never heard a word about it.

Joanna drove the short journey home from town, trying to think of a way around having absolutely no money left until next pay-day in a fortnight. This was going to be a tricky one she realised, as it dawned on her that it was another ten days until her next pay packet hit her account. Then she had a flash of genius. If she pretended that she'd lost her bank card, she could stall contacting the bank for a few days, using phrases such as "it can't have vanished!" and "it's here somewhere. It'll turn up in a minute!" Then it would take about a week for a new one to be processed and sent out. She smiled as she realised that this was the answer, she could probably blag her way out of all this with no hassle.

*****

Lee was sitting in his van, in a quiet little lay-by near Todmorden. He had no work on, the only job that he had lined up was the job that he'd blown the deposit for. The extension job was going to give him a month's work, at least, so he had turned several jobs away. He felt as though he was in no man's land and was genuinely scared about the future. The only chance he had of sorting this whole nightmare out rested with his big sister. If she could get the money together, as she'd promised the previous day, then he did stand a realistic chance of getting out of this mess.

And then Joanna's text arrived, letting him know that she had kept her word. She had managed to get the money together for him. Five thousand pounds had just been transferred into his bank account.

Lee's eyes were filling up with tears. Joanna was the kindest, loveliest, most genuine person he'd ever known. She'd never had loads of money, life had been a struggle for her and Tony. Lee had no idea how she had managed to get five grand together in such a short period of time but he was deeply touched that she had done. He kept staring at the text message, overwhelmed with emotion and gratitude as he read it over and over again. He started doing some sums in his head, trying to work out how he could get the money back to her, and make enough to live on whilst he was doing the extension job. He couldn't make the sums add up, he wasn't due to be paid for the work until it was completed. That was going to be at least six weeks away.

A sudden excitement stirred within him, as he worked out a way that he could solve this problem. If he used the five grand that Joanna had lent him, and put it on a horse, a dead-cert, then he could double the money, maybe even triple it. If he did that, he could give Joanna seven and a half grand back. He'd have his five grand for materials, and two and a half grand to keep everything going until the job was finished. It was a brilliant idea, he thought as he felt the electricity buzzing through his body. He felt giddy and restless. This was perfect.

Lee replied to Joanna's text. "Thank you Sis. You really are the best. Love you so much xxx."

He then opened the internet browser on his phone and started looking at the runners and riders for the day's horse racing. He wasn't too big on horse racing, he'd never really seen the attraction, but he did know that the chances of winning on the horses was far greater than the odds on a computer generated roulette wheel. Experience had taught him that lesson the hard way. He was scrolling through the races, looking for the horses with the best track record, the most wins, the smallest odds. There were dozens of excellent horses running later in the day. His hands were trembling as he continued looking at the lists. He spent over an hour working on this, his quote pad in the van was being filled with horse's names, their jockeys, their race history. After scrutinising all of the details, he finally settled on the horse he was going to back.

"Gerald's Girl" was running in the 13.20 at Chepstow. The odds of her winning were 2 to 1. This meant that the five grand would become fifteen grand, in just ten minutes. He'd win ten thousand pounds, plus he'd get the five thousand stake back. Lee's heart-rate was quickening, he could feel sweat pouring down his back and he felt completely exhilarated. This was perfect, this was the answer to everything. He just needed to place this bet, then kill a couple of hours until the race. And then, he would be sorted, and he'd be walking away from gambling forever. This was his way out of this mess.

Lee's heart was bursting out of his chest as he used his mobile phone to place the bet. He laughed excitedly when he saw the £5000 stake on the race. He decided that he had to go and have a bit of a jog on the canal for a bit, to pass some time and to use some of his hyper energy up. It was only half eleven. The race didn't start for over an hour and a half. He got out of his van and opened the side door and found his trainers. He sat down on the van floor and untied the laces of his heavy work boots, his adrenaline was pumping at full speed and he needed to start running, and start using this energy up, straight away.

Within minutes, Lee was running along the Rochdale Canal, running away from Todmorden towards his hometown. He felt brilliant, totally alive. All of his problems which had brought him down so low were sorted and now he felt as high as he ever had.

"Hello." He'd say cheerfully to dog walkers and cyclists as he jogged past them.

"Grand day!" He said to others. He would occasionally burst into a sprint for a few hundred yards, before slowing his pace back down to a steady jog. He felt amazing.

*****

Joanna was at work in the paper-shop in Hebden Bridge and was feeling a little anxious about the level of deceit that she would need to involve herself with in order to hide the fact that she'd given all of her fortnightly wage away, as well as every penny the family had stashed away for an emergency. It wasn't Joanna's style to be deceitful, but she had no other choice, she reasoned. She felt that she needed to plant the first seed anyway, if she was to get some cash out of Tony. She sent her husband a text. "Hi sexy gut, have you seen my bank card? xxx" She clicked send and placed her phone back in her handbag. She then took her bank card out of her purse and snapped it in half, before placing it inside an empty bag in the rubbish bin beneath the counter. She then pushed it under the rest of the rubbish to make sure nobody would accidentally find it.

"Good morning Jo, packet of Golden Virginia please, love." Joanna looked up from the bin. It was old Stan at the counter, his friendly smile and cheeky grin distracted Joanna from her stress and she smiled back just as warmly.

"What's up with you, lass?" asked Stan, as Joanna placed his tobacco on the counter and took his ten-pound note.

"Eh, nowt, what do you mean, Stan?"

"You, you don't seem yourself today. You look a bit fed up. It's not like you?"

"Oh, do I? Sorry Stan. Well I'll cheer up from now on."

"Aye, well a lovely face like yours deserves a nice big smile on it. Alright, see you tomorrow pet." Stan shuffled out of the shop and Joanna wondered how the regular customer had seen that she wasn't very happy. She wasn't very good with lies and deceit and all that and wondered if it was showing. Joanna took her phone out of her handbag again, and deleted her banking app. Now she would be alright, there was no way of Tony finding out. Joanna made a very conscious decision to put her usual smiling, charming face together and stop bloody worrying. Everything was going to be fine.

*****

Lee got back to his van dripping in sweat, despite his hands and face feeling frozen from the crisp autumn air. He opened the side door of the van and found a spare top. He pulled his sweaty top off and began drying himself off, before putting the fresh sweatshirt on. He looked at his watch, it was nearly one o'clock. He felt a fresh surge of excitement, knowing that he was only twenty minutes away from the race, and thirty minutes away from ending his short but stressful love affair with gambling, for good.

Lee drove the short distance to Todmorden town centre, parked his van and found the nearest bookies, surprised to feel absolutely no pull towards the roulette machine. He had no money on him anyway, and his bank was empty, so it was a good thing really, he considered. He checked that the race was all set to go ahead, and that his horse, Gerald's Girl was ready for the race, before sitting down on one of the stools.

The mood in the bookies was not dissimilar to that of the bookies in Hebden Bridge. It was full of sad looking old blokes, or "Gammons" to use the modern name for bitter looking middle-aged white men with high blood pressure. The name comes from their resemblance to, well, gammon. One old drunk was swearing loudly at another bloke, his voice broken from a life-time of cigarette smoking and drinking strong spirits. The two young ladies behind the counter looked completely disinterested in everything that was going on across the opposite side of their counter as one chatted away incessantly and the other one stared disaffectedly at her mobile phone.

Lee was tapping his fingers on the wooden shelf, desperate to hear the race gun, and desperate to see Gerald's Girl sort out all his problems once and for all. He felt brilliant.

"Have you got a runner?" asked an old bloke who sat down beside Lee.

"Yeah. Gerald's Girl."

"Oh, good choice. Strong horse that."

"Have you backed her?"

"No. I've gone for Nuts in May."

"How much?"

"Twenty quid. Six to one, so I'll be right if she comes in."

Both men stopped talking as the starting gun fired. The race had begun. Gerald's Girl was a dark brown horse, wearing yellow, the jockey was in yellow and white and Lee's eyes were trained on her as the horses set off.

"Come on!" shouted Lee, as Gerald's Girl gracefully moved to the front of the pack.

"Come on Gerald's Girl!" he shouted again. This was looking very good and Lee was feeling the full rush of the gambling buzz as his horse continued to romp away, focused, strong and powerful.

"Come on!" he shouted loudly at the screen, receiving vacant looks from the two girls behind the counter. Another horse was just behind, matching Lee's horse step for step.

"Is that yours?" he asked the old man who'd sat beside him.

"Yes, Nuts In May. Strong horse that."

The two horses were leading the way, as twenty other horses and their riders battled to stay in the race. But suddenly, Nuts In May seemed to find a bit more speed from somewhere, yard by yard, and was gradually pulling ahead of Lee's horse.

"What... come on! COME ON!" Shouted Lee at the screen, louder than ever. "COME ON!!"

Gerald's Girl was putting up a strong fight, her jockey was whipping her furiously. But she just couldn't match the speed and power of Nuts In May.

"COME ON!"

The commentator on the TV was yelling as the horses battled it out along the final straight. Nuts In May was still pulling away, as Gerald's Girl continued the battle with everything she had. But she just wasn't strong enough. Nuts In May crossed the finishing line a full width ahead of the nearest rival.

Lee just stared up at the screen. That was not supposed to happen.

"Can't win them all, mate." Said the old guy sitting next to him, as he climbed off the stool and headed over to the counter to pick up his winnings.

Lee just stayed rooted to the stool, staring up at the screen as the winning jockey stood up in his stirrups and cheered his victory in front of the TV cameras and press photographers.

Lee's adrenaline rush was slowing, the feverish excitement was rapidly turning to panic. He stared up at the screen, feeling a familiar dose of black emptiness replacing the euphoria that he'd been feeling only minutes earlier.

He'd just lost Joanna's money. Every fucking penny.

Chapter Twenty-Nine

Throughout the night of November 19th into the early hours of the 20th, the 999 police emergency number had been called almost nonstop in practically every county in the UK, to make reports of burglaries, looting and vandalism at betting shops. Police response units were sent out to investigate these calls, which were coming in from neighbours or passers-by who were witnessing the shocking incidents.

Gangs of people carrying heavy tools, dressed in hoodies and balaclavas were roaming the streets, smashing up bookies shops, in some cases two or three in one road. Police call handlers in every emergency call centre in Britain were being told that there were lots of people involved, and that they were armed with heavy tools and that they looked like they were drunk as they sang and shouted at the tops of their voices, waking up the entire community.

Police officers were mobilised to attend these calls. In the majority of cases, police officers were met with smashed up betting shops with burglar alarms blaring, the damage to each property ranged massively. From simply having all the windows smashed in, to having the entire shop pulled apart and smashed up, item-by-item.

The calls kept coming into the nation's emergency services throughout the early hours, the Manchester City police force alone ran out of officers to attend calls, as they were already en-route or engaged with a previous call. It was quite clear to the call handlers, the duty sergeants and inspectors, as well as the officers on the ground, that something quite extraordinary, and very well organised, was taking place.

Cities all across the country were seeing the same incidents, in some areas, just a few shops had been targeted. In others, such as Manchester, Leeds, Newcastle and Birmingham, there had been more than a dozen. The common theme of the night was that each incident involved "a gang" of men making a lot of noise as they went about their business of trashing the shops, seemingly without a care in the world. These gangs, as police officers discovered, ranged in numbers from 6 or 7 to as many as 15 and more. Another common theme was that each incident was extremely loud and intimidating, but only lasted for a couple of minutes. The people taking part in this were certainly not sneaking around, it was quite the opposite.

For every police force in the country, this was a remarkably challenging evening. Logistically, it was a nightmare. Understandably, incidents involving multiple males with weapons cannot be responded to by a single patrol unit for health and safety reasons. Each report had mentioned pick-axes, sledge-hammers and steel bars. This meant that each incident which was being reported required a tactical response from all of the police officers in that division and the timings of arrival and deployment had to be co-ordinated by the divisional inspector. What this meant, in many cases, was that a police patrol vehicle might well have been close to the site of the disturbance but was unable to engage until there was sufficient back-up available.

In several cases, officers had to sit in their vehicles and watch the offenders as they finished their attacks and then observe them as they made their getaways. This was unbelievable for the local residents who had made the 999 calls, witnessing the police staying put several hundred yards away from the scene of the crime and literally doing nothing about it. The residents were so incensed by this extraordinary scene, they made videos on their phones, which showed the gang smashing up the betting shop, and panned their camera up the street to show that police officers were sitting in their car, watching on. These types of videos were starting to trend amongst the late-nighters on Facebook and would later be shown on Sky News and BBC News channels.

The same situation had occurred at each incident. By the time that an adequate amount of police officers arrived at a job, the culprits had disappeared, in most cases ten, fifteen, or twenty minutes earlier. The same scenario was unfolding all around the country, police officers were being called by concerned, scared and angry residents near to the shops which were being trashed, but police officers had been instructed to stay back and could only attend long after the incident had concluded.

It had been a memorable night for every police officer on duty in the UK that night. They knew that they'd been caught up in the most audacious game of "cat and mouse" ever.

It was the early hours of Thursday morning before any kind of sense was being made of the unbelievable night of sudden pandemonium and disarray on the dark, normally silent streets of the United Kingdom. As ever, it was the media who had sussed out what was going on long before the authorities had. Over-night news editors began to link the activities of the nation's police forces and started their day of news reporting with some unforgettably sensational headlines.

They were to be assisted in their work by a Tweet from the now infamous Twitter account, Odds on Revenge which was sent at 6.07am.

"Awesome night! The nation's bookmakers will have a rude awakening this A.M. Their days of emptying bank accounts and forcing people to the edge of their sanity are coming to an end. This is just the beginning. We will strike again and we will strike again after that."

Chapter Thirty

"Good Morning, it's just after seven-thirty and this is BBC Radio Manchester. Our top story this morning. Hundreds of bookmaker's shops throughout Great Britain have been put out of business during a night of organised carnage which police inspectors have described as an unprecedented event. Here in Greater Manchester, it is reported that as many as twenty betting shops were targeted, but at this early hour we are as yet unsure of the accurate figure and we expect that we will have a lot more information as the day goes on and the full picture emerges. Naturally, we are linking this incredible news to the betting shops attacks that we have already seen here in the region over the past few weeks, and which were of course in the news just yesterday when the Odds On Revenge group claimed responsibility for four of the five attacks. I'm joined on the line by Denise Bailey who lives close to one of the shops targeted last night, in Stretford. Hello Denise."

"Good morning Alan."

"Well, I'm sure that came as a big shock last night?"

"You can say that again!"

"Talk us through what happened Denise."

"Well, it was horrible. It was really, really scary. I was in bed, with my husband, he was fast asleep, but I was still reading."

"What time was this at?"

"It was after midnight, about half-twelve I guess. I was just reading my book and I heard all this noise, it sounded like a load of yobs were coming back from the pub at first, so I didn't think much of it, you know, I just thought they'll soon be gone. Anyway, next thing I knew, I could hear all the windows being smashed at the BetSure over the road. I jumped out of bed, knocked the light off and went to the window to see what was going on. The alarm on the shop started going off and then this big cheer went up as though it was a football match and the home team had just scored. They were all laughing and joking and shouting as though it was a big joke."

"What were they shouting?"

"Don't know. I couldn't make it out with all the noise and the burglar alarm going off. Anyway, after bashing the windows in, they all climbed in and all you could hear was things getting smashed up, everything, you name it, the TVs, the counter, the glass on all the betting machines, the lights, all the panels on the walls and the ceiling. Honestly, it looks like a bomb has gone off over there. It's unrecognisable."

"You've been and had a look?"

"Yes, well, when the police arrived I went over to tell them. But, I must admit Alan, the police came about twenty minutes after these yobs had cleared off."

"It must have been a very scary experience, Denise."

"Oh, it was. Honestly, it's a dead quiet area this, normally. You wouldn't think something like this would happen round here."

"No, well, it was certainly a strange night. There are reports of these incidents happening all over the country throughout the night Denise, and the circumstances sound very similar, big groups of lads seemingly fearless of the law as they trashed these businesses. Tell me, what did the offenders look like?"

"Oh, I don't know Alan, they were all dressed the same, you know, hoodies, scarves over their faces, a few had ski-masks on. They were all carrying big tools like crow bars and sledge-hammers and stuff like that. The strangest thing is how quick it all happened, I bet it was all over within a couple of minutes."

"And what happened when they left?"

"Well, they were still laughing and joking and they just walked off up the street as though nothing had happened. It was really surreal Alan."

"Yes, surreal sounds like a great word to describe that. You're better with words than me Denise, because I keep saying that it's just unbelievable. Stay there anyway, because we've got Pamela Langton on the line, owner of Pammies Poodles, calling us from Worthington Road in Haughton Green. Pamela, I hear that you also witnessed one of these attacks last night?"

"Yes, good morning Alan. Yes, it's weird listening to Denise because it sounds exactly the same as what happened here."

"Talk us through it, Pamela."

"Well, it was about two o'clock in the morning. I was fast asleep when I heard all hell breaking loose outside. These thugs weren't scared about making a racket, it was as though they were trying to attract as much attention as possible. They've absolutely destroyed the shop, all the counters are smashed in, every window has gone through, the games machines thrown over and bashed in with big sledge-hammers. It was terrifying Alan, it really was."

"How many people did you see, Pamela?"

"Oh, it was a good ten of them. Easily."

"And tell us about what they did afterwards."

"Well, they weren't in there long, two or three minutes tops. They just wandered out of there, laughing and joking. They walked off towards town, bold as brass. Somebody has said they went and did the same thing to another shop further up the road."

*****

"Welcome to Good Morning Britain. Our major story this morning is still unfolding, and as each hour passes we are learning more about last night's extraordinary, co-ordinated attack against the nation's book-makers shops. The full story as we understand it will be covered in depth during the eight o'clock bulletin. But before that, we are joined by Gareth Barker from the charity Gamblers Support Network. Good morning Gareth."

"Good morning Piers."

"Well, I'd like to start by thanking you for coming along to our studios at such short notice. Before we start talking about last night's incredible crime-wave, I'd like to ask you first about your charity. Just what is Gamblers Support Network?"

"Sure, well, we started officially in 2007, but the seeds were sown a few years earlier, when myself and several ex-gamblers came together after realising that there wasn't really any help out there for people who were fighting battles against their gambling addiction."

"And so, you were a problem gambler yourself?"

"Yes, and I still am. There's no magic cure for this devastating addiction, so although I haven't actually gambled for over eleven years, I'm still very aware of the fact that I still have the overwhelming compulsion to gamble within me. And that's never going to go away, I just have to deal with it as best I can."

"It all sounds a bit, I don't know how to put it without causing you any offence Gareth. But it sounds a little bit daft. If you are a problem gambler, surely what that means is that basically, you're an idiot who doesn't know when to stop throwing your money away. Doesn't it?"

Good Morning Britain's host was forever trying to make headlines with his controversial and often provocative remarks. But Gareth Barker wasn't in the slightest bit phased as he smiled at Piers' typically idiotic comment.

"Well, I'm smiling because it's precisely that kind of suggestion which makes problem gambling so hard to talk about, particularly for those people who are going through the hell that this addiction brings. In so many cases that I'm aware of, people, quite often young men in their late teens or early twenties, have suffered this in silence, felt like they have nowhere to turn, nobody to talk to about their problems and their feelings. In many cases, these young people have found that the only answer is suicide, tragically."

Piers didn't seem at all sympathetic or phased as he ploughed on with his questioning. "But, there will be viewers at home watching this with their fingers covering their faces. Listen, if you have been gambling too much, and it's having a negative effect on your life, just stop. Okay? There, done. What's wrong with that?"

Gareth was an extremely calm and well-mannered guest. He smiled warmly at the TV host before talking very calmly. "That's an interesting point of view Piers, but I don't think you are quite ready to come along and volunteer on our help-lines just yet."

"Why not? Sometimes, the cold, hard truth is all we need to hear! Cruel to be kind may be an old-fashioned phrase, but it still works."

"Well, in my experience Piers, you've not taken a blind bit of notice to any of the cold hard truths that people have put to you, cruelly but kindly."

"Nice reply. Very good. But it's my show Gareth, I'll make the jokes."

"Thank you. But let's try and be a little more pragmatic about the situation. I seriously doubt that you would tell an anorexia sufferer to just have a cake and stop messing about. I doubt that you would suggest that a drug addict just stops injecting heroin and get on with their lives, nor would you tell an alcoholic to buy a can of Vimto and everything will work itself out."

"Well, no, I wouldn't actually. But those are entirely different things, Gareth. Let's try and keep a sense of perspective."

"I'm afraid that you are fundamentally wrong Piers. What we are talking about here is a very serious addiction. It doesn't matter if you are addicted to sex or drugs or cigarettes or brown sauce, it is still addiction, and you will still face the same barriers as any addict in trying to break the cycle of addiction."

"I'm sorry Gareth, but this is quite ridiculous..."

Gareth ignored the baiting and continued talking over his adversary. "And what we find, time and time again with problem gamblers is that the problem is usually well out of control before the person suffering from it realises that they have become addicted. And then a cycle of denial starts, where the gambler begins to hide their activities, they often tell lies and become deceitful, many of them begin stealing or selling their belongings to feed the habit. It happens at a time when the one thing that they really need to be doing is telling a loved one, coming clean about what's been going on. But sadly, what happens is quite the reverse, and those people very quickly find themselves isolated and confused and more often than not, finding the only salvation they can, in gambling. It's a vicious circle which has the most devastating effect on the people who find themselves in this situation."

"Okay, well, that's the plug done for your charity… what do you think is happening in Britain this morning, where bookmakers and their staff are arriving at work to find their shops in ruins and their jobs have been lost for the foreseeable future?"

"That's a great question, Piers. I like how you are somehow trying to imply that I am in support of the activities last night."

"Are you not?"

"Well, again, that's a very good question. I'm not in favour of this kind of activity…"

"But?"

"But, well, let's just slow down, I'm beginning to feel as though you are attempting to put words into my mouth…"

"I'm not. I just want to know what you think it's all about?"

"I think that it is quite simple really Piers. It's about anger, about anguish, about revenge, about loss, and not loss of money, I'm talking about the loss of family, friends, loved ones, jobs, homes. I imagine that the people who carried out these crimes last night will feel that they are justified in their reasons. There's every chance that these attacks were carried out by the silent victims of gambling addiction, the brothers, sisters, mums and dads of people who have found the only way out of their problem is to kill themselves."

"So, let's get down to the basic facts. You are coming on here, on national breakfast TV, as a trustee of the Gamblers Support Network, and you are saying that you can understand why these hooligans have caused millions of pounds worth of damage, and you are refusing to condemn them! Well shame on you Mr Barker, shame on you."

"That's not what I said at all…"

"Okay, I'll give you the benefit of the doubt. Would you like to take this opportunity to condemn the raving lunatics who carried out last night's attacks?"

"I feel that you are deliberately using extremely emotive language, Piers…"

"I am not. I am speaking on behalf of those viewers

who were woken up by this madness last night, who were terrified in their beds, and for all the police officers who had their shifts wasted last night, and on behalf of all of the people who needed a police officer last night but couldn't get one. But most of all, I'm speaking on behalf of the thousands of staff who will be facing a very uncertain future this morning, when the shop that they work at has been destroyed by a bunch of imbeciles who are angry with the wrong thing."

"Angry with the wrong thing?" asked Gareth Barker, his pleasant mood visibly slipping.

"Listen. I don't see fat people smashing up McDonalds."

"What's that supposed to mean?" Gareth's smile was gone now and his relaxed body language was visibly sharper.

"Well, smashing up bookies shops because they lost their money in them. The world's finally gone mad. Here's Sandy with the news."

Chapter Thirty-One

Miller was in an early morning meeting with DCS Dixon. Reports were still coming in about betting shops which had been wrecked, as the shop's staff arrived at work and discovered the carnage.

"This is a major incident, Andy. We still have no idea how many shops were done last night, but the national picture looks like two-hundred plus."

"Fucking Norah. Two hundred?"

"Could be more."

"I just can't get my head around it. Seriously, that's insane. We'll be talking about two hundred gangs."

"Well, not quite, there is growing intelligence that each gang did several shops. But even so, we are talking about a huge number of gangs who have co-ordinated this attack, very professionally as well, it has to be said."

"It's a fucking nightmare is what it is."

Dixon didn't respond, he just looked down at his desk-top.

"Where does this leave me then, with the investigation I mean?"

"That's the six-million-dollar question now Andy. I've got a meeting with the top team, being chaired by the Chief Constable. I'll know more after that."

"When?"

"Late morning is all I know. I think they'll be waiting for whatever reaction comes from the government. But whichever way this goes, it's going to be taken over by the NCA. There are no two ways about it. So, I'd prepare yourself for that news." Dixon was talking about the national crime agency, the nationwide police service which has significantly better resources for investigating organised crime, specifically when the criminals are covering numerous police force's geographical areas. In this particular case, it looked likely that at least one betting shop had come under attack within every single constabulary on the British mainland.

"Well, I'm not exactly gutted Sir. Wouldn't honestly

fancy trying to co-ordinate an investigation of this magnitude."

"Yes, but don't completely resign yourself from the task! NCA might want to borrow you."

"Sir, that's out of the question!"

Dixon held his hand up to mute his DCI. "I'll know more later. So, in the meantime, where is your investigation up to?"

"Which one?"

"The betting shops."

"Oh, I see. Well, we've got the small matter of not being one hundred per-cent sure if the people who are co-ordinating the shop attacks are the same people who killed the Ozols family."

"Yes. What are your thoughts on that?"

"I'm pretty convinced that the fire is unconnected to the betting shops. I think it's just a bizarre coincidence that they family lived above a bookies."

"A bizarre coincidence?" Dixon had one of his bushy white eye-brows raised high on his forehead as he held Miller's gaze, his contempt for such theories was well documented.

"Yes Sir. I know you don't believe coincidences exist. But let me remind you, for the umpteenth time, that Archduke Franz Ferdinand was assassinated in his car, and this event kicked-off World War One. The model was called a WW1 and the registration plate was A111 118. The war ended on the eleventh of the eleventh, eighteen and it is widely recognised as WW1. The A probably stands for Armistice, as well."

"Yes, Andy, I'm quite aware of this."

"But you still don't believe in coincidences?"

Dixon ignored the question, he wasn't in the mood for debating with Miller. Not today.

"What physical reasoning do you have to back the theory up that the fire was unconnected with the other shop attacks?"

"I'm still working on that, but there's a stack of evidence that this was a local issue. The car was stolen from Rochdale, it had fake plates which belonged to a local car. The stolen vehicle was found burned out in Hyde. So everything points back to the local area. I strongly believe that it's isolated, and I'm going to have a deeper look and find something conclusive."

"But what makes you so sure that the events at the other betting shops you've been investigating, are unrelated?"

"Well for a kick off, this was a completely different event. Nothing was smashed up, they just poured petrol through the letterbox and chucked a match in. I can see no plausible link to any of the other shops, other than the sign above the front door!"

Dixon considered what Miller was saying. A long moment of silence passed.

"Anything else?"

"I'm swayed by the Tweet that was sent out yesterday. I was already considering that the incidents were unconnected, and that Tweet has pretty much confirmed my suspicions."

"Okay, well, don't always trust everything you read on the internet Andy. That's a well-known quote from William Shakespeare."

Miller ignored the joke, he wasn't in the mood for mucking about.

"Right, well, I'll wait and see what the top brass have to say about our involvement in last night's eventualities. In the meantime, I suggest you drop the betting shops from your to-do list for the time being and focus all of the team's attention on the fire."

"Sir."

"I hope you're right about this Andy. Could really do with something solid to take into my meeting. If you could manage to come up with some compelling evidence, I think they will be able to break the investigation into two."

"Okay, well I'm pretty sure we have a couple of lines to chase up this morning, so I'll keep you posted."

"See that you do."

"Sir."

Miller stood and left his superior's office. He was still in a daze at the sheer magnitude of the previous night's vandalism, he couldn't think of anything that this nationwide night of civil disobedience could compare to.

As he reached the SCIU floor, he could see that his officers were also struggling to make sense of the event. They were all standing around Saunders' desk and watching the BBC News live-stream on his PC.

"Caught you!" Said Miller humourlessly as he approached.

"What the eff is going on, Sir?" asked Rudovsky.

"Search me." Said Miller, shrugging.

"What was Dixon saying?" asked Saunders.

"Not a lot, really. It's panic stations at the minute, I think the big cheeses are waiting for some instruction from the top."

"The top?" asked Grant. "As in the Home Office?"

"Precisely. Right anyway, shall we get started with this morning's team brief?"

Miller stepped across to the front of the office, standing before the incident room wall which was used as the noticeboard for every detail that the team had so far.

"All set?"

Miller's colleagues all nodded as they made themselves comfy.

"Right. Hands up if you think that the fire in Denton," Miller pointed at the photographs of the Ozols, and then at the photograph of their burnt-out home. "...is connected with these events." Miller stepped across a few paces to the pictures of the vandalised betting shops.

He seemed surprised to see that no hands were raised. "Not one of you?" he asked. Nobody spoke. "Is this anything to do with your inner-detectiveness, or is it more to do with those tweets yesterday morning?" asked Miller.

"Well, in my case Sir," said Rudovsky sticking her arm high in the air, "It's more to do with the nature of the attack in Denton. I'm not trying to say I agree with folk smashing up shops. But I can appreciate the fact that these betting shop attacks are against shops, fixtures and fittings, the biggest victim is the insurance companies. Nobody has been hurt, that we know of. If anything, the fact that last night's activities haven't involved a single fire that we know of, or a single injury against anybody tells me that we are looking at two separate crimes."

"Anybody want to add to that?"

"I agree one hundred and eighty-one per cent with Jo." DC Mike Worthington continued, "I can see why we all thought that the attackers had changed their tactics at that one," he pointed at the burnt-out shell on the photograph. "But, I'm of the opinion that this was just a very freaky coincidence. The news this morning sounds like these have been identical crimes to the first four shops. Jo's right, there wasn't a single fire last night, the BBC news reporters have been desperate to hear of one."

"Anybody disagree with that?" asked Miller.

"No."

"No, Sir."

"Well, let's throw in a curve-ball," said Chapman. "For the record, I'm in agreement that I don't believe the fire was started by the people who have trashed all these shops. But, I think it would be unwise to add weight to the fact that there were no fires last night. If this group are keen to distance themselves from the fire, sending out Twitter messages to that effect... well, they're not going to start any others are they?"

"Yes, that's a good point Bill. I don't think we should use that as the thrust of our argument." DC Mike Worthington agreed with his partner.

"I agree Bill. But to be honest, I'm not very concerned about the other shops right now. Dixon reckons we are going to be taken off this case any minute now, he's confident that the NCA will take it over."

Nobody looked surprised, and Miller assumed that they had all discussed this while he was with Dixon and had arrived at the same conclusion.

"It wouldn't be a justifiable use of resources for forty-odd separate CID departments to try and make any sense out of all this, so it would be sensible that the NCA run it." Miller's team were nodding and seemed glad to sense that a but was coming.

"But! I want to keep this case." He pointed again at the Ozols family. "I want us to send the bastards who did this to jail.

So we have until eleven o'clock, that's two and a half hours, to come up with some compelling evidence, Dixon's words, some compelling evidence that this crime was committed by people who are unconnected to the betting shops carry-on."

"You think we'll keep this case, if we can convince Dixon?" asked Rudovsky.

"Yeah, I think he's almost there, we just need to give him something good that he can take to the Chief Constable. That's all we need. So, come on team, what have we got?" Miller grabbed a marker pen and opened a fresh sheet on the giant A1 notepad which stood on an A frame beside the inquiry wall.

"The car on the motorway." Suggested DC Bill Chapman. Miller scribbled 'car M60' on the pad.

"The CCTV from the factories on Windmill Lane." Offered DC Peter Kenyon.

"There's the CCTV of the car being driven back towards Hyde, which Ashton CID got." Said Saunders. "Plus, the fact that it was burnt-out at a known location for this type of activity, suggesting a level of local knowledge."

"Brilliant!" Said Miller, as he scribbled the points onto the pad. "We need to take the argument to Dixon that whoever burnt that building down, did so because of an issue with either the Ozols, or another individual connected with that address. We need to come up with something that links these fucking psychopaths," Miller smacked the photograph of the four individuals on the motorway camera. "To this family. Or this address."

Miller's team had the usual look of enthusiasm and determination about them and he could see that they were keen to get cracking.

"Now I know we are doing this arse about face. Under normal circumstances, we'd have started the investigation at this point. But as we all know, the circumstances of this are very unique, so I don't want anybody feeling stupid or embarrassed that we are today starting this investigation afresh. We need to know everything about this man," Miller touched the photograph of the man who was killed in the fire. "We need to know absolutely everything, his friends, his associates, any links to any dodgy people. He's the number one line-of-enquiry. Number two is this lady," Miller tapped the photograph of Marija, who was still lay in a medically-induced coma in hospital. "Same goes for mum. Let's leave no stone unturned as we try to work out why this family was targeted by these four people. Okay?"

"Sir!"

"Yes, Sir!"

"On it!"

"You've got two hours. Off you go. Jo, can you co-ordinate what everybody is doing, I need a quick catch-up with Keith." Miller tapped Saunders' shoulder and set off walking across to his office on the other side of the SCIU floor.

"Bank stuff is the top priority, Jo. I think Tameside have requested the details so we've got a head start there." Said Saunders as he stood and followed his boss.

"Right, Keith, shut the door and sit down."

Saunders followed the instruction.

"We're going to lose all of this if we don't come up with a strong case."

"I know."

"Well, you said you wanted to see me."

"Yes, but it's a bit awkward now, if we're coming off the bookies shops."

"Why?"

"You're not going to believe this..."

"Oh, give me a bit of credit mate. You come up with unbelievable stuff every case! What is it this time?"

"Well... I've managed to get on the mailing list for the people who are trashing the bookies."

Miller laughed loudly. Even by Saunders' standards, this was fucking incredible.

"You what?"

"You heard."

Saunders explained the situation which had developed since joining the online forum a few days earlier. Miller sat and listened with a look of sheer admiration for his DI. Once Saunders had finished, Miller gave him a round of applause.

"That is something else, mate. It really is."

"Yes, but its pretty pointless now, if we have to drop that inquiry and focus exclusively on the fire?"

"Well, no. It's dynamite. If we give these details to Dixon, he's going to go into his meeting with golden tits. With a piece of intelligence like that, he can negotiate anything he wants."

"Suppose."

"You look a bit gutted Keith, I don't get it. This is amazing."

"I know... I know. It's just... I fancied us doing a bit of undercover stuff, you know... going out with them and smashing a few shops up, finding out who was who, getting all the best intelligence from the inside."

"Yes, sure, sounds great, but you couldn't do an undercover gig anyway. It's the price you pay when you're the second-best known detective in Manchester."

"After you?"

"Yes. Second best-looking, too."

"After you?"

"No, Bill Chapman. Anyway, stop sulking, this is the dogs bollocks Keith, I can see you getting a commendation off the back of this."

"Shall I go and get stuck in to finding out who started the fire?"

"Please. We need something urgently. I don't want to lose this case and I'm sure you don't. We were there when they were still damping down, when we could still smell the tragedy."

"I know. Okay, ciao ciao."

Miller smiled as he watched Saunders walk across the office floor. He never ceased to be amazed by the stuff that his DI was capable of pulling up out of thin air. He was reminded that his DI was destined for great things and that it wouldn't be long until he was offered a DCI role somewhere else. The thought thrilled Miller and gutted him at the same time. His department would really miss this talented detective.

"Jammy bastard," said Miller under his breath as he lifted his phone to update Dixon to this incredible opportunity.

Saunders headed straight over to Rudovsky. "Got that bank stuff, Jo?" he asked.

"The DCI is being a bit stroppy. Said she needs clearance from you or Miller before she can proceed."

"Fucks sake," said Saunders as he looked for DCI Katy Green's number in his phone. He sent a text, he couldn't be arsed getting bogged down with a chat. "Hi DCI Green, it's DI Saunders, SCIU. Please forward the Ozols bank details to my colleague DS Rudovsky as requested. Thanks Keith."

"Should have it in a second. She's not being a pain, she just does everything by the book."

"Anal."

"Nah, doubt it. She's a good detective though. A lot better than you."

"Cheers." Rudovsky held her middle-finger up, inches away from Saunders' face.

"Anyway, while we wait, we need to think about that registration plate on the stolen car. If it is still attached to the one in the scrap yard, we need to work out some options that can explain that."

As Saunders finished his sentence, he heard Rudovsky's e-mail notification. "You have e-mail!"

"Okay. Forget that. Go and see what Mr Ozols bank details can tell us."

"Sure. By the way, there was a phone call to the incident room about the number plate of the car, I didn't read it because I got distracted by all the stuff on the news. Someone said they'd seen the car before or something. Like I say, I didn't really read it. Check the logs."

Saunders thanked Rudovsky and logged into his PC and checked the incident room call logs. Sure enough, there was a note on there about the registration plate for the car, but it didn't make a great deal of sense. Saunders decided to phone the caller.

"Hello, Big Baps?"

"Er, hello." Saunders had a weird look on his face. Who the fuck was Big Baps, he was thinking.

"How can I help?" The lady sounded friendly.

"Erm, yes, sorry, I'm a detective sergeant at Manchester City…"

"Oh, hiya! Yes, it was me that called, last night, Tina Parsons. It was the weirdest thing…"

"Go on."

"Well, I was cleaning the café last night while North-West tonight was on…"

"Ah, is this, have I called a café?"

"Yes. Big Baps in Mossley."

"Oh, I see." Saunders was blushing.

"So, yeah, like I say, it was the weirdest thing. As the telly people were talking about this car, I looked up saw a poster on my wall for Radio Cars. It's only the same flipping car, same registration number!"

Saunders was stunned. "Honestly?"

"Swear on my husband's grave. I'm looking at it now. It's MT15 FPG."

Saunders looked across at the photograph of the car on the wall. The registration plate was spot on.

"This is unbelievable."

"I know, I got dead giddy when I saw it. I don't think the copper I phoned understood what I was trying to say."

"No, no the note was a little bit confusing. But it's great news. You wouldn't take a photo of the poster and e-mail it to me, would you?"

"Yes, course. God, it's dead exciting this!"

Saunders gave Tina his e-mail address.

"You'll have to give me five minutes though, I'm rubbish at out like this. I'll have to get one of the girls to help me."

"Yes, well, I'll really appreciate it. I can't tell you how helpful this is!"

"Right love, leave it with me."

"Okay, I'll phone you back when I've got it."

Saunders logged onto Google and searched out "Radio Cars Mossley" and within seconds he was on the cab firm's website. Sure enough, the home-page had a photograph of the Vauxhall Zafira, complete with the number-plates.

"Clever bastards." Muttered Saunders under his breath

as he headed across to Miller's office. He knocked twice before walking straight in.

"Sir, development."

"Oh?"

"Yes. Turns out this cloned number-plate has been nicked off a cab firm's advert. Stick Radio Cars Mossley into your search engine."

"Right..." Miller followed the instruction.

"Now click on the website."

"Fucking hell."

"Yes. That's where they've cloned the plates from. It's nowt to do with the scrap-yard. It's just bad luck that the car is off the road."

"Bloody hell, how have you come up with this?"

"Oh, some woman phoned it in last night. She saw it on the cab firm's poster in her café."

"So, here's another solid local link to the area."

"Precisely."

"Doesn't give us much chance of catching them, though?"

"No. No, I agree with you on that. But it's an extra layer of information that links the people who were in that car to the area."

"Yes, don't get me wrong Keith, it's great. But it's not like we can investigate who has seen this website or the poster and cloned the plates."

"No. Okay, well I'm going to phone the firm anyway, see if I can find anything out about the car. It's pretty young to be scrapped."

"Yeah, but they're on the road twenty-four-hours a day. I imagine it'll have done half a million miles!"

"So, it's a dead end?" Saunders looked as though his sense of momentum was fading.

"Yes. Probably. It's good that you've sussed out how they came about the number-plate. But I can't see how it can progress much from there."

"Fair enough. I'll go and see what Jo's finding out."

"Cheers, I'll tell Dixon though."

"Ta."

Saunders had a bit of a sulk on as he stepped back across the office floor.

"What's up with you? You look like Geri Halliwell has just listening to one of her albums back." Rudovsky was smiling but Saunders ignored the observation.

"Anything?" he asked.

"Cheer up and I'll tell you."

Saunders smiled widely. "Better?"

"Yes. And before we go any further, I thought you said that DCI Green in Tameside was good?"

"She is."

"You said she was better than me!"

"She is."

"Well she's not managed to pick up on the fact that Andris Ozols hasn't paid any rent for the previous four months."

"You what?" Saunders sat down beside Rudovsky.

"Here's his bank statement." Rudovsky handed the document that she had printed out to her DI, several lines were highlighted in fluorescent yellow pen. "Rent goes out every month on the first, every month without fail, all year last year, then all through the beginning of this year. Then, look. Stops dead at the start of May."

"Jesus! How's that been missed?"

"I'll tell you how it's been missed, Sir. Because I'm better than DCI Green. Way better."

"I can't believe this..."

"I'm waiting for a call back from Bingley's Estate Agents in Ashton, they manage the property on the landlord's behalf. Hoping they can shed some light."

"How long ago did you ring them?"

"Ten minutes since."

"Come on, let's get down there."

"Serious?"

"Yes, totally serious Jo. You'd think the small matter of Andris Ozols not paying any rent for five months might have been mentioned by the fucking estate agents at some point. Let's go."

Chapter Thirty-Two

"We are very pleased to welcome the newspaper columnist Greg Harris onto Sky News, good morning Greg."

"Good morning."

"Well, an incredible night. What are your thoughts on the breaking news this morning?"

"Thank you, Andrea. Well, I must firstly point out that what we have witnessed throughout the night is the biggest and most organised riot that this country has ever seen."

"Riot?"

"Absolutely, without any shadow of a doubt. This shocking event has been described as 'attacks' thus far. But what we are actually talking about is a very sophisticated and brilliantly organised riot, one which will cost many millions of pounds to clean up."

"We have of course seen the Tweet by the organisation who are keen to take responsibility for this riot, as you describe it. They appear to be very pleased with the outcome of last night's activities and are promising much more of the same. What are your thoughts on that?"

"I think that it is extremely worrying, not only for the bookmaking industry, but for the British authorities as well and the government will be discussing these matters in the most serious manner this morning. What we have seen here is a brilliant demonstration against government policy and the gambling industry's modern methods of practice, which allows people to feed their gambling addictions without any form of redress."

"Forgive me, Greg, but that statement almost sounds as though you are congratulating the people who have carried out these appalling acts on hundreds of shops last night."

"Well, I wouldn't go as far as that Andrea. But what I am saying is this. There are two ways to go about changing government policy in this country. One way, is to protest and make a great noise about an issue, which will ultimately be ignored anyway, I'll use the Iraq war demonstrations as the case in point. On the fifteenth of February 2003, over a million British citizens marched to demonstrate their opposition to the war. More than a million people cheered, shouted, sounded horns and banged drums, waving signs with slogans 'No War On Iraq' and 'Don't Attack Iraq'. And we all know the outcome of that demonstration. Every single voice was ignored and history has gone on to show us that the government were wrong and that every single protestor was correct. So that's an example of trying to change government policy through the traditional, peaceful channels."

"Okay."

"But let's compare that with the poll tax riots of 1990. I'm sure you are too young to remember the shocking events which unfolded in the Spring of that year?"

"I can just about remember!" said Andrea with a flirtatious smile.

"Well, for those viewers who weren't around then, this was a dark moment in this nation's recent history. This was a full-scale riot, when thousands of protestors fought running battles with the police. They trashed all the shops and businesses around Trafalgar Square, smashing up shops, turning cars upside down, setting fires to shops and restaurants. It was a very ugly event, the police found themselves being pelted with bottles, bricks, huge metal fence panels. It was a very disturbing incident."

"And this was in response to the new poll tax which was being introduced at the time, which is now better known as the council tax?"

"That's absolutely right. And the community tax that we all pay today is an extremely watered-down version of the poll tax which was being proposed in 1990. It is a fair assessment to say that this riot had a huge impact, the government revised their plans, and the Prime Minister of the day, Margaret Thatcher was forced to resign within months. So here we have two very different outcomes. With Iraq, a peaceful civilised protest involving a million people achieved nothing. By contrast, a full-scale riot which caused many millions of pounds worth of damage in London, involving a couple of thousand people, had a much more successful outcome. There are dozens of examples that we could use, such as the Strangeways riot in the same year as the poll tax riot. This single event, which destroyed Manchester's famous Victorian prison in 25 days, achieved much more than the previous two decades of polite protesting at the appalling conditions in the overcrowded jail. Not only that, but that riot led to improved prison conditions throughout the land. So, although it may seem barbaric to say, it is these kinds of activities which bring about change."

"Interesting points Gareth. You do realise that making statements such as these could attract criticism, and even accusations of incitement?"

"Well, I'm not inciting anybody to riot Andrea, I'm merely stating facts. Another fact is that several campaigning groups have been lobbying the government for some years regarding the behaviour of the gambling companies, asking for tighter regulations, particularly around the topic of problem gambling. I make no apologies for stating the facts, and the facts, as we understand them today, is that a group of campaigners have demonstrated that they are determined to bring about change, using the most effective method, which is, and always has been, civil disobedience."

"So, you think that last night's activities…"

"I'd call it a riot, Andrea."

"Okay, but to get to your point, you are suggesting that the group calling themselves Odds on Revenge will succeed in changing the government's regulations on betting?"

"I have absolutely no doubt in my mind that they will be successful, particularly as they are threatening to do the same thing again. I cannot see how any government minister can come out and defend the policy of allowing people to spend every penny they have with online gambling within an hour, when you or I cannot withdraw more than three hundred pounds at a cash point in one day. Make no mistake how dangerous this matter is, when somebody can literally spend all of their money in an online game. Imagine being sucked into a nightmare world where you have lost so much money that your only thought is about winning it back, so you gamble more. There are hundreds, if not thousands of appalling stories out there, about people who have destroyed their entire lives an have even taken their own lives after falling victim to the vicious cycle of gambling addiction. This is a very serious problem, and if we compare gambling addiction to any other serious addiction problem, we will very quickly see that the rules are there in support of the gambling companies, at the cost of the gambler. You could compare it to the drinks industry, which is currently seeing major regulation changes surrounding the price per unit. These are government changes which are designed to help people make better choices about what drinks they use. But it is not all about government intervention, there is a moral aspect to these things as well as the regulation aspect. When Heineken became aware of the enormous health and social problems that their super-strength cider White Lightning was having on its drinkers, they stopped making it. Nobody made them do it, they just realised that this was a bad product which was having very bad consequences for its consumers, so they withdrew the product. I think we can all agree that this was a very good ad responsible decision, which put the public interest above profits. By the same token, it is impossible to defend the gambling industry at a time when they have never been so profitable due to their unashamed marketing tactics and relentless pestering of customers. I cannot imagine Heineken e-mailing customers who were trying to give up drink, offering them a free case of cider. But that is precisely what the gambling companies are doing. Their automatic computer systems recognise when one of their customers hasn't placed a bet for a few days and entices them to gamble using free voucher codes or fifty-pound credits. It is quite diabolical really, and in my opinion, morally indefensible. The NHS have released their own statistics which suggest that this relatively new problem is becoming a major crisis affecting half a million people in the UK. Something urgently needs to be done, and it looks as though Odds on Revenge are determined to see that something is done, once and for all."

"So, what do you suggest that the gambling companies are doing wrong?"

"Well, that's an incredibly complex question Andrea. The simple fact, the statistic which is driving the conversation is a very sobering one. Two people a day are committing suicide because of their problem gambling."

"Good heavens." The news presenter looked visibly shocked.

"If we go back in history, say twenty years ago, thirty years ago, and further, we would not be seeing this tragedy unfolding."

"But gambling is hardly new. The earliest examples of gambling that we are aware of date back to China in 2300 BC. Why now, when human beings are at their most intelligent and sophisticated, are we seeing such a problem?"

"Yes, that's an excellent point you make Andrea. Of course there is a long history of gambling and there have always been gamblers, likewise there have always been heavy gamblers, but we did not see these people killing themselves, certainly not in the numbers that we are seeing today. What we are currently witnessing is a gambling epidemic which takes people to the very edge of their sanity and this behaviour is being actively encouraged, rather than discouraged."

"But why, if the issue is so serious, are the gambling companies continuing down this route?"

"Well, forgive me for saying this Andrea, but that is quite a naïve question. It is about money, nothing else. It is a very new problem which is driven by greed and nothing else. One gambling company owner recently hit the news headlines when it was revealed that she had paid herself a salary of two-hundred and sixty million pounds, for the past year. It is no secret that the gambling firms have a very specific target market. They see young, impressionable, low-income consumers as their golden goose. They know that some young bloke who is struggling or is just about managing financially will be lured into their world by a simple advertisement which suggests that they will have no more financial problems if they sign up now. This is a very slick and organised operation which actively targets this demographic with neon coloured dazzling, exciting adverts which feature bright lights, super-cars, young men having lots of great fun and sexy young women. They are paying third party data companies for the e-mail addresses of people with low incomes. The people affected are targeted out of the blue, usually with a personalised e-mail, which is written by psychologists who know exactly the right words to trigger a reaction. That reaction typically ends up as a financial transaction, and the person who had never even considered gambling before will quickly find that their money problems haven't improved at all, they've actually worsened, and that they will have a very human instinctive reaction to try and win that money back. Safe in this knowledge, the gambling company will e-mail them again, and tell them that they could have twenty-thousands pounds from a free bet, and the person clicks on the offer and they get sucked in again. As I say it is a very sophisticated operation, and it doesn't take a genius to see how the gambling industry is more successful than ever, at a time when people have never had so little disposable income. The sinister part of course, is that the gambling companies know that their product is highly addictive, so they are literally looking for new victims that they can exploit, using very sophisticated means, and the most sinister part is that it is all perfectly legal. It is genius, but it is a very dark and evil kind of genius, in my opinion."

Chapter Thirty-Three

Saunders and Rudovsky entered the offices of Bingley's estate agents in Ashton town centre. Jo still hadn't received a call back from the firm. It was beginning to smell a bit iffy.

"Good morning, we're police. I'm DI Saunders, this is DS Rudovsky. We're from the serious crimes unit."

The young lady on reception looked quite scared. The two senior detectives picked up on her nervousness immediately.

"We need to talk about the property which was destroyed in the fire the other night. Who is the best person…"

"I've told Tim, my boss, he said he'd call you back. But he's gone on an appointment." The young lady sounded extremely insincere. Her voice was quivering and her eyes were all over the place. Whatever it was that was going on with this arson attack, she knew something about it, it was written all over her flushed, panic-stricken face.

"Who is Tim?"

"Tim's the manager. It's his dad's business."

"And are you in a relationship with Tim?" Rudovsky was sharp, and she'd sussed this set-up out already.

"What… I'm, well, yes. But…"

"But what?"

"Well, what's that got to do with anything?"

"Where's Tim now?" Saunders interrupted the discussion with his own question.

"I told you, he's had to…"

"Can you show me his diary?"

"What, well, we don't… he keeps his diary with him." She was a shit liar.

"Bullshit alert."

"Wha…"

"Just to be clear, you don't keep an integrated online diary system, so staff can see where other members of staff are, or when they're already booked in for an appointment? I'd have thought that was a basic requirement in this line of work, unless of course it's actually 1987 and I've imagined the last thirty-odd years?" Saunders was going in hard and Rudovsky was keen to keep the pressure on.

"Can you phone Tim please and tell him to get back to the office toot-sweet?"

"I can't... he's with a client."

"Look love, I'm sure you're aware that we are investigating the murder of three people, and the attempted murder of a fourth, at one of the properties that you manage. So stop mugging us about, phone Tim and tell him to get back here before you end up in the back of my car with a pair of handcuffs around your wrists."

The young lady was in tears as she lifted her mobile, her hand was trembling so violently, it looked as though she might drop the phone. Saunders and Rudovsky looked at one another. They both knew that they had just taken a gigantic step closer towards solving this mystery.

"Tim, yes, the police are here... detectives... no, they are going to arrest me if you don't come back here straight away. I don't know...."

Saunders leaned forward and grabbed the phone out of the receptionist's hand.

"Tim. This is DI Saunders. Can you come straight back to your office right now please?" He pressed the call end button and looked at the screen. The phone number was still lit up. Saunders took a photo of the screen using his own phone, before handing it back to the young woman.

"Jo, just ring comms, get a GPS satellite location for this number. It's 07...."

This was bollocks, but Rudovsky went along with what she was asked, giving the receptionist the impression that she was going outside to call "comms."

"Right, while we get a location for Tim, just in case he isn't on his way back here, let's talk about Andris Ozols."

The young woman just stared back at him, she still looked frightened, so that was good.

"He's a bit behind with his rent, isn't he?"

"I don't..."

"Oh come on! Don't play silly beggars with me. It's only

a small little firm this. What is it, just you and Tim?"

She nodded, and then said, "And his dad. But he's part-time."

"What's he called? The owner?"

"Clive."

"So, it's just you and Tim, and Clive, part-time?"

"Yes."

"And in a business this small, you haven't heard a word mentioned about one of your clients not paying their rent for the past five months?"

Suddenly, the receptionist seemed to grow in confidence. Her next sentence told Saunders that she wasn't taking any flack for any of this, whatever the "this" was. "You need to speak to Tim. Seriously, I'm starting to get a bit pissed off..."

"Not as pissed off as Marija is going to be when she wakes up out of her coma and learns that she's lost her whole family in an arson attack, and that her face was so badly burnt, they've been taking skin grafts off her buttocks to try and rebuild it."

She just stared ahead, her eyes were filling with tears and her chin was quivering. She had no reply to that powerful come-back. There was a tense silence as Rudovsky stepped back inside the shop.

"Sorted?"

"Yes, they're scanning him now."

Suddenly, a stressed-out, but smart looking young man walked into the shop.

"Look, listen... this..."

"Ah, you must be Tim!" announced Rudovsky theatrically. "Where was the meeting with your client, next-door-but-one?"

"Yes, yes, I'm Tim, but, we're in serious danger. Listen, I can't help you with this unless you help me." Tim's eyes were sincere, he looked genuine and he looked scared.

"What's..."

"I need you to do a full raid, I mean the full works, police cars, vans, sniffer-dogs, armed police. I need every single person in Ashton going on Facebook asking what's going on at my shop. Please, my life is in danger if you don't do this." Sweat was pouring from Tim's face as he spoke. Saunders and Rudovsky recognised immediately that this bloke wasn't a criminal. But he was definitely scared of criminals. They'd seen this look of terror on folk before.

"Deal. I'll give you the full treatment, I'll try and get the chopper up as well if that helps. But you need to give me the file on who owns on that house."

"How do I know I can trust you?"

"Because I've just agreed to what you've asked, rather than arrest you and take you down to the station in my unmarked car and then come back here and raid your offices."

"Oh..."

Saunders liked this young guy, and he wanted to help him. The DI suddenly felt as though he understood what was going on.

"Please, make your call and I'll give you everything. But I need people to see that this was a police raid or it'll be my house next."

Saunders lifted his phone out of his pocket. He dialled Miller.

"Ah, DI Saunders! Nipped out for a fry-up without inviting me?"

"Alright boss. No, me and Jo are in Ashton, literally a couple of minutes away from arresting the people behind the fire."

"You what? I thought you were looking at bank statements."

"Long story. We're in Ashton. Have you got a pen?"

"Yes."

"Right, it's Bingley's Estate Agents, Cavendish Street, OL6 7DB."

"Go on."

"We need a big police drama at this address, it's the offices of the estate agents who were managing the Ozols address."

"Okay?"

"The manager is willing to help us, but he's worried about repercussions if it doesn't look like a full-on police raid, out-of-the-blue."

"Has this got legs?"

"Yes Sir, and knees and toes."

"Leave it with me. Are you staying at the address?"

"Yes Sir."

"Nice one. I'm on it." Miller hung up.

Saunders looked at Tim. "Right. Sorted. Now let's have this information."

"Am I going to be arrested?" asked Tim.

"I don't know yet. Depends what you've done."

"He hasn't done fuck all!" shouted the receptionist, her emotions getting the better of her. Emotions were starting to get the better of Tim too, tears were rolling down his cheeks.

"Shut up a minute Charlotte. Listen, we've been praying for this moment, since we first heard about the fire. We thought this place would be next... or our house." Tim was completely genuine. Both Saunders and Rudovsky could spot a liar a mile away. Tim wasn't one.

"Are you saying you want to be arrested?"

"No, I... I don't know. If I'm seen to be arrested, well, it might look like I've grassed. But if you guys just burst in here and make a big scene... removing files and computers and stuff, well, I don't know. Like I say, I've never been caught up in any of this type of thing before."

"Right, let's sit down while we wait for the drama, and you can tell us what's going on." Rudovsky grabbed Tim's arm gently and guided him back to the row of red seats in front of the window.

"Let's start at the beginning. Andris Ozols hasn't paid his rent since May. Why?"

"Because his boiler wasn't working. He's had no hot water."

It was clear from the look on Saunders' face that this wasn't the answer he had anticipated. "Okay. And presumably, your job as the tenancy manager is to see that work like that is carried out?"

"Yes, naturally."

"But it wasn't?"

"No. The landlord refused to pay to fix the boiler, he said it's the middle of summer, it can wait."

"And Andris Ozols presumably said that the rent can also wait?"

"That's pretty much it. Only…"

"Go on."

"Well, I loved these guys, they were my best tenants without a shadow of doubt. Andris and Marija have been in here half a dozen times about this broken boiler issue." Tim's eyes started filling up with tears again. He wiped them away with his sleeve, but the emotion was still clear in his voice as spoke. "They were brilliant tenants, honestly. They were lovely people. And… the kids were so lovely… well, I couldn't do anything about this awful situation with the boiler, I explained that it was the landlord's responsibility. So Andris asked me to find him a different landlord, which I did."

"You did?" Rudovsky sounded surprised.

"Yes, I didn't agree with this attitude of the landlord's either and Andris knew that."

"So, what happened?"

"Well, I found them a property, a house on St Annes estate, so they were really excited, they were finally going to have a garden for the kids to play in and it was nearer to the kids school and the rent wasn't that much more. Everything was looking great. But…"

"What?"

"A couple of days before the fire, Andris e-mailed the landlord. He blind-copied me into it so I was aware, and said that he was moving out at weekend, and that basically, if he thinks he's getting his back-rent, he must be living in a dream-world. Something like that." Tim started crying, he leant forward into a foetal position with his head between his knees. His shoulders and his back were heaving as the tears ran freely, dropping onto his well-shined shoes. "If he hadn't sent that e-mail… God! He…he could have just done a midnight flit."

"Jesus. Is that all this was about?" Saunders looked

shocked.

"Yes. Fucking sick bastard." It was Charlotte who was speaking now. Tim was too upset to continue. Rudovsky stroked his back, gently, she could feel the raw tremors of emotion coming through his suit jacket.

"You say you feared for your own safety after this. Was this because of the e-mail?"

Tim was still in a state but he nodded to confirm. After a big sniff, he lifted his head slightly. "It wasn't the e-mail so much, I don't think the landlord knew I was blind-copied. But obviously, he knows that I know about the problems with the rent. I've not slept since I heard about it, waiting for something terrible to happen."

"Well, don't worry Tim. We've got this now. I think it will be an idea to give us that file now, so we can arrest this person before he gets wind of your offices being busted. It'll be a shame to give him a head-start." Saunders' phone was vibrating in his pocket. He held his hand up as he took his phone out of his pocket. "One-sec." He pressed the answer icon. It was Miller.

"Hi Sir."

"Alright, I've got DCI Green setting up a raid now, she thinks its going to take a good half-an-hour to sort out."

"Half an hour?"

"Yes, there was a big job on earlier apparently so Tameside haven't got a lot of bodies. Anyway, it's happening, she's on it. So, what can you tell me?"

"One sec, Sir. Tim, can you please get me the name and address of the landlord please mate."

Tim stood slowly and wiped his tears away again. He looked like shit.

"What's going on?" asked Miller.

"I need a real raid to happen, have you got a pen?"

"Go on."

Tim returned from the tiny office at the side of the reception desk and handed over the file for the address in Denton, his hand was visibly shaking as he did so. Saunders placed the battered old folder on the reception desk and opened it. Tim pointed at the information that the detective was looking for.

"Okay Sir, prime suspect for the fatal fire in Denton. This individual and any associates or family members at the address should be arrested at the earliest opportunity. He's called Adrian Wilson, address is fifteen, that's one-five Sterling Street, Guide Bridge, OL7 0HN. I think we need to move quickly on this, Sir."

"Anything else?"

"Tim, anything else we need to know? Is he likely to be home?"

It was quite clear that Tim was shitting himself. This was too much and it was obvious that he was worried about how deeply he was becoming embroiled in this horrific situation.

Saunders read the signs and decided to take the pressure off the estate agent. He knew that Miller would quickly find out everything he needed to know just from the name and address. "Yes, I think that's all we know about him. I trust you'll find more out on the PNC."

"Well, this is a turn-up Keith. I'm looking forward to hearing how the fucking-hell this all came about. Speak later."

"Cheers."

"Okay, that's my boss informed. You'll both be able to relax soon."

"Listen, I know this is all very intense at the minute. But you'll be fine. You'll see." Rudovsky was trying to calm the stressed-out couple. She could see they were expecting the place to be fire-bombed at any moment.

*****

"Hi Sir."

"Andy, got anything for me?"

"Are you sitting down?"

"Yes. Why?"

"I've got the name and address of the person we believe is responsible for the fire."

There was a pregnant silence. DCS Dixon sounded as

stunned by this extraordinary outcome as Miller had upon taking Saunders' call earlier. "Go on?" said Dixon, finally.

"I don't know the exact details, this is very much a live operation at this moment Sir. But it's come in from Saunders and Rudovsky so it'll be right."

"What do you need?"

"ARU and Tactical Aid on blue lights right now. The address is in Ashton but Tameside are all tied up on another job connected to this so it will have to be either Stockport or Manchester division."

"Understood. Address?"

Miller gave his boss the particulars and ended the call by reminding Dixon that this information required a grade one response.

Miller called DCI Katy Green at Tameside and told her to stand-by with the raid on the estate agents.

"What the hell is going on?" she asked grumpily. She sounded extremely frustrated.

"I don't know the specifics, I'm in my office. But I think your job is a decoy. DCS Dixon is arranging a grade-one response at the home of the prime suspect for the fire." That shut her up.

"Oh, right. Well it would be nice to be kept informed."

"I am informing you now. You know as much as me. Anyway, got to go, I'll phone you back when you're clear to proceed." Miller hung up. He'd really warmed to DCI Green at first, but now that initial positivity was cooling. Miller was beginning to realise why she was so good at managing her team. She was a total ball-breaker.

Miller raced out of his office and shouted his officers. "Guys, stop what you're doing please. Time to make some arrests for the fire."

The SCIU team members looked stunned. That enormous announcement had literally come from nowhere.

"Chapman, Worthington, you travel in your car. Kenyon, Grant, you can jump in with me. Come on let's go, blue lights and sirens to Guide Bridge."

Chapter Thirty-Four

As the convoy of police vehicles approached the address, they were ordered to kill the blues and twos. The last thing anybody needed was the suspect receiving a tip-off that he was about to get a visit from over thirty police officers, some of which would be wearing riot gear, whilst the others would be holding loaded guns or barking dogs.

The vehicles pulled up quietly around the corner from the address. This area of Manchester was predominantly made up of the old Coronation Street style terraces. Fortunately, these types of streets were the perfect kind of address for a police operation of this nature, as a solid police presence around the front and back made it extremely easy for kettling a suspect inside their own home.

There was no messing about, every officer had been briefed on the way to the job. They all knew exactly what was required, so within seconds of the vehicles being parked up out of sight of the address, the van doors slid open and the officers filed out, running straight to their specified locations. The first team of TA officers, fully suited up in their helmets and riot gear ran along the junction at the top of the street and headed down the back ginnel behind the suspects address. A few seconds later, every officer's radio crackled alive.

"Rear of property secured, over."

On that, the rest of the police officers headed down to the street, running the short distance to number 15 Sterling Street, the home of Adrian Wilson. Two ARU officers followed, carrying their Heckler and Koch firearms proudly across their chests.

"Standby." Said the TA Sergeant as the officers assembled in single file along the front doors and windows of neighbouring properties. The silence on the street was eerie, but that was soon to change with the next instruction from the sergeant.

"Engage."

Upon hearing this instruction, the TA officer carrying the "big red key" stepped forward and gave the battering ram an almighty swing at the front door. The wooden door flew open on impact, which was always satisfying for the officers. The armed police stepped forward and walked into the address with their guns pointed.

"ARMED POLICE!"

"GET DOWN ON THE FLOOR!!"

Inside the property, a fat, middle aged man with frizzy grey hair was sitting in his armchair, the sudden intrusion clearly came as a huge shock as the drink in his hand had jumped out of his cup and was being worn down the front of his t-shirt.

"GET DOWN ON THE FLOOR!" Screamed the firearms officer as the TA officers began filing noisily and boisterously into the living room. The fat man did as he was told, kneeling slowly from his seated position and then slowly making his way onto the floor. It sounded as though he was sobbing.

"ARMS BEHIND YOUR BACK."

With the fat man's arms placed on the small of his back, he was quickly cuffed by the sergeant.

"WHAT'S YOUR NAME?"

"Adrian... Wilson..."

"WHO ELSE IS IN THE PROPERTY?"

"No-one."

The suspect was left on the floor for several minutes whilst police officers checked every room in the address for other people. They quickly established that Wilson had been telling the truth, there was only the suspect in the address. The huge police presence very quickly slipped away, as officers were stood down and advised to return to their units and back to their respective divisions. As they returned to their vans, minibuses and cars, it seemed that the whole neighbourhood had come out, people standing in their doorways or glimpsing out from behind net curtains. A significant crowd was gathering at the end of the street, not far from the police vehicles. Many of the spectators were taking photos and videos of the drama on their phones.

One of the neighbours had a theory already. "It's a fucking terrorist raid! Our Susan always said he was a fucking Javadi, that one." Said one of the ladies in the general direction the crowd.

A few minutes after all of the drama had unfolded, an MCP custody van pulled out of the convoy and headed down Sterling Street, its driver blaring the siren as it parked up outside number 15, alerting the TA officers inside that Mr Wilson's lift had arrived.

"You should be ashamed of yourself! Fucking muslamic bastard!" shouted the woman in the direction of the police van. Several of the by-standers looked at her quizzically.

"He's white. And he looks like he lives off bacon butties." Commented another member of the group, to much amusement.

Moments after the overweight, scruffy looking white man was locked in the van, the police van pulled off and headed down the street slowly, before turning left and disappearing out of sight. Not long after, several of the other police vehicles set off in the same direction, this unexpected commotion resulted in some impressive videos for Facebook.

Miller arrived a couple of minutes later, with his officers right behind him. The scene that he found in the house was one of relative calm and tranquillity. The TV was still on, and it looked as though the man suspected to be responsible for the tragic and devastating fire a few miles up the road in Denton, had been watching "A Place in The Sun" on television whilst eating chocolate digestives with a cup of tea.

"Don't touch anything." Said Miller.

"We know how a crime scene works boss!" said Worthington.

"I know. But that comment was directed at Bill when I saw those biscuits."

Chapman leant forward and pretended to take one, which received a good laugh. The tense drive here had heightened everybody's mood. It felt good to relax now, safe in the knowledge that Manchester's most wanted had been arrested and it had all passed off peacefully.

"So, it looks like the man behind the arson attack is in custody. I can't wait to see what Saunders and Rudovsky have got on him. But while we're here, let's have a snoop about, see what we can find out."

The SCIU officers had a quick look around the small, two-bedroomed house. There were just two rooms downstairs, the living room was at the front of the property and the kitchen was situated at the back. The place was quite tidy, but the décor was tired. It instantly presented as a single man's address, there were no feminine touches around the place and it didn't look as though there was much money knocking about either. The bread on the kitchen work-top was the supermarket's budget brand and the kitchen lino had a big hole in the middle which was covered with brown parcel packing tape. There was a dirty pan in the sink, the contents of which were dried hard inside. It felt very cold and lonely in there. Miller stepped on the pedal-bin lever and its contents were exposed. It was filled with empty cider cans.

"Okay, I think I've seen enough, it makes me feel a bit sad this place. Let's go and see what intelligence we can find out about this chap. Helen, can you get on to Tameside nick and sort out a thorough SOCO examination?"

"Sir."

"Bill, you find out which nick they've taken the suspect to."

"Yes Sir."

"I need to ring Dixon."

Chapter Thirty-Five

DCS Dixon's meeting with the Chief Constable, the Assistant Chief Constables and the Greater Manchester Police and Crime Commissioner had been postponed for one hour, subject to the outcome of the very live developments which were unfolding. It looked like it was going to be positive news as far as the arson attack was concerned. The issue of the over-night bookies attacks still remained, but that wasn't MCP's major concern at this moment in time, not now that there was some compelling evidence which backed up Miller's view that the shop attacks and the fire were two separate things. It was certainly looking like that theory was coming up trumps.

But there was still a great deal of confusion and speculation about the matter. The only people who really knew exactly what was going on were the four people standing inside an estate-agents shop on the outskirts of Ashton town centre, waiting for a very public raid and the very public arrest of its manager, Tim Bingley. It was all arranged, and Tim was in agreement that it was for the greater good. Saunders had come to the conclusion that if the suspect had been arrested first, which Miller had now confirmed, then there was absolutely no reason not to carry-out a fake arrest on Tim Bingley, and his partner Charlotte. This event, coming after Adrian Wilson's arrest, would make a very authentic smoke-screen intended to shut down any "grass" claims before they could even get started.

It was all arranged. Bingley would be dragged about in the street, then thrown in the back of a police van, then after arriving at Ashton nick, he'd be given a brew and a look around the police station, before being released without charge a few hours later, with a press release apologising for MCP's "heavy-handed" arrest and an acknowledgement that his arrest had been based on incorrect information. It all made perfect sense, and the timeline of the events would prove to any of Wilson's associates that any "tip-off" which had resulted in all of this had nothing at all to do with Tim Bingley.

One hour after the drama on Sterling Street, close to

the border of Ashton and Denton, the fake police raid commenced on Cavendish Street in Ashton town centre, in the most unrestrained of circumstances.

The news broke, as it so often does, on Facebook. The Tameside Hangout page, which had twenty-five thousand members went crazy for the dramatic story.

"What the fuck is going off in Tameside today? First a million police storm an house in Guide Bridge, and now there's a million of them in the town centre raiding an estate agents!!!!"

"Chopper's up as well. Can hear it from here."

"Armed response, sniffer dogs, tactical aid, they're all out. Something proper big is going down!"

One member of the group posted a shaky video from their mobile phone. It was hard to make-out what was going on with all of the police officers running about, the shouting and the deafening roar of the police helicopter overhead, but the person who had taken this footage zoomed in on the pavement outside the shop where two people were laid down being handcuffed. One thing was abundantly clear; the police were not messing about. The man looked distressed, but the woman in the footage was screaming and struggling, shouting "fuck off me now! Fuck off me!"

It seemed that everybody in the Facebook group was watching the video, as it kept stalling and buffering. But the nosey neighbours of Tameside persevered and waited for the next few seconds of film to load on their Facebook feed.

Once people had watched the thirty-five second clip, it didn't take long for all the gossiping to start-up again.

"That's Tim Bingley they are arresting! From Bingley's estate agents. WTF is going on???"

"It's his girlfriend as well."

"She's fit."

"She seems a bit moody though!" added one joker.

"Not being funny right, but I rent my house off him, he's a proper nice bloke. This is mistook identification."

"Someone said they were planning to shoot the Prime Minister!!!!"

The Facebook debate continued, while fresh videos of

the incident continued to appear on the social media platforms. It didn't take long for the local press to learn about this extraordinary action on the streets of Ashton-Under-Lyne and headed off to try and find some factual explanations for the events which were unfolding this morning. Thankfully, MCP's press office were all ready with a statement, which was published on the press-office section of their website within seconds of the raid on the estate agents commencing.

This story was about to become much bigger than the Tameside Hangout group members could possibly have anticipated. This was not just a local story, the official police statement was to have a major impact on the national news headlines.

"MCP OFFICIAL PRESS STATEMENT

This morning, our officers arrested a number of people in connection with the fatal arson attack on Seymour Street in Denton during the early hours of the seventeenth of November. This incident resulted in the murder of three members of the Ozols Family and the attempted murder of a fourth.

MCP would like to reassure the local community that the high-visibility raids today were in connection with this major investigation and would like to thank the public for their patience and understanding whilst these arrests were made. We cannot reveal the identities of the people arrested at this stage and would remind the public that naming people on social media may result in you committing a criminal offence. We are not connecting these suspects to the betting shop incidents which have taken place in the past twenty-four hours, nor the previous four incidents which have occurred in Greater Manchester over previous weeks. WE WILL PROVIDE MORE INFORMATION REGARDING THIS ONGOING INVESTIGATION LATER."

*****

"We need to leave it there Lisa, sorry. Some breaking news now on Sky and a statement has just been released by Manchester City Police." The newsreader read out the statement from MCP, whilst the TV screen showed the dramatic footage of the raids, taken from Facebook. The news editors had blurred out the faces of the people arrested, but this didn't downgrade the level of drama in each video as dozens of police officers were seen storming the small shop, and a woman lay on the floor screaming, with an officer knelt on her back. Her words were bleeped out.

"Joining me on the line is retired Detective Superintendent Ken Chiswick, Ken, what's your reaction to this breaking news story?"

"Ah, yes, good morning. Well, I think we can all agree that this is good news, if charges are brought of course."

"It seems like a very powerful police presence in Manchester this morning. Is it normal to see so many officers deployed on an operation such as this one?"

"I think so. Let's not forget the heinous crime that these individuals are allegedly involved with. The murder of children, as they slept in their beds is about as dark as crime gets, so no, under the circumstances, I am not surprised that MCP have deployed this amount of officers and have thrown absolutely everything at making sure that the arrests went ahead smoothly. They wouldn't have wanted to get a single aspect of this operation wrong."

"What can you tell us about the timing of these arrests, bearing in mind last night's nation-wide public disorder surrounding betting shops?"

"I think that MCP's hierarchy will be taking a huge sigh of relief this morning, the pressure to find the arsonists responsible for this tragedy will have been quite overwhelming over the past few days. I think they will be hoping beyond all hope that they have taken the correct people into custody."

All of the news channels were broadcasting the same BREAKING NEWS story. This was high-octane stuff, and a very welcome development to all of the news broadcasters, who had by now been getting a little bit bored of reporting live from smashed up betting shops up and down the country, especially as they didn't have an official "line" nor a dedicated spokesperson from the police or the Home Office to focus their attentions onto. That story, as sensational as it was, had remained stuck in limbo for several hours as no "official" wanted to step forward and claim ownership of it, at least not yet.

The timing of MCP's press release was excellent content for the broadcasters and newspapers, it was finally official that the fire which had broken the hearts of the nation was not part of the extraordinary developments throughout the night. That realisation also downgraded the seriousness of the betting shop attacks considerably. Now that people could make a clear distinction between the two separate things, it began to appear that most people weren't massively concerned about the shops and the damage that had been done to them. There was just a sense of relief that the arsonists were off the streets and would face justice for the appalling crime that had been committed just three nights earlier.

Chapter Thirty-Six

"Right, I think you'd better tell me what in God's name has gone on!" Miller had a huge smile on his face as he met up with Saunders and Rudovsky. It didn't take them long to explain the circumstances of how they had ended up with Manchester's most wanted suspect in a cell before brew-time.

Rudovsky took great delight in rubbing it in that Tameside CID had failed to spot the missing rent payments on Andris Ozols' bank statement, mainly because she was standing in Tameside CID's offices, within ear-shot of DCI Katy Green who, In Rudovsky's opinion, deserved the ribbing after she had started the day being a dick with her.

"Jesus. This is the jammiest arrest of all time, and I really do mean all-time!" Miller was buzzing, this was an incredible outcome.

"Hey! Cheeky bastard. Good solid detective work is what led us to this point. Job's not done yet though, there were four of them on that motorway, we've still got three of these twisted fuckers to pull in." Rudovsky looked keen to get to work, she wasn't a fan of back-patting when there was still plenty more to do.

"We're sure that it's right, though?" Miller suddenly looked serious, for the first time since he'd entered the office.

Saunders answered. "Nearly almost a hundred per-cent. We've got a motive, as stupid and pointless as it was, plus the damning question mark over Adrian Wilson's property being the most famous burnt-out property in Great Britain, yet he hasn't even phoned the estate agent about it. We'll have to see what he's got to say when we go in."

"Got a plan?"

"Yes, working on it now. We just need evidence of him out and about on the night of the fire, so we've got the details for his motor and we're just waiting to run it through ANPR, see if anything turns up."

"We'll need more than ANPR."

"Relax, boss. We've got this." Rudovsky seemed a bit pissed off that Miller was wading in and throwing bad vibes into the mix, particularly as the ground work had been done without his input.

"Sorry, yes, it's just... I didn't get the impression from the guy's house that he's the right man."

"Why?" It was Saunders and Rudovsky's turn to look a little concerned.

"Don't know. Can't put my finger on it. It just seemed a bit, I don't know. Not the kind of bloke who can sort out nicking cars, getting fake plates made up, or..."

"Or what?"

"Or even having any mates to go and do all that with him. It just seemed like a very lonely house, lots of cider cans in the bin."

"Well, maybe he's turned to cider to blot out the fucking evil that he's responsible for. It's him, I'll bet my next two wage packets on it. The estate agent is terrified of him and he's very wary of what he says. Besides, my gut feeling is always spot on. If I had any doubts..."

"I know... I know. It's just, I need to update Dixon, pretty sharpish. There's a lot riding on this, I need to be totally convinced that the information I'm presenting to him is legit."

"Well just tell him that we need a couple more hours and we'll have a bomb-proof charge sheet ready for the CPS."

"A couple of hours?" Miller glanced at his watch.

"A day, then." Rudovsky's massive upgrade to the time scales received a big laugh from her colleagues.

"You want twenty-four hours cooling off period?"

"Look, boss, it's your call. But all I'm saying is, we've got the man who owns the flat in custody. He's been playing dickheads with the Ozols family for months and now they announce they are moving out of his property, and he isn't getting his back-rent, the place burns down in a fire-bomb attack and the man we have in custody hasn't even lifted the phone to police or the estate agents to ask what the fuck is going on. That's enough of a starting point for me, Sir."

Rudovsky's passionate speech worked. Miller's face relaxed as the skilfully presented monologue painted a rational overview of the facts as they were presently known.

"Okay. That's a reasonable point of view to present. I'll go and see Dixon now while you guys figure out the next stage of this investigation."

"Well I've got it pretty much sussed Sir." It was Saunders' turn to speak. "We need to build up a full picture of Adrian Wilson, his lifestyle and history, criminal past or associations. We'll get back what we can from ANPR on Wilson's vehicle while his house is getting the full-works from Forensics, every finger-print in the address will need explaining, as will every trace of DNA. His computer, his phone and laptop have been seized and are being examined now, IT investigators will be looking through e-mails, phone contacts, text messages etc. We'll work out who his accomplices are and build up a solid picture. All the while, he'll be sat in the cell stewing it over. He's been booked in now and he's already asked for a solicitor, so he knows that there's going to be some turbulence ahead."

"Any thoughts about the interview?"

"I think we'll set all these wheels in motion first, then let Jo give him a few things to think about in the interview room, and once all that is completed, we'll have a charge sheet good to go."

"Fair enough. I'll pass that onto Dixon, there's not too much to complain about there, looks like you guys are on it." Miller looked happy again.

"Cheers."

"Thanks Sir."

"I'll go back to HQ and organise the troops, so e-mail me what tasks you want doing at our end and I'll give you a call in a few hours to see how things are progressing."

With that, Miller turned and set off walking out of the office, bidding farewell to DCI Katy Green as he went.

*****

ANPR technology has revolutionised police work in the UK over the past decade. The automatic number plate recognition system has been at the heart of intelligence gathering by the authorities for a variety of sophisticated reasons. As far as the general public are concerned, ANPR is just an easy way for the police to do people for not possessing car insurance or a valid MOT. But this is only one of the advantages of the technology, and by no means the main reason that millions of pounds are invested each year in installing thousands of new cameras in every part of the UK.

Very little is known about the locations of ANPR cameras. They are not required to be "hi-vis" like the speed trap cameras. They are in fact, quite the opposite, and their fixed locations are kept secret, to such an extent that their locations cannot even be disclosed in court-cases, even if the information provided by the ANPR is the strongest piece of evidence in the prosecution's case. The technology is only allowed to be used to assist the police to build cases and provide clues. The rest of the story has to be told by good, old-fashioned detective work on the ground.

Many police forces have found so much benefit from the ANPR technology that they have installed the cameras into retired undercover vehicles, and park them in locations which are recognised crime hot-spots. These discreet vehicles keep a constant eye on every vehicle going in and out of an area, which in turn helps the police to understand who is behind drug dealing activities, or burglaries, or terror-related activities and as such, these hidden cameras make life very hard for people who are up to no good.

With this remote, automated and completely undercover police work taking place by computer software, it enables police officers to identify who is who, what they are up to, and can carry out investigations into people without even making an arrest. It is this power that ANPR technology has unleashed which makes the scheme so shrouded in secrecy. You cannot go into a city-centre without your vehicle details being logged, nor travel more than ten miles without being "pinged" by one of these invisible devices.

It is not just used for criminal investigation, either. Supermarket car-parks have installed ANPR cameras to help make sure that visitors don't stay longer than the two-hours permitted. If they do overstay their welcome, Tesco, or

Sainsburys buy the car owner's details from the DVLA and send out a £100 fine in the post. It is almost as though George Orwell gave the authorities the idea for this incredible surveillance system himself. The only down-side was that they had to wait the fifty or so years for the technology to arrive.

Today, MCP's ANPR software was being asked to look into the activities of a certain Mr Adrian Wilson of 15 Sterling Street, Guide Bridge. His vehicle, a black Ford Mondeo, registration, BK12 JBC was having its past twelve months of activity scrutinised by the software.

Extremely good news came in quickly. The vehicle was active on the night of the fire, for several hours before, and several hours after. The vehicle had pinged a number of cameras near Hyde, close to the location where the Vauxhall Zafira was burned out. It also pinged a camera at the all-night McDonalds in Ashton, where it stayed for twenty-five minutes between 2:18 and 2:43am, before passing several other cameras around the Tameside district in the following hour. The vehicle, it appeared, hadn't been used again since the early hours of the night of the fire.

In short, what the ANPR logs told DI Saunders and DS Rudovsky was, to put it bluntly, that Adrian Wilson was well and truly fucked. They high-fived each other as they headed out of the small office that they'd been "hot-desking" in Tameside CID dept, their next location was McDonalds, about five minutes around the corner.

*****

Less than an hour later, DI Saunders and DS Rudovsky were back at Ashton police station, sitting in interview room 2, face to face for the first time with Adrian Wilson and his duty solicitor. Once all of the interview room formalities were out of the way, it was finally time to see what kind of opponent Adrian Wilson was likely to make for the SCIU senior detectives.

"You have been arrested on suspicion of three counts of murder and one charge of attempted murder. Do you understand the reason that you are here?" asked Saunders, who was taking care of this section whilst Rudovsky planned her strategy.

"No comment."

"Are you the owner of the property at the junction of Seymour Street and Windmill Lane, which was destroyed by fire in the early hours of Monday morning?"

"No comment." Adrian Wilson looked scared, and stressed, but defiant none-the-less.

"Either you own it or you do not?"

"No comment."

"Can you tell me your activities on the night of Sunday 16th of November, into the early hours of Monday the 17th of November?"

"No comment."

"Did you go out at all on Sunday evening, or in the early hours of Monday?"

"No comment."

"Okay, I can see that your solicitor has advised you to provide a no comment interview, so we know the score. You know that you don't have to answer our questions and all that, so don't worry, we won't take very much more of your time up at this stage."

This comment appeared to induce a flicker of something on Wilson's face. Rudovsky was studying him closely, but she couldn't be sure what that flicker was, whether it was relief, or humour, or what. But Saunders' rather vague comment about Wilson's time had certainly gained a positive reaction.

Rudovsky decided to chuck the hand-grenade in.

"Sorry Detective Inspector Saunders," said the DS. "Before you make plans to release Mr Wilson..." that flicker of something in the suspect's face was there again. It was a conceited look that she'd seen so many times before on arseholes who were getting away with stuff because the police didn't quite have enough evidence to charge them. The difference on this occasion was that Saunders had just been toying with Wilson. The horrible bastard wasn't going anywhere.

Rudovsky genuinely couldn't wait to slam that smug, piss-taking look into reverse. "...I just wanted to ask Mr Watson a few questions about these photographs." Rudovsky took her time opening the A4 wallet on the desk, before taking a similarly relaxed amount of time taking the photographs out of the folder. She began placing them on the table-top, facing Adrian Wilson.

"These photographs show yourself and three other men enjoying a laugh and a Big Mac meal at a McDonald's restaurant, not very far away from here. Could you please confirm that this person is you?" Rudovsky pointed at the blatantly clear photograph of Wilson. He looked a bit unnerved by this sudden change of direction in the proceedings.

"No comment." He sounded stressed as he said it.

"What about these people? Any idea who they are?"

"No comment." He didn't look at the pictures.

"For the benefit of the tape, these photographs are stills taken from the McDonalds CCTV. The time that these images were captured are two-twenty-one, two-twenty-seven and two thirty-three am, respectively. This was just over an hour after the fatal fire at Mr Wilson's property in Denton. Do you still not recognise any of these people Mr Wilson?"

The suspect took a long time to reply this time, but eventually he did. "No comment."

Rudovsky noted that the flicker of smugness had been extinguished, which pleased her greatly. Her detective experience told her that in these circumstances, nobody, other than a guilty person, would sit and no comment a question like this. Miller had been wrong in his assertion that Wilson didn't "seem right" and she couldn't wait to get out of here and show him the proof.

"We do have the full video of this very jolly and humorous encounter. It does look like you and your mates are having a bloody good laugh here..."

"No comment."

"Would you like to watch the full video?"

"No comment."

"Now, I know this is going to sound bonkers. But, did you pay for this food on your debit card?"

"No comment."

The solicitor huffed loudly, it was clear that he'd been fed a load of bullshit by Wilson thus far and now he was seeing the true magnitude of what his client was involved with. The sound of the huff suggested that Wilson was going to have to find another solicitor, pretty soon.

Rudovsky pulled out another photograph and placed it with the others on the table. "Is this you, paying for food at McDonalds, using contactless?"

Wilson refused to look at the picture. "No comment."

"Do you think that when we seize your bank details, your statement will show a purchase from McDonalds at two-twenty-three hours on the seventeenth of November?"

"No comment."

"I think that's enough for now, DS Rudovsky." Saunders began collecting the pictures off the table. The DS knew what her superior's tone of voice implied. It implied that she should go in for the kill.

"Okay, well, I'm not saying that this is you, or it isn't, that will be for the jury to decide. But what I will say Mr Wilson, is that if you think you're going to get away with this, as your no commenting suggests, then you really are as thick as your own shit, aren't you?"

"No comment."

"See you on Britain's dumbest child-killers, you sick, evil, depraved bastard."

"Interview suspended at 13.01 hours. Mr Wilson will be taken back to his cell as our enquiries continue. Thank you."

Wilson's solicitor stood, nodded politely towards the detectives and walked out of the room without so much as a glance at Wilson. That smug look was well and truly gone from the suspect's face.

Chapter Thirty-Seven

"And... breathe..." Rudovsky was pleased with how that had gone, it was always a pleasure to mess with evil people. She and Saunders were walking towards the Tameside CID office after escorting Wilson back to the custody sergeant, who was going to bang him up in a cell, for the first night of the rest of his life.

"Reckon Miller's managed to get anything from the McDonald's CCTV yet?" Asked Saunders.

"Hope so, but if not, he can stick the faces on a press release. It won't take long to round those bastards up. I'm more interested in letting Tim and Charlotte go now, I bet they're ready for home."

"We'll need to sort out an announcement first. They might have trouble at the door when they get home." Saunders was concerned, he knew that the public were often keen to take the law into their own hands, particularly on a case such as this.

"Miller's on it. The press release will have gone out by now. Anyway, I was talking to them both before we went in with Wilson. Tim says he's going to check them into a hotel and stay there until we've got the others banged up. Just to be safe."

"Bloody hell, where was I while all this was going on?" Saunders looked mildly irritated at the realisation that he was out of the loop.

"You were flirting with that DCI Green."

"I wasn't flirting! God, you boil my piss sometimes Jo!"

"Okay, well, you were talking to DCI Green, whilst blushing and fidgeting with your hair and laughing at her every sentence, the whole fucking time. It was excruciating to witness."

"Bollocks. Anyway, what was said with Miller?"

"Basically, he said that he was sending out an urgent press release which would explain that the arrests of Tim and Charlotte were a mistake, with an unreserved apology for any distress caused, and an offer of compensation for any damage at the office."

"Sounds good."

"He also told me to send the CCTV from McDonalds over as a matter of urgency and he'd get the geeks to run it through the automatic facial recognition system and see if any of the three have any snaps on the PNC."

"Heard anything on that?"

"Not yet, but he's only had forty-five minutes."

Saunders was scrolling through his phone. He stopped in the corridor as he found what he'd been looking for.

"Ah, here we go. The press statement has gone out."

"Let's have a look."

Saunders and Rudovsky stayed rooted to the spot as they both read MCP's press release about Tim and Charlotte.

"URGENT PRESS STATEMENT

Following our arrests earlier today in connection with the fatal arson attack in Denton, MCP would like to apologise unreservedly for the arrests of two individuals in Ashton town centre this morning. These arrests were made in error, following incorrect information which had been shared with officers at Tameside police station. We apologise for any distress, loss of earnings or damage to the premises, and will be working closely with those people affected by this mistake. Our unreserved apologies are sent to these individuals and we would like to assure the public that these individuals have been released from police custody without charge and we wish to make it clear that they have absolutely no involvement in any police inquiries. This statement is exclusive to the incident at Bingley's Estate Agents in Ashton town centre this morning, and in no way refers in any respect to any other arrests made in Tameside in relation to the fatal fire in Denton in the early hours of Monday the Seventeenth of November."

"Bloody hell. That's pretty selfless of the press office!" Rudovsky was stunned by the flamboyant language used in the press statement. MCP weren't known for such flowery apologies.

"Miller's written that. I can tell."

"Well, it's good news for Tim and Charlotte I guess. But it makes us look like dicks."

"Who cares? It doesn't matter really, does it? As long as

they don't get any come-backs. It's a pretty unforgettable crime to be implicated in. No, I think it's a great press release. Let's go and show Tim and Charlotte."

*****

Miller was at HQ, working with "the geeks" as they were affectionately known, although the official title of their department was the "AFR Technology Team." They'd earned their nicknames due to their consistent enthusiasm for their work, and because they were, without any shadow of a doubt, the biggest dorks in the city of Manchester.

AFR is a relatively new and emerging technology which has been carefully developed by the US Government since the 1980s. Today, many British police forces are signing up to the technology as the benefits of the system have been hard to resist. In essence, AFR or Automatic Facial Recognition software is a revolutionary new biometric system which scans the police service's database of hundreds of thousands of police "mug-shot" pictures for possible matches to CCTV or photographic images in order to hopefully identify a person in a CCTV clip, just from their police mug-shot.

The technology has an unrivalled success rate and is regarded as yet another technological breakthrough which will eventually make the streets much safer. The only technical requirement that AFR needs is clear, good quality footage, so it relies heavily on decent CCTV systems as it cannot read the data of older, grainier systems.

The consistent arguments against the fact that there are not enough police officers on the streets, is countered quite passionately by those who understand the extraordinary power of modern technology in assisting with and solving criminal investigation cases.

And today, AFR was wowing DCI Miller, as he watched first-hand how it all works. The geeks were running the McDonald's CCTV footage through their software, and the facial recognition software was naming the people in the clip. People who weren't even part of the investigation into the four men in question were suddenly getting a red frame around their faces on the computer, followed by an information card on that "suspect." Basically, if a person had ever had their photo taken by the police, this technology worked in much the same way as a finger-print record does in identifying them.

One of the geeks was explaining it all to Miller as the DCI watched on in awe of the "AFR Locate" system, which was still relatively new to MCP, and was Miller's first "live" encounter with it. "You see, bone structure, facial features, hair, ears, neck and skull circumference, they all make each person completely unique, just like their DNA does. What this little baby does is analyse the data from every measurement on the face and skull and works through all of the possible matches on the database, scanning a hundred thousand faces per minute! It's totally awesome!"

There could be no criticism of the geek's enthusiasm for the computer system. But Miller wasn't here to buy it, he wanted to know if any matches had come up.

"Yeah, it's great, absolutely. But have we got anything?"

"I'm just printing out a report for you now, Sir. I think you're going to be very happy!"

*****

Miller *was* happy. All four of the men had previous. The AFR confirmed that Wilson was definitely one of the men in McDonalds that night, but that wasn't really an earth-shattering revelation. His registration plate's details on the ANPR had already placed him there, and it was just a matter of hours before his bank confirmed the McDonalds transaction. So, he was goosed.

The three men seen with Wilson had all been spoken to by the police before, numerous times. Their names and last-known addresses were on the piece of paper in Miller's hand. The best news of all was that they were all local, so this could, in theory at least, all be sorted out by home-time today. That would be an excellent conclusion to an extremely distressing case, which twenty-four hours ago looked nigh-on impossible to figure out.

Miller's plan now was to round the three individuals up. With Wilson safely locked up, and the information being public, Miller felt safe in the knowledge that they'd be ringing and texting one another non-stop to find out if they'd been sussed, or grassed on, or even better still, writing incriminating text messages to one another trying to offer reassurance that they were going to be okay. If this was the case, and Miller felt sure that it would be, then this current "down-time" was yet another fantastic evidence gathering opportunity and would prove invaluable when their phones were seized. There was no mad panic to start kicking doors in just yet as far as Miller was concerned. The longer these men had to stew, the bigger the hole they were likely to dig for themselves.

The crucial thing now was trying to place these men at the scene of the crime. There was plenty of anecdotal evidence which suggested that Wilson had a reason to start the fire. There was also plenty of proof that he was out and about in the Tameside community with three other men, before and after the fire. In short, there was lots of circumstantial evidence but nothing in terms of rock-solid physical evidence that placed any of the four individuals at the address, pouring petrol through the letterbox. This was now Miller's number one priority. He thought back to the CCTV of the four men walking up Windmill Lane and considered whether this was enough to bring a water-tight prosecution. He decided to review the grainy footage from the nearby factory which had been the only line of enquiry in the hours following the tragedy. Miller had been so sure that the peculiar walk of one of the individuals would eventually become a part of his evidence and had decided not to release it to the press. He wanted to look at the clip again.

Miller loaded the footage on his screen and began watching it through. He was instantly reminded of the casual, almost comical way that the men walked. An early theory had been that they were older, and possibly drunks heading home from a lock-in at the nearby working-men's club. Miller scrutinised the short section of film and analysed each of the men's physical profiles. He began making notes on his pad, referring to the individuals as numbers 1-4, from left-to right on the screen.

Number one was a little taller than the others. He was quite slim and had noticeably big feet. There was no clue as to his facial details as his hood was up. His clothes were generic, dark jeans and a hoody.

Number two was the slowest walker, he looked quite small, certainly fat and he appeared to walk with a limp. It wasn't a fully pronounced limp, but there was certainly some sort of an issue with the way he walked and Miller considered that he might have some kind of a back-related problem. Again, the clothes were very nondescript and gave nothing away and his hood covered any clues as to facial details.

Number three was the sprightliest of the gang. He was also quite short, a similar height to number two. He was walking faster, then stopping for the others to catch up, before stopping once again. He would burst into a bit of a jog, before berating the others to keep up with him. It was quite clear to Miller that this man was likely to be younger and judging by his behaviour, was experiencing the most amount of fear from the event which had just taken place. Miller had the feeling that this man was possibly the son of one of the men, his whole gait was different.

Number four was an interesting character. Out of the three, he looked the most drooped and least enthusiastic. This man was by far the fattest and without question the physically un-fittest. There were no other clues about him, the clothing, the hoody, there was nothing of note other than the fact that he looked like he wanted a lie-down.

Miller was hopeful that the physical attributes of the people in this video would convert perfectly when he met the three individuals in the coming hours. Presently, this bizarre CCTV footage of the four men was all he had that placed them close to the crime scene and he needed to make a plan of how he was going to match all this up.

Lee Riley's Story - Part Three

Nobody had seen or heard from Lee Riley for two days. His girlfriend, Olivia was being comforted by her family at the home that the couple shared. The hours were passing by very slowly, and despite everybody's best efforts, her parents, her siblings, friends and neighbours, it was proving impossible to provide any form of comfort to Olivia. This usually beautiful young woman was lost. She looked ill and desperate.

Lee's elder sister, Joanna was finding this even harder to cope with than Olivia. Widely acknowledged as the go-to person in a crisis, everybody in the family, and the wider circle of family friends gravitated towards Joanna for the latest news or to offer help. She felt that it was her duty to remain strong and positive, but Lee's disappearance was made all the harder for Joanna, because she was pretty sure that she knew exactly why Lee had disappeared and for what purpose. Due to the circumstances, Joanna didn't feel able to share this information with anybody. But, being a naturally optimistic and positive person, she wasn't prepared to confront any dark thoughts just yet.

The police had been good. Not brilliant, it had to be said. But it was understandable that the West Yorkshire force hadn't dredged the rivers, organised land searches and sent the helicopter up looking for Lee. After all, the missing man was a very able-bodied, strong, fit, well liked and respected builder. This was not a case of a six-year-old girl going missing and the reaction to the situation was in proportion to the circumstances, as the police officers kept repeating.

West Yorkshire police had released a recent photograph of Lee, in the form of a missing person's poster. The police were extremely cautious about releasing such details in the case of a 28-year-old man going missing, because usually, it was simply a case of free-will. Thousands of men, and women, take themselves off for a few days at a time, particularly in times of stress or worry. Almost ten times out of ten, they turn up with a sheepish expression and an awkward explanation a few days later. However, due to the nature of Lee's disappearance, and his usually reliable and dependable nature, the police officers decided to release a mis-per announcement, regardless of what damage this could potentially have on his personal and his business reputations.

The police officers who were looking after this missing person's report were based at Halifax, about ten miles away from Hebden Bridge. Lee had been reported missing the previous day, twenty-four hours after he was last seen, or was last known to be in contact with anybody. The last person that he had contacted was Olivia, his long-term girlfriend. He had sent her a very vague but troubling text message which had filled her with terror. It read;

"So sorry Liv. I love you so much."

His phone had been switched off just after it had been sent and Olivia had tried over three hundred times to ring him since. She was 100% confident that Lee's phone had not been switched back on, purely due to the amount of times that she had tried, and it had not connected.

Despite the public appeal, the police had very little to go on. All they had were four lines of enquiry. The first was the troubling text message to his partner, the details of which had been kept secret from the public. The second notable line of enquiry was the discovery of Lee's van, which was parked up on the pay and display in Todmorden town centre, the parking ticket he'd purchased was only for one hour. There was CCTV footage of him inside the BetPower betting shop on Rochdale Road, where he was seen leaving in a very troubled-looking state at 13.41. The parking ticket for his van was due to expire at 14.04, but there was no evidence of him going back to his van. The final line of enquiry came in the form of several witness statements which had been phoned in to the police, following their public appeal for information. The callers had phoned to say that they had seen Lee earlier that day, running along the canal towards Hebden Bridge, or running away from Hebden Bridge towards Todmorden. In almost all of the calls, Lee was described as happy, friendly and even "bubbly." One of the callers described Lee as "manic," going on to explain that the missing man seemed over-friendly and a little unhinged during the brief encounter.

A strange picture was emerging. Instead of going to work on the day that he went missing, Lee had instead driven his van to Tod, then ran back along the canal to Hebden, and then ran back to Tod. This amounted to a ten-mile run. Following this run, he had driven his van from a lay-by on the outskirts of Todmorden to the town centre, before parking it up and going into a bookies. There was no record of Lee making a transaction at the bookies, and the CCTV showed that he walked in, sat on a stool for fifteen minutes, and then left again, looking extremely agitated as he went. He turned right as he left the bookies, a detail which attracted a lot of attention because his van had been parked in the opposite direction. The investigating officers were considering all of these details and were being led to the conclusion that the explanation for Lee's disappearance was consistent with a significant mental health crisis.

The police had to be open and honest with Olivia. As the time went on and their investigations presented more details, the mood of the police officers was becoming colder. Where it had all started two days earlier with "don't worry" and "try to stay calm" the words of the police were now much more controlled. They were now saying things like "that is a major line of enquiry" and "we are looking into that." Something had changed, and Olivia was acutely aware of it. Despite the officers earlier attempts at putting her mind at ease, she was now resigning herself to the thought that when the news finally came, it was going to be the worst possible, most unimaginable kind of news.

Joanna was in a state. She felt that this was all her fault, that if she hadn't given Lee that money, he wouldn't have done whatever it was that he had done. Her mind was filled with regret, guilt and an overwhelming sense of grief. She couldn't get the images of her brother, crying in his van as he told her all about his problems three days earlier, out of her head. The hardest thing was that she couldn't tell anybody. All she wanted to do was break her silence, explain to Olivia, and to everybody, what had been going on in Lee's life in the days leading up to his disappearance. She also wanted to cleanse her own conscience regarding the money that she had sent to his bank account. But as each hour had passed, as each conversation about Lee had been concluded with "it's just not like him," she felt that it was now impossible to say anything. The guilt generated by her own deceit on top of everything else was really weighing her down. It was becoming intolerable.

It came as something of a relief when the police officers knocked on Joanna's door and asked in soft, gentle voices, if they could speak with her. She had dreaded, but anticipated this conversation for the past twenty-four hours. Now, it seemed that it was finally time to face up to the darkest of all possibilities.

"Hello Joanna. We need to speak to you."

"Yes, sure. Come in." Joanna was visibly trembling, her teeth were chattering together as the two uniformed police officers entered her modest terraced house. Joanna's husband, Tony, had a real panic building up. He sensed that this was bad news, and he also had serious concerns for the state of his wife. She was in a bad way, mentally, emotionally and physically.

"Kids, go and play in your rooms please," said Tony as he opened the front-room door. Ellie and Ben did as they were asked quietly and respectfully, where normally there would be a five-minute debate ending with a door being slammed. Despite their youth, they knew that things were very serious.

"Sit yourselves down," said Tony to the two officers.

Joanna sat down on the arm-chair by the gas fire. Tony stood behind the chair. He decided to prompt the conversation that he sensed nobody wanted to start.

"Any news?" he asked.

The older of the two police constables leant forward slightly. "No. Nothing new has come to light, I'm afraid. However, there has been a development, which we need to make some further enquiries about."

Joanna needed this over and done with, she needed this information to come out. She had internalised a million arguments with herself over the decision to keep it a secret from her family, from Liv, and most importantly, the police. She sounded frightened as she spoke. "Is this about the money?"

The two constables glanced briefly at one another. The half-second interaction between them told Joanna everything she needed to know. It *was* about that.

"Can I talk about this at the station?"

This question threw the police officers. "What, well…"

"I need to talk in private about it."

Tony looked puzzled. "What's all this about?" he asked.

Finally, despite her best efforts not to, Joanna broke down. The pressure had been building and building within her since the moment Liv had first phoned her, telling her about that distressing text message. The emotional turmoil had been developing relentlessly since that moment, over 48 hours earlier. And now, the dam had finally burst.

"Love, what's up?" asked Tony as he kneeled on the rug before his wife. But Joanna was a wreck, she couldn't speak as the huge wave of emotion came crashing over her.

"Love?"

"It's… me… it's… my, my… fault…"

There was now no need to speak in private at the police station. Joanna had done the hardest part, she'd got past those first few difficult words. Words that she felt had now opened the floodgates to allow a full, honest and frank discussion about Lee's frame-of-mind the day before he disappeared. She felt wretched, and stupid for keeping it all back, but she knew that her reasons had been honourable. She'd wanted to protect Lee's reputation with his nearest and dearest, at first thinking he'll turn up and explain all to Liv after a few hours. And, naturally, from a selfish point of view, she wouldn't have to confess to giving every penny she and Tony possessed to Lee, which it looked like he'd gambled away within a couple of hours.

But now, it was all finally out in the open as Joanna spent twenty emotional minutes telling the police, and her husband, what she knew. Tony's reaction to all of this was the biggest surprise of all. He was calm, understanding and supportive. Whilst Joanna appreciated his strong, loving hugs and soft words of encouragement, she also felt stupid for keeping this awful secret for the past two days.

The police officers had only come around on an errand

for CID, to find out why Lee had received a bank deposit from Joanna for £5,000 on the day he went missing. They got a lot more than that, as the full story of Lee's addiction came out. The officers looked keen to leave when Joanna had finally finished her explanation. As they stood to leave, Joanna was desperate to hear some encouraging words. Something like "don't worry, he'll soon be home." Or "little brothers eh?" But there was nothing like that. All the older officer said as he left was, "we'll pass all of this on. Thanks for your time."

Tony was great about everything. He sat comforting Joanna for the following hour and reassured her that she had done nothing wrong, and that he completely understood her reasons for keeping quiet about the gambling problem, and the money.

"You need to stop beating yourself up, love."

"Lee would still have managed to get hold of the money from somewhere else."

"Come on love, this isn't your fault, all you've done is tried to help your brother."

"Liv doesn't need to know. Not yet, anyway. The main thing is finding Lee."

Tony did a great job of calming and comforting his wife. His gentle, supportive reassurance, along with the police's lack of information regarding Lee's whereabouts was helping to bring a renewed sense of optimism at a time when she had resigned herself to hearing the worst possible kind of news less than a couple of hours earlier. For the first time that day, Joanna was feeling calm, collected and thoughtful.

The Hebden Bridge Facebook Group had become the number one place to find out the latest news and gossip regarding Lee's disappearance. Comments about Lee on this local community group was testament to the good regard he was held in locally. In the hours following the announcement of his disappearance, the page was littered with well-meant comments.

"Top lad Lee. He'll be home soon."

"Saw him yesterday, seemed his usual friendly self. It'll be right."

"I've known Lee all my life. Can't believe this. But he won't have gone far. Stay positive."

But the facts were looking very disheartening. Lee had not been seen since he stepped out of that bookies shop in Todmorden. His phone hadn't been switched on, and that text message he'd sent to Olivia was extremely concerning for all who had been made aware of it. For Lee's nearest and dearest, it was becoming increasingly hard to keep that positive, optimistic faith going for a happy ending.

However, a beacon of hope emerged later on that night, just a few hours after the police had left Joanna and Tony's house. It came from the Facebook page and it lifted everybody's mood, especially as it had been written by a well-known and respected member of the local community.

"Hi, just been talking in the pub with a guy who's navigating the canal on his barge. He said he saw somebody who fits Lee's description walking along the towpath towards Manchester yesterday. He said he was talking to him at a lock near Rochdale and that he seemed a bit down but was still friendly. He said he was from Hebden Bridge and that he's going through a bad time."

This was a brilliant announcement. This was the first sighting of Lee since the bookies in Tod. Naturally, this news brought a great deal of positivity, not least to Olivia, and to Joanna and Tony. But this was just hearsay. This needed verifying properly, one way or another.

Joanna had been alerted to the Facebook post by a phone call from Liv at 11.20pm. As soon as the call ended, Joanna and Tony logged into Facebook and searched out the post. Joanna sent the author of the post a private message.

"Hi, this is Lee's sister. Do you know which boat this man is on? And where it is moored? Please help!"

Within minutes, the man replied. "Hi Joanna. I didn't get the name of the boat, but the guy is called Frank and he's moored up near the Stubbing Wharf. Hope this helps."

"Come on, we need to go and find this Frank," said Joanna, leaping up off the settee. "Go and check the kids are asleep."

Tony ran up the stairs two at a time and popped his head around each of his children's bedroom doors. All was still and quiet, but that didn't necessarily mean they weren't wide awake with their phones burning in their hands under their quilts. Tony ran back down the stairs, grabbing his coat off the post at the bottom.

Joanna suddenly had a renewed look of life about her. Where her appearance had gradually been worn down over the previous 48 hours, now, it was as almost as though nothing had happened and good, old Joanna was back, the blood pumping stronger than ever through her veins.

Tony opened the car door as Joanna got into the passenger seat, before slamming it shut and rushing around to his own side. Within seconds, the car was travelling at speed through the town centre, heading past the Co-Op and out of town.

Stubbins Wharf, the place that the Facebook contact had mentioned, is a pub on the banks of the Rochdale canal, roughly half a mile away from the centre of Hebden Bridge. Several barges were moored up along this stretch of the canal, which was handy for the famous pub, whilst still in a relatively quiet and rural setting.

Tony indicated left, and pulled into the car park of the pub. He and Joanna had their doors open as the car was still coming to a stop. They jogged past the pub and up the little lane which led to the canal towpath.

"Put your torch on your phone!" said Joanna, as the pitch-black darkness of the towpath became apparent.

"Frank!" said Joanna loudly, as Tony switched the light on and shone it at the muddy walkway alongside the still, silent canal.

"FRANK!" she bellowed, making a few geese flap loudly and splash unceremoniously into the cut.

Joanna started knocking on the window of the first canal barge she came to, just ten metres or so away from the pub.

"Hello. Hello." She shouted as she continued tapping. But the boat was in darkness. She walked on towards the next one, Tony was keen to stay close behind with the light, worried she might trip on one of the boats ropes which were tied up to the canal bank.

"Hello!" said Joanna loudly, as she started tapping on another window. Suddenly, the curtain inside twitched and a scared looking woman appeared in the glass. "Is Frank with you?" asked Joanna, unaware of how intimidating this kind of activity was for the boat-owner. Regardless, the woman gestured to Joanna to wait and a few seconds later, the barge's doors could be heard being opened from the inside as the big heavy bolts were being released.

"What the..."

"Sorry, sorry, I know it's late, I didn't mean to alarm you..."

"Well you have done. Where's the fire?" The lady was fuming, and it looked as though she'd been asleep prior to this rude awakening.

"No, there's no fire. I'm looking for a man called Frank. He's on one of these boats."

"I don't know of any Frank. But there's a new boat moored up tonight, down there, under the railway bridge."

"And you know all these other boats?"

"Yes, we're all permanent this side of the bridge."

"And none are called Frank?"

"How many times? I don't know about a Frank. Now go on, and keep your noise down."

"Sorry, sorry, but..."

The lady on the boat wasn't interested, she closed the heavy doors with a crunch as Joanna was about to explain.

"Come on," said Tony, shining his torch down at the floor as they walked hurriedly towards the last boat, about thirty or so yards away from the grumpy woman's.

"Here we are, the lights are all on." Tony tapped lightly on the glass. His gentle knocking provoked a reaction and the canal barge suddenly rocked outwards as somebody walked along the corridor inside the vessel. It was an elderly bloke with a bushy beard.

"Hello?" he asked as he reached the top step and lifted

his hatch.

"Hi, are you Frank?"

"Depends who's asking? If it's the tax office the answer is no." The man laughed at his joke.

"No, we're not from the tax. Are you Frank, then?"

"Yes, allow me to be Frank. I am Frank, frankly."

Joanna rolled her eyes at Tony. This Frank seemed a bit pissed and she wondered if he was going to talk any sense.

"Hiya Frank, I'm Joanna, this is my hubby Tony. I believe you were talking in the pub tonight, about the man who's gone missing?"

"Oh right, yes, come in." Frank unbolted his cabin doors and opened them, gesturing the cold, sad looking couple on board.

"Thanks a lot," said Tony as he led the way, shining his torch on the deck for Joanna.

"Mind your head as you come down," said Frank. "Can I offer you a hot drink?" He seemed nice enough.

"No, no, we're aright, thanks."

"Right, well, how can I help?" Frank sat down on a small stool, gesturing the sofa to his unannounced visitors.

"The lad who's missing, Lee, it's my brother."

"Oh, I see. I'm very sorry to hear that."

"Somebody on Facebook said that you were in the pub earlier, saying that you've seen him?" Joanna's face was filled with hope.

"Yes, well, what it were, a few people were talking about it in the pub, they had his picture on their phones. So I mentioned that I'd seen a bloke who looked just like him yesterday. He helped me through a lock."

"And it was definitely him?" asked Joanna.

"What did he look like, if you don't mind me asking?" asked Tony, he was becoming increasingly concerned that this Frank was just talking shit to impress strangers in the pub.

"Right, let me see. He was a big lad, I'd say six foot if not a bit bigger. Big lad, like I say, looks like he can handle himself. Dark hair, had a reasonably good tan for this time of year so I imagined that he was an outdoors type of bloke."

"What was he wearing?" asked Joanna, desperate for this information to be genuine.

"Ah, what was he wearing? You've, God, that's a good question. I'm guessing it was work wear, yes, he had a phone number on his back."

Finally, this conversation was bearing fruit and both Tony and Joanna sensed that this friendly old drunk really had seen Lee.

"I was just pulling up, ready to open the lock, up by top end of Littleborough, coming towards the tops.

"Go on."

"Anyway, I saw him, this bloke, he was sat on the balance beam of the lock. He looked a bit sad and lost, so I started talking to him, asked him if he would help me to open the lock."

"Did he?"

"Oh, yes. Couldn't do enough to help me."

"That's our Lee!" said Joanna to Tony, with a warm smile.

"Like I say, he seemed pretty upset."

"In what way?"

"Well, it was just his demeanour. I spent about five or ten minutes with him, he didn't say much, I was doing all the talking."

"Did he say what he was doing?"

"No, he just said he was headed for Manchester. I told him it's a fair old walk, as I'd just come up from that way. He didn't seem phased by it though."

"How far is it? Littleborough to Manchester?" asked Joanna.

"Oh, I couldn't say. I measure distances by locks these days!"

"It's about twenty miles." Tony spoke confidently.

"What time was this?"

"It was earlier, before lunch I'd say."

"And this was yesterday?"

"That's right."

"Aw God, you really don't know what this means. It's

the first sighting of him since he was last seen, officially." Joanna grabbed her phone out of her handbag and started looking through her photos. After a few moments of silence, she finally held the phone out, showing Frank a photo of her brother. The picture had been taken a few months earlier. Lee looked happy and relaxed, holding a beer in one hand while his other arm was wrapped around Olivia's waist.

"Yes. That's him. Definitely." Frank was 100% sure that the man in the photograph was the same person he had met near to Littleborough, about twenty locks away.

"Are you totally sure?" asked Tony.

"Honestly. I wouldn't say it if I wasn't. That's the lad I spoke to yesterday. He told me that he's having a bit of trouble with a job he's supposed to be working on."

"Aw, Tony, it's definitely him." Joanna broke down in tears, the emotions that she had been trying to suppress since hearing of this possible sighting were now flowing freely. Tony comforted his wife as Frank watched on, looking a little embarrassed and unsure of what to do with himself.

This was the news that Joanna had craved so desperately. Her darkest thoughts had tortured her for the past two days, question marks about where Lee might have gone to end his life had been at the forefront of her mind, although she had not uttered a word about these dreadful thoughts. Now, thanks to Frank, she had a real glimmer of hope that Lee had survived the first day of his mental anguish. It now seemed appropriate to start considering that there might, just might be the possibility of a happy ending to this ghastly, nightmare scenario.

"Come on, let's head home. Busy day in the morning." Joanna stood from the little sofa seat that she had perched on.

"Have you got a phone number, Frank? Just in case we need to ask you something else." Tony was being his usual, calm and practical self.

"Er, yes, just a minute." Frank walked across to the kitchen and started looking through his phone. Eventually, he came back with the retro looking mobile. "Here we are, oh I can never work these bloody things..."

Once Frank had figured out how to find his phone number, Joanna and Tony thanked him for his help. Tony kept the phone's torch on as he led Joanna along the towpath. He was relieved to see such a change in Joanna's spirit. She didn't stop talking all the way along the towpath, still chattering away as they reached the pub car park and she was still going on with herself as Tony drove them back towards town, and home. Tony wasn't complaining though, it meant the world to see her back to her usual positive, pragmatic self.

"I'm going to print some pictures of Lee off. We can hand them out to boaters. If we get the bikes out, we can ride the whole way along the canal, see if we can work out where he's gone. You never know, we might find him. He'll be ready for home now, ready to face the music. Is that tyre still flat on your bike? How long does it take to ride to Manchester from Tod? No, do you know what we'd be better setting off from here, he might be on his way back. How much ink is there in the printer? Will you be alright taking the day off tomorrow? It gets light about half-seven now, so I'll make some butties and we go as soon as it gets light. I'll have to text Barbara and tell her I won't be in tomorrow, she'll be alright about it, she knows what's going on."

"Yes, no probs, love."

The following morning, Tony and Joanna set off on their bike ride at first light. Joanna had set the printer off before she'd gone to bed, printing the photo of Lee that she had shown to Frank on his canal boat. Underneath she had written, "Missing. Lee Riley. Loved and adored by his family. If you have seen Lee, please phone Joanna, his proud sister." Beneath that she had typed her phone number. Her idea was that the poster would have two purposes. One purpose was for handing to people along the canal. The other was to pin up along the way, in the hope that Lee would see it and realise how much he meant to everybody. Especially Joanna, and to Olivia, who was standing in the photograph with him.

The Rochdale canal, which starts in Manchester city centre and ends in Sowerby Bridge, is one of the nation's most picturesque waterways. From Hebden Bridge, it makes its way through the stunning Calder Valley to the foot of the Pennines, where more than thirty locks elevate the canal over the top of the peaks, before they drop it back down again on the Manchester side.

The bike-ride is usually one of the most beautiful rides in this part of Britain. But not today, as Joanna and Tony's attention was not on the picturesque surroundings. Instead, they were more concerned with looking behind the dry-stone walls, the little fishing huts and old, broken sheds and garages.

As they neared Littleborough, the small town on the Manchester side of the Pennines, the opportunity to speak to boat-owners and tourists who had hired vessels, as well as dog-walkers and oncoming cyclists was really starting to slow progress down.

Joanna soon realised that she didn't need to spend the first few minutes introducing herself and explaining the circumstances of her being on the canal today. As time went on, she began to realise that a simple, "have you seen this man anywhere along the canal?" was a much faster, and productive opening gambit.

Sadly, the reaction was disappointing. Of the first twenty or thirty people that the couple had approached, not one of them had seen Lee. Annoyingly, none of them seemed too bothered, either, which really wound Joanna up at first. But she soon got used to the apathy that people who had never even seen her before felt about her missing brother. It was just life. Nobody actually said "I couldn't give a shit, mate." But they may as well have done.

Joanna continued to put the posters up, using drawing pins or Sellotape depending on the surface she was fixing the home-made poster to. She felt confident that somebody along here would have seen Lee, after all, this was the place that he'd been sitting only two days earlier, when he'd been helping Frank open the lock.

She kept checking her phone, to see if anybody had called her. It was a disappointment each time. It really felt as though nobody cared. Nobody gave a toss about this, the scariest, most nerve-wracking time of her life.

Beyond Littleborough, the canal flattened out somewhat, and Joanna and Tony were pedalling on the flat for several miles as they made their way steadily towards Rochdale. There were fewer people around now, fewer boaters, fewer joggers or dog-walkers and hardly any cyclists along this long, relatively straight section of canal which went on for as far as the eye could see without deviating from its perfectly straight line.

They would stop, regularly to check any suspicious looking locations. There were dozens of little hidey-holes along this stretch of canal, be them old, dilapidated sheds or dens built by kids which had long since been abandoned. The high-hopes were fading fast, and although nothing was said between Joanna and Tony, they were both beginning to have their doubts about Frank's information. But what sort of a sick, twisted bastard would give people false hope like that? Well, it took all sorts to make up the human race, considered Joanna as she continued to pedal behind Tony, determined to overcome these nagging doubts and try to keep a positive outlook.

"A fit, strong bloke like Lee could walk thirty or forty miles in a day," said Tony, slightly breathlessly as he rode beside his wife. "He could have made it to Manchester by last night." He was trying to keep Joanna's hopes up. But her hope seemed to be fading, and Tony sensed it. He continued talking anyway. Joanna interrupted him as they got closer to Rochdale.

"Tony, what's that up ahead?" Joanna's voice was cold, it didn't even sound like her.

Tony looked up from the towpath that he'd been concentrating on. He quickly realised why his wife's voice had sounded so detached. Up ahead were several police officers, wearing their hi-vis jackets. A police car and a tactical aid van were parked up along the grass verge beside the towpath. Beyond them, Joanna and Tony could make out a crime-scene tent. A big white and yellow tent like the ones off the TV news appeared to be set up right across the middle of the tow-path.

"Aw fucking hell Tony. What's happening?" The panic was clear in her voice. Joanna's flushed complexion from the cycling had suddenly turned a deathly shade. "What's going on,

Tony?" she repeated. Her husband said nothing. It was obvious that they were both thinking the same thing as their bikes arrived at the police cordon line. A police officer was signalling at them to slow down with a gentle wave of his hand. He was standing behind a section of blue and white tape which was flapping in the wind. POLICE LINE – DO NOT CROSS was written all across it.

"There's no access through here at the moment I'm afraid. You'll have to turn around..."

"What's happening?" asked Joanna as she squeezed her brakes, despite fearing the answer.

"We are dealing with an incident. The towpath is closed. If you turn back you can..."

"I'm... I'm looking for my brother. He's missing." Joanna pulled a poster out from the breast pocket of her waterproof jacket. She handed it to the officer, her hand trembling as she did so.

The police officer was thrown by this sudden and extraordinary encounter. Joanna was staring at him, trying desperately to read every expression on his face, every twitch, every muscle spasm. Every movement of his eyes.

The policeman looked at the poster for a long time. Eventually, he looked up in Joanna's direction.

"Have you reported him missing?"

"Yes, yes, two, no three days ago."

"I see. Where are you from? You sound like you're from over the hill?"

"Yes, we are, Hebden Bridge."

"Ah, that'll be why I've not heard about your brother yet."

"That's, that's not...." Joanna was pointing at the tent.

"Oh, I see." Suddenly, the police man offered a warm, reassuring smile. "No, don't worry, this is nothing to do with your brother."

"Well, what is it?"

"It's a crime scene, a serious incident occurred here last night. It's not connected with your brother, so don't worry."

It was easy for this copper to say don't worry, while

Joanna's heart was bursting out of her chest.

"What was the incident? I need to know that Lee wasn't involved."

"Trust me, it's fine. This has nothing to do with your brother, some kids were fighting here last night and one has been stabbed, it's not life-threatening but we still have to set up a scene and carry out a forensic examination. We've got all the kids who were involved in custody. You can stop worrying."

Joanna collapsed onto the grass verge, her bike fell across the towpath. She was overwhelmed by the overpowering cocktail of emotions. Tony placed his bike down carefully and kneeled by his wife.

"Ssshhhh. Come on now love, shhhh."

Joanna was sobbing uncontrollably as the policeman tried to make small-talk with Tony, presumably in an attempt to neutralise this unexpected drama. Or maybe he just felt awkward. "I can see why you'd think... must have been a shock to the system... just take a few deep breaths." It was obvious that the copper didn't have a clue what Joanna was going through. He was only a young bloke himself.

Joanna's meltdown was distracted by the ping of a new text message on her phone. She wiped her tears away with her sleeve and unzipped her pocket.

The text was from Olivia. "Lee's home, looks like shit, really sad, just walked in. Don't know what's happened yet, just running him a bath. I'll phone you as soon as I get chance. But he's home safe and in one piece. Love Liv xxx"

Joanna handed the phone to Tony and collapsed on the grass verge once again.

The policeman was amazing, he radioed his sergeant and explained the situation which was unfolding at his cordon line, and his superior officer organised a van to come down and pick Joanna and Tony up and take them back to West Yorkshire. It was a tight squeeze getting the bikes into the prisoner cage in the back of the police van, but the police officers persevered and Tony and Joanna were soon sitting up front in the vehicle, on their way back up the road to Hebden Bridge.

Chapter Thirty-Eight

The British Home Secretary stood before the invited media reporters in the small press briefing room at Number 10 Downing Street. This much anticipated press conference was being presented from inside Number 10, rather than on the packed-out street outside, where every member of the 160 press representatives with Downing Street security clearance could have recorded it and shouted their questions at the end.

The fact that this was being held inside told the media professionals exactly how Number 10 were planning to play it. The government weren't looking for any awkward questions, and so they were only inviting their most trusted reporters and journalists along. The ones who generally tow the line and write or present their news from a very biased angle. Every single one of the thirty or so reporters and journalists, most of them very familiar faces from the TV news, knew that they were in a privileged position. It was a great honour to be invited through the door of number 10, which is widely regarded as the most famous front door in the world. The address dates back to 1735 and has been the home to over 50 Prime Ministers.

Each press member sitting inside here today knew exactly what was expected. Without a word being spoken on the issue, these journalists all knew that they were to be nice in their reports. Otherwise, next time, they'd be out on the street, in the cold, with no story, like the vast majority of their colleagues. This wasn't a particularly sensible decision from the Number 10 spin-doctors and advisors. It just meant that the reporters outside would be even more critical and negative than they might otherwise have been. But this was a government which was widely renowned across the globe for its complete disregard for logic.

"Good afternoon," said the Home Secretary, stepping up close to the lectern in the cramped, but luxurious press briefing room which had started life as a dining-room. Through the years it has been instrumental in entertaining the world's most powerful and influential people.

"Thank you all for coming along today. I am very

shocked to announce that over the course of last night, in almost every county in the United Kingdom, a total of two-hundred and forty-seven betting shops were ransacked and wrecked by gangs. I'm sure you are all as shocked and angry about this as I am, the television reports today have shown sheer devastation in these businesses and the clean-up operation required to get these shops back in business will be in the tens of millions of pounds."

The Home Secretary paused and let that figure hang in the air a moment, before continuing with the prepared statement. "Let me make something very clear. The people responsible for these unacceptable and despicable acts will be caught by our police officers and they will be dealt with in the most severe manner that the law allows. There is nowhere to hide. Let me remind you all that the last time that we saw anything like this was during the riots of 2011 and I would like to take this opportunity to remind the perpetrators of last night's hooliganism, that over 3,000 arrests were made then, and over 1500 people were sent to serve maximum sentences in our prisons. I will have no mercy at all in replicating this unparalleled level of punishment again. I urge every single person who was involved in last night's outrageous activity to listen to my message. I am asking you to wrestle with your conscience and hand yourself in at your nearest police station. Anybody who appears at their local police station voluntarily will be treated more leniently than those who try and evade the law, which will inevitably prove to be a futile exercise. My colleagues in the police force will be tackling this crime-wave in the most profound manner." The Home Secretary paused again, in order to let that point dominate the speech.

"I would like to take this opportunity to send my sincere and heart-felt sympathies to all of the business-owners, staff and neighbours of the shops who have been dealt an unimaginably damaging blow as a consequence of this shameful and reprehensible night of mindlessness. I know that many of the shops targeted are small, independent, family-run businesses, as well as shops from the larger, national bookmaker chains. Whether yours was a large, or small shop, I offer you my full assurance that this shameful behaviour will not be tolerated. Thank you."

With that, the Home Secretary offered a gentle nod of appreciation to the tiny audience, turned and left. The reporters didn't say anything.

*****

"Well, that was quite a strong message from the Home Secretary, a stark warning to those who took part in last night's devastating betting shop attacks. There was no mistaking the message, those responsible will be facing the full power of the law, when, not if, they are caught. Our Home Affairs correspondent Graham Jones was at the press briefing and joins me now live in the studio. Well, Graham, what do you make of what the Home Secretary had to say earlier?"

The vision switched from the head and shoulders shot of the famous Sky News anchor to the face of the channel's veteran politics correspondent.

"Thank you, Kay. I think that this was a speech which demonstrated a huge amount of defiance and at times, was rather mocking of the people who caused so much damage and terror in neighbourhoods throughout the country last night. I think that the Home Secretary said just enough to leave anybody involved under no illusion that they are going to face some very harsh consequences for their actions if they don't take themselves into their nearest police station and admit defeat. One thing which was made unequivocally clear is that this kind of behaviour will not be tolerated and I get the distinct impression that the police service will be instructed to cancel all leave until these people are rounded up and put safely behind bars."

"What did you make of what the Home Secretary had to say about those businesses which have been affected by these mindless actions?"

"Not as much as I might have expected if I'm perfectly honest Kay. I thought that there may have been some announcement of an emergency fund to help some of those smaller, independent bookmakers get their shops back up and running as quickly as possible. So I must confess that it came as something of a surprise that there was no actual offer of financial aid, which I had thought that the Home Secretary was leading up towards announcing."

"Okay, Graham Jones, thank you."

Chapter Thirty-Nine

DCI Miller had met with Dixon and updated his superior officer with all of the information regarding Adrian Wilson and his three accomplices. It was agreed by Dixon that there was "compelling" enough evidence to justify the SCIU department's continuation of the investigation into the four men laughing and joking in the McDonalds restaurant CCTV footage.

As had been anticipated, the wider investigation had been taken over by the NCA, under instruction of the Home Secretary's department. It was something which Miller and Dixon were both pleased about. They strongly suspected that the NCA would not be particularly over-joyed to be handed this case, however. The National Crime Agency typically manage major investigations into organised crime, large-scale drug dealing, child-sex gangs and people-trafficking. Public disorder and vandalism, as part of a political protest was not something they would be too enthralled to be taking on. But Miller couldn't care less about that, or the damage to the betting shops, really. It was annoying for the betting shop owners, without doubt, but Miller didn't view this as a crime which was worthy of his department's involvement. What Miller really cared about was building the strongest possible case against the people who had killed the two kids and their dad in Denton.

Miller had officially relinquished his department's involvement in the betting shops investigation, and had stood down the senior detectives in Tameside, Bolton, Stockport, Manchester and Salford with whom he had been working with since Monday. He did this task by e-mail, thanking them all for their excellent support throughout the week. Their instructions were to wind down their investigations with immediate effect and to hand over all of their case-notes and evidence to the NCA.

With that, Miller was officially done. But there was one loose end which needed tying up. He called Saunders through to his office.

"Sir?"

"Sit down Keith."

Saunders sat and listened as Miller explained everything which had been agreed with Dixon.

"So, that just leaves this peculiar situation with the website you signed up to. I'll need you to do a report, for the NCA, with all your log in details and everything."

Saunders looked disappointed. He'd been really excited about this, he felt that his access to this information via the e-mail list would prove invaluable in discovering who the people behind all this were. He explained his dissatisfaction to Miller, who listened patiently, despite not giving a shit.

"Fair dos Keith, I know that you wanted to be the one who brought them in. You wouldn't be you if you didn't feel disappointed. But cheer up! You've cracked the arson case, that's the crucial one. I've told you before, you can't have them all."

"I know Sir. But someone from the NCA is going to crack this one, using my lead."

"What's wrong with that?"

"I... I don't know. I just don't like the idea of handing my leads over."

"Well my advice to you is this. There's no way on God's earth that this Odds on Revenge group are going to share any sensitive information on that e-mail list now. That ship has sailed."

"I'm not so sure..."

"Listen mate. That e-mail list you've signed up to won't be recruiting any new members now, when every single police force in Britain is trying to find out who's taking the piss out of them. It's dead in the water."

Miller had a valid point, and Saunders knew it. The tactics that the gangs had used the previous night had seriously under-mined every police officer on duty. Whoever was behind all of this obviously knew something about the police's health and safety at work directive. They must have known that individual officers are prohibited from engaging with a gang of people carrying tools which could easily be used as an offensive weapon. The organisers had been clever enough to plan the attacks around this loop-hole, making so much noise and bother in the local community to ensure that every concerned resident who dialled 999 would provide details which subsequently ensured that the police were aware that each incident was a "high-risk" deployment. It was a very clever plan, and well thought through.

"There's no way they're going to e-mail you mate. If you'd had the foresight to sign up to it six months ago, then we'd be having a different conversation."

"But I didn't know about it six months ago…" Saunders had missed the sarcasm, probably deliberately.

"It was a joke. Anyway, sorry to piss on your chips but you've got five minutes to send me an e-mail with all the details regarding this, I want the website link and the e-mail address, plus the e-mail and password you used to sign up. Okay?"

"Okay, fair enough."

"Don't look so glum." Miller had known that this was likely to be a disappointing announcement for his second-in-command, so he revealed the positive news which he had skilfully withheld, anticipating Saunders' negative reaction to the first bit. "When you've done that, come back and we'll start planning the arrests of Adrian Wilson's horrendous little mates. You're going to like this, I'm thinking of doing some undercover surveillance work on the three suspects, a bit of an evidence gathering exercise before we make the arrests."

Miller was right, Saunders suddenly looked refreshed and ready to go again. "Oh?"

"I'll tell you in a minute when you've sent me that stuff for the NCA."

"Right, okay. No problem." Saunders stood and headed out of the door. It was as though he'd found a new lease-of-life as he stepped quickly across the SCIU office floor to his desk and began flicking through his notepad looking for the information which had been requested. Miller knew exactly how to manage his enthusiastic and energetic DI. Just give him more work to do.

A couple of minutes later, Miller's e-mail notification sounded. He had a quick look and it was the information that he'd requested from Saunders. After giving it the once-over, he forwarded the e-mail to the DCI at the NCA, who was taking care of the betting shop attacks now. He was glad when the "e-mail sent" message popped up on the screen. That was officially the end of that, a case which he would have hated having to continue with, largely due to the trivial nature of it. Miller always preferred working on things that had a bereaved family member involved, somebody he could really get stuck in and work for. Today, that person was Marija Ozols.

"Right, what's the plan?" asked Saunders as he burst in through the office door.

"I'm glad you asked me that. Sit down."

Chapter Forty

"Good evening, this is Channel 4 News. Our leading story tonight focuses on the Home Secretary's statement earlier this afternoon, in response to last night's unforgettable destruction at two-hundred and forty-seven bookmaker shops in every part of the country. Unfortunately, Channel 4 News were not allowed in to Number 10 to take part in this press-conference and ask questions. And we think we know why. We've reviewed the footage of this speech several times now, and not once does the Home Secretary, one of the most powerful people in British politics, attempt to make any reference to the reported reasons behind these betting shop attacks. Even the government's most trusted journalists who were invited inside Number 10 were denied the opportunity to ask any questions. As stated, the only reporters allowed in there were those who habitually support the government's policies in their reporting. So, as we always like to do on Channel 4 News, let's take an alternative look at this powerful speech. I'm joined by Lisa Ledger, the Chief Executive of the gambling addiction charity GSF, which stands for Gambling Support Family. Lisa, tell us what you made of the speech this afternoon?"

"Yes, good evening John, thank you for inviting me along. I think the most striking detail that I took away from this press statement was the complete lack of any acknowledgement of what the Odds On Revenge people are campaigning about. As far as I was concerned, the Home Secretary talked about this incredible story as though it was just a random event involving gangs of hooligans."

"And in your view, you think that there should have been a mention of the issues that are reported to be behind all of this?"

"Oh, absolutely. Even if the government didn't mean it, they could have at least put the idea out there that they were listening, that they were aware of the concerns that the Odds on Revenge people are trying to raise awareness of. Instead, this statement has basically side-stepped the bigger issue at play and said that the people responsible are going to jail for a very long time. It was a wasted opportunity to demonstrate that the government are aware of this enormous problem, in my humble opinion."

"Ah, but your opinion isn't humble at all. You set up and run the nation's biggest charity that exists to offer support to people suffering from gambling addictions?"

"Yes. And their families. This is such a major issue, not just for those people who are struggling with their own gambling problems, but also their loved ones who suddenly find their lives turned upside down once this disease presents itself."

"And, I'm sorry to bring it up, but you started this charity due to a very personal reason?"

"That's absolutely right. Mike, my husband was suffering with a serious gambling problem, which started out with him downloading a betting app to his phone. I had absolutely no idea what was going until I received a final demand letter from the bank for almost thirty thousand pounds. I thought it was just a mistake. When I confronted my husband to ask him what this letter was, he broke down in tears and told me what had been going on and explained how he had managed to run up these debts after applying for numerous loans in my name, just to feed his gambling craving."

"And I'm very sorry to hear that your husband is no longer with us?"

Lisa was very calm and collected as she spoke about the worst thing that had ever happened to her, some years earlier. It was clear to the TV viewers that this was a story that she'd had to tell a great many times before.

"No, sadly not. Mike took his own life. He just couldn't cope with his problem. I wasn't able to help him, I didn't understand the sheer magnitude of this crippling disease and unfortunately, I did what so many people do when they find themselves in this position. I was incredibly unsupportive and quite nasty and bitter towards him, because I just didn't get it, I thought he was an idiot, quite frankly. I really do feel that my response to his problem contributed towards his decision to end his life. It was only after he died that I began to realise what an immense problem this is, and the shocking number of people who are facing this misery every single day. I also learnt that most people who suffer from the inescapable compulsion of gambling addiction are treated with anger and frustration, rather than calm, measured support, which just makes the problem worse as the addict will do everything they can to keep their problem secret. When I began to realise just how big a crisis this is, and the enormous numbers of people affected, I wanted to do something to try and help, not just the gamblers, but the relatives of those who are living in the dark shadow of this overwhelming illness. I think I owed it to Mike, who I called a moron and an idiot on a daily basis, and my behaviour probably did contribute to the decision he took." As she reached the end of her point, Lisa did sound emotional and it was clear that she carried a very heavy burden of guilt.

"Your charity is doing very well. One of the main services that you offer is a free-phone twenty-four-hour telephone support service, and I read earlier that the line is in constant use, around the clock?"

"Yes, that's right John. We have six lines on the scheme, all manned by people who have suffered from gambling addiction themselves, all of whom volunteer their time to provide free help and support to people who need to speak to an understanding and reassuring voice at the end of the line. We also run a safe-house scheme in a number of places around the UK, which is effectively a rehab centre which we operate to help people to come off gambling, whilst providing a safe, understanding and non-judgemental place for them to really focus on recovery and start to rebuild their lives."

"It's fascinating to hear you speaking so passionately about your work. Most of our viewers will probably be quite surprised that this problem is so big. It's generally unheard of."

"I think the public are becoming more aware of it, the topic hits the headlines every few weeks. It's usually the subject of fixed-odds machines in the bookies, but that activity is taking place online with just as much damage being caused inside the minds of the players."

"Yet, despite all of this going on, affecting around two-million people, the Home Secretary has today completely ignored the issue in his press conference. How does that make you feel?"

"Disappointed. But not surprised, I deal with members of the government on this issue regularly. We did have a very supportive Minister in Tracey Crouch, but she resigned from her post as the Sports Minister because the government just won't take this matter seriously. It's a crying shame because Tracey Crouch really did care passionately and wanted to tackle this problem once and for all. But in the end, as far as this government are concerned, the tax revenue receipts are much more appealing than demonstrating some basic human compassion."

"What would be your message to the government on this complicated issue?"

"Well, make no mistake John, people in the relevant departments of government are fully aware of my message. There is such a lot that needs to be done around this issue, and let's be completely honest it doesn't have to all fall at the government's feet. The gambling companies themselves own most of the blame and could do so much more in terms of showing a reasonable level of responsible behaviour, but of course they are making ridiculous amounts of profits off the back of this tragedy so although it sickens me to my core, I can understand their reluctance to behave in a responsible manner. But there are so many ways of tackling this, for example the banks could practically stop this madness in a heart-beat, just by limiting card payments to a reasonable sum. If gambler's cards were declined after they'd hit a daily limit, that alone would be a massive help. But they allow people to place ridiculous sums of money on online bingo games, or TV poker games, or on the bookies websites. It's an absolute tragedy that the banks aren't stepping up and helping with this. It cannot be right that somebody can spend their full month's salary in one day's gambling, can it? If I was trying to spend a full month's salary on shoes and handbags in one day, I know for a fact that the bank's computer would recognise that I was having a bit of a breakdown and decline my card."

"And what would you like to see the government doing?"

"Well, as today's performance by the Home Secretary has confirmed, the government appear to be in a great deal of denial about the sheer scale of this problem. In fairness, they can't really be blamed for this enormous public health crisis which is affecting around two-million people, this has come about really due to the advancement of technology and the previous government's relaxation of gambling laws just over a decade ago, it probably wasn't planned that way, but the two worlds have collided and the result is a major public health crisis."

"That's a very good point you make. It was the Labour government under Tony Blair, who watered down the gambling rules to allow the TV advertising and so on. It does seem rather ironic that the present government, who opposed these reforms, are today facing the backlash?" The Channel 4 News presenter was keen to bring some balance into the discussion, despite being locked out of the press conference earlier in the day.

"No, I agree with you that they cannot be blamed for introducing the problem, that will remain the Labour party's dirty stain. But the present government *can* be blamed for taking billions of pounds in tax revenue from the gambling companies whilst looking the other way and wilfully ignoring the fact that most of that money is coming in through the most irresponsible and unsavoury methods. A simple thing the government could do is tax profits much higher on irresponsible games, such as the fixed-odds betting machines and the online casinos. It's very simple mathematics that if a fixed-odds betting machine, the crack-cocaine of gambling as it's become known, was taxed at say 60% of all profits, then there would suddenly be a very different attitude from the bookmakers and the machines would disappear overnight. They serve no other purpose than to fleece the customers and the great tragedy is, those customers become addicted to them."

"It's been very interesting talking to you tonight, Lisa

Ledger. One final question. What advice do you have for any families out there, who have a loved one who is going through this right now?"

"That's a great question John. Firstly, I would say that although you will feel alone, lost, confused and probably scared and angry, you should know that you are definitely not alone. There are millions of people out there, feeling exactly the same way. The second thing I'd say is, don't do what I did, and fly off the handle and blame your loved one. You wouldn't tell somebody who is suffering from depression to cheer up, and you shouldn't tell somebody who is suffering from gambling addiction to stop gambling. If it was as easy as that, there wouldn't be depression, and there wouldn't be gambling addicts."

"Lisa Ledger, from Gambling Support Family, thank you."

Lee Riley's Story – Part Four

As the Manchester Police van travelled across the Pennines, taking Tony and Joanna home, Olivia phoned. She was talking very quietly and the emotion was clear in her voice.

"Hiya."

"Hiya, thanks for phoning Liv. Everything okay?"

"Yeah, I think so." She sounded sad, but calm and relieved.

"So, what the hell's been going on?"

"I'm not sure. I think he's been sleeping rough, he looks like shit. He seems really low and embarrassed, but he gave me the tightest cuddle ever when he came in, he was crying his eyes out. He's in a proper state, I've not found out what's going on yet."

"Where is he now?"

"In the bath. I'm just giving him a bit of breathing space. I don't want to do his head in just yet. That can wait. I'm going to have his guts for garters!"

Joanna laughed. Despite the fact that tears were streaming down her face, she still thought it was hilarious that Liv was already planning to bollock Lee, good and proper. "Cheers love. Give him a big cuddle from me and T. Love ya Liv."

"Love you too Joanna. And thanks for everything these past few days. I don't know what I would have done without you."

Joanna and Tony sat in silence for the rest of the journey home. They were just relieved to hear that Lee had turned up safe. They didn't want to go round there and intrude, they felt that it was important that Lee explained himself to Olivia before any visitors came knocking, especially visitors who had just lost five grand in trying to help Lee with his problems. It wasn't going to help matters in any way, certainly not with Lee's current frame of mind.

As the police van neared home, Joanna posted on the Hebden Bridge Facebook group.

"Hi all, Lee is home. Thank you to everybody who has helped in trying to track him down over the past few days. It looks like Lee is having a bit of a tough-time, so we ask that you respect his privacy for the time-being. Main thing is he's home and he's well. Thank you all so much, love, Joanna xxx"

As soon as the couple arrived home, Joanna went into the kitchen and wrote a note for the kids.

"Kids, Uncle Lee is safe and well, mum and dad are in bed catching up on some much-needed sleep so keep the noise down or I'll brain you. And do your jobs (quietly!!!!) Love mum and dad xxx."

*****

The following day, Joanna woke up at 4am and couldn't get back to sleep. She felt very strange, her head was whirring with all sorts of stuff going around and around. All of her pent-up anxiety regarding Lee's disappearance was gone now, thankfully. All those horrible, grisly thoughts that she had tried so hard to fight off, the mental images that had painted in her mind of Lee hanging from a tree, or lay in a hedge, full of tablets, or jumping in front of a train had finally stopped torturing her. She had also stopped reliving that heart-stopping moment when she'd first caught glimpse of the police crime-scene tent on the canal near Rochdale, but thankfully the innermost dread from all of those terrible thoughts was gone now and had been replaced with a fresh anxiety over what was to come and how Lee was going to recover from this.

Joanna decided to give up on trying to get back to sleep, she was up in an hour anyway for work. She got out of bed and sat on the edge of the mattress and took a moment to thank whoever it had been that she'd been praying to. Joanna wasn't a religious person, at least she didn't think that she was. Unless something *really* serious was happening, that was. She had prayed many times since learning of Lee's dark text message a few days earlier, and now she was feeling thankful that her prayers had been answered.

But now, she was in limbo. Her fears were gone, sure. But she had no idea how to deal with the situation now. Lee didn't need her going round there, not now anyway. It was quite apparent that he had a lot of shit to deal with, the last thing he needed was a guilt-trip about the five grand. And after all, it wasn't the end of the world. As Tony had said the previous day, in the police van coming back from Rochdale, "I'd rather we lost five grand than we'd lost our Lee." That simple sentence said so much, and it really hit home to Joanna that her husband was a good man, with good thoughts.

Unsure of how to proceed and feeling quite confident that paying Lee a visit would be difficult for both of them, but mainly for him, she decided to take some advice from her Gran. Joanna and Lee's Gran, Elsie was no longer with them, but her sage advice and words of wisdom still lived on, long after her death. Elsie used to say, "the hardest things to say are the easiest to write down." And Joanna had realised many times that this was true. She decided it was time to break the stalemate of the current situation and put pen to paper.

Joanna had tears in her eyes and a bulge in her throat as she wrote her note.

"Dearest Lee,

Yesterday was the best day of my life. The best thing that has ever happened to me was receiving a text message from Olivia saying that you were home, and that you were okay. I'd had some very sad thoughts about what you were planning to do and I'm just so relieved that you have gone home, to a lass who absolutely adores you, in a street surrounded by family and friends who truly think the world of you.

I don't want to talk about anything we discussed the other day. But all I do want to say is that you have always got me to use as a shoulder to cry on, or to have an argument with, or to pull my hair like you used to when you were little. Don't you ever take yourself off like that again, you have no idea how much you mean to everybody in this family, and in Liv's family and in Hebden Bridge.

You've got some tough days ahead, but I'll be with you every step of the way, always by your side. So please don't ever forget that or I'll give you the worst Chinese burn of your entire life.

Phone me, when you're ready. No rush.

Love you mate.
Joanna Diana xxx"

Joanna put her middle-name in because she knew it would make Lee laugh out loud. That name was forbidden to be mentioned in the family, following the compromise which had been reached when she was very young and had threatened to leave home if anybody teased her about it one more time.

Joanna read through her letter. She wondered if she needed to change a few bits, just in case Lee had not mentioned his gambling problem yet. It wouldn't do if Olivia read the letter and started asking questions about certain things, particularly the bit about what the two had discussed. After several re-reads, she wrote it again, keeping the sentiment strong, but removing a few of the more cryptic comments.

Once she was happy with it, Joanna made a coffee and had a shower. She decided that the letter was a great idea, it managed to say all the things that she wanted to express, whilst avoiding any awkward moments that could potentially damage Lee's mental state any further. As Tony had said, Lee was worth so much more than five grand.

At work, Joanna asked the paperboy who does Lee's street to deliver the letter. Sadly, the paper-boy in question was the worst one the shop had. He was forever posting the wrong paper through the wrong door and was known by the staff members as "shit-for-brains." Joanna told the lad to take a photo of himself, on his phone, posting the letter. She wanted to be sure that Lee got it, and that it didn't go into some random house up the lane.

A couple of hours after the paper-boy had set off on his relatively simple round, Joanna received a text message from Lee. It was short and to the point. "Thank you, Big Sis. I'll sort this out, all of it. Love you xxx."

It took a few days for things to calm down, for the emotions to settle and for the community to stop gossiping about Lee and his disappearance. Life was returning to normal. Olivia had been around to see Joanna and explained the situation. Joanna was pleased to hear that Lee had confessed to everything, in great detail, as painful, humiliating and as emotionally draining as it had been. This news had come as a huge relief, as did Olivia's graceful acceptance of Joanna's questionable silence regarding the issue whilst Lee was missing. Olivia respected the fact that it was Lee's problem and that the explanation should come from him. Besides, it would have only worried her more. When all was said and done, it had been the right thing to do.

The best news was that Olivia was 100% supportive and was determined to help Lee deal with this overwhelming problem, a task that had already begun in the form of Olivia taking complete charge of Lee's financial affairs. This resolution that the two had come up with was borne out of Lee's completely open honesty about the severity of his problem, coupled with a rather starling confession. Lee had explained that despite knowing the hell and misery that his gambling unleashes, he still had an overwhelming desire to go and do it again, an intense compulsion to try and win all of his money back. Even stronger still, Lee had an overpowering need to win back Joanna's money. In amongst all of this torment, Lee was battling with himself over the fact that he'd let a lot of people down through all of this and that didn't sit well with him either. As far as Lee's mental health was concerned, he recognised that he was at crisis point, but he was determined to put everything right and come through this in better shape than he'd been in before it all began, just three and a half weeks earlier.

Lee had promised Olivia that he wouldn't trust himself with anything more than his dinner money until he felt absolutely sure that he had been completely released from the suffocating grip of this shockingly powerful addiction.

Olivia went with Lee and signed up for a bank loan of six thousand pounds and as soon as the money hit their joint account, Olivia transferred five thousand pounds into the account of Lee's building materials supplier and one thousand into Joanna's account. The rest would be repaid in instalments over the following months, but Olivia was aware that Joanna had literally no money at all because of this, so the first thousand was just a down-payment to replace her wages and tide her over for now.

Lee made a startling confession to Olivia, which really demonstrated to her that he was taking all of this seriously. He signed his van over to her, filling out the log-book and asking her to sign her name in the "new keeper" section.

"Why?" she asked.

"Because I'll probably sell it otherwise."

It was at this moment that Olivia really, truly felt that she grasped the enormity of Lee's problem and she respected him for being so brutally honest and open about just how vulnerable he had become to this gambling problem. It was extraordinary that a man as grounded and sensible as Lee Riley was talking in such a way. But none the less, it was greatly appreciated and it served as the strongest sign yet that Lee was determined to overcome this. "Deeds are stronger than words!" said Lee, borrowing a phrase that his gran, Elsie used to say.

Joanna finally sat and spoke with Lee four days after he'd turned up. It wasn't planned as such, she just called around at Lee's house out-of-the-blue, as she often did. Lee was a bit awkward at first, it was clear that he felt an immense deal of shame. But Joanna was an expert at putting people at ease. She walked in, held her brother in a tight embrace before saying, "Well, don't just stand there like a mouldy old dildo. Tea, two, plenty of milk."

The conversation which followed lasted hours. Joanna was absolutely thrilled to see that Lee had made such a positive start in beating these demons. The tears and the self-pitying that she had witnessed in Lee's van the previous week, high on the moors above the town, were gone. Now, Lee was talking openly and frankly about his plans to beat this, the online researching that he'd been doing, the stats and figures of how many people he had discovered were in exactly the same boat as him.

Most encouragingly of all, Lee was talking about all of this clearly and confidently and he seemed much more accepting of what he had gone through, thanks in part to realising that there were a lot of people just like him, who had experienced the very same problems. Lee had learnt that there were many, many thousands of people in the same boat as him. People who'd had everything one minute and had fallen victim to one of the most addictive activities on planet earth.

Lee explained how it works, how the adrenaline buzz grips you and how the money lost never really feels lost, because a gambling addict's mind hasn't accepted that it is lost, it's just temporarily being held by the bookies until you win it back, next time. He explained that games are addictive, pointing out that Joanna was forever filling her spare time playing Word-Cookie on her phone. No money was changing hands, but Lee explained that her compulsion for playing "just one more game" at bed-time, was no different to what Lee had found himself doing, when it was all boiled down. The only difference was that Lee's "one more game" issue had been much more exhilarating because of the money and had also resulted in a loss of more than twenty-thousand pounds in under a month.

"If it was a quid a game, but you could win a tenner if you won, do you reckon you'd play it as often as you do, or more?" he asked. It was a very good question because Joanna won most of the time on it. She didn't honestly know the answer, but she understood the point and realised with quite a start that she was, indeed, addicted to the game without even realising it.

The chat went on for ages, and Joanna was relieved that the tears were none existent. He had made a promise to himself, and Olivia, and now Joanna, that he wasn't going to try and get the money back. He had to accept it was gone, forever, and as hard as it was going to be, he had to deal with the fact that every penny he had, every penny that he had saved, and every penny that he had borrowed off Joanna, was gone. "I have to face that, I have to treat it as though it was in a house-fire. It's lost and if I can accept it's gone, and that I'll never get it back, I'll be okay."

The final part of Lee's plan was the most productive. He was going to start attending meetings with Gamblers Anonymous. The nearest group was in Halifax, and Lee told Joanna that his first meeting was the following night, at 7pm. "The first part of recovery is accepting that there's a problem, admitting it, speaking openly about it, celebrating the fact that I'm aware of it, rather than trying to pretend I've got things under control. I can't start to get over this until I'm completely open and honest about that."

All in all, this was a fantastic chat and Joanna was so pleased with how things were working out. There were lots of questions that Joanna really wanted to ask, and there were some that she really didn't want to ask, but she wanted to know the answer to. As depressing and distressing as it would be, she really wanted to know where Lee had gone, when he'd disappeared, what he'd been doing, and what he had been planning to do.

But there was no way. That would have to wait for another day. The main thing now, was that Lee was in a better frame of mind. And, even if he lost this first battle and wanted to relapse, it wasn't going to be easy because Olivia was holding the money. Joanna left Lee's house feeling a thousand times lighter than she'd felt when she'd arrived. She walked out there knowing that things were going to be okay.

Chapter Forty-One

Friday

The SCIU team were sitting in the incident room, waiting to hear about the operation that Miller and Saunders had hinted at the previous evening. Miller was still pinning pictures and maps up on the incident room wall whilst his officers were taking part in some general office banter to pass the time. Worthington and Kenyon were having a go at one another over something that had happened at the previous year's Christmas do.

"You can't say anything after you asked if the roast pork was halal, you stupid fuck-wit!"

"I did not… everyone knows I didn't say that so… if you've got to start making stuff up, you've lost your argument already! Knob rot."

"Right, guys settle down please." Miller had finished what he was doing and turned to face his team. "Okay, let's get busy, we've got a lot to achieve today. I want you all to take a good look at this man." The mood in the incident room became much more serious as the officers realised that Miller was in full, no-nonsense mode. "This is Adrian Wilson, the man who owned the flat that was destroyed by fire in the early hours of Monday morning." Miller reminded his team as to how it was that this individual had arrived in police custody. As he concluded, Saunders and Rudovsky stood and took a bow.

"Yes, well done Keith, Jo, amazing result. But we're not quite there yet. It's nine am, which means we've got little more than an hour and a half to get this arsehole charged." Miller looked at every member of his team, they all looked extremely concerned. The DCI smiled at them, sensing that they were all starting to feel a panic. "Thing is, that's not going to happen, so I've applied for a warrant to extend his detention for another twelve hours, taking it to thirty-six hours." The detectives all knew that because the offence that Wilson was suspected of was so serious, there was no risk of the application being turned down. But even with the 12 hour extension, it still meant that the clock was ticking, and that he only had until half-past ten that evening to gather enough evidence against Wilson to press charges.

"So today, our primary objective is going to be focused on arresting these three men." Miller gestured at the police mug shots on the wall, before he patted the photograph next to Wilson's. "This man is forty-six year-old Terence Bright. He's got a list of previous as long as Blackpool front. He's been done for all sorts of mindless shite, from shop-lifting to car-theft. He was once caught stealing a mountain bike on Market Street in town, the bike was chained to the CCTV post. His surname is quite ironic, considering he's about as bright a two-watt bulb." Miller allowed a moment to accommodate his team's laughter at the brutal observation.

"Terry two-watt!" said Rudovsky as the laughter died down, "I'm keeping that!"

"Nice one Jo. Terry two-watt's last known address on the PNC is close to Wilson's, less than a two-minute walk away. He lives at 44 Henrietta Street, Guide Bridge. This guy, I believe is the man who is sat here next to Wilson in Ashton McDonalds, visibly enjoying some good crack over a Big Mac meal and a milkshake, just after burning two little kids and their father to death as they slept. I also believe that this man is the person I have numbered 4 on this photo." Miller pointed to a different photo, this time he held his hand next to the grainy black and white image which was taken from a still of the Hat Factory's CCTV. Number 4 was on the extreme right of the four people. Miller wrote "Bright?" on a post-it note and stuck it on the image, right above the number 4.

"Okay, stick with me, there's a lot to learn here. This man," Miller slapped another photograph, "is called Callum Dewhurst. He's thirty-two and again, from the Guide Bridge area of Ashton, address we've got for him is 27 Jubilee Street. He's a reformed heroin user with a long list of previous. Most of it is predictable stuff really, burglary, shop-lifting, common assault, breach-of-the-peace etcetera. But most interestingly, he's got previous as a serious car-thief. He started out as a joy-rider and has graduated to stealing high-performance vehicles to order.

He now appears to be quite heavily into his alcohol, he was last picked up by MCP officers three months ago for trying to get out of Asda in Ashton with a crate of Special Brew under his jacket." This comment didn't attract a laugh, or even a smile. It may have sounded quite bizarre, but this was ordinary behaviour from somebody with a drink problem and a low sense of self-worth.

"Are we all jotting these addresses down and making notes? There's a test later."

"Sir!"

"Yes, Sir."

"Okay. Now, I have Callum here in McDonalds." Miller pointed to the photograph and smiled as his team all nodded their agreement. Callum Dewhurst's nose had been broken so many times, it looked like it was trying to get away from his face. It was certainly going to be difficult for him to deny that it was him in McDonald's, his hooter was quite unique. "Callum's nose is so misshapen, I think if he painted it yellow, he could get a job promoting bananas." Miller's cruel jibe received a hearty laugh.

"Now then, simmer down. I have Callum on this photograph as number 3." Miller repeated the process of writing the suspect's name on a post-it note and stuck it in position on the picture. "In case anybody is wondering, number 1 is Wilson, in my opinion and based on the physical profile. So, onto number 2. This man." Miller repeated the same procedure of tapping the police mug shot which was pinned up on the wall. It may have seemed like a patronising gesture to an observer, but Miller knew from experience that it was a good way of making sure that everybody locked eyes on the picture that he wanted them focused on, burning that image into their retinas.

"Another bonny looking bloke, this one. This is 57 year-old Barry Hughes, a petty criminal with over twenty charges to his name, possession of stolen-goods, mainly stolen vehicle parts, there's also quite a few investigations into dodgy activities that didn't amount to any charges. Most interestingly, Barry has been banged up for offences centring around the motor-trade. In 1998 he served six months for providing fake MOT certificates, and received a fifty-grand fine, which closed-down his garage. From what I can gather of his life story, certainly as far as the PNC tells me, he's been on the wrong side of the tracks since he was released from custody twenty years ago. The most interesting thing of all, he still works as a mechanic at a garage in Droylsden. So, I think he could have easily knocked up some dodgy registration plates at work."

The SCIU team seemed impressed by Miller's ground-work. "There's another thing as well. I've been a bit puzzled by the whole fake-plate scenario. It wasn't adding up that this Zafira was stolen, and had plates made up for a local taxi which has been in the scrap yard for months. So, I had a bit of a play around on Google. The taxi comes up as the first result in a Google image search for a dark silver Zafira Ashton. Try it now, get your phones out."

Miller's team followed the instruction and within seconds, they had all nodded their agreement that this was how the fake number plate had come about. The fact that the vehicle had been scrapped had added a layer of intrigue to the investigation, but now it appeared to be nothing more than an unfortunate coincidence. One which had knocked Miller and Saunders off course for a short time.

"So, once we've arrested these three men and seized all of the phones and computers connected to them, we've potentially got a solid piece of evidence if we discover that search term in the internet browsing history. Agreed?"

Miller's team were very vocal and enthusiastic as they chanted "Sir."

"Right, nearly done on all this. The final thing I want to talk about is this man. Barry Hughes' and his funny walk."

This comment was met with confused looks from the SCIU detectives, but Miller was about to explain. He walked across to the window and pulled the blind down, blocking out the panoramic city-centre view which was framed by the moody and foreboding Pennine hills in the distance. Miller turned on the projector and the incident room wall was suddenly filled with a black and white image of the CCTV footage from the factory, which was situated just yards away from the scene of the arson attack on the opposite side of the road.

"Now, it's only a short clip this, but it is the only piece

of evidence we have that potentially places these four men at the scene."

"Potentially?" asked Chapman.

"I'm coming to that Bill. I want us to study this footage a number of times. Firstly, watch person number two. I don't want you looking at anybody else, just focus your eyes on number two, okay?" Miller pressed the play button on the laptop and the detectives all trained their eyes on the footage being projected against the wall, watching the man that Miller was convinced was Barry Hughes limping along. The limp was unmistakable as Hughes tried to keep up in between Wilson and Dewhurst, though slightly behind. Once the four men had walked out of view, Miller paused the playback.

"Okay, who wants to describe number two for me?"

Grant put her hand up first.

"Go on Helen."

"He's overweight, looks quite old to me, from the way that he carries himself. He's definitely got something wrong with him physically, he seems to do a strange hop with each step he takes on his right foot."

"A hop! That's a great description. I had it as a limp, but a little hop is a much better way of describing it."

"Thank you, Sir."

"So, as trivial as it might sound, this man's gait is extremely important to this investigation. I need some undercover footage of him walking normally, just as he does in day to day life. If we bring him in, he'll probably start putting on a different walk, you know what these types of reprobates behave like once we bring them into custody. I strongly suspect that this one will start doing some exaggerated limping on both legs as soon as we meet him, or he might even pretend he can't walk at all. So, I need some video footage of him to see if we can match it to the individual on the CCTV."

Everybody looked as though they understood the requirements of this peculiar operation. "Who is volunteering to sit in the back of an undercover van outside his home or workplace for a few hours, filming Barry Hughes? The mission is simple but incredibly important. I need one of you to bring back some footage that absolutely nails Hughes to this CCTV clip."

Several hands went up. "Good, well I think I'll choose Bill and Mike for covering the home address, Helen and Pete, you can cover the work address. Okay?"

"Sir!"

"Yes, Sir."

"In theory, this little hop of Hughes could be the strongest piece of evidence we have if used in combination with the McDonald's CCTV showing them all together. It will be enough to charge these horrible bastards, and once we've brought charges, they'll all be remanded and we'll be able to relax a bit as we gather the rest of the evidence for trial. Understood?"

"Yes, Sir."

"Brilliant. Well you lot go and see surveillance, I've booked two vans out, a United Utilities and a Manchester City Council one. You'll be given some uniform to wear as well. As soon as you've got the footage, and you've checked it looks good enough to prove that Hughes is the man walking on that clip, phone me and I'll organise his arrest. Good luck."

Chapter Forty-Two

Whilst Chapman, Worthington, Grant and Kenyon were out of the way, doing their crucial under-cover work on Barry Hughes, Miller, Saunders and Rudovsky were trying to work out the best way to arrest Terence Bright and Callum Dewhurst.

"We know that Callum doesn't work, at least not officially. Terence, despite his surname, isn't bright enough to hold down a job. So, this looks like it should be a case of carrying out a straight-forward raid on their houses. I've got every suspicion that they'll be sat there waiting for us. After-all, it's no secret that Wilson is in custody. They will be sat there chewing their nails, waiting for their doors to go in."

"Why don't we just get on with it?" asked Rudovsky. The DS was always more interested in getting stuck in, as opposed to sitting around doing arrest plans.

"Well, the simple answer to that is we will, just as soon as we've got video evidence of Barry Hughes' funky walk. The footage from McDonalds doesn't show much as he's obscured most of the time and he sat down right near the door. Once I've got some footage of that to compare to the CCTV, we can get every available officer in Greater Manchester involved in the arrests if we want. But until then, we're in no man's land."

"Fair enough."

"I know what you mean though, Jo. I'm keen to get them in as soon as and start the examinations of their communications devices." Saunders was just as eager to get on with the job.

"Patience is a virtue." Said Miller.

"Why isn't 'hurry the fuck up' a virtue?" Asked Rudovsky, smiling.

"Tell you what, the minute I know we've got that video, you can go in and eat these silly bastards for breakfast. I want us to pull off the biggest con-trick in this department's history. I want to blag each of these scrote-bags that we are blaming it all on Barry limpy-legs, and the only piece of evidence I need is a name for the man in the video, which our technical colleagues are currently trying to make of Hughes limping up the street.

They are attempting to airbrush the others out of the shot."

"Can they do that?"

"They think it's possible, as the CCTV footage is so shit. If they manage it and then we get the other suspects to agree that it's Barry Hughes on the video, then we've got enough to press charges. These dumb twats won't know that they've just embroiled themselves into the scenes from the Hat Factory and the McDonalds CCTV."

"It's a great plan boss," said Rudovsky. "But there is a lot resting on whether they'll grass on Hughes."

"There's also a lot resting on whether they fancy spending the next twenty-years in Strangeways, though." Countered Saunders. "We need to present it nice and cosy, act like we really give a shit about them. You'll be the secret weapon in this tactic, Jo."

Miller looked across at his DI and DS and nodded slowly, he looked as though he was deep in thought. "Okay, I think we need to hold a vote. All those who feel completely satisfied that these four men killed Andris, Juris and Inga Ozols, raise your hand in the air."

All three raised their hands. "All those who don't think... oh wait, there's not going to be much point in doing that." Rudovsky and Saunders smiled politely at Miller's attempt to lighten the mood, as he continued. "Listen, we all know they did it, the only obstacle in front of us is the CPS agreeing with the evidence we have, which they could argue is tenuous in its current format. We all know how awkward the CPS can be if there's nothing concrete. I'm not that concerned about building the entire package today, we just need enough to guarantee charges for all four of them..."

Miller stopped talking suddenly as his phone began vibrating on the desk. It was DCI Katy Green at Tameside.

"Aw, for... what does she want? Thought I'd seen the back of her for now," said Miller under his breath as he lifted the phone.

"Hello Katy, what a nice surprise, how can I help?"

"Hi Sir. Just had a very interesting call from the duty desk here at Ashton."

"Go on."

"A man has just wandered in, says he wants to speak to you. He's under the impression that you're based here, I think."

"What does he want to talk to me about?"

"He's not saying much, but he is insisting that he'll only talk to you."

"Have you got a name?"

"Yes. Well, he's quite well-known to us actually. Callum Dewhurst."

The line went silent, as Miller's mind tried to process the enormity of DCI Green's statement.

"Are you there?"

There was a further pause before Miller spoke. "Yes, yes, I'm here. That's a shock. So, what, he's there now?"

"Yes, he's sat in reception, he seems quite agitated."

"This is weird. I'm sat in a meeting with Keith and Jo, planning Callum's arrest, right now."

Saunders and Rudovsky's mouths opened as they read between the lines of the conversation Miller was having.

"Oh, well, saved you a job!"

"Yes, absolutely! Can you get him inside the nick, in case he has a change of heart? If he does have a change of heart, arrest him on suspicion of murder. I'll be over in fifteen minutes."

"Sure, I'll stick him in an interview room."

"Please, just, whatever you do, don't give him any clue that I even know about his existence. See you in a bit."

"Understood. No problem, Sir. Speak later."

Miller ended the call and looked across the desk at his colleagues. "Callum's just walked into Ashton nick, he wants a word. Come on."

Chapter Forty-Three

Miller stepped into the interview room where DCI Green had left Callum Dewhurst, followed by Saunders and Rudovsky.

"Hello Callum."

"Alright?"

"Yeah, not bad mate, what's all this about wanting a word?"

Callum Dewhurst looked like any other generic scrote that the Manchester police had endless dealings with. His dirty fingernails and the shit tattoo on his neck were the first things that the detectives noticed after his hideously disfigured nose. He had a very sad, scruffy looking face with lots of long wispy hairs dotted around. Whether this was a conscious decision to grow a beard, or the result of not having any razor-blades was impossible to guess. His trainers looked worn out and his clothes were filthy. The urban scum-bag look was completed with a faded La Coste baseball cap and a ripped Adidas tracksuit top.

"What's all this, who are these? I just wanted a quick word with you. That's all."

"Oh, right. Sorry, I had no idea. These are my colleagues, DI Saunders and DS Rudovsky from Serious Crimes. They're working with me on the investigation into the fire the other night. Is that what you wanted to talk to me about?"

"Well, like... I just wanted... do they need to be here?"

Miller turned around and looked at his colleagues, flicking his eyes at the camera in the corner of the interview room. "Can I ask you guys to give me a minute while I find out why Callum wants to speak to me please?"

"Yes, no problem. I need to make a phone call anyway." Said Saunders.

"To the wife?" said Miller, smiling. Saunders laughed. "You spend so long on the phone to her, I don't know why you don't just bring her to work with you and save on your phone bill!"

"Well, if I did that I'd have to buy her dinner!"

Miller laughed loudly at Saunders' joke and Rudovsky

joined in. The job of telling Callum Dewhurst that they knew nothing about him, or what he'd done had been completed with this rather shite office banter bravado.

"It's nowt against yous." Said Callum charitably, as Miller's colleagues turned to leave the interview room.

Rudovsky closed the door behind them and Saunders ran along the corridor to the custody desk. "Can you take us somewhere we can watch the live-feed from interview room three, please? We need to monitor the conversation. Now!"

Saunders and Rudovsky were quickly led along to a small room adjacent to interview room three, where Miller had arranged the discreet recording of Callum's chat with him.

"Cheers!" said Rudovsky as they sat down hastily and trained their eyes on the monitor screen before them. They were pleased to learn that they'd not missed much, as Miller had engaged Callum in a conversation about something completely irrelevant in order to compound the impression that the SCIU staff were unaware of this child-killing arsonist's existence.

"So, anyway, forgive me waffling on. DCI Green said that you wanted a word, off the record."

Callum leaned back in his chair, his nervousness was abundantly clear, but he looked as though he was determined to try and blag his way through it.

"Yeah, well, you're the main guy about the arson attack aren't you?"

"Yes, that's right. Why, do you know something about it?"

"Well, not exactly. But I've heard summat. About that Ady Wilson."

"Adrian Wilson?"

"Yes."

"What do you know?"

"Well, first of all, is he the guy you arrested yesterday?"

"Where have you heard that?"

"It's all over Facebook and that."

"So, you've answered your own question."

"Yeah, yeah, I know but people are chatting shit and I

just wanted it straight."

"Well, forgive me Callum, but that kind of information is strictly confidential. We don't release names of suspects until charges have been brought." Miller was playing with Callum, trying to see how well he understood the law.

"So, he's not been charged?"

"Listen mate, I'm not being funny, but you can get all this on Facebook. Why have you asked to see me?"

"Listen, yeah, what it is, cards on the table yeah, I can tell you what you need to know about that fire."

"How do you know anything about it?"

"We'll get to that in a minute, yeah. But all I'm saying, is I know what's gone on, and I'll tell you. But I need some fucking what's it called? Like animosity."

"Anonymity?"

"Yeah, that's it. So, I'll do a deal with you, yeah. You tell me what you know and I'll tell you if its right or not. That way, there's no way of me being accused of grassing, innit?"

Miller acted dumb and kept a straight-face as he laid his first trap. "Callum, listen mate. I really appreciate you coming down here and everything, but I need strong information about this guy. He's a complete mystery to us, he won't talk about the fire which has destroyed his building. We don't think for a second that he was involved on the night, there's no evidence of that and he doesn't fit the bill anyway. But since he's not giving us any answers, we're starting to think that he might know who was involved. And we need to know."

"Yeah?" Callum was trying to play it cool. He'd come here for information, trying to figure out what the police knew. This version of what the police knew, the one which Miller was presenting was music to his ears. At least that's the way Miller read it, as did Saunders and Rudovsky who were eavesdropping in the booth next door.

"Yes. Our theory is, wait… You're not going to breathe a word about this out there are you?"

"No, course not man." Callum was physically relaxing before Miller's eyes, his stiff body language was softening and that shaky nervousness that he'd started with was becoming less pronounced with each passing minute. The comment about going "out there" had completely reassured this repugnant man that he was in the clear, safe in the knowledge that Wilson was staying silent.

"Okay, well, we're working on the idea that Adrian Wilson has upset somebody, you know, pretty bad. And they've got their own back by torching his flat. Would you know of any arguments or disagreements that he may have had with anybody recently?"

Callum's face began heating up. It was as obvious as the nose on his face that he was excited at hearing some incredible information here. Information that showed what a set of useless twats the police were.

"Listen right, Ady has pissed everyone off. I'm telling you, he's got more enemies than friends. So yeah, that's quite a good theory that you've got."

"And is that what you wanted to speak to me about?"

For the first time since this conversation had started, Callum had to try and think quickly and the stress of this sudden question manifested itself in the form of Callum's upper-body suddenly stiffening up again.

"No, well, like I say..."

"You said that you'd heard something."

"Well, it might be bollocks, do you know what I mean?"

"Try me. You can't have thought it was that much of a load of bollocks if you've come all the way down here and insisted that you speak to me about it."

Callum looked down at the floor. He was suddenly on the ropes. He'd only come here to see if these detectives were looking for him, his morbid curiosity had gotten the better of him. Now, he was feeling satisfied with what he had heard from the main plod and he didn't really feel the need to say what he'd originally intended.

"Come on Callum, help us out mate."

"No... it's not that, I just... I think you're right what you said. It's probably spot on."

"Just tell me what you've heard. It'll never come back on you, I swear down."

Callum looked down at the floor again, his hands were trembling. He was beginning to realise that he needed to say something or he would look extremely suspicious. He opened his mouth and started speaking.

"It's just, what I heard yeah was that Ady's flat had come empty and it was fucked inside and he couldn't afford to do it up. That's all. Then someone else said that it was burnt down for an insurance job, right, but whoever it was that done it didn't know that anyone was inside it. They were supposed to have moved out a few days before."

Miller was staring at Callum, waiting for more, but that was it.

"Where did you hear this Callum?"

"No names."

"Yes, I know. But *where* did you hear it?"

"I overheard some mates of Ady's in the pub."

"Which pub?"

"Which pub? The, er, the Corporation Arms."

"When was this?"

"The other day."

"Can you remember which day?"

"Dunno, Wednesday I think."

"But you've only decided to come and speak about it today?"

"Yeah, well, like I said. It's all this shit on Facebook about Ady being arrested. It's got me thinking."

"Do you know who was supposed to have done it?"

"Nah, nah, nothing like that. It's just, Ady's a cunt and that, everybody knows. But I believe the story I heard. I don't think he's capable of killing a family. Not kids. So, if he is under arrest for murder, that's probably why he's saying fuck all."

Callum's confidence was beginning to build back up, Miller got the distinct impression that the little scrote felt that he had done enough to blag his way in and out of this police station. Miller was about to give this Callum Dewhurst a little surprise.

"Well, I'm grateful to you for coming in and talking to us. It's really appreciated, as you know this is a very serious crime. They don't get much more serious than this one."

"Yeah, yeah, I know what you mean."

"Do you know what I was doing when you asked to speak to me?"

Callum shrugged.

"I was planning your arrest!" Miller smiled widely, but his eyes contained no warmth.

Callum's face changed instantly, that rosy-glow he'd been developing was suddenly turning a shade darker. The cocky-glint in his eyes was replaced with an unmistakable expression of shock.

"What... *my* arrest?"

"Damn right! Your arrest, Barry Hughes' arrest and Terence Bright's arrest. Your mate Ady has told us everything about yous! He's been singing like a demented canary!"

"What, that's fu..."

Miller's jovial and pleasant demeanour suddenly disappeared. He locked eyes with Dewhurst and stared at the man, there was no longer a tactical requirement for hiding his utter contempt and hatred for this evil, pathetic man. "It was you four. You killed them two gorgeous little kids and their dad. You left their mum fighting for her life in the hospital, even though she's got nothing left to live for."

"This is total bullshit!"

"You reckon?"

"I fucking know it is!"

"Was it your bright idea to come in here and try to suss out if you were on my radar, or Smithy's?"

"Who the fuck is Smithy?"

"Smithy? He was the thick one out of The Bash Street Kids."

The man sitting opposite Miller looked confused, almost as though the room was spinning for him.

"Callum Dewhurst, I am arresting you on suspicion of three counts of murder and one count of attempted murder. You do not have to say anything..."

Chapter Forty-Four

"Hi Sir!"

"Alright Bill. Anything?"

"Oh yes, just e-mailing you something now. We've got Hughes walking all the way up his street from the bus stop. If it's not the same guy limping as the one in your CCTV, then you can strip me naked and call me Susan!"

"Erm, that's great news Bill, but why have you just put that visual impression inside my head?"

"Where are you, anyway? Sounds a bit echoey."

"We're over in Ashton, I'm in the corridor, we've been having some incredible developments. Callum Dewhurst popped in to try and work out if we were onto him."

"What a fucking whopper!"

"I know. He's set us up for a fantastic set-to with Wilson though. We're beginning to think that they thought the flat was empty. It might have been an insurance job that's gone very wrong."

"Jesus."

"Anyway, Jo's about to go in and have a word with Wilson, so I'm just going to have a quick chat with her and then I'll be heading back."

"Right. Well, we're still here outside Hughes' house, ready to make the arrest. He's home alone."

"Perfect, give us five minutes and I'll send you some cavalry. Great work Bill."

*****

Saunders had driven the short journey from Tameside police station to The Corporation Arms, a big old Victorian era pub on the border of Guide Bridge and Audenshaw, just yards away from the famous old railway station.

"Hello love," said the barmaid. "What can I get you?"

"Hiya, I'm not here for a drink, sorry, I'm a detective." Saunders held up his warrant card as a couple of old blokes on the bar-stools began muttering to one another.

"Oh, right. What's up?"

"I'm just wondering if you recognise this man?" Saunders showed the barmaid a mug-shot photo on his phone.

"Yes, unfortunately. Everyone knows who he is."

"Do you have a name for him?"

"Just a minute, I'll get the landlord." The barmaid smiled politely as she walked across to the phone at the end of the bar. "Brian, can you pop down a minute love? Ta." She placed the phone on its cradle and walked around to where Saunders was standing. "He'll be down in a minute, would you like to follow me through here? You can talk privately."

"Sure, thanks a lot."

Saunders was led through to another part of the pub, a small bar with just a couple of stools, a pool table and a dart board.

"I didn't want to say anything in front of the customers. It's Callum Dewhurst on your photo. Biggest pain-in-the-arse around here."

"Right. Does he come in here often?"

"No." The lady laughed. "He's barred, I think he's barred from every pub in Tameside, likes to start with his mouth after a couple of pints."

"So, he's definitely not been in here this week then?"

The barmaid smiled warmly. "Definitely not. He wouldn't dare come in here. Anyway, Brian will tell you more."

"Cheers. In fact, do you know what, that's enough. That's all I needed to know. He's using this pub as an alibi, says he was in here Wednesday afternoon."

"Well, I work every day, opening til' six. We've got CCTV on the door as well so we can prove he's not been in. He's lying."

"Brilliant. Okay, well, I've a lot on. Tell your boss it doesn't matter."

"Okay love, well, if you need anything else, just ring up and ask for Brian."

*****

Rudovsky was facing Adrian Wilson in the interview

room. He had a new duty solicitor with him, so she was fully prepared for a no-comment interview.

"Okay, it's just a brief interview Adrian, I just need some facts confirming."

"When are you letting me out?"

"Well, that would depend on how co-operative you are. If you refuse to answer my questions, it's only going to slow things down, isn't it?"

Wilson didn't answer, he just stared aggressively at Rudovsky. It didn't put her off her work.

"So, a bit of breaking news for you. Callum Dewhurst popped in..."

Wilson's steely-stare was disrupted by this announcement. His eyes looked away from Rudovsky and down towards the table-top. That comment had knocked his confidence.

"He has made a statement. In it, he says that you told him that the flat was unoccupied, and that you were burning it out because it was going to cost too much money to fix up for a new tenant."

Wilson's hands began trembling and he moved them from the table-top, quickly placing them on his lap. His eyes were filling with moisture as the colour drained noticeably from his already pallid complexion. As devastating comments went, Rudovsky had just hit the jackpot. But she wasn't done yet.

"He's a right wally, isn't he? He came in thinking he'd be able to drop you in the doo-doo. But he hadn't anticipated that we were already on to him. And Terence Bright. And Barry Hughes. Do those names mean anything to you Mr Wilson?" Rudovsky smiled as she waited for a reply. It felt good to see how devastating her words were to the man facing her.

Eventually, Wilson replied, he sounded as though his emotions were affecting his voice. "No comment."

"Well, just so you know, the others aren't no commenting. They've got a lot to say about the fact that they are facing multiple murder charges off the back of your fibs."

This comment forced an involuntary tick from Wilson, he did a very noticeable twitch which seemed to start in his shoulder but made his entire body twist quickly. He was rattled, there was no question about it. Rudovsky could see that she was close to ruining this evil bastard's day and decided to get on with it.

"How sick do you have to be? Getting your mates to help you burn down a building, knowing that there are kids sleeping inside?"

"YOU FUCKING BITCH!" Shouted Wilson as he leapt to his feet, his chair flew back and clattered against the floor. Wilson's eyes were filled with rage as he pointed his finger at Rudovsky. She stayed put, looking up at him from her seated position, deliberately wearing an expression of indifference.

"THEY SAID THEY'D MOVED OUT!"

As he shouted it, Rudovsky's tummy flipped. She hadn't expected a confession, not just yet anyway.

"Just calm down or I'll press the alarm and you'll be tasered!" Rudovsky held her hand over the red strip which was fixed all around the wall. "Sit down."

Wilson's duty solicitor realised that everything had just gone about as badly as it could. "Can I request a break please?" he asked calmly. Rudovsky gave him a death-stare across the table as Wilson picked his chair up from where it had fallen and sat down on it.

"No, fuck your break. I'm not fucking having this murder bullshit. I've got a fucking e-mail, right, that says this prick who was living there had moved out. I didn't fucking know they were in, did I?"

"You didn't check though. Did you?"

"Listen, you smart-arse little bitch. He sent me a fucking e-mail that said he's fucking moved out and I aren't getting my rent, which was three grand! So, I admit it, yeah, burning the flat out. But I didn't mean to kill anyone, so fuck off."

* * * * *

Terence Bright was sitting on his door-step, smoking a roll-up when the police arrived at his terraced street. He took a long hard drag at the cigarette as he realised that the huge

Tactical Aid van wasn't driving past. It was slowing down. He stood up, threw the cigarette on the floor and held his wrists out for the officers as they approached him. He saw no sense in running or putting up a fight. If anything, he'd been looking forward to this moment, ever since he'd heard about those people who'd been in the flat when it had gone up in flames.

He'd only agreed to go along and be a part of the whole thing because he was bored. Ady had promised to give him "a wedge" when the insurance money came through. All he had to do was sort out an alibi for where they had all been when the fire had started. It had all seemed like a genius plan to Terence, he was impressed by how much thought had gone into it all. The stolen car with a local taxi's plates on. When does a taxi ever get pulled by the police? The petrol cans in the boot, parking on the motorway. They'd even gone as far as to make sure the petrol needle was showing as empty if any police stopped on the motorway. Terence Bright had really felt like a serious gangster that night, it was all so well organised, and the buzz they'd all felt afterwards, in McDonalds. It was brilliant, the most professionally organised crime he'd ever been involved in. And Ady was looking at about £100,000 in the bank within a week. Maybe he'd give Terence a grand. Maybe even two. What did a wedge mean anyway? Might even be five grand! It had been one of the best nights of Terence Bright's life.

But the next day, when Terence got up around dinner-time and heard the news on the radio. That was the worst moment of his entire life. He couldn't take it in at first. He ran downstairs and put the telly on. Seeing the footage on Sky News, seeing all those police and fire engines and all those sad faces at the cordon line had helped him to accept the horrific news. As he stared at the TV screen, the cameraman had zoomed in on a group of little kids in their school uniforms placing a bunch of flowers next to the policeman's feet. That was when he realised what he'd done.

From that moment, Terence Bright wanted nothing more than to hand himself in, just go into the police station and explain the mistake, just to look in another person's eyes and tell them that he was involved, that it wasn't supposed to have ended that way. But he knew the consequences would be even worse than what he was already going through. His past experience of prison had learnt him one thing, there's nowhere to hide if you're a grass, the word gets around.

The news people were confusing everything, saying it was some gang who had something against betting shops. Even though Terence was struggling to control his breathing, it looked like they were going to get away with it, that some other people would take the blame. But that still didn't make him feel any better.

The best that Terence Bright had felt all week was when that massive copper in the riot helmet threw him down on the floor and put the cuffs on his wrists, tighter than they'd ever been put on before. It was over.

*****

The mood in the SCIU office was flat as the shift came to an end. The sudden news that Marija Ozols had passed away in hospital had been devastating for all of the investigating officers, all of whom had been in high-spirits about the arrests. This awful news had come through from the hospital whilst Miller and his team were celebrating the fact that they had at least one piece of good news for Marija when she woke up. But now, that wasn't to be.

Chapter Forty-Five

There had been no Twitter activity from the people behind the "Odds on Revenge" moniker for several days. The last message which the account had posted had been in the hours following the unforgettable night of pugnacious damage which had seen over two-hundred of the nation's betting shops put out of business within just a few short hours.

Despite the lack of activity on Twitter, the account had still managed to attract over two hundred-thousand followers.

But today, some five days on, the Twitter account was back in action. At 6am precisely, the following message was sent to a number of high-ranking Twitter news accounts in Great Britain;

"NEWS ALERT! @bbcnews @skynews @itvnews @bbcworld @bbcr4 @r4today @mcpolice @skynewsbreak @channel4news @cnni @TheSun @dailymirror @independent @thetimes @MENnewsdesk MAJOR NEWS STORY TO FOLLOW #oddsonrevenge STANDBY FOR MORE"

And that was it, that was all it said. This Twitter handle was supposedly being used by the people responsible for the chaos that the nation had seen over the past week. On the previous occasions that it had been used, it had served as a facility to comment on events that had taken place. This tweet was announcing that something was *about* to happen. And it was being taken very seriously.

The only clue as to where this "major news story" was taking place, came from the inclusion of the Manchester City Police twitter account, as well as the Manchester Evening News newspaper. All of the other @ addresses included in the tweet were the Twitter account names of the biggest newsrooms throughout the UK.

The Tweet was soon retweeted by the nation's earliest risers, and it didn't take long until it was going viral. The newspapers, talk radio stations and TV breakfast shows began making reference to it, dropping little hints and teasers that this was probably worth staying tuned into their channel for. The betting shops news story had been so big in this past week, it was perfectly legitimate to upgrade this simple news alert into a story in its own right.

Several of the Twitter addresses which the message had been sent to had replied. "@OddsOnRevenge thanks for news alert. Any more information? From @skynews"

But these speculative tweets were being ignored. There was no further activity from the Twitter account for well over an hour and a half, until 7.48am to be precise, when a further Tweet was sent.

"NEWS ALERT! People of Manchester, England. If you are in the City Centre this morning, please look above."

This rather ominous message was met with derision from the news editors and reporters who had been waiting impatiently for the next message to arrive.

"What the fuck is that supposed to mean?" asked Sky News' Managing Editor of his staff.

"Look above. All there is above is the last Tweet. What does it mean?" asked a Good Morning Britain news producer.

It took several minutes before the message began to make any sense to the news teams who were desperately trying to understand what this cryptic message meant. The first message which made sense came from a member of the public in Manchester city centre, who Tweeted a photograph with the hashtag #OddsOnRevenge.

The photograph was quite dark and not very clear, due to the fact that daylight was only just breaking in the city. But despite the poor-quality image, it was still possible to make out what the image was.

The famous Arndale Centre tower, in the heart of Manchester, had dozens upon dozens of people standing on its roof-top. These people looked as though they were holding hands, right on the edge of the flat roof.

Another picture was Tweeted just minutes later, taken by another passer-by. This time it was the roof of Manchester One, another city-centre high-rise office block on Portland Street, about a quarter of a mile away from the Arndale. There were dozens of people standing all the way around the top of this building as well, holding hands and looking down, they were literally inches from the edge, standing around all four sides of the twenty-one story building.

And then another Tweet was published, this one showed the rooftop of City Tower, the famous office block in Piccadilly Gardens which stands thirty-stories tall. It too was adorned by dozens of people, all standing by the edge, holding hands, staring down at the ground below.

"What the actual fuck is going on?" screamed the BBC North news editor in the general direction of his production team, as more images began appearing on his computer screen. He had an unmistakable look of terror about him. "Is this... do we think this is a suicide pact?"

Then another Tweet appeared, showing the rooftop of the CIS Tower. Then another quickly followed with a picture from the Civil Justice centre, the weird office block which looks like a filing cabinet with a couple of drawers left open. On every dimly-lit photo, all of which were being taken by shaky hands on mobile phones, the images all appeared to show the same, bizarre thing.

It was such a surreal sight, it took a few seconds for viewers to register what they were actually seeing. Dozens, no, hundreds of people were standing on the edges of the most famous high-rise rooftops in Manchester, all of them were looking down at the ground. It was impossible to make out the faces of the people on these camera-phone images, the people taking the photos were too far away and the morning light was still very faint.

It wasn't long before a few professional and amateur photographers in the area started snapping the scene with their top-quality cameras and their super zoom lenses. Their high definition images soon began surfacing on the various social media platforms. These pictures began to tell a better story of what was going on.

The first HD picture which was published on Instagram allowed viewers to zoom right in and see what was happening. The people standing on top of the Arndale centre, some 80 metres above the ground, appeared to be talking and discussing matters casually, as though they were merely waiting for a bus.

They certainly looked relaxed. The people ranged in ages, there were young adults and older folk, male and female. It was even more of a bizarre sight when viewed close-up.

"Do you know what this reminds me of?" The Manchester Evening News editor span around in his chair and spoke to his closest colleagues. "Who remembers that guy who did the nude installations all around Manchester a few years ago? Spencer Tunick, that was his name. It looks just like one of those... only, well, all these people have got their clothes on." The MEN editor had a point, this did look some sort of a modern art installation, which quite frankly, was a much cheerier explanation than a "suicide pact" which the North West Tonight editor was fearing, just a few miles up the road.

Just over ten minutes after the photographs of this random spectacle began circulating, the MCP helicopter, India 99 was air-borne and was beaming footage of the tops of the buildings back to HQ. The live footage made for interesting viewing as the senior officers of MCP, including DCS Dixon, watched on in the incident command centre in puzzled silence.

The deafening roar of the aircraft's rotor-blades chopping through the early morning air made it impossible to hear anything, which was frustrating for the senior police men and women as it was quite apparent that many of the people on the rooftops were looking up and shouting something at the personnel on board India 99.

The footage kept coming in, as the force's helicopter switched from one building to another, hovering high above the people. The Tactical Flight Officers were instructing the pilot on where to fly, as they endeavoured to catch every face on their recording equipment. The pilot's key task was to follow the TFO's instructions whilst ensuring the helicopter kept a safe distance away from other buildings and hazards, as well as the people that they were here to observe. The powerful down-wash of the rotor blades could easily sweep these people off these roof-tops if the aircraft got within seventy metres of the buildings. Whilst the pilot had an absolute nightmare of a job on his hands, it wasn't a particularly difficult task for the TFOs making the video recordings, as most of the people, out of the hundreds upon hundreds, were looking directly at the helicopter. It made chilling viewing for the TFOs on board, as well as the senior police officials who were watching all of this back at HQ.

Once all of the recording was done, and the TFOs were confident that they had captured images of every single person present, across ten buildings in the city-centre, it was time to start phase 2 of India 99's mission. This task was to warn the people to step back slowly, and carefully, away from the edge of the building that they were standing atop of.

Despite the roar of the aircraft hovering 100 metres above them, the message was heard loud-and-clear by all of the people, thanks to India 99's powerful Tannoy system which is positioned beneath the aircraft. The sound system was so loud that the TV cameras which had arrived on the streets and were capturing this dramatic footage from the ground in the city-centre, could clearly make out the TFO's message.

"Danger! Step back, slowly and carefully, away from the edge of this building." The TFO in charge of the announcement kept repeating his message, but nobody was taking any notice, most of the faces were just smiling back in the direction of the helicopter. It was a very unnerving and unsettling sight, and the helicopter crew couldn't wait to receive their orders to retreat back to base. This was a strange and eerie job and the India 99 crew all sensed that something truly horrible was about to happen.

The first broadcaster to go-live from the city-centre was the BBC, thanks to their OB van being quite close to the area when this news story broke. As the local presenter went live on the national BBC News Channel, it was quite apparent that she, like everybody else in the nation, didn't have a clue what was going on, other than the fact that hundreds of people were standing on the edges of Manchester's tallest buildings, holding hands.

While the journalists waffled on relentlessly, trying to pad for time and make it sound as though they knew what was going on, and failing miserably, one young news journalist phoned her boss at BBC Radio Manchester to announce a major scoop.

The reporter was patched through to the broadcast desk immediately and was live on the local radio station within seconds, announcing her news.

"We'll leave you there Harriet as we've got another reporter on the line, Kiera Stewart, one of our junior reporters is in the city-centre and has got some fresh information. Kiera?"

"Yes, thank you Alan, I hope you can hear me okay over the helicopter and police sirens?"

"Just about Kiera, where are you?"

"Well, I'm on Market Street, in Manchester city centre, just at the foot of the towering Arndale Centre building, the police helicopter is directly above my head right now…"

"And what have you learnt about this extraordinary event which is unfolding in our city this morning?"

"Well, we're… sorry… I'm just being moved back now by police officers, we are being escorted away from the foot of the building… there are dozens of police officers standing in a line, walking us back, trying to clear the area."

"This is just crazy, I started this morning's show wondering what we were going to talk about, and now this."

"Yes, well, this is an extremely scary story Alan, the police are saying that we have to move away from this area in case the people on top of those buildings are planning to jump."

The adrenaline and terror in Kiera's voice was unmistakable. The veteran presenter was lost for words, he didn't know what to say to that bewildering comment. Kiera sensed that she needed to keep talking. "Just as I started talking to you Alan, I was with one of the Arndale Centre's security staff who told me that his colleague has been taken up onto the roof with the people. They stormed the building at around half-past seven this morning. The security guard I spoke to said that he was on patrol, doing his routine checks around the building whilst his colleague was left on the security desk, he says that there were several people knocking on the door and when he went to ask them what they wanted, they literally ran into the building, and then dozens more people rushed past. The security guard told me that he has heard that similar tactics have been used at other buildings in the city centre this morning too, and looking around, it's just... all I can see is hundreds upon hundreds of people stood above my head, on every flat roofed building, and they are all holding hands and staring down. It's quite shocking Alan, and the scariest part of it all is that nobody seems to know what is going on, not even the police."

MCP's top officials had no idea what they were witnessing in the major incident command centre. The Chief Constable was now in attendance and didn't take long to declare himself the Gold Commander and announce this extraordinary event as a major incident. Within seconds, this dramatic announcement kick-started the police force's well-rehearsed MIRE instruction, the "Major Incident Response Exercise" which was the little used, but regularly practised drill for any major incidents in the city. The MIRE training covered everything from terrorist attacks, rioting and civil disobedience, to serious rail or motorway crashes. As soon as the MIRE instruction was circulated, every single operational police officer on duty within the Greater Manchester county was required to make their way into the city-centre and meet at their divisional check-point to await further instruction.

Facebook and Twitter were going wild with the story, as members of the general public decided to explain what was happening, rather than wait for some kind of an official explanation.

"Easy to see what's happening in MCR, all those people on top of the buildings are going to jump off holding hands, it happened in America a few years ago at that Waco. They'll be God-botherers or summat."

"I've been told that they're on Spice and they've been told to go there and show the world that they can fly, it makes sense I suppose."

"My mate's a copper and he's just told me that the people on top of the buildings are asking for the release of a tiger at Chester Zoo or they're going to dive off."

"Hasn't this been organised by the people who've been trashing all the betting shops? I think they're going to threaten to jump unless the police drop all charges against them. Bet you a tenner. Whoops, sorry."

It was quite easy to see that nobody had a clue what this was about. It was just so odd, so out-of-the-ordinary and nobody knew what to make of it. The police, the tv crews, the Facebook commentators. The only people who knew what the hell was happening here were those hundreds of men and women, holding hands and staring down at the deserted streets beneath them.

The mood in Manchester was strange. Other than the non-stop blare of police sirens, there was an unnerving quiet and stillness all around this normally bustling, busy place. There was no other sound in the city, but for the dramatic blasts of sirens from the emergency vehicles. Buses had stopped, their drivers had switched their engines off. The passengers just gazed out of the double-deckers, looking up at the sky. The roads were all closed in the city centre, part of a "lock-down" exercise in line with the MIRE procedure. Cars, taxis, delivery vans and trucks were all parked up on the streets and roads all around the area. People were standing by their vehicles, looking up, or holding up camera-phones, filming the eerie scenes. Members of the public who were talking to one another were doing so in hushed tones and whispers. Every person in town looked shocked and frightened. This was such a freaky situation, and although everybody was looking up, none of them wanted to see what they feared was about to happen.

Odds on Revenge Tweeted at 8:15am. It was a short message which did nothing but heighten its readers anxieties even further. "#Manchester have we got your attention?" That was all it said. Everybody who was following this extraordinary spectacle, be it from Piccadilly Gardens in Manchester, or on TV in the Outer Hebrides, were all desperate to know what the hell was going on. That Tweet didn't help. It did however attract thousands of replies.

"WTAF is going on?"

"Don't jump! PLEASE! Come down and talk."

"Step back from the edge!"

Thousands of random people were Tweeting Odds on Revenge, desperate to try and have some kind of an input into this terrifying situation which was unfolding live across TV news channels, social media and the internet.

The Sky News director in London was shouting the channel's most senior staff members into the gallery, where TV screens filled the walls, each screen showing a different angle of a different building as they monitored all of the incoming footage from various cameras and sources. He had a very concerned look on his face.

"I'm not sure we should broadcast this footage live. If they jump off, that's going to be traumatic for the viewers." He said.

"Just put it on a delay," suggested a producer.

"Yes, that would work. Replay the same footage from five minutes ago." Added another member of the team.

"Yes, yes, that's the answer. Do that now please!" shouted the director at his staff at the controls.

"What do you think is going on?" asked one of the news editors.

"They're going to jump. I wasn't sure at first, but that last Tweet has spooked me."

Another member of staff interrupted. "Oh, here we go, another Tweet." The senior officials of Sky News gathered around their colleague who was holding the phone. The looks on all of their faces confirmed that this wasn't good news.

The Tweet read "DANGER! To any people beneath the buildings we are occupying in #Manchester, please move out of the area immediately. You have two minutes."

"Oh my fucking God! What the hell is happening?" asked the Chief Constable in the MIRE control room. He didn't receive a response. Everybody in the room was stunned into silence. The only sound was the thundering beat of every one of the senior officer's hearts.

"Gold Command to all officers in the city centre, urgent message, retreat away from the foot of all occupied buildings immediately. Repeat. Urgent message, all officers are to retreat from beneath the buildings, immediately! Over."

It was the longest two minutes of every single one of the senior MCP officers lives, each second passed with a terrifying sense of dread and alarm. Some of them tried to fight pictures of the unimaginable horror that could soon devastate the city's streets and pavements.

There was a loud, upsetting sound from the corner of the control room as the Assistant Chief Constable knelt-down and vomited into a waste-paper bin. As several colleagues offered support to their colleague, the Chief Constable pointed to his watch. The two minutes had elapsed.

"This is Gold Command. Standby."

A few seconds passed before another Tweet appeared on all of the screens which were monitoring the Odds on Revenge account. The senior police officers all had one eye on the video-camera feeds from the roof-tops, and another on the Twitter screen.

The Tweet that had just appeared didn't say anything. It was a link to a website. The Chief Constable stepped over and with a trembling hand, clicked the mouse on the link which had appeared. It opened-up a new window, which was loading a very basic looking website. As the police chief's eyes were focusing on the website, a voice behind him alerted him to the video monitors.

On the screens, which were providing live feeds from all of the rooftops, there was activity. The people who had stood still, holding hands with the person on either side of them, had suddenly let their hands go. The dramatic vision of all of these people holding hands now looked even more dramatic, as they had all released their grips. Now, every single person was standing alone, looking down onto the deserted streets beneath the tower blocks. The silence was electrifying. Each of the figures suddenly reached into a coat pocket, or their jeans pocket and produced something, throwing whatever it was ceremoniously away from themselves and out into the cool November air.

"Zoom in, Zoom in" said the Gold Commander into his radio, the unmistakable stress and anxiety in his voice was broadcast to every serving police officer in the city. As the camera operators followed their instructions and zoomed their lenses in on the people on the rooves, it became clearer what was happening. The items which were being thrown to the ground were mobile phones. Hundreds of them, each one landing with a loud crunch on the streets below.

After several seconds of loud crunches, bangs and pops, the sound ceased and the eerie silence was restored. Nothing else was raining down from the towers above, but the streets were suddenly covered with the debris of the mobile phones which had smashed into hundreds of thousands of little pieces.

Suddenly, the people on the roof-tops slowly stepped backwards and began walking back to the doors and access-points that they had entered the roof spaces from, forming orderly queues as they waited patiently for their turn to step off the roof space and go back inside.

"Thank Christ!" said the Chief Constable, before lifting his radio to his mouth. "This is Gold Command. The protestors are now leaving the roof spaces, I want all available officers deployed to each tower block and each protestor needs to be arrested. Over."

The Chief Constable put the radio down on the desk and held his head in his hands as he tried to get his breath back.

"This is BBC News, and I'm relieved to say that this distressing incident in Manchester city centre appears to be over. The hundreds of men and women who have been standing at the edge of several tower-blocks for almost forty minutes have now stepped back from the edge and appear to be coming down. Gina Phillips, our North of England correspondent joins me. Gina."

"Yes, thank you Sue. Those were quite alarming scenes which we've been witnessing, and thankfully, it looks as though everything has come to a positive conclusion."

"Do we understand what this was all about, Gina?"

"Yes, we are starting to make some sense of that now, the final Tweet which the organisers of this incredible spectacle sent out contained a link to a website which appears to contain a statement that might explain what has been happening in Manchester in the middle of the city's rush-hour."

The BBC News channel switched from the head and

shoulder shot of Gina Phillips standing in Manchester, to a shot of the website. The screen turned white, this was an extremely basic webpage - it looked more like a Microsoft Word document. At the top, in capital letters it read; ODDS   ON   REVENGE – STATEMENT.

Beneath, there was a single paragraph;

"This morning, 730 people stood on the top of key buildings in Manchester to help raise awareness of gambling addiction. These 730 people are the relatives, friends or loved-ones of people who have ended their own lives as a result of their gambling addiction. 730 people, who some of you may have feared were going to jump, were standing there in tribute to their loved-ones who are no longer with us due to the poison that is gambling addiction. We're glad we got your attention. We're sad that you would take so much notice of this, because it looked like 730 people were going to die in front of you. Why aren't you taking notice of the 730 people who kill themselves because of gambling addiction, every year in Britain. That's two a day, every day, every year. This has to stop. Please, contact your MP and tell them to back us, tell them they have to clamp down on the gambling industry robbing our young people of their money and leaving them so broken that the only answer to their problems is suicide. This has got to stop and to the government, we say this. Make it stop, clamp down, just like you did with cigarettes a decade ago, or how you are attempting to with alcohol now. And how you do with drugs. If you do not fix this appalling situation, we will be back and we will do much more damage next time. Gamble responsibly stickers don't work, but fining gambling companies a million pounds if they allow somebody to gamble irresponsibly *would* work. Fining them a million pounds if they fail to act when somebody is in distress because of gambling would work in forcing the industry to behave responsibly. Clean this disgusting mess up and sort this evil out, once and for all, or we will be back and we will make our activities over the past few weeks seem like a teddy bear's picnic by comparison. Thank you, from the members of Odds on Revenge."

Epilogue

Billy Nolan pleaded guilty to the crimes that he was accused of at Manchester Crown Court and was sentenced to two concurrent life sentences for the murders of Graham Hartley and Lindsey Nolan. In summing up the Judge said that Nolan was a wicked, calculated and depraved individual, and stipulated that he must serve a minimum sentence of 28 years before he would be considered for parole. He wept openly in the dock as the sentence was handed down.

The trial against those responsible for the deaths of the four members of the Ozols family was held at Preston Crown Court in a trial which lasted over two months. Adrian Wilson was the only defendant who faced charges of murder. The others, Terence Bright, Callum Dewhurst and Barry Hughes all pleaded guilty to charges of manslaughter. A major part of the trial focused on the details surrounding Wilson's understanding of whether he had deliberately coerced his friends into assisting him to murder, or if this tragic incident was nothing more than a dreadful misunderstanding. The details of the e-mail from Andris Ozols were examined at great length. Long and complicated arguments about the understanding of the contents dominated several weeks of the trial. In the end, the jury decided that if there was so much confusion on the matter, then setting fire to the property without first checking to see if it was unoccupied had been the deciding factor around this technicality, of which all of Wilson's defence rested. Adrian Wilson was sentenced to four concurrent life sentences. His accomplices, who had all given evidence against Wilson, faced five years each.

Wilson maintains that the deaths were never intended and plans to appeal.

Not long after the Odds on Revenge website had appeared on the TV news and online news pages, it disappeared. The address was replaced with an "error 404" message. Investigators trying to locate the source which had hosted the page soon discovered that it had been hosted on a public access server located in Russia and was impossible to trace back to the original source.

The British government announced a "far-reaching review" into the practises of the gambling industry and how it is reacting to the new and emerging "online financial opportunities" which are currently unregulated. Several High Street banks have agreed to "explore" the "potential" of placing a gambling limit on their customers accounts, in a similar way to how they manage daily cash withdrawal limits. A number of smaller banks who have set-up similar schemes, such as Monzo the online bank, have offered to help the bigger banks introduce this technology to their services. There remains a small number of opposing voices who claim that any such changes are "further encouragement a nanny state."

The loudest voices of opposition against any significant changes to the status-quo come from the owners and shareholders of the gambling companies who know that new legislation will spell the end of their "golden era."

There has been no further communication from the Odds on Revenge Twitter account, which was deactivated soon after the website disappeared. Every person who took part in the stunt on the city centre roof-tops was arrested as they tried to leave the buildings and all received a police caution for trespass in a police operation which took several weeks to conclude due to the numbers of people involved.

Police investigators were told by every single member of the roof-top protest that the reason they had thrown their phones hundreds of feet down onto the ground was because it would make it impossible to identify the individual who was managing the protest group and sending the Tweets. The authenticity of this detail is still being investigated, as data-communication details from Twitter suggest that the messages sent out on the morning of the protest had not originated from anywhere in Greater Manchester.

Twitter had the source location as a mobile phone mast 45 miles away, in the West Yorkshire area. The person sending the Tweets had been somewhere within or between Halifax, Keighley and Todmorden.

The End

A short note from the author…

As has happened a few times whilst I've been writing books regarding contemporary issues, a major news story broke about the topic featured in this story, while I was half-way through writing it. I was so impressed and surprised by the news that I did make a small reference to it in the story.

On the 1st of November 2018, Tracey Crouch, the Conservative MP for Chatham and Aylesford resigned from her very well-paid Cabinet position as "Minister for Sport." The reason, she explained, was because the government were delaying the implementation of important changes regarding Fixed Odds Betting Machines, changes which would reduce the maximum stake of £100 to £2 (per 20 seconds.) This was a change which would lose the betting shops and the Treasury a heck of a lot of money, so they pushed it back 6 months.

To quote her; "From the time of the announcement to reduce stakes and its implementation, over £1.6bn will be lost on these machines. In addition, two people will tragically take their lives every day due to gambling-related problems and, for that reason as much as any other, I believe this delay is unjustifiable."

This matter is clearly very important to Tracey Crouch and welcome proof that there are some politicians who care deeply about the role that they play in public life, even though it's depressingly rare that we get to see it.

The Archbishop of Canterbury Justin Welby tweeted that Tracey Crouch was "principled and courageous" adding: "May God bless her commitment to doing right."

If you have been affected by any of the issues raised in this story, there is support out there. Whether you are facing problems yourself, or if it's regarding somebody close to you. Please get in touch with the National Gambling Helpline. They can genuinely help. Freephone 0808 8020133.

Printed in Great Britain
by Amazon